PLAINS OF TYBRUNN

THRICE BORN

By Summer Hanford

Martin Sisters Publishing

PLAINS OF TYBRUNN
Martin Sisters Publishing Company

Publishing History
First edition published in 2016

Published by
Martin Sisters Publishing Company
Kentucky, USA

Martin Sisters Publishing Company
ISBN: 978-1-62553-092-9

Science Fiction/Fantasy/Young Adult
Printed in the United States of America

Visit our website at www. martinsisterspublishing.com

DEDICATION

To my nieces and nephew, Isabelle, Penelope, Lillie and George. May there always be magic in your lives.

THRICE BORN SERIES
MARTIN SISTERS PUBLISHING COMPANY

Gift of the Aluien
Hawks of Sorga
Throne of Wheylia
The Plains of Tybrunn
Shores of K'Orge (2017)

COMPANION SHORT STORIES
BY SUMMER HANFORD

The Forging of Cadwel
Hawk Trials for Mirimel
The Fall of Larkesong
The Sword of Three

ACKNOWLEDGEMENT

My gratitude, as always, to Martin Sisters Publishing for their continued confidence and support, and to Simply Marcella, the Baltimore Woods Nature Center and Sycamore Hill Gardens for allowing me to participate in their events.

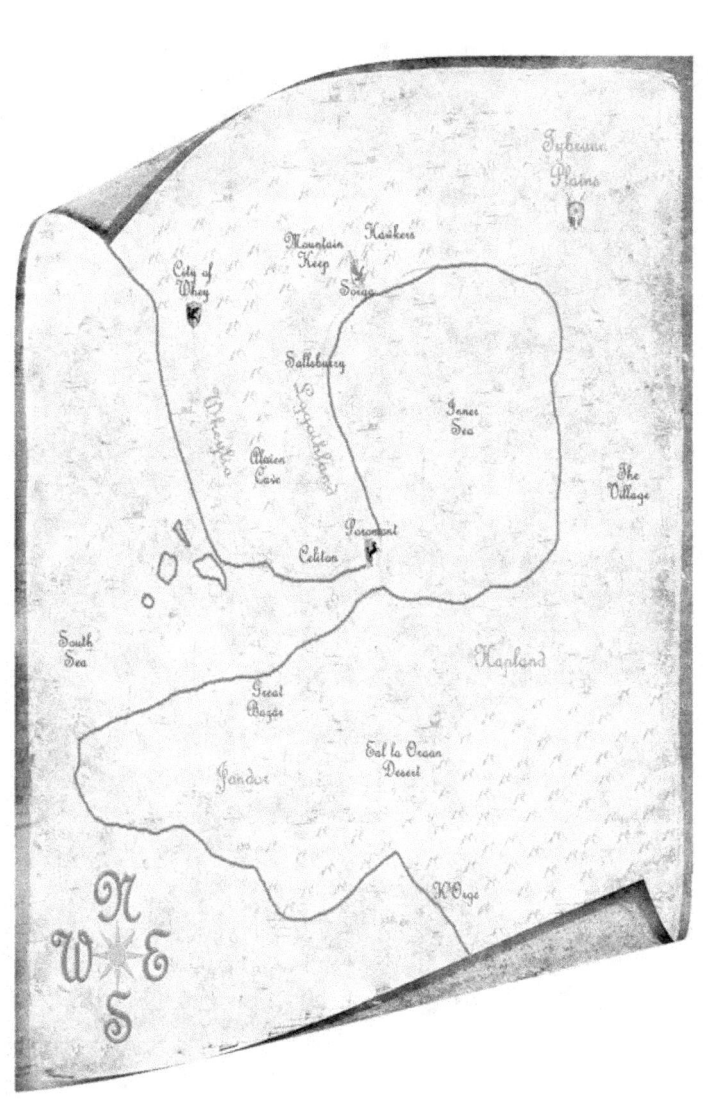

Chapter 1

Aridian drew in a deep breath as he rode, taking in the smells of spring. The air was filled with the scent of churned earth mingled with the sharpness of new growth. Though it was several hours shy of dawn, the star-spattered sky offered more than enough light for travel. Not that Ari, his companion Larkesong, or their Questri steeds needed light to navigate the dark ribbon of roadway. All were touched by magic.

They didn't employ excessive haste, although Ari was anxious to reach their goal. He'd been summoned by the Lady, an ancient magical Aluien who had always taken a keen interest in him. It was the Lady who'd saved him from death at the hands of an Empty One three years ago, and in the process turned him into something more than human. It was also she, he was sure, who'd rescued him nearly eighteen years ago, on the day of his birth, when his parents were murdered by a different Empty One.

Both of those foul Empty Ones were dead now, at Ari's hands, but he still had few answers. Why were his parents murdered, and why had the Lady saved him and not them? When the bard, Larkesong, summoned him to the caves of the magical Aluiens, he said the Lady wished to speak on subjects Ari cared greatly about. Ari was sure his questions were about to be answered.

He curtailed his impatience, knowing the pace they kept, which his horse Stew and Larke's gray could maintain without pause, was the fastest way to their goal. Indeed, under the turning constellations, rolling grassland to either side, the dirt roadway sped by beneath Stew's hooves. They drew ever closer to the Aluiens' caves.

Sooner than Ari thought possible, they came to a halt at the base of the winding trail that led to Larkesong's people. Ari looked up at the tall peaks separating his home of Lggothland from neighboring Wheylia. His imagination filled with memories of the ethereal caverns hidden within.

Sliding from his saddle, Ari slapped Stew on the neck affectionately. "It's a nice time of year for running, if a bit messy," he added, noting the mud that splattered his shins and Stew's belly.

Stew shook his mane and snorted, seeming impatient.

"All right," Ari said, chuckling. "I can see you want to be well rid of me." He removed Stew's bridle. "Thank you for putting up with a year in Wheylia. I know it wasn't as much fun as most of our work."

Stew turned large brown eyes on him, and Ari got the impression his horse would have shrugged, if horses could. Ari did shrug, wishing he could understand the Questri the way Larke could. Ari, though changed by Aluien magic, didn't seem to have any magic of his own. Without it, he couldn't master the art of communicating with other sentient races, like the Questri or the Sorga Hawks. With another pat for Stew, Ari divested the bay stallion of the rest of his tack.

Stew gave him one last look before trotting away. Larkesong's gray, whose name the bard never mentioned, was already disappearing east across the grassland, melding into the sudden light of day. Ari squinted, but he couldn't keep track of the Questri against the brilliant glow of the cresting sun. His eyes stinging from peering into the dawn, Ari turned toward the secret trail leading to the entrance of the Aluien caves.

"Ari, lad, this way," Larke said, his lean form disappearing behind a large boulder. "That way's too long with all this gear."

His interest piqued, Ari followed the Aluien bard, leaving the path behind. The back side of the boulder was nearly cleaved in two by a large opening, big enough for horses to enter. Ari was rather sure he wouldn't be able to see it without Larke. He'd certainly never noticed it on the other occasions he'd sought the Aluiens.

"Where does this lead?" he asked, following Larke inside.

The bard, taller even than Ari, ducked his head slightly, though he didn't need to. "We've a place for gear." Larke turned from the curved tunnel into a hewn-out room. Iron hooks decorated with scrollwork were driven into the rock. Few were in use.

Ari hung Stew's tack on an empty hook beside the one the bard used. "I'll need to clean this." He tried to brush off some of the dirt.

"Will you?" Larke grinned.

Muttering under his breath, the bard drew a glowing rune in the air before their gear. The leather and metal seemed almost to shiver. In moments, rings gleamed and hide glistened. Ari watched in awe as, at another gesture from Larke, the pile

11

of dirt that formed beneath their gear swirled into a small cyclone and whirled out the door.

"Show off." Ari kept his tone light. He tucked his thumbs into his sword belt, hoping the trembling inside him wasn't obvious. He still wasn't accustomed to such blatant displays of power. Plastering a smile on his face, he fought down surprise and, he hated to admit, the sting of envy.

"It's so much more civilized my way." Larke's smile refuted his affected tone.

Turning from the tack room, Larke led the way back into the tunnel, which curved into the mountain. They passed several other openings, one a stable with a natural spring. All were lit by increasingly bright and convoluted patterns of light, as Ari knew the majority of the Aluien caves to be. Though Aluiens needed no light to see by, they seemed to enjoy using it to decorate their realm.

"So, all those times we climbed up that steep mountain trail, even carrying Clorra, in the snow and wind." Ari allowed accusation to fill his tone as he followed the bard. "There was an entrance right at the base of the range?"

"Well, it's a secret entrance."

"So is the other one."

"Yes, but it was important to make you work to find us, you see, to test your resolve."

From behind, Ari couldn't see the bard's face, just his blond curls jutting out from beneath a garish yellow and red plumed orange hat, but he knew Larke well enough to hear both amusement and apology in his tone. "I see," Ari said.

"It wasn't up to me, you understand."

"No, it wouldn't be."

"I would have let you in the easy way" Larke's tone was growing more apologetic.

"Of course."

"We should never have given Cadwel the rearing of you," the bard muttered, referring to Ari's gruff mentor. "You were such a biddable lad."

Ari smiled. In truth, he hadn't become page to Sir Cadwel until his fifteenth year, but he was honored for anyone to imply he took after the great knight. Even if it was Larke and the bard didn't necessarily mean it as a compliment.

"Where did Stew and your gray go?" Ari asked as they walked, the tunnel angling upward. He'd tried to find out where the horses went before, never receiving a clear answer, but sometimes he could wear Larke down. The bard didn't actually like keeping secrets. He did it only because it was the law of his people not to do anything to interfere with the human race, which most took to include passing on knowledge.

"They're off to see others of the herd."

"The herd?"

"You know those two and Sir Cadwel's Goldwin aren't the only three Questri in the world, don't you?" Larke's tone held only amusement now.

"Of course, but aren't the rest on the great plains beyond the northern range?"

"Not all. There are some here and there about Wheylia and Lggothland, for their own purposes and ours."

"Does Stew have a family?" Ari asked, realizing it was something he should have wondered long before now. He felt a pang of sorrow, thinking of his friend Peine. Ari knew his estrangement from Peine was in part due to his preoccupation with his own life. He should have learned more about Peine's aspirations and family when he had the chance. He didn't want to make the same mistake with Stew.

"Oh, aye." Larke glanced back at Ari. "But with Questri it's a different sort of thing."

Ari didn't find the bard's answer very enlightening, but his next question scattered, half-formed, as they emerged into the central cave of the Aluiens.

The sight of the large cavern that was the heart of the Aluiens' home stirred as much awe in Ari as the first time he'd seen it. Aluiens filled the vast hollowed-out mountain before him. Alone or in groups, they chatted and read, or walked along with their slow gliding steps. A blue-white glow emanated in an aura around each, filling the cave. As if seeing them reminded him he was no longer out in the mortal realm, Larke began to glow as well. Above them, illuminating the vaulted roof, shimmering runes floated in elusive and beguiling patterns.

Few Aluiens paid attention to them as Larke and Ari crossed the main cavern, though some nodded in greeting. As always, Ari felt a stab of bitterness that his memories of the brief time he'd lived among them had been taken. It was disconcerting, knowing they knew him but he would never recall those first meetings.

He knew that when the Aluiens took his memories, they'd done it to keep their secrets. While he logically understood the council's actions were dictated by their laws, he still resented not being able to remember what it was like to dwell among them. Nor could he recall the feel of having Orlenia, the magical substance that infused their very veins, flowing through him.

Maybe it was for the best, Ari thought as he and Larke turned down a side tunnel, leaving the majesty of the central cavern behind for a rune-lined and vaulted corridor. Every time he saw the glow of the Orlenia, he felt a longing deep within. Although his mind couldn't remember having Orlenia, it was as if his body could. Even now, following Larke down the corridor, his hands shook slightly with the desire to reach out and touch the gleaming runes around him. Ari recalled, with a shudder, how close he'd come to desecrating the Wellspring of Wheylia, the most sacred object in their kingdom, so he could try to capture the glowing Orlenia for himself.

Wrenching his mind away from thoughts of Orlenia, Ari realized the downward sloping hall they walked was one he couldn't recall traversing before. Far away still, he saw a single door. Even at a distance, he could make out runes carved into the dark wood. Tracing his and Larke's path in his mind, he thought they must be walking deep into the heart of the range above.

Larke halted, turning to face him, surprising Ari with the worry creasing his handsome face.

"Something is wrong?" Ari could discern nothing amiss, but his hand moved to rest on his sword hilt, fingering the three empty sockets where stones had once resided. He glanced over his shoulder before turning back to Larke.

"Nothing like that." Larke's eyes moved to Ari's greatsword. "When did you grow so quick to fight, lad? Even Cadwel will tell you that swords aren't always the answer."

Ari shrugged. It wasn't as if he'd drawn. Besides, most of the troubles he faced were from Empty Ones, the evil opposite of Aluiens. His sword worked fine on them. "Then why are we stopping?"

A grin lightened Larke's expression. "Firstly, you're covered in mud and, if I may be so bold, a bit pungent. I myself am used to it, having traveled with you, but the Lady is, well, a lady. Her sensibilities run more toward the delicate."

"If you wanted me to take a bath, you should have thought of it before we walked half a mile down this corridor."

15

"I rather thought I could, well, magic you." Larke wriggled his fingers at Ari.

"Uh, what will it do to me?" Ari asked, a bit leery. Larke had a habit of working magic on Ari without permission, something he'd requested the bard not do. Ari wasn't sure how to respond, now that he was being asked first.

"I'll demonstrate on myself, my trepidatious companion." Larke's nimble fingers wove runes in the air, each glowing symbol disappearing as it was completed. In a whirl of dust and debris that left Ari choking, dirt rose from the bard and swirled away down the corridor, much as it had in the tack room.

Ari sputtered, coughing. "You could have warned me to move."

"My apologies, lad. It didn't occur to me you wouldn't. Are you sure you're in full possession of your mental faculties?"

"I'm fine." Ari felt a scowl pulling at the corners of his mouth. In fact, he'd been so busy watching Larke use the Orlenia, he hadn't thought about moving out of the way of the resulting whirlwind.

"Shall I?" The bard gestured to Ari. "I hardly dare say it, but now you're worse than ever."

Ari nodded, bracing himself. He wondered if Larke had any spells for shaving, knowing he looked a little scruffy in that respect as well. Aluiens, as far as Ari knew, didn't need to shave. Some had mustaches or beards, though. He wondered if their facial hair stayed the way it was when they were transformed from human to Aluien.

He didn't voice that question, watching as a web of glowing runes encircled him. Ari stood as still as he could, fascinated by the warmth that accompanied them, enveloping him. It was as if a desert wind wrapped itself about him, lifting dirt and fatigue away. Against his chest, the rune-covered

16

amulet he wore under his tunic grew cold. The amulet, a gift from the Lady, kept anyone, Empty One or Aluien, from using magic to scry out Ari's location. It also offered some protection from malevolent spells and grew cold anytime magic was worked nearby. His father, Ari learned last spring, had possessed one as well.

The wind stopped and Ari looked over his shoulder to see an embarrassingly large cloud of dirt whirling away. Glancing down, he noticed his boots gleamed. Even his fingernails were clean. "But that isn't the only reason we stopped," Ari said, realizing uncleanliness alone couldn't account for the worry he'd seen on Larke's face.

Larke looked down, lowering Ari's spirit with his gaze. It was never good when the lighthearted bard looked dejected. Ari held his peace, waiting for Larke to speak.

"I knew your parents," Larke finally said, his voice low.

Ari stared at him, startled by both the information and the subject. "You never told me that."

Larke's lips curled in a wry smile. "In spite of what you may think, I try to adhere to my vows, both to my people and to the Lady."

Ari ground his teeth, but as much as he resented Aluien secrecy, he knew he shouldn't take it out on Larke. The bard had already stretched and mangled his vows to help Ari, earning himself punishment by order of the Khan Dar, the ancient leader of the Aluiens.

"What I want to tell you, lad, is that while I've not always agreed with everything the Lady has done, I've played my part in shaping your fate. I make no excuses. I just wish to extend my apologies." Larke's melodic voice was nearly a whisper.

Not giving Ari a chance to respond, the bard turned away, long strides taking him down the corridor. Ari didn't follow, unsure if Larke could have been any more unsettling. Had he just criticized the Lady? No one ever criticized the Lady.

At the end of the hall, Larke swung the door open, its massive size now apparent as it dwarfed the tall bard. Looking back, he gestured for Ari to follow before disappearing inside. Squaring his shoulders, Ari marched down the corridor to his fate.

Chapter 2

Ari pushed the heavy door open, surprised by the thickness of the wood. The flimsy-looking filigreed hinges securing it to the stone of the mountain all but reeked of magic. He stepped into the room, aware that the door swung closed behind him.

The cavern he found himself in looked natural, not carefully sculpted as most of the Aluien caves, although the floor was worn smooth. Though the space was large, the sloping walls, rising to form a dome, made it feel closed in. Unlike other parts of the Aluiens' home, here, Ari could feel the oppressive weight of the mountains above.

The sensation was somewhat alleviated by shimmering veins of quartz that rose from the floor, tree-like, stretching up to mingle at the summit of the dome. The glowing crystal lines created the feel of being in a forest glade, only the trees were bright and the sky dark.

Dropping his gaze, Ari took in the ring of stones in the center of the cave. They were piled as a farmer would pile rocks from his field, creating the low walls that separated a man from his neighbor. These were not ordinary stones, though, or they had spells upon them. The ring was filled with clear dark liquid, yet none seeped from the many fissures between the rocks.

The Lady, looking as ancient and regal as ever, perched on the wide brim of the pool. Ari would have found comfort in the sight of her, save for the immobility of her normally kind features and the shadows in her deep brown eyes. When first she turned toward him, a tremor touched his limbs, for there was no compassion on her weathered face.

She blinked, and the coldness was gone. A smiled curved her lips. Recognition shone from her eyes. Ari wondered if his first impression had been false, or if her uncustomary coldness was the result of the deep sleep she was forced to endure when Larke left the caves.

As punishment for breaking the laws of his people, Larkesong was under a thousand day internment, but the Lady had bartered relief from that sentence. In exchange for allowing Larke to occasionally travel the lands, the Lady must enter into the deep sleep. She was held, in effect, as a hostage on Larke's good behavior and quick return. Ari knew the Lady feared the sleep, claiming that, while it extended Aluiens' already long lives, it also stole their humanity.

Ari came forward, bowing low before the Lady. Larke already stood at her shoulder, his usually expressive face still, his eyes troubled. Ari straightened, murmuring, "My Lady," in greeting. He wished someone else would speak or indicate what was expected of him. He felt odd, looming over her diminutive form. He stepped back so she wouldn't have to crane her neck to look up at him.

"My Aridian." The Lady's voice was lyrical with an ancient Wheylian lilt. "It is good of you to answer my summons so speedily. Please, sit beside the pool."

Ari did as she bade him, though wary of the dark water. "There are none who wouldn't answer a summons from you with all the speed they could bring to the task," he said, wondering if he sounded eloquent or foolish. He'd been working on his courtly affectations, this past year in Wheylia. For most of his time there, he had precious little else to do.

The corner of her smile twitched, leaving him further in doubt of the success of his speech. "You must wish to know why I have called for you, Thrice Born."

Ari nodded, swallowing. Things always seemed dire when someone called him Thrice Born. It wasn't a name Ari had given himself. He'd first heard it from the lips of the sorceress queen of Wheylia. It referred to Ari's several reincarnations. Having been born mortal, then reborn as an Aluien, and once again as . . . well, whatever he was now, had apparently robbed Ari of his fate. This seemed to make those who wielded magic nervous around him, as they couldn't control or predict him as they could a normal man.

"I have some truths to tell you, Aridian." The Lady's gaze slid past him to the pool. "I am afraid not all of them shall paint me in a glorious light. In truth, I fear you shall be cross with me."

Ari blinked. "What?" he blurted, surprised by the mere suggestion of anger toward the Lady. He ran a hand through his unruly brown hair, trying to calm his nerves. "Why?"

Behind the Lady, Larke snorted, some of the strain leaving his face. "Lad, the correct response is denial that crossness with the Lady is even possible."

"Right, yes," Ari agreed. Were they trying to make his head hurt? "I'm sure I won't be cross with you, my lady."

Her eyes were on his face, searching his features. "I think we must begin with a history, before we can properly reach your part in this tale."

Ari nodded, not interrupting. Perhaps he would finally discover why an Empty One had murdered his parents, or who the master of the Empty Ones was and why he kept sending people to try to kill Ari, and to threaten those he loved.

"You recall, I'm sure, the recounting of how Empty Ones came to be?"

Ari nodded again. He knew the Lady referred to the accident, the act of a violent and long forgotten warrior, that had caused the transformation of a human into an Aluien to go awry, creating the first Empty One.

"The man who became the first Empty One was known as Tal Mraken. He was selected for transformation because he was a powerful sorcerer, nearly as powerful as the Aluiens themselves." The Lady's musical voice soft.

That didn't sound unusual to Ari. The Aluiens perpetuated their race by selecting the most accomplished humans and, when death was about to overtake them, offering them a place among the ranks of Aluiens as an alternative to the unknown beyond.

"He was, when first he awoke as an Empty One, a mindless beast, driven by hunger, consumed by the emptiness within him. That is the tale we told you, and it is a true one, but it did not end there." She looked away again, sighing. "Tal Mraken was a man of great power and even greater will. He did not stay a beast. He returned to his life, his mortal life, while our council argued what course to take. Was it not the height of interference to allow a man who should be dead to live on? Or would trying to rectify the accident of his life be compounding an unfortunate interaction with yet more meddling? While we argued amongst ourselves, Tal Mraken studied the change he'd undergone, learning the extent of his powers."

There was bitterness in her tone, though Ari couldn't read her eyes, trained as they were on the still water of the pool. He knew how the Lady despised the Empty Ones, but she was in the minority. Not in her dislike of them, but in her insistence that since Aluiens had played a role in the creation of Empty Ones, they should play a part in the creatures' destruction as well. Most Aluiens followed their leader's will, staying sequestered in their cavern and studying the wonders of the world, but not interacting with it.

"It must have been apparent to Tal Mraken that he was now something more than mortal, for he soon set his will to creating others like himself. It was at that point, when we learned he was forming new Empty Ones, that I could restrain myself no longer." She lifted her gaze to meet Ari's.

He nearly flinched from the fierce hatred contorting her features. He'd never seen the Lady like this.

"I gathered those loyal to me, those whom I had brought into the fold, and we went to Tal Mraken's lair. There, we slew all the Empty Ones we could. We tried to scour their evil from the world, and to learn how to prevent it from ever returning."

Behind her, Larke shifted uneasily.

"As you must realize, we failed," the Lady said, some of the anger leaving her face, replaced by bitterness. "I lost many friends that day, those I had hand selected to join the ranks of the Aluiens. I counted the price paid, painful but necessary, for the end of such evil. It wasn't until later that I learned Tal Mraken had survived."

23

Her features folding into lines of sorrow, she lifted a hand. In a seemingly idle gesture, she drew a swirl in the dark water of the pool. The swirl captured Ari's attention, crests of water spinning outward, forming patterns from the light reflecting off the veins of quartz.

It took Ari a moment to realize the patterns weren't without meaning. The water flattened, mirror-like again, but no longer dark. He saw forms moving within in, people. They wore unfamiliar garb as they went about their daily tasks, from milking cows to transcribing faded scrolls, and all were Wheylian. He looked up at the Lady, awed by the display but unsure why she chose to show this to him.

"It seems Tal Mraken learned I had an unseemly obsession with my descendants." She watched the images play out, still looking dejected. "I wasn't even disobeying the rules of the Aluien by watching them. As the first human to enter their fold, I had no such restrictions placed upon me. There was not yet any edict staying me from continuing to interact with their lives."

Ari remembered the Khan Dar saying the Lady was the first of his children, but he hadn't fully realized what that meant. He didn't know how long the Aluiens had been increasing their ranks through the careful selection of humans, or why they began doing it, but he had the impression it had been going on for a very long time. How old was the Lady?

"One terrible night, after rebuilding the ranks of his followers, Tal Mraken struck," she said. "He worked a spell, a deep and abiding magic, that alerts him to any descendants of mine. Using it, he marked where my people dwelled. He sent his minions throughout Wheylia and, all at the same horrible moment, they attacked my descendants and their families in their sleep. Over a hundred people. Anyone with a drop of my blood flowing in their veins had it spilled that night."

Ari gaped at her. "All those people in the pool?" No wonder she hated Tal Mraken. Even for an Empty One, he was a monster.

"All save one. One managed to escape." She sighed. "Their images used to be so bright." She touched the water and the pictures moving in it dissolved, leaving it dark and smooth once more. "They are but memories now. When, long ago, I used to watch them while they lived, the images were vivid with life."

"Do you still watch people in this pool?" Ari asked, momentarily distracted from the horror of her tale. "Do you watch me?"

"Sometimes." Her lips twitched as if she might shed her melancholy and smile. "But I do have many other things to tend to."

Ari wondered how often she conjured up his image in the pool, and when. It was disconcerting to think someone could be watching him at any moment. Did his amulet prevent it now?

He surely hoped so. What if the Lady had seen him kissing that Wheylian girl? All of the guilt he'd been working to suppress over kissing someone who wasn't Ispiria surged to the front of his mind. He fought it back, trying to focus on the Lady. There would be time to make amends with his fiancée when he got back home to Sorga.

"Do not worry, Aridian," the Lady said, an amused glint in her eyes. "I cannot scry you in the pool while you wear the amulet I gave you."

Ari swallowed his unrest, relieved. He did appreciate the Lady looking out for him. He wasn't comfortable with the idea of her viewing his every action, though.

The Lady's face turned melancholy again. "The battle between Tal Mraken and myself waged for many years, I'm afraid. I hunted his minions, he those of my line. I soon learned the weaknesses of his spell. It only seeks out the blood of my descendants once they reach adulthood, and I can craft amulets to protect them from his foul magic, even after that. Yet, with his spies, he still found them and killed them."

"Amulets?" Ari asked, reaching up to touch his where it lay under his shirt. "Like mine?"

"Exactly like yours, Aridian." The Lady's eyes fixed on his.

"But, do you mean . . ." Was the Lady trying to tell him that he was of her line? "But, you're a Whey, and I'm Lggothian."

"Nearly a thousand years ago, I moved the last child of my line to Lggothland. I thought it might fool Tal Mraken's spies. I thought as well that perhaps diluting my Wheylian blood with Lggothian stock would deceive his spell."

"You're saying that my father was of your line?" Ari asked, his face hot but his hands ice cold. For once, he wouldn't settle for evasion. "I am of your line?"

"Yes." She regarded him with fathomless eyes. "When your father removed his amulet the night of your birth, to place it on his newborn son, Tal Mraken was instantly aware of him, as was I. Unfortunately, Tal Mraken's minion, the Caller, was nearer to your parents."

"I am your descendant." Ari lifted his gaze to Larke, who stood, unmoving, behind the Lady. There was pity in the bard's expression, and guilt.

26

Ari had grown up thinking he was the orphaned nephew of innkeepers. He loved his adopted family, but the comfort of thinking he was truly one of them had been taken from him two years ago when he'd learned he'd been left in their care by a stranger. Since then he'd made a home for himself in Sorga, but he never gave up the idea of discovering who his parents were, where they'd come from and why they were killed.

"So, my father died because he removed his amulet?" Ari asked, trying to force his mind to take in the implications of the Lady's words as he scrutinized her. "Why would he remove it?" The guilt flickering over Larke's face sparked a horrible suspicion. "Did he even know why he wore it? My father died without knowing the truth, didn't he? My parents died because of your secrets."

The injustice of it sent him surging to his feet. Ari hadn't realized he had so much feeling for a man and woman he'd never known. His parents had nothing to do with Empty Ones, Aluiens or anything else. They were farmers. No one deserved to die in a war they didn't even know they were a part of.

Unable to vent his churning emotions in any other way, he turned and paced away from the Lady and Larke, then back, then away again. Looking down, he could see a trail worn into the stone. He wondered who else had paced here and how long it had taken to wear the path.

"They died because they disobeyed me." The anger in the Lady's tone spun Ari back around. "I protected my line. I kept them safe," she said, her visage as fierce as her voice. "To them, I was a wealthy great aunt who paid their way in the world. I made demands, true, such as forcing them to wear their amulets at all times, or live where I asked them to live, but those demands were necessary."

27

Ari took a deep breath, steadying himself. The Lady wouldn't have wanted his parents to die. There must be more to the story. "What happened?"

Color rose in her cheeks, but he couldn't tell if she was angry or abashed. "I didn't wish your father and mother to marry," she said. "Your mother was the daughter of a minor noble, but one of rising prominence. She drew too much attention, from too many, especially for allowing a man in the trades to court her. What good does it do to wear an amulet that hides you from magic if you become well known to all?"

Ari nodded. He could see the value in that. Yet, if his parents had loved one another, what could be done?

"For hundreds of years I kept my line safe, using a careful web of spells to guard them, and to keep the line small. Always a single child, so I could steward them."

Ari wondered what sort of magic could accomplish that. He feared he didn't truly wish to know. He eyed the Lady, she who always seemed so noble, calm and wise. Her face was flushed and her eyes narrow with remembered anger, giving her a coarser, crueler look. He blinked, hoping that would dispel the image.

It did, for she seemed sad again, almost frail. She looked up at him beseechingly. "I couldn't let your father and mother marry. I threatened to disinherit him, and his parents. I knew that wouldn't work, of course, but I lack the subtlety in shifting human emotions that some Aluiens have." She gestured over her shoulder.

Ari looked up at Larke.

The bard wouldn't meet his eyes.

The Lady sighed, recapturing Ari's attention. "I sent Larkesong to your father. I knew he, if anyone, could scour love for your mother from the man's soul."

She said it as if it wasn't at all an evil thing to do. Turning away, Ari went back to his pacing, confused to have anger toward the Lady building in him. He wondered what Larke had been apologizing for earlier, agreeing to make Ari's father stop loving his mother, or failing to do so.

"Alas, they'd already run off. I admit, I was too furious to follow them. What did I care if the line ended at last?"

As Ari came round once more to face her, she dipped a finger into the pool, drawing up new images. Behind her, Larkesong turned his face away. Ari peered into the pool to see a man, only a year or two older than he was, walking up to a farmhouse. A beautiful blonde woman came out, heavy with child, and handed him a flagon. From the man's mop of brown hair, his hazel eyes and familiar even features, Ari knew they were his parents.

He watched them speaking words to each other he couldn't hear, but with looks of happiness and love. Without conscious thought, he found himself on his knees beside the pool, scrutinizing them intently, trying to memorize their faces. He cleared a suddenly tight throat, aware of tears mounting in his eyes.

His father handed back the flagon, kissing his mother before moving away. She watched him go for a moment, then reentered the house. Ari stared at the empty image of the porch steps, seen before only as a charcoaled mass in his dream, or a grown-over clearing he'd once explored.

"Which brings us, my Aridian, to your story," the Lady said.

Ari moved his eyes back to her face, finding it creased with compassion. He retook his seat on the lip of the pool, beside her. Surreptitiously, he blotted his eyes, clearing his throat again.

Doing his best to appear as composed as she did, he asked, "And what is my story?"

Chapter 3

"I will not hide the truth from you," the Lady said. "I did not come that night for the purpose of saving your parents, but to make war on Tal Mraken, or whichever minion he sent to do his bidding. Finding you was a great inconvenience to me, for I couldn't pursue the Caller with a babe. I rid myself of you as quickly as I could, but the Empty One had already fled back to the sanctuary his master has built."

Ari stared at her, stunned by her admission. She could easily have claimed to have made all haste to save his unsuspecting parents. He would never have known the brutal truth. He wasn't sure he was happy he did. Still, one question remained. "Why did my father remove his amulet and put it on me?"

If only his father had left it on, his parents wouldn't be dead. Ari wouldn't have been raised by innkeepers. Not that they hadn't been more than kind to him. They treated him as their own. It was just . . . he knew he was not.

"He thought of it as a family heirloom," Larkesong said, speaking for the first time. "We shall never know his mind, but I imagine it was a simple thing, an act of love, to place such a family treasure about your neck. Certainly, it kept the Caller from realizing you were near."

"But the Caller wouldn't have come if he'd left the amulet on." And Ari's father wouldn't have removed it if he'd known the truth. Ari pressed his lips firmly together to keep from voicing that accusation aloud. He knew all about the Aluiens and their maddening secrecy.

He looked down at the pool again, but the water revealed nothing. He almost wished the Lady hadn't shown him an image of his parents. Last spring, when he'd journeyed to the clearing where the charred and timeworn rubble of their farm lingered, he hadn't felt much of anything. Now, having seen them, watched them move and interact, sorrow swelled inside him.

"But he could not know that," the Lady said. Her eyes narrowed, as if she could read his accusatory thoughts. "They could never know who I was, nor that they were even in danger, let alone from whom. Aluien law forbade it, and the Khan Dar was already allowing me to break the new laws, made for the once-human like me, so that I might watch over them."

Ari nodded, but inside he was still cursing Aluien law. Cursing Tal Mraken, yet he couldn't bring himself to curse the Lady or Larke. "So, you failed to kill the Empty One who murdered my parents, and you left me with an innkeep and his wife." Ari stated it as a fact, aware of the harsh edge to his voice.

"But, to my even greater shame, it did not end there."

Ari raised his gaze to the glowing pattern of lines above them, seeking calm. He couldn't believe the Lady, the only being he trusted as much as his mentor Sir Cadwel, had plotted to steal his father's love for his mother, failed to avenge their deaths at the hands of her enemies, and abandoned him. Slowly, Ari unclenched fists he hadn't realized he'd made, resting his palms on his thighs. He lowered his gaze to find both the Lady and Larkesong watching him with worry. "Where did it end, then?"

"The spring before your fifteenth summer."

Ari frowned. That was the spring his life had changed. He'd snuck out into the woods, disobeying the orders of the man he thought of as his uncle, and been mortally wounded by an Empty One. That's when he'd met the Lady, for she saved him. She'd changed him into an Aluien, replacing his body's spilled blood with glowing Orlenia, so he would be reborn. Only, the Empty One who'd slain him had used a poisoned blade, coated in a substance lethal to Aluiens. In order to save him a second time, the Lady had convinced the council to change him back into a mortal, with the unexpected consequence of leaving him more than human.

All this, she'd done for him. He'd always thought she'd done it because it was right, because she was a noble being. Now, he didn't know what her motives may have been. They were probably too convoluted for him to follow, even should he want to.

"As I told you, I was angry with your father." She sounded more abashed than ever. "I deemed it time to let my line end, if fate should have it so. I did not make myself known to you. Did not come to you. Most importantly, I cast your father's amulet aside when I found you, leaving you without protection."

Ari digested that for a moment. He wouldn't have needed any protection, though. Not until he became a man.

Memories sprang up in him, pulled free from the spells of forgetfulness woven through his mind. He looked up at Larke. "That winter and spring, you were there in my uncle's inn. You played every night. I remember now. My aunt said she could hardly keep up in the kitchen, for everyone in the village was coming to hear you perform."

The bard nodded, guilt overshadowing his features, pain in his blue eyes.

"And you told me to go out into the forest." The realization stunned Ari. He remembered it all, now. Larke meeting him in the dark hall of the inn after Ari had finished his chores, murmuring into his mind about the forest. Go, Larke had said. Go to the woods. Be free. Run. Play. Disobey your uncle. "I was bait." The pieces fell into place. "I was nothing more than bait."

Ari folded his arms across his chest, glaring at them, a part of him sure they would deny it. There must be another explanation. The Lady and Larke wouldn't treat his life as no more important than that of a fisherman's worm.

They didn't deny it. Larke looked down, clearly miserable.

The Lady met Ari's gaze, regal and defiant. "I did save you."

"And I thank you for that." Ari stood, his anger at their betrayal a fiery ball in his gut, his mind blank of anything but the need to get away from them. "I thank you for everything you've done for me. I wish you could have been as kind to my parents." He strode toward the door.

"Aridian," the Lady called. "There is something more you must know."

Ari stopped. Obedience to the Lady warred with his desire to leave that closed-in room where the weight of the mountains

34

and the past pressed so heavy upon him. He turned back. "What more must I know?"

"My enemy is your own."

"No. Your ancient feud has cost too much. It ends with me. I want nothing to do with it."

"I doubt Tal Mraken will allow you the decision."

"There were months when I had no amulet," Ari said, speaking the thought as it came to him. "He didn't attack me then."

"You crossed out of fate, my Aridian. I have told you that. When you did so, you moved beyond his spell's ability to find you."

"Then he knows nothing of me." Ari wished she wouldn't refer to him as her Aridian, as if he was a thing she owned. He used to think the words almost an endearment.

"He knows nothing of your heritage, but of you, I am sure he knows much. He knows you are my creature, and will believe I have created you to end him. He proved as much by sending the Caller to retrieve the stone guarded by the Sorga Hawks. He's trying to collect all three before we do, to stop you from assembling a weapon with which to defeat him."

Ari's hand went to his chest, touching the small white stone he kept in a pocket sewn inside his tunic. The year before last, the Caller had attacked Sorga, destroying an entire village and orphaning Ispiria's cousin Mirimel, all to claim the stone. Though Ari and Mirimel had defeated the Caller, many had died. Ari had never learned what prompted the attack. "Why does he think I am your creature?"

"Because he knows Larkesong is, and my bard nearly died to save you from his spawn."

"Larke saved me from Tal Mraken?" Ari asked, taking a step closer. He glanced at Larke, but the bard's face was downcast.

"You went to his keep."

"Lord Mrakenson," Ari said, recalling the fiendish Empty One who'd almost killed him, Larke and Sir Cadwel. He took a deep breath, the Lady's revelations swirling in his head. "And is he right? Did you create me to end him?"

"That would be a vast task, even for me." She drew a finger through the water. "How could I know you would be struck down while I was near enough to aid you, and by a knife coated in poison formed to kill Aluiens? How could I know the council would agree to save you, or what you would become? Was it not coincidence that, on the day you were sent back into the world, you met Sir Cadwel, a man capable of training you to be a great warrior?"

Behind her, Larke shifted uneasily.

Ari pressed his lips together. It did seem like a farfetched plot, ranging over years and requiring the manipulation of human, Aluien and Empty One alike. Yet, if anyone had the time or perseverance to carry it out, wouldn't it be the Lady? And what to her if she failed? She'd already confessed willingness to let her line end, as she put it. Ari rubbed at his throat, recalling the Empty One's blade slitting it open when he was not yet fifteen.

"He plots against you even now, Aridian. In your fateless eyes, he sees the power to at last lay him low."

"But you saved Larke that day in his keep. Why didn't you kill him then? If you know where he is, why not go fight him? Why use me to draw him out?"

"I cannot overcome him in his keep. The walls, the ceilings, the very foundation on which it stands, are woven with

36

spells. His fortress gives him a strength greater than I may withstand."

Ari recalled well the strange patterns decorating the surfaces of the place, even the doors. At the time, he hadn't even considered they might be magic, but looking upon them had been unsettling. "But he's afraid of me?"

"He's afraid I will help you gather the stones, so you may recreate the power they give the sword you bear, and he is right. I will help you find them, so you may bring an end to this battle at last. I shall guide you."

Ari drew himself up straight. It mattered not that he knew he must hunt down Tal Mraken to stop his evil and seek vengeance for his parents and Sorga. He wanted nothing more to do with the Lady's machinations. With her talk of ending her line, and her willingness to use him in her plots, he was coming dangerously close to wanting nothing more to do with her at all, ever. "I am champion of Lggothland. I will take the matter of retribution for Tal Mraken before my king. It is he who must decide who I battle. I am not yours to command."

"No? Yet what of your children?"

She was angry, he could see. Angry with him for not giving her blind obedience. "What of them?" Ari wondered what threats she would unveil. He didn't bother to point out that he wasn't yet married and had no children. He knew these things would come. He was heir to the dukedom of Sorga, and would need an heir of his own.

"His spells of seeking may hold no sway over you any longer, but when your offspring come of age, he will know. Do you really think he'll not seek them? His hatred for me has lasted centuries. It will not dim now."

"So you will make them amulets," Ari said, not giving in. In all likelihood, King Ennentine would order him to confront the villain long before amulets for Ari's children were needed. Ari would find a way to lure the monster from his keep and then he would slay him, as he had every other Empty One who'd threatened the lands and peoples he loved. All without subservience to the Lady's dubious aid.

"Is that what you want to hinge the future of Sorga on, amulets? One slip, a moment of thoughtlessness by one of your offspring, and he will know them. Then, the line of Sorga shall be forced to fight or run and hide. The lords of Sorga are not some insignificant family of artisans I can secret away. No, you must fight him, Aridian, and believe me when I say you shall not overcome him without the stones."

Ari ground his teeth, scrubbing a hand through his hair, unsure if he believed her. It was clear the Lady wanted to use him, to make him into a weapon to do what she could not, but should he let her?

He let out a long slow breath. Why not take her aid? Salving his pride wasn't worth failure.

Yet, it was more than his pride that was ravaged by her truths, as she called them. Before now, he'd thought her interest in him purely benevolent, but the revelations of the day showed he was a fool. Why he'd thought an ancient magical being such as the Lady had taken an interest in him for motives only pure and kind, he couldn't fathom, but he knew the truth now.

He looked at Larke. The bard's face was a mixture of sorrow and guilt. Larke met his eyes and nodded. He was agreeing with the Lady, but could Ari trust the bard any more than he should trust her?

He did trust Larke, though. Somewhere, deep within, Ari knew that Larke was always on his side. Larke had risked himself for Ari often enough to prove his loyalty. "What must I do?" he asked through a jaw he had to work to unclench.

"You have the stone the hawks gave you?" Her face transformed from anger to eagerness.

Ari nodded.

"Place it in one of the empty fixtures on the hilt of your sword. It matters not which."

Carefully, Ari drew the massive blade. For most men, it would be impossible to wield it with one hand, but Ari managed with ease. He owed his extra strength, his speed, his tolerance for heat and cold, quick healing, and his ability to see in any amount of light, to the Lady. Whatever her true motives, she had given Ari many a priceless gift.

Sword in hand, he used his other to extract the pouch carrying the gleaming white stone from the pocket sewn into his tunic.

"Lay the sword here." The Lady tapped the stone next her. "Place the hilt beside me and set the stone into it."

Ari did as she bade him. The Lady pulled a pin from her coif. Swiftly, she jabbed the pin into her finger. Ari gasped, his hand half extended to stop her. Giving him a little smile, as if to let him know she'd observed he still cared, she turned her gaze to the sword's hilt. Squeezing her finger, the Lady spilled a glowing drop of Orlenia, dripping it onto the stone.

The blue-white luminescence of the Orlenia seeped around the stone, light shining from it. Peering through the bright glow, Ari could see the stone fuse into the hilt. As the light dimmed, he reached for his sword, but the Lady laid her hand over it.

"Now, my Aridian, you must travel to the vast northern plain, where the Questri dwell, and gain the stone they guard. You must gather all three in order to defeat your enemy."

"To link mind, body and intent," Ari said, recalling Larke's explanation of the stones. He eyed her bitterly. He didn't see how such magic would help him defeat Tal Mraken, but he didn't think the Lady would lie about this. No, in this he could trust her, for Tal Mraken's death was her goal.

"Yes," she said with a nod.

"But no one knows where the third stone is."

"I know how your Prince Parrentine came to possess Fwellian, the sword you now carry, and the tale is steeped in clues. Larkesong and I shall endeavor to unravel them while you journey north, but it is almost certainly across the ocean, and that is where you will need to go to claim it. Do you agree to seek the second stone?"

"I shall think on it," Ari said, though he knew he must. He eyed his sword. The Sorceress Queen of Wheylia had called it Fwellian as well, and had told him it was a sacred object to her people. It seemed odd to have a sword with such a history and a name. She'd also declined to ask for Fwellian's return, saying the Lady must wish Ari to have it and she, the most powerful sorceress in a kingdom of sorceresses, feared to cross the Lady.

Ari looked down at her, trying to see her as she truly was, his eyes now less clouded by awe and love. She drew her hand away from his sword, frowning at him. He took up the blade, the stone the hawks had given him warm against his palm, and sheathed it. "My lady, Larke." He gave them each a half bow. This time, no one called him back as he strode from the room.

Ari didn't know where he was going, just that he was going away from the Lady. He tasted bitter betrayal on his tongue and while he longed to be rid of it, he also couldn't allow himself to sink back into the oblivion of blind trust. His thoughts so turbulent he hardly saw his own path, barely acknowledging those who waved as he passed, Ari soon found himself before another door.

It, too, was marked with runes, for it led outside and must therefore be guarded. Ari pushed it open all the way, propping a rock against it so it wouldn't close. Only an Aluien could open it from the outside, and Ari wasn't one.

He was in the small practice yard he'd used the previous year when he and Sir Cadwel had dwelled in the caves for a time. Sir Cadwel had been learning magic, for he was secretly an Aluien now. Ari had honed his sword work and learned Ancient Wheylian, spending his days half alone and half with Larke. Ari had been a bit bored then, but looking back, it seemed a time of happiness and innocence.

He glared at the practice dummy standing in the center of the yard, wondering if he wanted to lose himself in sword work. Somehow, he needed to think through what he'd learned about himself, the Lady, and his apparently lifelong enemy, Tal Mraken. Behind him, Ari heard light footfalls he easily identified as Larke's, but he didn't turn. His gaze roamed over the rough stone walls of the yard, which hemmed it in shadow.

"I don't want to be placated," Ari said as Larke's footsteps halted behind him.

"I didn't come to placate you. I came to offer to tell you how to find your family."

Ari whirled. "My mother and father?"

Larke shook his head, surprise flittering across his face. "Your parents are dead, Ari." His melodious voice was rich with sympathy. "I mean your grandparents, and aunts, uncles and cousins, on your mother's side."

Ari hadn't thought to ask about that. It hadn't occurred to him to wonder past his parents' death. He looked around, feeling shaky, but there was no place to sit in the practice yard.

"Why don't we adjourn to my chambers?" Larke asked.

Mutely, Ari nodded, following the bard back into the tunnels of the mountain.

Chapter 4

Ari didn't know what he'd expected Larke's sitting room to be like, but it wasn't the chaos that greeted him. The bard closed the door behind them, saying, "Sit wherever you like," but all Ari could do was look about in shock. It was as if one of Larke's mini whirlwinds had been trapped inside the room, trying to escape.

The myriad of mismatched tables, chairs and couches were, Ari supposed, to be expected. It was the sheer volume of things, however, that boggled. Piles upon piles of papers, manuscripts, charts, scrolls and works of art were stacked everywhere, assuming you could call the teetering towers stacks. Some of them had clearly fallen over and never been put right.

Shelves wouldn't have gone amiss, Ari supposed, but he couldn't see anywhere to put them because, to add to the pandemonium, the walls of the room were covered. One, the shorter wall that was to Ari's right when he entered, was layered with images and objects stuck to the stone. The others were aglow with flowing script crafting what appeared to be poetry, with strange notations below it. Not poems, Ari realized as he read, but ballads, and the notations must have something to do with singing or music.

He turned to Larke to ask if they were ballads and if he was allowed to read them, but stopped when he saw what the bard was doing. Larke was working a spell on the door, and it was a spell Ari knew. He'd seen the bard etch the very same runes on Sir Cadwel's chamber door two years ago, when Larke had wanted to make sure other Aluiens couldn't hear what they were saying within. Seeing him working that enchantment now, here, made Ari instantly wary.

"It's to be a very private conversation, then?" Ari tried to keep his tone light. He was feeling somewhat dizzy with the revelations of the morning swirling about in his head. He wasn't sure how much more he could take.

Larke finished the incantation before turning to him. "Please, lad, sit."

"Where?" Ari looked around. There was one chair not piled high with objects, a very worn but plush looking green fabric covering it, but it was obviously where Larke sat.

Larke looked around too, surprise growing on his face. "It has gotten a bit out of hand, hasn't it?" He turned to a couch, then to a chair, then back to the couch. At a gesture from Larke, the heap of parchments filling one end of the couch became a neat stack and floated over to rest on a teetering monolith of tomes. "There you go."

Skirting similarly unstable looking formations, Ari maneuvered to the couch, sitting carefully on the edge to keep the hodgepodge of items on the other end from sliding toward him. Larke crossed to sit in the green chair. The bard leaned back, his long fingers tapping out a beat on one armrest while he gazed over Ari's head.

Abruptly, Larke smacked his hand down on the chair arm, blue eyes focusing on Ari. "The Lady did intend for you to meet Sir Cadwel that day." Larke's voice was tight, as if he had to force the words out. "Although, at the time, she told me it was because she feared for him. There was no mention of any desire for you to receive training." His fingers resumed their tapping, his face creasing with unfamiliar lines of anger.

"Well, Sir Cadwel did need help." Before Ari met the knight, despair over the long ago murder of most of his family and the more recent death of his brother had pressed Sir Cadwel into a deep despondency. Ari frowned, wondering why Larke was quite so livid, his own anger dimming in surprise. He'd never seen Larke truly angry before.

"Yes, but is that all she was mindful of?" Larke rubbed at his forehead, his other hand drumming increasingly complex rhythms on the chair arm. "As I have said, I am not so deep in the Lady's counsel as you may suspect."

"Is this about my family?" Something had Larke quite agitated, enough so that he'd bespelled the room. The revelation about Sir Cadwel didn't seem that dire a secret.

"It is. It's about . . ." Larke looked away again. "I don't know where to start," he muttered.

Ari leaned back on the coach, putting out a hand to push away the pile of parchment and books threatening to fall on him. "How about at the beginning, because I'm getting a little tired of being misled and lied to."

Larke's expression became a bit hurt.

"I'm sorry, Larke," Ari said before the bard could speak. "Just, please, tell me what's going on."

45

Larke nodded, but didn't speak, his brow creased in thought. Ari let his head tilt back, finding a glittering star-like pattern of Orlenia on the ceiling. In fact, the more he looked at it, the more it seemed to him it wasn't a pattern, but a detailed recreation of the night sky, and it was rotating ever so slowly.

"I don't know any more details of her past battles than the Lady told you. That was all long before my time here." Larke's melodious voice was low, but filled the chamber. "What I do know, is that I was her first new mark in years. So many of her followers died in her war with Tal Mraken, the Khan Dar punished her by forbidding her any new ones for over a thousand years."

"That seems like an awfully long time." In truth, Ari could hardly conceive of how long it was. Larke may as well have said ten thousand.

"Well, there were other rumors, but I'd discredited them until this past year. Rumors she may have begun to hasten some of her chosen along."

Ari's head snapped up. "You mean, killed them?"

Larke shook his head. "I don't think it ever went that far, but she did insist I argue Sir Cadwel's case for premature admittance to the council when you both came here last year, declining to do so herself."

Ari laid his head back again, gazing at the glowing blue-white stars above, set against the gray stone of the mountain. He was having trouble feeling much. He wondered if Larke had cast a spell on him, or if his mind and heart simply couldn't stand any more turmoil. "So you were the first in hundreds of years, and that involves my family because?"

"Because, even though he punished her, the Khan Dar never rescinded the Lady's right to watch over her family. She talked him into extending that right to me, and allowing me back into the world long before our rules dictate, that I might aid her in the task." The bard's tone was bitter. "Of course, I was sworn not to see my own family or any who knew me. I was sent to your family as a liaison, but not allowed to offer any comfort to my mother, who had lost both husband and son in such short order."

Ari heard the bard sigh. Even when Larke was angry or bitter, two emotions Ari wasn't accustomed to from him, his voice still flowed about the room in well-modulated tones.

"But that is neither here nor there, as they say, for it is not my story I tell. It is yours," the bard said.

Normally, Ari would have encouraged Larke to speak of his own past, but the numbness inside him made him too tired to care.

"You see, Ari, it's my fault your father fled the Lady's protection."

Ari sat up, his malaise gone, books spilling over him. "Your fault?"

Larke nodded. "The Lady did send me to dissuade your father from marrying your mother, but they had not already fled."

"And you told them to." Ari didn't even make it a question. Of course Larke had told them to flee. To Larke, using his magic to try to make a man forget the woman he loved would be too evil. The bard's romantic soul would never allow it. "You lied to the Lady to protect their love?"

"I'd known your father since he was a boy, younger than you were when first we met." Larke glanced nervously at the bespelled door. "We were friends, so when I began to broach the subject of your mother, trying to learn where best to lay my spells, your father told me the whole truth." Larke leaned forward, elbows resting on his knees.

47

Ari pushed the books back to their side of the couch.

"They'd already married, in secret, and your mother was with child. I dared not tell the Lady. I could imagine her anger and couldn't bear to think on what steps she might take to have her way." Larke was speaking faster than Ari had ever heard him speak before.

Ari realized the bard had kept this secret, and all the guilt that accompanied it, for eighteen years.

"I gave your father some coin and the aid of a Questri mount and told him to take your mother and leave. I wouldn't let him tell me where he planned to go, but promised him he might write after you were born and return then, if they wished."

"Because, by then it would be too late," Ari said. Too late for whatever the Lady might try to do to separate them. "I know my father had an amulet, but why didn't the Lady search out my mother instead? Was she protected from being sought by magic?"

Larke smiled, though with little mirth. "That very thought plagued me the entire journey back. In truth, I hadn't resolved it beyond deciding that I would interrupt any attempt the Lady made to do so. A poor plan, and one that proved unnecessary. She was so angered by what your father had done, she decided to leave him to his fate."

"Until he removed his amulet and she saw a chance that Tal Mraken would come forth from his lair deep in the Northern Range," Ari said.

Larke sat back in his chair again, looking tired. His gaze turned toward the picture covered wall. "And now you know the full tale of how your parents came to be farming outside of Sallsburry."

"Was the Questri Stew?"

Larke's face flickered with the barest of smiles. "It was Stew's father."

"Oh." Ari realized he should say more. His mind felt slow and blundering as he sought the proper words. "Thank you for telling me, Larke." Ari swallowed. "You didn't kill them. You didn't start the feud, or make my father take off his amulet, or force him to marry in secret. You saved them."

"A fine savior I made."

Ari didn't know what else to say. He leaned back again, gazing up at the stars on the ceiling. "I didn't realize she could be so heartless."

"She is very old, lad."

Ari wasn't sure what that had to do with it, and his head hurt too much for him to work it out. Above, the familiar constellations revolved ever so slowly. Ari picked out his favorite, Verillia, and envisioned the majestic sailboat it depicted floating above him.

"I'm sure you aren't headed for Poromont when you leave here." Larke's voice broke into the imaginary oceanic battle Ari was conjuring in his head. "But would you like me to write to your father's parents and your mother's family, letting them know of your birth and your parents' fates? I'm known to your father's parents, and I can guarantee you that your mother's will believe my letter."

Ari squeezed his eyes shut. Behind his lids, they burned, threatening tears of the sort he hadn't shed in a long time. "Tell me of my father's parents."

"Well, your grandfather is a portrait painter, rather a good one, and your grandmother assists him. He was training your father in the art, which, of course, is how he met your mother. In fact . . ."

Ari heard the bard stand. Cracking his eyes open, he saw Larke cross the room and start rummaging behind a pile of books near one wall. Ari blinked a few times, quickly wiping his face on his sleeve while the bard's back was turned. He was almost eighteen, he reminded himself, and king's champion. He didn't cry.

"Here it is." Larke turned back, holding a portrait of the same blonde woman Ari had seen in the Lady's pool, looking even younger and prettier than before. "Your father asked me to keep it until they returned." Larke angled the painting so he could see it, sorrow pulling at his features. "I ought to have given it to her parents, years ago, I suppose. I think you should have it now, lad. I don't have one of your father, but your grandfather does."

Ari stood, crossing the room to take the small painting. "Cyanna," he said, trying out her name. "They were Arden and Cyanna. Mother and Father."

The carved wooden scrollwork of the frame indented under his fingers and Ari realized he was squeezing it too hard. Relaxing his grip, he took in a deep breath, staring down at the painting. It all seemed so hollow. So inadequate.

He'd found his parents final resting place, killed the Empty One who'd murdered them, learned the story of their deaths, and none of it did anything to fill the desolate corner of his heart that had always hoped, always believed, that someday it would turn out everyone was wrong. Someday, he would find his parents and they would embrace him and he would know the love he'd seen in other people's eyes. That special look a parent gave their child that let him know there was someone who loved him beyond constraint, or conditions, or reproach.

Ari cleared his throat. "Thank you, Larke. Do you have something I can wrap this in?" He held out the painting. "I think I'd like to go now."

"Now?" Larke's voice was high with surprise, his face creased with concern. "Lad, you've been traveling for days. At least stay till morning."

Ari realized he had no idea what time it was. It was impossible to tell inside the caves. It seemed as if a hundred suns must have set since he'd entered the realm of the Aluiens. "No." He shook his head. "I'd really like to go home."

If Sorga is home, his mind whispered, but he bristled at the thought. Sorga was his home. Sir Cadwel was there, at least for now, and Ispiria, and his people. He was Duke of Sorga, and he would make it his home. Even if he'd had a normal childhood, he would have grown up and made a new home for himself somewhere, away from his parents. He had to stop wishing for childish things that could never be and make a life now, with Ispiria.

"Tell the Lady I will seek the second stone," he said, making his voice firm. "The Caller may be dead, but Tal Mraken must pay for ordering the deaths of my parents, for Hawkers, and for all of his other crimes."

Larke nodded, but his face was still etched with worry.

"And please do write to my family, both sides," Ari continued. "Let them know who I am, and give them some reason I didn't come forward before. Tell them I'll see them next time I'm in the capital, or they can come visit me in Sorga. You're the eloquent one. I leave it up to you. Please."

"Yes, of course lad. Leave it to me. I'll send you copies, so you'll know what was said. Are you sure you won't stay?"

"I'm sure. I think I need some time alone." Holding the painting in one hand, he held out his other for Larke to clasp.

"Thank you, Larke. I know you always watch out for me, though I'd never realized quite how much."

Chapter 5

It didn't take Ari long to realize why knights traveled with pages. It wasn't for help with armor, or brushing horses and setting up tents, for Ari could do all of those things himself. It was for sanity. His and Stew's.

Halfway through their first full day of travel, tired of turning the Lady's words about in his mind, Ari related the entire exchange to Stew. He knew he'd been charged with keeping many things secret, both by the royal family and the Aluiens, but as a magical Questri, Stew must count as part of the secret already. Besides, no one but Aluiens could understand Stew, not even Ari, so who would his horse tell?

The way Stew angled his ears toward Ari's voice, seeming to take in every word, was much more satisfying than letting the words tumble around in his own head. Soon, Ari found himself telling Stew everything.

He spoke of his life growing up in the inn, and his adopted aunt, uncle and cousins. He told Stew about traveling with Sir

Cadwel when the knight was still in his drink-fueled depression. Although Stew had been there for much of it, Ari recounted the quest to save Prince Parrentine's first bride, and the vengeance Ari took against the Empty One who'd tried to murder him just before his fifteenth birthday.

Ari spoke, too, of the Caller, the Empty One who'd slain his parents. Ari had faced that enemy deep in the forest, without Stew, and his horse seemed enthralled by the tale of how Ari had ended the Caller's mad existence. He realized how unfair he'd been to Stew. The Questri was always there when needed, more dependable than almost anything else in Ari's life, yet Ari hadn't thought to tell Stew about important events that took place without him. If Stew could speak, Ari was sure he would have asked to know how the Caller had finally been defeated, as any friend would.

Encouraged by his horse's interest, Ari at last turned to one of his innermost torments, his betrayal of his fiancée, Ispiria. "I don't know what to do," Ari said, twisting the reins in his hands. "It's not so much that I kissed that Wheylian girl. I had too much bubbly wine and I don't even know her name. That meant nothing. It's Siara's kiss that worries me."

Stew tossed his head.

Ari realized he was pulling the reins tight. "Sorry." He let them go. Most of the time, he didn't actually use the reins. It wasn't as if Stew didn't know the way. "I know it meant nothing to Siara. She's in love with Parrentine and that can never change. I mean, she's magically bound to him. Her life depends on him loving her."

Ari sighed. He pondered, not for the first time, how awful that must be. Fortunately, Parrentine had come to love Siara and they were happy. Still, it must be a terrible thing to have your heart belong so completely to another that you would die without their love, yet not have them bound to you in the same way. Ari wondered how Wheylian woman lived with it. Would he trade magic for that formidable curse?

Yes. He would trade anything to be able to reach out and grasp the Orlenia, bending it to his will, as Larkesong could. Ari shook his head, throwing off that thought.

"The trouble is, it meant something to me," he said to Stew. "I don't know if you realized, but when I first met Siara, when she traveled with us, I sort of fancied her."

Stew's snort was as close to a laugh as Ari supposed a horse could get.

"Yes, well, I suppose everyone noticed. Which is bad, because that means if I tell Ispiria that Siara kissed me, she might realize I liked it."

He fell into gloomy silence again. Stew plodded down the lane. They were traveling the same back roads they'd ridden over a year before, after Sir Cadwel's initial training with the Lady. Ari took the route for the same reason they had then. He wished to encounter as few people as possible, even if it meant sleeping on the ground many nights, instead of at inns.

It was an early spring. The ground under Stew's hooves was muddy, puddles dotting the rutted roadway. Ari looked across the fields sweeping away from them, a quilt of matted yellow grass and patches of snow. The air was crisp but the sky bright. Usually, he would have been immune to any sorrow on a sunlit spring day, but the question of whether or not to tell Ispiria he'd kissed Princess Siara and that girl at the party weighed on him.

Fragile looking purple and white flowers poked up along the side of the road, petals open toward the sun. Ari turned his face that way too, closing his eyes. "It's just, I've kept so much from her. I try not to lie, but I've been entrusted with so many secrets. Peine was right. I should have told her the truth from the start. The lies have grown so deep, they're going to smother our love."

"Spouting poetry, Lord Aridian?" a familiar voice called. "It is a fine spring day, but I hadn't pegged you with a lyrical bent."

Ari's eyes flew open, a smile forming as he took in a dark-haired Wheylian man on a piebald horse waiting in the lane ahead. "Cooro," he called, urging Stew forward at a swifter pace.

The Wheylian weapons master leaned across the space between them as Ari and Stew drew near, reaching out to clasp Ari's hand in greeting. "Well met, Ari."

"What are you doing here?" As soon as the words left his mouth, Ari realized he'd fallen back on youthful habits. He was a knight now, and king's champion. He really should try to greet people with more decorum.

Lines crinkled about Cooro's brown eyes as he grinned. "Looking for my favorite sparring partner. It's been more than dull since you left Wheylia."

"I'll take dull any day. I've come to appreciate those moments when someone isn't trying to kill me."

"I don't believe a word of it." Cooro turned his piebald mare up the lane, in the direction Ari was traveling. "A man of your skill cannot help but love the challenge of danger."

Ari smiled, shrugging as they headed up the road at a walk. In truth, he didn't love danger, but he did love dueling. Cooro was the most skilled opponent he'd faced, aside from Sir Cadwel. Twice Ari's age and a head shorter, the Wheylian swordmaster was thickly muscled and, Ari knew, deadly fast. His best weapon was the estoc, a light, quick blade favored by the Wheys. During the months Ari had dwelled in Wheylia as

Princess Siara's protector, he'd spent many an afternoon in fierce competition with Cooro, dueling for the pure joy of it.

"Where are you headed?" Ari asked, still wondering what his friend was doing on a back road deep in Lggothland. Not that it was uncommon to see Wheys in Lggothland. Many, like Peine's family, even lived there. Relations between the two kingdoms were stable, and had been for many years. It seemed too much of a coincidence to find Cooro in his path, though.

"I spoke truly. I've come seeking you."

"Me?" Ari's pleasure at seeing his friend dimmed as uneasiness put a pall over the sunny day. "How did you even know where to find me?"

Cooro looked away, tension in his shoulders, which only served to increase Ari's apprehension. "Queen Reudi sent me."

Ari didn't like the sound of that. Why would the Witch Queen of Wheylia send her best swordsman to find him? "Oh?" he prompted, when Cooro didn't continue.

"My queen wasn't clear on why she sent me, I must admit. She claimed you were to embark on a great journey and suggested I accompany you. She said no more than that, but one does not question our queen."

Ari couldn't blame Cooro on that score. He'd met few people more intimidating than Queen Reudi. Since she'd already pressed Ari to go north seeking the stone, as the Lady willed him to, it wasn't much of a leap that she'd sent Cooro to help. "Well." Ari shrugged off anxiety in favor of being happy to have a friend to travel with. "The queen's inscrutable reasons aside, I'd be glad for your company, for so long as you like."

"And I look forward to seeing the vaunted halls of Sorga," Cooro said, the tension leaving him. "And this woman who has inspired such tumultuousness in the mighty Lord Aridian, champion of the Lggothian throne."

Ari shot his friend a grin, but he wished Cooro had spoken a moment sooner upon sighting him, so he wouldn't have babbled about love and secrets in front of the weapons master.

They headed north, Ari steering their talk to more idle ground than his relationship with Ispiria. Cooro possessed a gregarious nature and, in his nearly forty years, had amassed enough stories to be a fine travel companion, especially as most of his tales involved sword fights of one type or another. Ari supposed someone else might find miles passed in the description of a single duel tedious, but martial studies were one of the cornerstones of his life.

Stopping early, they tended their horses and set up camp, then fashioned quarterstaves and set to practicing. Ari knew he wore a foolish grin as they fought back and forth across their small camp, but he didn't care. As much as he'd enjoyed traveling with Larke, the bard didn't claim skill with any type of weapon, and Ari loved to practice.

Cooro wasn't as strong as Ari, who had the hidden advantage of Aluien enhanced musculature, but he somehow managed to be just as quick. Plus, the Whey had a repertoire of acrobatics that Ari would never even attempt. As Wheys traditionally used lightweight weapons and wore only light armor, not the heavy suits of plate a Lggothian knight would employ, Cooro's fighting style was almost a form of dance.

Ari hoped his own armor had arrived safely in Sorga. He'd left the care of that to Prince Parrentine's steward. Sir Cadwel had commissioned the son of the man who once made his armor to make Ari's. His armor was among Ari's most treasured possessions.

"Ow." Ari yelped as Cooro's staff came down on the back of his head. How had the Whey even gotten behind him?

"Woolgathering in the middle of a bout? Please, sir, you insult me with your lack of attention. Is a duel with Cooro now so commonplace to you?"

In answer, Ari spun, dropping low to sweep Cooro's legs out from under him. Ari was too slow, though. The weapons master launched himself into the air, flipping right over Ari. He winced as another blow smacked him on the back of the head.

"The light fails us, my lord," Cooro said, his tone amused. "Perhaps we should halt for the night, before I rattle loose your brains."

"You just want to quit while you're winning." Ari rubbed his head as he straightened, turning. "And I still say jumping and flipping shouldn't be allowed in a duel."

"You are the great knight, my lord, with the great weights of honor, and armor. Cooro never claimed not to cheat."

Ari shook his head, lowering his quarterstaff. "Well, I guess if you're conceding because of poor light, I'm willing to stop." He hid his smile at the look of outrage Cooro crafted his face into.

In truth, Ari hadn't been aware of the lack of light. More so than his enhanced speed and strength, quick healing, or even his lack of sensitivity to cold and heat, it was his ability to see in almost any light that he found hardest to hide from others. He simply didn't notice when it was too dark for most people to see.

"Let's build up the fire," Cooro said. "You can tell me all about this woman you're languishing for."

Putting aside his staff, Ari tossed wood on the small fire they'd made earlier. Maybe it would be useful to speak to Cooro about his worries. Though they weren't as close as he and Peine had been, or as he and Larke were, Ari and Cooro had spent many hours sparring. Ari counted the weapons master as a friend, and Cooro did have a reputation for being popular among the ladies of the court.

"I have a fiancée in Sorga," Ari said. Sitting, he idly tossed a few more twigs at the blaze, watching them curl and burn.

"The Lady Ispiria, grandniece to Sir Cadwel," Cooro said, lowering himself to the ground on the other side of the fire.

Ari nodded. He didn't recall if he'd mentioned Ispiria to Cooro before, but he wasn't surprised the weapons master knew of her. He'd come to realize his marital status was the gossip of two kingdoms. "Well, I did some things I shouldn't have while I was in Wheylia, and I don't know how to tell her, or if I should. Really, they were nothing."

"Some things?" Cooro repeated, his tone a question.

"I kissed someone else. At a ball."

"Lady Leola."

Ari grimaced. He hadn't even known her name. To Ari, she was the girl in the blue dress. "I suppose so."

"Oh, it was her, my young friend. For weeks, she could speak of nothing else but your strong embrace. All the court heard the tale."

Ari groaned, rubbing a hand over his face. Still, it was the Wheylian court. No one there knew Ispiria. It wasn't as if anyone would have written her. He hoped. "That's not all. Princess Siara kissed me. It meant nothing," he hastened to add. "We were meeting in secret, to discuss who might be poisoning the queen, and were discovered. She kissed me merely to create the illusion we were keeping a different sort of secret than knowledge that a murderer was near the throne."

"Of course." Cooro brushed the matter aside with a dismissive gesture.

Ari had known the Whey wouldn't take Siara's kiss seriously. It was common knowledge she was magically bound to love none but Prince Parrentine. The trouble was, Ari wasn't magically bound to love anyone, and Siara's kiss had sparked far too many feelings in him. Feelings a man who deserved Ispiria shouldn't have for another woman, even the one who would be his queen.

"And that is all?" Cooro asked, eyeing him with a slightly amused expression. "Two kisses?"

"Well, er . . ." Ari swallowed. "I did kiss Lady Leola more than once. I'm not actually sure how many kisses were involved. I wasn't exactly counting."

"My point remains the same." Cooro tilted his head back, looking up at the stars with a serious expression. "In the nearly four seasons you were in Wheylia, you kissed two women, one of them not even of your own volition."

"Yes."

"And you hold, I believe, seventeen years to your name?"

"This summer I will be eighteen," Ari said, unsure what that had to do with it.

"I know Sir Cadwel is your benefactor. The world knows the tale of how he plucked you, an orphan, from the obscurity of a stableboy and trained you to be the greatest knight Lggothland has seen."

"Sir Cadwel is the greatest knight Lggothland has ever seen," Ari said, defending even the hint of a disparaging remark against his mentor.

Cooro shot a glance his way and Ari stilled, a bit embarrassed by his aggressive tone. He looked back at the fire, tossing in another twig. It twisted into a brittle knot before igniting in bright orange flame.

"Be that as it may," Cooro continued. "This marriage to Sir Cadwel's grandniece, is it one of convenience or love?"

"Love," Ari said, not needing to think about it. He'd fallen in love with Ispiria, with her wild red hair, sparkling green eyes and effusive personality, the moment they'd met. Being with her, having her smile at him and laugh with him, was like being in the sunlight, and he knew he couldn't live without it.

"And do you plan to continue kissing women who are not your fiancée?"

"Of course not," Ari said, a trifle offended.

"Well, then, it is simple."

"It is?" It didn't seem simple to Ari.

"You cannot tell your lady of these kisses."

"I can't?" That wasn't the advice Ari had expected. He'd been waiting for a discourse on honor and honesty, and his duties as a knight and her future husband. "Why can't I?"

"If it was a marriage of convenience, and you meant to go on in this manner, seeking your amusements where you may, you would have a duty to inform the lady of how things stand between you." Cooro's tone was patient. "But in a union of love, where the lady's heart is committed, it behooves you to never speak of what you have done. You shall endeavor not to repeat your mistakes, so why torment your beloved? What good could possibly come of such a truth?"

Ari studied Cooro, whose face was serene and sincere, then turned his gaze back to the fire. He hadn't thought of it that way, of what was best for Ispiria. He'd only thought in terms of honor and absolute morality. He was a knight, sworn to uphold those philosophies.

Keeping more secrets from Ispiria definitely wasn't what Peine would advise him to do. Of course, Peine had broken the heart of just about every girl in Sorga, so what did he know of love? When you loved someone, you kept their heart safe, and Ari loved Ispiria.

Chapter 6

Though Cooro was a pleasant travel companion, he forced Ari and Stew to make the journey north at a slower pace than they would have alone, and spring was nearly over by the time they drew in sight of Sorga. Ari had been watching the northern range grow on the horizon for days, his eyes straining for the moment he could detect some hint of the keep of Sorga at the base. The evening before their final day of travel, he discerned the two long arms of the mountain which reached out to embrace the keep and knew he was almost home.

The following day, as they rode across the lush plain that rolled away from the foot of the range, Ari's sharp eyes finally picked out the outermost wall of the keep. Shortly thereafter, he could see the flags fluttering from each turret, although he couldn't make out the blue and white of Sorga yet, or the brown hawk emblazoned on each. He knew the moment they sighted him as well, for flags on the outermost wall dipped, signaling to those on the inner fortifications that riders approached. The same flags fluttered in a different sequence as he drew near, letting those within know that the lord of the keep had returned.

The guards cheered as Ari and Cooro rode under the thick outer wall. It spanned the gap between the arms of the mountain, using those natural formations to create a long empty yard. The yard was aptly referred to as the killing zone, across which anyone wishing to gain entrance to Sorga must travel. At the other end of yard stood a second wall, topped by more cheering guards. Ari could see the keep beyond, half-built of gray stone and half-carved from the mountainside itself, and people flooding out to greet him. He grinned, happy to be home.

As he and Cooro passed into the shadow of the inner wall, Ari saw Sir Cadwel standing on the steps to the keep, looking as solid and formidable as ever, his gray mustache drooping over his smile. Sorga's handsome chief steward, Natan, stood to the knight's left, and Sir Cadwel's trusted hounds, Canid and Raven, lounged to either side of the two men. Ari took in the blue light of Orlenia surrounding the giant dogs, aware that only he and Sir Cadwel could see the magic infusing them. With no regard for Aluien sensibilities, Sir Cadwel had employed spells to grant his stalwart companions eternal life.

Stew held his head high, arching his neck as his hooves rang out on the cobblestones of the courtyard. Ari ignored his horse's tendency to put on a show, scanning the crowded steps of the keep for Ispiria's bright red curls, but in vain. He swept his eyes across the back row of those who dwelled in the keep, knowing her great-grandmother usually stood there, but the disapproving Lady Enra was also absent.

Ari supposed the old woman was making Ispiria attend her, deliberately keeping her away. As Ispiria's guardian, her great-grandmother didn't approve of Ari's attachment. Ari wished Lady Enra could be happy for them, like everyone else in Sorga, or would at least decide to leave them alone.

Not that it mattered. He and Ispiria were both of age. They could marry whenever they chose. In fact, if Ispiria didn't mind a bit of a rush, they could be married now, before he headed north to look for the second stone. The thought served to widen Ari's grin even more.

He slid from his saddle as Stew halted before the steps. Canid and Raven came trotting down to greet him, followed by Sir Cadwel and Natan. Ari turned to Stew, murmuring, "Thank you for a safe journey," as a stablehand came to take him away. Over Stew's back, he could see Cooro dismount and hand over the reins of his piebald mare.

"Ari." Sir Cadwel pulled him into a brief, gruff embrace. "You're overdue, lad. We've had your armor returned already, but no sign of you."

"I had a stop to make."

Sir Cadwel nodded. "Aye, so the prince wrote me."

"Welcome home, my lord," Natan said, bowing slightly. "Sorga has missed you."

Ari winced, feeling a stirring of guilt. When Ari was away, the chief steward, once a knight himself, shouldered the burden of managing the dukedom. To cover his discomfiture, he turned and gestured to Cooro. "Sir Cadwel, Chief Steward Natan, this is Swordmaster Cooro of the queen's court in Wheylia."

"My Lord Cadwel, I am humbled to be in the presence of the world's greatest knight." Cooro bowed low, but Ari could see a look of gleeful calculation in the swordmaster's eyes as he assessed Sir Cadwel. "Perhaps, during my stay here, I might have the honor of testing myself against your might?"

Sir Cadwel grunted in response, giving Ari a look that clearly said, where do you come by these idiots?

Ari chuckled, clasping the swordmaster on the back. "I can save you the trouble, Cooro. Sir Cadwel will win."

"You sound so certain." Cooro looked hurt.

"We're all certain," Natan said with a quirk of his lips.

"And it is an honor to meet you as well, Chief Steward Natan." Cooro bowed to Natan. "It is not every day a man gets to meet the most notorious rakehell in Lggothland."

Sir Cadwel let out a bark of laughter.

"Your friend is remarkably well informed, my lord," Natan said to Ari, his tone indicating he didn't appreciate Ari passing on rumors.

Ari shrugged. "Not by me." He declined to add that the follies of Natan's youth had nothing to do with him. Ari hadn't even been born when Natan was stripped of his knighthood.

"Ari," Sir Cadwel said. "Say something to your people."

Ari raised his head to survey the steps again, realizing most of Sorga had spilled from the keep to greet him. Squaring his shoulders, he turned to his people. "Last spring, I left you as Lord of Sorga, a greater honor than any man could ever expect to claim, and one I strive to live up to." Ari knew they would have received word of his success at last spring's tourney long ere now, but they deserved to hear it from him as well. "While I hold my duties here foremost in my mind, I am happy to say I have secured another honor for Sorga, one long held by our dukedom. Just as Sir Cadwel before me, I, Aridian, Duke of Sorga, won the title of King's Champion, protector of the royal family and defender of all of Lggothland."

The people of Sorga cheered. Ari let the warmth of being home wash over him. It wasn't that he wanted adoration, for he didn't, nor did he think of this as such. They cheered for themselves and for Sorga as much as for him. He was their leader, their figurehead, and his successes were for them. He glanced around for Ispiria once more, hoping to see pride in her bright green eyes, but she still hadn't come out.

"A feast tonight," Natan called when the crowd finally began to still, causing the cheering to redouble. "For the Lord of Sorga is returned in triumph."

The cheering died more quickly this time. It became a happy murmur as people reentered the keep, knowing Natan's proclamation for the dismissal it was.

The chief steward turned back to Ari. "Do you wish to adjourn to your study, my lord, or would you care to refresh yourself first?"

"I'd prefer to wash up, if there's nothing pressing."

"Nothing that can't wait," Natan said. "Shall I show our guest to a room?"

"Yes, thank you. Put him somewhere in the upper hall, so I can keep an eye on him." Ari gave Cooro a quick grin. "Gentleman," he said, remembering at the last instant to incline his head, not bow, before turning away.

Peine would be proud of him for remembering that he was lord of the keep and there was no one there he should bow to, Ari thought as he headed inside. He looked around the ancient stone foyer, angling for the steps leading up to the noble's wing. It was strange not to have Peine chattering away beside him. He considered calling for a page, but he'd never really liked having help bathing and dressing anyhow.

He paused outside Ispiria's door, filled with the urge to put his ear to it to listen for her. He was starting to worry about her lack of an appearance. Could she be away? He didn't think she would go anywhere when she knew he was due to return, but her great-grandmother could have convinced her to make their yearly trip to visit their ancestral home of Hawkers earlier than usual.

Looking down at his mud spattered breeches and travel worn tunic, Ari turned resolutely away from Ispiria's door and toward his own chambers. He would find out where she was soon enough, and it would be more considerate of him to be clean when he saw her. Usually, she ran up to him and kissed him, something he was rather looking forward to. He wouldn't want to ruin one of her gowns with the grime of travel.

Spurred to haste by the thought of seeing Ispiria, Ari made short work of bathing. He folded his dirty clothes, opting to set them on the floor where they could do the least damage to the carpet and furnishings. He realized he didn't actually know where laundry was cleaned in Sorga, something he should remedy. Peine had always seen to things like that.

Turning to his wardrobe, he faced another quandary as he tried to recall which tunics Peine would match with which pants. On his journey back, Ari had very few items with him, having sent most of his possessions ahead to Sorga. Now he was faced with an array of tunics, doublets, breeches, shoes, boots and more, and he wasn't sure what to do with them. Growing up, he had two pairs of trousers and two tunics, all in various shades of brown and off white. Then, he'd never dreamed of having someone help him choose what to wear. He sighed, wondering when he'd become so helpless.

Finally, getting a bit cold just standing there, Ari pulled out a plain white tunic and dark blue breeches. He opted to ignore the doublets altogether, as he didn't like the heavy brocade and he knew he'd only choose the wrong one. He supposed he would have to get another valet. As Lord of Sorga, it was his duty not to walk around looking like he'd fought a battle with his wardrobe, and lost.

He was pulling on a clean pair of boots, having also elected to ignore the confusing array of shoes, when he heard the door to his sitting room open.

"Ari?" Ispiria's voice called.

Ari shoved his second foot into a boot and stood, hurrying across his sleeping chamber. He flung open the door separating the two rooms, her name on his lips, and stopped, staring at her.

Ispiria was dressed in a black gown, the fabric bunched about her waist, as it was too large for her. Ari had never seen her wear black before, and it didn't suit her pale complexion at all. Her red curls were woven into a thick braid, which was wrapped about her head in an austere style. He didn't know if it was the braid or the year since he'd last seen her, but her face looked thinner, her high cheekbones more pronounced. Worst of all, her green eyes were ringed with red, as if she'd been crying.

Had he been wrong when he thought word wouldn't reach Ispiria about what he'd done in Wheylia? Did she already know he'd kissed the girl in the blue dress? For the hundredth time, Ari wished he hadn't drunk so much bubbly wine, hadn't gone out on the terrace with Lady Leola and had never, ever kissed her.

"Do I look that terrible?" Ispiria asked. She stood in the doorway, one hand toying with the pendant she wore.

Ari recognized it, a flower sculpted of green stone, which he'd given her as a betrothal gift. Ispiria loved the pendant, but to him it was a constant reminder of the secrets between them. She didn't realize that Larkesong had crafted the piece. It was imbued with spells, both to keep Empty One magic out of Ispiria's head and to make sure she would never want to take it off.

"What's wrong?" he asked, crossing the room to greet her.

She stepped inside, closing the door. Strictly, they shouldn't be allowed alone like this, unchaperoned, but Ari didn't care and he doubted she did, either.

"You didn't get my last letter?" She held out her hands.

He took them, finding them ice cold. "I didn't return via the King's Way. I don't suppose any messenger would have been able to find me. What is it?"

"My great-grandmother died." She swallowed and looked down.

Ari let go of her hands and pulled her close. "I'm sorry." He wished he knew something else to say, anything, to make her feel better. He held little affection for Ispiria's great-grandmother, but she'd raised Ispiria, and he could tell his fiancée was heartbroken. She started to cry against his chest, and he squeezed her tighter, wishing, as well, that he hadn't had such uncharitable thoughts about Lady Enra earlier that day.

Ispiria pulled back, wiping her cheeks with the backs of her hands. "But that's not all." Her lips pulled down at the corners as she gazed up at him.

Ari's heart stuttered in his chest, his guilt over kissing Lady Leola slamming into his misery over Ispiria's tears. "Wh- er, it isn't?" That was all he could manage with her angry green eyes glaring at him.

"How could you let such terrible things happen to Peine?" she demanded. "When I read what happened, I couldn't believe it was actually you writing, Ari." She poked him in the chest, as if to emphasize her annoyance. "First, you allowed him to be embroiled in some sort of conspiracy, against a queen, no less. Then, you let him be banished from Wheylia, and then you let him just up and leave."

Poke, poke, poke, until he thought, if he didn't have magical healing, he would have a bruise.

"Ari, how could you?" Poke. "He's your best friend."

He caught her hand, wishing he dared to kiss it. The way things usually stood between them, and after being away from her for so long, this wasn't how he'd pictured their reunion. "I didn't let him do any of those things. He just did them."

"You're a lord and a knight and he was your valet. You should have stopped him."

"But I didn't know." He dropped her hand, rubbing his own over his face. "If I'd known what he was doing, I would have stopped him. And I didn't let him be banished from Wheylia. Queen Reudi banished him as a favor to me, instead of chopping off his head."

"Oh." She looked a little deflated. "Would she really have done that?"

"He was involved in a conspiracy to kill her."

"Well, yes, I don't suppose people take that well." She pursed her lips. "But how could you let him leave? Will he ever come back? I daresay you can't even pick out a doublet without him."

Ari winced at the truth in that observation. "He had to go tell his parents that his brother is dead," he said softly. He hadn't written Ispiria about the details of how Peine's brother Gauli had died, for it involved some of the secrets he was sworn to keep.

"It just didn't seem like you not to find a way to save Peine from the trouble he got himself in, and save his brother, and, well, make everything right again."

"I did my best." Ari looked down at his boots, realizing Peine would have polished this pair before they left last spring. Would his friend ever return to Sorga?

"I--" She broke off.

Ari brought his gaze back to hers to find her staring at him, a look he couldn't interpret on her face. His eyes moved to her lips, but he didn't lean toward her to kiss them, raking a hand through his hair instead. He was too full of guilt, he realized. Guilt for not saving Peine from his own choices, even though there hadn't been a way to. Guilt for having to kill Peine's brother, though it was at Gauli's behest. Worst of all, he couldn't kiss Ispiria with the guilt of kissing Lady Leola hanging over his head. He'd sworn to keep many secrets, but not telling Ispiria that he'd kissed another woman wasn't one of them and, he realized, he couldn't do it.

"I need to know you're more consistent than that, Ari," she said, her green eyes wide and serious. "Letting Peine walk away isn't something a loyal friend would do."

He hardly heard her. Now that he'd made his decision to confess, the words he needed to say churned in his mind. He drew in a deep breath, gathering his courage.

"My great-grandmother's dying wish was that I not marry you," she said, at the same time as he blurted, "I kissed a girl in Wheylia."

His words hung in the air between them, irrevocably free of his tumultuous mind. Ispiria's eyes were so wide he could see red-rimmed white all the way around the green. Letting out an inarticulate shriek, she spun away from him. He reached for her, but somehow the door was already slamming behind her. He could hear her sobbing as she ran down the hall.

Chapter 7

Ari wasn't sure how long he stood there, his mind entertaining a dozen inadequate ways to apologize, before Sir Cadwel burst into the room, Natan behind him. The look of resigned disappointment on Sir Cadwel's face hurt nearly as much as Ispiria's reaction.

"Sit," Sir Cadwel barked, pointing toward the array of furniture assembled before the fireplace.

Ari moved to the other side of the large couch, dropping himself into it. Natan took one of the high-backed chairs, the smugness of his gaze needling Ari. Looking away, he watched as Sir Cadwel moved to stand before the mantel, drumming his fingers on the stone. The knight turned his formidable frown on Ari, his drooping gray mustache adding even greater severity to his downturned mouth.

"Are you aware that my grandniece stormed into my study and informed me that you have betrayed her trust to the utmost and she can never marry you?"

"No, sir, but I'm not surprised." What did she mean, not marry him? Surely, she would let him apologize.

"Oh how far the virtuous fall." Natan sounded almost gleeful.

Ari's hands fisted at his sides, but he restrained himself from any other reaction. He deserved whatever torment they devised for him. He should never have betrayed Ispiria.

"What have you to say for yourself?" Sir Cadwel asked.

"I'm sorry, sir." Ari had to work not to choke on the words like a child, realizing that he'd played into her great-grandmother's hands with his folly. If it wasn't ill-omened to curse the dead, Ari would give voice to how he felt about her. "I should never have kissed that girl."

"Kissed?" Natan repeated. "As in, kissed?" The smugness dropped away from him and he slouched back in his chair, rolling his eyes toward the ceiling.

"Kissed," Sir Cadwel stated. "And?"

"And, er, I shouldn't have drank so much bubbly wine," Ari added, unsure what else his mentor wanted him to apologize for.

"Let me see if I have this correct," Sir Cadwel said. Ari couldn't read his gruff tone. "You drank too much and kissed a girl. How many times?"

"Uh, I'm not sure. I mean, I wasn't counting at the time." Why did everyone ask that? How much detail could they possibly want? For that matter, what exactly counted as one kiss ending and another starting? "At least six times?"

Sir Cadwel's heavy brows were quirked in an odd way, making him look almost confused. "What I mean is, how many times did you drink too much and betray Ispiria's trust?"

"Well, once, and Siara kissed me once, to make it look as if we were having an affair and not colluding about who was

74

poisoning the queen, but Ispiria ran away before I could tell her about that." He may as well tell Sir Cadwel everything, so whatever punishment his mentor came up with could encompass all of Ari's transgressions.

Stepping away from the mantel, Sir Cadwel sank into the chair opposite Natan.

"You were away for a year," Natan said, eyeing Ari. "And you kissed one girl, at one party?"

"I try not to repeat my mistakes," Ari said, a little angry at how disappointed Natan sounded. What right did Natan, a man so notorious for philandering that he'd been stripped of his knighthood for it, have to be upset with Ari for kissing one girl?

"He's hopeless," Natan said, looking over at Sir Cadwel. "I couldn't be more disgusted. I think there might actually be something wrong with him."

Ari clenched his fists tighter, reminding himself that he'd resolved to take their censure as part of his punishment. He glanced at Sir Cadwel, hoping the knight's reaction wasn't as severe. Ari blinked, surprised, for the unreadable look on Sir Cadwel's face seemed to have transformed into something resembling a smile.

"Well." The knight stood. "I'm sure Ispiria wouldn't have reacted so badly if not for my mother-in-law's absurd dying wish. Just talk to her, Ari."

"You aren't angry with me, sir?"

"Don't break Ispiria's heart and don't sully the bloodline, and I won't have to kill you," Sir Cadwel said, his grin affable.

"Yes, sir," Ari said. He unclenched his fists.

"For the sake of all the gods above and below, Ari, just don't tell her next time," Natan said, as he too stood.

"There won't be a next time," Ari said, turning his head to watch them leave.

"If only that wasn't true," Natan muttered, Ari's keen hearing picking out the words.

"We'll be in the study," Sir Cadwel said as Natan shut the door behind them.

Ari leaned back on the couch, going over what they'd said in his mind. Were they implying he betray Ispiria as much as he liked, so long as he didn't create any illegitimate offspring or upset her by telling her about it? That sounded like terrible advice for how to have a happy life with the woman he loved.

None of them knew what they were speaking of, Ari realized. Not a one. None of his friends, not Larke, Sir Cadwel, Peine, Natan or Cooro, had wives. There was no reason to take advice about Ispiria from a single one of them. He would have to forge his own way forward, and it wouldn't include betraying and lying to Ispiria.

It would include apologizing to her, though. Standing, he left his suite. He went to her door, but his knock received no answer. As he tried again, he could hear women's voices whispering inside.

"Ispiria," he called. "Will you please talk with me?"

The voices fell silent. Ari waited a while longer before turning away. Even his keen hearing couldn't pick out the words of the whispers, or be certain one of them emanated from Ispiria. It could be her maids were inside and she was not. Either way, it wasn't as if he was going to break down her door.

Trying to let go of his frustration, he turned and headed down to the foyer and Sir Cadwel's study, readying himself for another unpleasant task. Natan wouldn't take kindly to learning that Ari must leave again as soon as possible, but if he intended to seek the second stone, it was best done now.

Everything bespoke of this being the time for his quest. The kingdom was at peace, the mountains would be most passable from spring to early fall, by which he hoped to return, and the sooner he went, the more likely he was to beat Tal Mraken. The leader of the Empty Ones had already tried to take the stone the Sorga Hawks had guarded, so he was almost certainly after the one the Questri possessed as well. Ari felt depending on Tal Mraken having no knowledge of the stone's location was too scant a hope.

Of course, Ari was sworn to keep the existence of Aluiens and Empty Ones secret, so he wouldn't be able to tell anyone, save Sir Cadwel, the facts of what he sought or why. Instead, he would have to dance around the truth, deliberately keeping his own chief steward, his fiancée, and the rest of Sorga ignorant. Ari pushed a hand through his mop of brown hair, wishing life wasn't quite so complicated.

Nodding to the footman standing outside, Ari swung open the door to Sir Cadwel's study. The green walled room, with its comfortable leather furnishings and walls lined with books and weapons, contained more people than Ari had anticipated. Natan and Cooro sat near each other, their conversation breaking off as Ari entered. Sir Cadwel was by the fire in his favorite armchair, a book in his hands and Canid and Raven sleeping at his feet. Most importantly, Ispiria sat at a table near the other and of the room.

Ari smiled, hoping desperately she would return the expression. She didn't, looking away from him to drop her gaze to the chessboard on the table before her. Ari hadn't realized, until she did, that someone sat opposite her. The man, of average height and a slightly more slender than average build, peered toward him with curious brown eyes. He had poorly cut brown hair, shot through with gray, and his clothing appeared quite rumpled as he stood.

"My lord," the man said, making an awkward bow. "I'm honored."

"Ari." Sir Cadwel set his book down. "I'd like you to meet Lord Kenmar, our guest this past winter."

"Pleased to meet you, my lord." Ari bowed. Hearing the name, he recalled both Sir Cadwel and Ispiria mentioning the man in their letters to him. "The cartographer, I believe?"

Lord Kenmar smiled, looking pleased. "Yes, yes indeed. I make maps, you see. I plan to expand our knowledge of what lies directly beyond our borders. Our current depictions are quite inaccurate, you know."

"Mostly water," Natan said, looking amused.

"Well, yes," Lord Kenmar said, sitting back down.

Ispiria shot Natan a glare, her gaze passing coldly over Ari.

"No, no, it's true, my dear." Lord Kenmar reached out to pat Ispiria's hand with a familiarity that rankled. "Lggothland and Wheylia share a peninsula, so, by definition, they're nearly surrounded by water. That's why I'm here, of course, for Sorga's holdings in the mountain mark the northernmost extent of our detailed maps."

"How detailed can a map of the Great Northern Plains be," Natan said, reaching to pour himself a drink. He glanced at Cooro, who nodded, watching the exchange with what appeared to be mild amusement. "I've never been, but they say it's just a lot of grass in the summer and a lot of snow in the winter."

Ari's eyes narrowed. He hardly listened while Lord Kenmar and Natan entered into what seemed like an oft-revisited argument about the value of mapping the plains. Ari had learned by now not to be content with coincidence. How was it this afore unknown lord was here, in his home, wanting to go north at the same time as Ari planned to? He shot a look at Cooro. The swordmaster met his eyes and nodded, seeming to say he thought it a bit suspicious as well.

"When did you say you arrived in Sorga, Lord Kenmar?" Ari asked, not caring that he was breaking into Lord Kenmar's and Natan's discussion. Obviously uninterested, Sir Cadwel had already returned to reading his book.

"Last fall." Lord Kenmar gave Ari a timid smile. "I set about corroborating the maps I had of the mountains, but, you see, the snow came before I could reach the other side and lay eyes on the plains."

"And a good thing, too," Natan said. "As it was, we had to put out a search for him. Found him half frozen out in the snow. If you don't mind me saying, my lord, you're a bit of a disaster when let out of a library."

Lord Kenmar coughed, making a show of studying the chessboard between him and Ispiria. "I'm sure I don't know what you're speaking of."

Natan grunted, shaking his head. He opened his mouth.

Ari preempted him. "Well, this is a fortuitous turn of events, then." Realizing he was still standing just inside the doorway, he moved to sit on the opposite end of the couch Cooro occupied, facing the chess table. "For Swordmaster Cooro and I were about to travel north ourselves."

The hand Ispiria held over the board jerked, knocking over several pieces. "You're leaving again already?" Her voice was high. She was finally looking at him, but her face was full of hurt and anger.

Ari winced. What was he thinking, blurting out his plans in front of her like that, instead of taking her aside to tell her first?

At this rate, it wouldn't be her great-grandmother's fault if she wouldn't marry him.

"The crown has need of you again so soon?" Natan asked, setting his glass down. "Does the king not realize that you have a dukedom to run?"

"It isn't for the king. Actually, uh, I have news." He shifted in his seat, adjusting his thinking. What was he doing, eyeing the people around him with suspicion and deliberately making startling declarations to test their reactions? This wasn't Wheylia. He wasn't on a mission. He was home. These people were his family, and Lord Kenmar was their guest.

"What sort of news?" Sir Cadwel asked, setting aside his book.

"I've learned what happened to my parents." Now everyone was staring at him. "They were murdered."

Ispiria gave a little gasp.

"The story . . . I'd rather not tell it now." Ari redirected his train of thought, for he couldn't blurt out the whole truth before everyone in the room. "Suffice it to say, I need to go north as part of my quest to avenge them."

"And the king has given you permission to do this?" Sir Cadwel asked, his tone stern.

"Well, I haven't asked him, exactly. I mean, I'm a free man, am I not?"

"You are also the sworn protector of this land," Sir Cadwel said. "What if you're off on the northern plains and something urgent transpires in Lggothland?"

"But I must go. A certain Lady charged me to, and I agreed."

Sir Cadwel nodded his understanding, frowning. He was probably thinking the same thing Ari was. They owed obedience to the Lady, yet also to the crown. "We'll require a way to reach you quickly, should the king have need."

"Do you mean the queen charged you to?" Natan asked. "For, in Lggothland, the queen's word bears nearly the weight of the king's."

"If I may intrude," Cooro said. "I know this isn't a matter for my people, but Queen Reudi also suggested Lord Aridian journey north, and sent me to aid him."

Natan smiled slightly. "I say two queens are at least as good as a king, if we can devise a way to reach you speedily. I can manage things here well enough without you for a few more seasons, assuming you'll tend to a small amount of pressing business before you depart."

Ari glanced at Natan, surprised he was being so agreeable. He usually lamented being left alone to govern. The chief steward shrugged. Picking up his glass, he drained the content before refilling it.

"Mirimel," Ispiria blurted out.

Ari turned to look at her.

"When I was in Hawkers for the . . . the funeral, Mirimel told me the hawks could always find her, no matter where she went." She tapped her cheek, frowning. "I think maybe it was a secret, so don't tell anyone."

Natan coughed, taking another large sip of his drink. Across from Ispiria, Lord Kenmar looked to be doing his best to stay unnoticed and small. He reached out and set the chess pieces she'd knocked over to rights.

"The idea has merit," Sir Cadwel said, drawing their gazes.

Ari nodded. He should have thought of it. He knew of Ispiria's cousin's magical-seeming affinity for the hawks, though few others did. Mirimel could feel their emotions, and call them to her. She would be the perfect person to accompany him, and not just because of her skill with the Sorga Hawks. Hawk Guardian Mirimel was an excellent tracker, well trained with sword and knife, a scratch shot with a bow, and Ari trusted her.

"Yes, Mirimel has to go." Ispiria sounded oddly intent. "She knows the way through the mountains, she has her hawks." She turned angry eyes back to Ari. "And I don't know if there are any women on the northern plains, but she can also keep an eye on Ari."

Ari stared at her, wondering if she would come aside and speak with him. He didn't really appreciate her implying, in front of everyone, that he needed supervision. In fact, he was beginning to feel a little put out. It was just a few kisses, after all, and he was well and truly sorry about it. He would tell her how sorry, if she would let him.

Deciding he didn't wish to address their argument in public, he turned to Natan. "We can begin attending to the business of the keep tomorrow, if that's soon enough for you. I'll write Hawk Guardian Mirimel and put together supplies, and a plan. I would like to leave soon, as the weather seems fairly stable. Lord Kenmar, you're more than welcome to travel with us, though I can't say how map-worthy our course will be."

Ari looked around the room, finding everyone watching him again, though Ispiria looked sullen. He came back to Natan. "Keep an eye out for a missive from my bard friend, Larke. He's looking into locating members of my family for me. He believes I have grandparents on my father's side, in the trades, and that I belong to a minor noble house on my mother's." He stood. "And please assign me a valet while I'm here, but let him know I won't be taking him with me. I'm assuming my armor has already arrived?" Natan nodded, looking bemused. "Have him bring it up to my chambers for me to inspect. That will be all. I'll see you at dinner."

Ari knew he sounded pompous, even a bit harsh, but his temper was in danger of deserting him. He'd waited so long to be here, with these people, and Ispiria was making it impossible to be happy. He knew it was his fault, but it still hurt.

With a last glance around, he marched from the room. He didn't really have anywhere to go, or anyone he wanted to spend time with who wasn't in the study. He did, however, want to be alone with his sullen musings.

Chapter 8

Ari rose before dawn, the chill air in his chamber reminding him that it wasn't truly spring yet, though the snow had mostly receded. He dressed himself instead of ringing for his new valet. He didn't need a fancy doublet for his morning practice, after all. Belting on his sword over serviceable brown attire, he strolled from his suite.

He went first to check on Stew, filling him in on the happenings of the day before. Ari couldn't be sure his horse cared about what went on inside the keep, but he didn't want to exclude him. It wasn't Stew's fault he didn't fit into Sir Cadwel's study.

Back outside the stable, Ari stretched, bringing warmth to his limbs before turning to the dilapidated practice dummy. Behind him, the sun would take time to crest the arm of the mountain, but the sky was already aglow. Drawing his sword, he inhaled deeply, taking in the smell of wood smoke mixed with that of fresh baked bread wafted from the keep, mingling with the muddy scent of spring. Ari couldn't believe it had been a year since he'd stood in this spot, ready for a morning of practice.

In the mood to exert himself after yesterday's frustrations, which had included a dismal dinner sitting beside a frosty fiancée, Ari took his heavy greatsword in one hand. It wasn't something he did often, for he didn't like to emphasize his enhanced strength. Today, though, he was filled with restless annoyance, and no one was about yet.

He saluted the dummy, then launched into a series of attacks better suited to a sabre than the giant sword he held. Ari focused on speed and precision, for he could never unleash his strength. One full swing of his sword would smash the dummy into a useless heap, and he'd just have to assemble a new one.

The morning sun was full upon Ari by the time he halted, his arms weary and his forehead streaked with sweat. He glanced up at the sky, realizing he must have practiced right through breakfast. A smattering of applause behind him caused him to whirl, raising his sword.

Cooro and Sir Cadwel stood on the steps of the keep, a semi-circle of guards and other castle folk behind them. The people of Sorga wore expressions ranging from pride to awe, making him feel a bit embarrassed. So much for no one being around, Ari thought as Sir Cadwel and Cooro descended the steps. Sir Cadwel's pair of giant shaggy gray hounds meandered down behind him.

"He really is quite extraordinary, isn't he?" Cooro was saying to Sir Cadwel as they drew near. "Oft-times, I flatter myself that I may equal him in some way, but I know it's merely a fantasy."

"He's passable," Sir Cadwel said.

"Sir, Swordmaster." Ari bowed. He eyed the large wooden practice swords the knight carried. To Ari's eyes, they glowed with Orlenia. "Did you wish a bout, sir?" he asked hopefully.

"If you aren't too fatigued." Sir Cadwel held out one of the blades. "I've been working on these, anticipating your return. They're well-crafted to be stronger than the average practice blade."

"I'm not tired at all, sir." Ari took the sword eagerly. If he understood Sir Cadwel, the knight was saying they could practice using their full strength, without worry of shattering the wooden blades.

The rest of the morning passed amicably for Ari. It was one of his greatest joys to practice sword work, and Cooro and Sir Cadwel were the only two people he'd ever found who presented true challenges.

Ari and Sir Cadwel tied their bouts, while Ari beat Cooro more often with the quarterstaff, but less often when they brought out the estocs. Sir Cadwel had greater success against the Whey, much to Ari's chagrin. Ari would have kept up their bouts all day, but at lunchtime his stomach growled so loudly, it startled Canid and Raven to their feet.

"Your gut has more sense than you do, lad," Sir Cadwel said. He stood between the hounds, watching Ari and Cooro circle each other.

Cooro lowered the tip of his estoc to the earth. "Maybe we ought to call it a morning."

Ari nodded. He really did wish to carry on, but he shouldn't push Cooro, a mortal man, too far, and he was very hungry. Reluctantly, he handed over the estoc he held to the guard Sir Cadwel waved over.

"I can help put all this right," Ari said, looking about at the mess they'd made of the practice yard, various dulled weapons littering the area.

The young guard pulled the weapon closer against his chest. "We'll tend to it, my lord. It's the least we can do after the privilege of such a display." He bowed to Ari before turning to deliver the same respectful gesture to Sir Cadwel and Cooro.

"The men can see to it, Lord Aridian." Sir Cadwel emphasized Ari's title.

"Thank you," Ari said to the guards. He didn't like anyone clearing up after him, but he supposed staying would only make them uncomfortable.

"After lunch, I'd like you to ride out to look over some of the holdings with me," Sir Cadwel said as Ari drew alongside him.

Ari frowned, but nodded. He hurried to his room to change, wondering at the request. Sir Cadwel had sworn to have nothing to do with the running of the dukedom, and the knight always kept his word. Not interfering in mortal lives was part of his agreement with the Aluiens when he joined their ranks, and that specifically included the people of Sorga.

His enjoyment of the morning effectively dampened by the knight's strange request, Ari made hasty work of lunch before excusing himself from Natan's and Cooro's company and heading to the stable. Rather than call a groom, he saddled Stew and Sir Cadwel's horse, Goldwin, leading them out as the knight was descending the keep's steps.

Sir Cadwel nodded in greeting, accepting Goldwin's reins. Wordlessly, he mounted and led the way from the keep. Without direction from Ari, Stew kept pace beside them.

Sir Cadwel took them east, the afternoon sun at their backs, and Ari wracked his mind for what the knight's goal could possibly be. There wasn't much east of Sorga save the rocky coast. That did appear to be where they headed, for they crested a cliff overlooking the dark northern sea and halted. Below, the surf smashed against the shore in an endless rumble. The wind whipped across the ocean toward them, the combined forces of air and water occasionally strong enough to bring a dusting of sea spray surging into the air before the horses' hooves.

"Natan is stealing money from the coffers," Sir Cadwel said.

"What?" Ari choked out, so startled the word caught in his throat.

"I've been pretending not to touch the ledgers for over a year, and you've been absent." The knight shrugged, the movement matching the nonchalance of his tone. Glancing at him, Ari could see hurt deep in Sir Cadwel's hard blue eyes, belying his detachment.

"He's been steward of Sorga for . . ." Ari trailed off, unsure of the number of years. Longer than he'd been alive. "Why?"

"I don't know. It began with so little, I thought the error was mine. He doesn't know I've been keeping track, of course. I daresay the only why is because he can. He's always had a difficulty with honesty."

Ari stared out over the restless ocean. He recalled Natan's lack of concern the day before, when Ari said he would have to leave again almost immediately. "What should I do?"

Sir Cadwel shrugged again. "I'm not in a position to say. It's wrong enough that I told you, but it's nothing you wouldn't have figured out, if you'd the time."

There was no censure in his mentor's tone. Sir Cadwel didn't begrudge Ari the months he must be away doing the king's bidding. Of all people, the great knight knew what it was like to place the good of the land before the good of one dukedom, even their own. Sir Cadwel had, after all, done that very thing for twenty-five years.

"I'll have to confront him," Ari said, grimacing. How could he confront the man who ran Sorga for him? A man twice his age with ten times his knowledge and experience when it came to running a dukedom?

"Not immediately."

"No. I'll have to make a show of going over the ledgers first." Ari sighed, pushing a hand through his hair.

Sir Cadwel nodded.

They both resumed their perusal of the endless rolling sea, the northern waters dark and cold under the clear blue of the spring sky.

"Larke knows your family, then?" Sir Cadwel asked.

Ari nodded, recalling he had more to worry about than a pilfering steward. "He has all along, of course." He turned to find Sir Cadwel looking at him with compassion on his gruff face.

"May I ask who they are?"

With that little prompting, Ari divulged the whole tale. He spoke of the Lady's confession, of how she'd arranged for him to meet Sir Cadwel. He told the knight about his parents' flight, and his grandfather the painter. "I have a picture of my mother," he added, at the end. "Larke gave it to me. I should have it reframed and hung."

"I can understand your suspicion of Lord Kenmar now." Sir Cadwel wore a contemplative frown. "I never thought to question if the man is what he seems to be."

"Was I that obvious?" Ari frowned.

"And your new friend, this Wheylian swordmaster?" Sir Cadwel asked, not bothering to answer Ari's question.

"Cooro?" Ari shot a surprised look at Sir Cadwel. "As far as I know, Cooro is simply Cooro. He's the best swordsman in Wheylia. Queen Reudi sent him to help me with my quest to find the second stone."

"The Witch Queen of Wheylia has never been known for her altruism."

"Even if she has other goals, I don't think Cooro's a part of them." Cooro was the only friend Ari had for most of the past year. Already, when faced with danger, he'd trusted the weapons master with his life.

"I suppose there's no help for it but to take the two of them, and Mirimel, and head north," Sir Cadwel said. "I know you'll keep your wits about you as this unravels."

Stew snorted, pawing at the earth with one hoof.

"And Stew," Ari said. If he was going to find the Questri, he wanted Stew with him. He couldn't communicate with his horse very well, but he trusted Stew to be on his side and to help him with the other Questri.

"Of course," Sir Cadwel said. "Have we covered everything we can't speak of in front of the others?"

"I think so. Thank you for the warning about Natan."

With a nod, Sir Cadwel urged Goldwin away from the edge of the cliff, directing the great steed back toward the keep. Ari didn't follow immediately, his thoughts in turmoil as he gazed out across the waves.

During the next several days, Ari surreptitiously went over the ledgers. It wasn't that he didn't believe Sir Cadwel. Rather, the accusation he had to make toward Natan was too great for him to do it on anyone's word but his own, even his mentor's.

In addition to the time he spent closeted with those volumes, he practiced with Cooro and Sir Cadwel in the mornings, tended to the matters Natan brought before him for ducal approval, organized his foray north, and tried to find a chance to speak with Ispiria. Normally, she employed an uncanny ability to appear places she shouldn't be so they might have a few stolen minutes.

Apparently, she was just as good at avoiding him as seeking him out. It wasn't that he didn't see her, of course. He never saw her in private, however, and the conversation he wished to have wasn't one he desired an audience for. As the days passed, he started to despair she'd allow him to speak with her before he left.

Natan, however, was another matter. Ari had no difficulty knowing where the chief steward was. Other times aside, they'd specifically taken to meeting each afternoon in Sir Cadwel's study to discuss the business of Sorga. The day after Ari finished his examination of the ledgers, he arrived there early, wanting to ensure the room would be vacant of all but Natan and himself. His reprimand of Natan was another conversation he didn't feel would be improved by witnesses.

At first, Ari thought the dimly lit room was empty but, as he walked toward the table he and Natan usually met at, he made out the form of Lord Kenmar. The gentleman sat, a burned down candle beside him and his gaze fixed on nothing, several maps laid out before him on the tabletop. He was so still, and that corner of the room so dark, Ari blinked several times to bring him into focus. He coughed and Kenmar's head swiveled toward him.

Ari stopped midstride, almost flinching at the pain reflected in Kenmar's eyes. The older lord gave himself a shake, a smile easing his expression. Ari ran a nervous hand through his hair, wondering what the matter could be and if he even wanted to know.

"Lord Kenmar." Ari crossed to the table. "I didn't see you there, at first. Your candle has burned out."

Kenmar looked at the slightly smoking stub, appearing a little bemused. "So it has. I must confess, I was too deep in thought to notice."

"Is something troubling you, my lord?" Ari hoped his reluctance didn't show. The last thing he needed was another problem, and he hardly knew this lord.

"We are all of us troubled by some things, are we not?" Kenmar's eyes dropped to his maps. "One of my troubles does, I confess, seem more immediate." He looked up at Ari, his narrow face pinched further by worry. "I know it isn't my place to give advice, Lord Aridian, but, in the nearly half year I've been among your people, I've grown fond of Lady Ispiria, you see."

Ari stifled a sigh, nodding. He didn't see this conversation going anywhere he wanted it to. Natan was coming to meet with him soon. How rude could he be without giving true offense? "Yes, well, she's easy to care for."

Kenmar smiled, but his eyes still reflected sorrow. "Yes, yes indeed. She reminds me so of my own daughter. She had red hair, you know, like her mother. I'd forgotten what it's like, having such a spirit about."

"Did she leave home to wed, then?" Ari didn't really care, but maybe the question would derail the lord from whatever he planned to say about Ispiria.

"Ah, no." Kenmar dropped his gaze again, but Ari could hear something hard in his voice. "No, um, you see, my family was struck down by a terribly malady, of sorts. My wife and children were taken from me, including my elder son. My younger son survives, but he is in a state of constant suffering."

"I'm very sorry to hear that, my lord," Ari said, stunned. He'd no idea the scholar had known such loss.

"Yes, well, I was sorry to live through it," Kenmar muttered. "Fate is ever cruel."

"Is that why you travel, in hopes of finding a cure for your son?" Ari asked as the idea came to him. He recalled Prince Parrentine's mad dash about the kingdom, seeking aid, when his first betrothed was ill. Maybe Kenmar did the same, albeit more sedately.

Kenmar looked up at him, his face surprised. "I hadn't thought of it. I suppose, possibly, in a way, though I know there is no remedy for him."

"Still, no one can sit idly and watch a loved one suffer." Ari drew in a deep breath. The conversation had definitely taken a turn he hadn't expected.

"Right, yes, and Ispiria is suffering."

"What?" Ari pulled out the chair across from Kenmar, sitting. The man was tenacious. "I mean, I know she is, and I want to make it right, but she won't let me."

"I . . ." Kenmar pressed his already thin lips into a line of worry. "May I be so bold as to ask, rumors abound, but what did you do?"

"I drank too much and kissed a girl at a ball." Ari scrubbed his fingers over his forehead, aware of the tension there. It really wasn't any of Kenmar's concern, but if rumor abounded, as the lord put it, he may as well get in his side of things.

"This is not so grave an offence." Kenmar's face became stern. "You shouldn't have done it, nor should you again, but it is mendable."

"And I wish to mend it, but she won't speak with me."

"I will attempt to persuade her, if I may?"

Ari shrugged. For all he knew, she would listen to Kenmar. She seemed fond of the scholar, and he was persistent. No one else had offered as much, he realized. "Thank you."

"And you shall say you're sorry, and all will be well." Kenmar seemed certain.

Ari wasn't. Ispiria had never been so angry with him before. "I don't see how saying I'm sorry will fix things when she's this angry. I think I should explain what happened, so she'll understand."

Kenmar shook his head. "Start with sorry. When you say you're sorry to a woman, you're really saying more. You're saying that, even if she was also wrong, you acknowledge that you were. You're saying that her feelings have value to you, and you respect them and her right to have them. You're saying you love her."

"I am?" Ari asked, a bit surprised. He wasn't sure two words could mean that much. On the other hand, Lord Kenmar once had a wife and a daughter, so he might actually know of what he spoke. "Thank you for the advice, my lord. I'll take it into consideration."

"It is but a small payment on my debts to you."

"Debts?"

"I have been living in your keep for nearly half a year, Lord Aridian."

"And, from all I've heard, a pleasant addition to it." Ari mustered up a smile. Discussing Ispiria with Lord Kenmar wasn't how he'd meant to spend his last moments before confronting Natan, but the cartographer seemed sincere in his desire to help. "Um, could I ask you to leave the room now, though, please? I have a meeting with Chief Steward Natan."

"Yes, of course. I apologize, Lord Aridian. I'll just move these." He stood, reaching out ink-stained hands to pull his maps and notebook to him.

"You really can just call me Ari. I mean, we're both lords, after all. Actually, if I had my way, everyone would call me by my name. This whole lord business is a bit arrogant." Ari realized, as he said it, that he might be giving offense. "Er, for me, not you, of course. You're from a long line of lords, I'm sure, and deserve every honorific, my lord."

Kenmar clasped his pile of parchment to his chest, turning thoughtful eyes on Ari. Some strange emotion swirled in their dark depths. "You aren't what I expected, Ari." He bowed, turning away.

Ari watched him go, not really sure how to reply to that. What should he be like? If he wasn't what was expected, did that mean people had been talking about him? Was he better or worse than expected? Ari looked about him, but the empty room offered no answers.

Realizing they'd never remedied the lack of light, Ari stood. He stirred up the fireplace and lit a few candles, declining to summon a servant to do what he could easily do himself. Last, he went to the door and asked the page without to please turn anyone away except Natan, and not to allow anyone else in until he and Natan were done discussing keep business.

Ari retrieved the heavy ledgers from their shelf, arranging them on the table. He sat back down to wait for Natan to arrive. The chief steward came in with a smile, but it dimmed when he looked around the nearly empty room. It extinguished completely when his eyes fell on the open pages in front of Ari.

"Please, sit," Ari said quietly.

Natan cast a glance toward the door.

"I insist," Ari said, gesturing to the seat across from him.

"Going over the ledgers, my lord?" Natan crossed to take the seat. He was smiling again, but Ari could see the strain in it. "May I ask how far you--"

"Far enough." Ari leaned back, gripping the arms of his chair. He hadn't expected the tightening in his chest, and realized it filled him with sorrow to have to confront a friend like this.

He'd thought long and hard, and he knew what he must do. He needed Natan to run Sorga. There wasn't time to find anyone else with the skills, nor anyone he could trust even as much as he trusted this man.

Natan's eyes darted about the room. He cleared his throat as his gaze came to rest on the decanter at the end of the table. "May I?"

Ari nodded, watching the Natan pour himself a drink. He downed the content of the tumbler in two swallows, setting it back on the table. He folded his hands in front of him, looking at Ari, who was surprised to see fear in Natan's eyes.

"My lord?" Natan asked.

Ari realized he'd been staring for too long, studying the signs of age that had begun to blur Natan's striking features. "I would like you to increase your pay."

Natan flinched. "Pardon me?"

"I see here." Ari tapped the ledger. "That, as duke, I receive a large sum of money from the dukedom. An unfairly large sum, that is. I wish you to take a portion of that, at your discretion, and add it to your own wage. A fixed amount," he added, lest he encourage Natan to take more and more.

"I . . . that's very generous of you, my lord. I don't understand."

"At this time, you do most of the work of managing the dukedom. You should be properly compensated."

"Ah, thank you." Natan looked down at his hands.

Ari could tell how tightly they were pressed together by the strained white skin of Natan's knuckles. "It's my understanding that the income of the duke should be employed as he sees best for the dukedom. I feel paying you more adequately for your service is a good use of the funds. At this time," he said again.

Natan raised his eyes as Ari reiterated that point. Tension making the movement jerky, the chief steward nodded.

Ari leaned forward. "But you are going to return every coin you took from the people of Sorga, and if I ever find you stealing from my people again, I'll hang you." Ari let all the anger he felt at Natan's betrayal flow into those words. He locked eyes with the older man for a long moment before leaning back. "Are we clear?"

Natan stared at him, seeming stunned into immobility by the threat. Ari reminded himself how angry he was, not just at what Natan had done, but because the actions forced Ari to issue threats. He didn't think he actually meant what he'd said, but he couldn't allow Natan to realize that. If morality wouldn't guide the man, fear would have to do.

Finally, Natan nodded.

"Good." Ari snapped the ledgers closed. He pressed his lips firmly together, hoping the shakiness he felt inside didn't show. "There's one more issue."

Natan was sitting stiffly now, looking more hurt and angry than guilty. Ari wondered if he'd gone too far with his threat. He knew it was what Sir Cadwel would have done, but did that really make it the best approach? He wanted to keep Natan from stealing, not create animosity between them.

"My lord?" Natan prompted.

"Why did you do it?" Ari shook his head. "Do you need money for something? You could have written me. I'll give you all the money you require."

Natan looked away, his eyes roaming over the shelves of books to his left. He sighed. "Because it was there, and no one was paying any attention. Cadwel can't be bothered with any of it. You're never here. I've been managing this dukedom for years, with little thanks and no real privileges." He shrugged, meeting Ari's eyes again. "It was there," he repeated.

"Well, it's still going to be there. You're still in charge of the funds coming in." Ari realized he was tapping his finger on the ledger and stopped. "Natan, I need you to run Sorga. More than that, you're my friend. Can I trust you?"

Natan swallowed. "Yes, my lord."

Ari let out his breath. "Good. Thank you." He grimaced. He probably shouldn't be thanking the man he'd just dressed down for robbing Sorga. "You're excused. I don't feel like discussing any additional business today."

"Yes, my lord." Natan's chair scraped back as he stood.

Ari stayed sitting. He did his best to look tired, or bored. Anything but what he was, which was miserable and a little nauseated. Under the table, his legs were shaking. "I'll see you at supper."

"Yes, my lord." Natan crossed to the door. "My lord?" he asked, not reaching for the handle.

"What?" Ari wished Natan would leave before the controlled facade he'd adopted could crumble.

"Did you tell Sir Cadwel?"

Ari raised his eyebrows. Apparently, as daunting as he'd tried to make himself, there was still something Natan feared more. "No, I did not tell Sir Cadwel," Ari replied, going with the strict truth, both to spare Natan and to maintain the anonymity of his informant.

"Thank you, my lord." Natan pushed the door open, hurrying from the room.

Resting his elbows on the table, Ari dropped his head into his hands, scrubbing them over his face. He hoped Natan hadn't seen him shaking. Ari had never tried to intimidate anyone before, though he'd seen Sir Cadwel do it many times. It felt even worse than he ever imagined.

The door swung open again. Ari popped his head up, trying to muster a look of flinty indifference before Natan could see how hollow his threat was, but it wasn't Natan.

In a swirl of black skirts, Ispiria spun to shut the door before turning back to face him. "I've come to speak with you, my lord," she said, her tone frosty.

Chapter 9

Ari gaped at her. Now? He'd been trying to find time alone with her for days, and she wanted to speak to him now? Had Kenmar been so persuasive, and so quick? Ari could wish it otherwise, for his meeting with Natan had left him dispirited.

She frowned at him from her position by the door. "You look awful, Ari."

He rubbed his hands over his face again before placing them flat on the table. "You look beautiful," he managed, although he doubted flattery would help.

Her eyes came to rest on Natan's empty glass. "Have you been drinking?"

"No." He stared at her, wondering how long she would wear the somber tones and severe coif of mourning. That wasn't all that was different, though. She seemed more grown up and less . . . fun.

Ari winced. He may not be the most brilliant when it came to speaking with the opposite sex, but he knew that wasn't something he should even think when in Ispiria's presence, lest she somehow read it in his eyes. "You want to speak with me?"

"I do." Setting her jaw, she marched over and pulled out the chair so recently vacated by Natan, seating herself across from Ari. Wrinkling her nose, she pushed the empty glass aside.

Ari scrutinized her face, wishing she'd smile. He hadn't seen her smile in over a year, which seemed quite unfair, really. He'd dreamed of it often enough. He realized he was drumming his fingers on one of the ledgers again and stopped.

"You're supposed to start," she said, sounding annoyed.

"How can I start when I don't know why you came to speak with me?"

"Ari, you're leaving in two days. Who knows how long you'll be away this time. I've come to give you a chance to explain yourself which, really, I thought you would have done by now."

"Explain myself? You mean apologize? How could I have done that by now when you keep avoiding me?" He couldn't keep the frustration from his voice.

"You were supposed to find a way." Her lips formed a pout. "You're supposed to show me how much you care by overcoming all obstacles."

"But you placed them." He drew in a deep breath, aware his voice had become almost a wail.

"That's not the point." She tossed her head. "You're king's champion. You're supposed to be unstoppable and steadfast."

"I am steadfast, and I'm sorry," he added, recalling Lord Kenmar's advice. "Really sorry." Even though her eyes softened, he searched for more words, still sure sorry wasn't enough. "And I should have tried harder to see you. I know that now. It's just, I've been so busy and--"

"Busy?" It was only one word, but it was filled with more venom than he would have thought Ispiria could unleash.

Maybe he should have left things with sorry. He shut his eyes, his thoughts vacillating between the idiocy of using being busy as an excuse, and anger that she wouldn't let him apologize. Did his exact words really matter when he was trying so hard to speak what was in his heart?

"You've been away for a year, you're only here for a handful of days, and yet you're too busy to speak with me?" she said, bitterness still in evidence.

"You grew up here, with Sir Cadwel. I thought you said you know what it's like to be married to the king's champion."

"We aren't married yet," she snapped. "We were supposed to be married this spring, but now you're too busy."

Ar stared at her. Was that what this was really about? He would marry her any day she wanted, if she would stop being angry with him for long enough.

"Not too busy to kiss other girls, though," she added, her tone sullen. She crossed her arms over her chest and stared down at the table.

"Ispiria." He reached across the table, but her arms were folded, so he couldn't take her hand. "I'm very, very sorry I kissed that girl. It will never happen again."

"Why did you do it?" she asked in a small voice, still looking down.

"I don't really know. I drank too much. I'm not even sure how it started."

"That's not very reassuring. I spent the past year without even anyone to dance with, except Lord Kenmar, because everyone is so afraid of you, and you've been off drinking and kissing people."

Ari took in her red-rimmed eyes, trying to understand what it must be like to be Ispiria. He'd come to love Sorga. He wasn't one for fancy parties and crowds of people, but Ispiria had been here her entire life, save for one brief trip to the capital. Would he love Sorga as much if he wasn't forced to spend so much of his time away from it? Would the familiarity and solitude of their northern home seem like the sanctuary he found it to be, or would it feel like a prison? "Maybe you should return to the capital."

She shot him a look through narrow eyes. "Are you trying to get rid of me?"

Ari shook his head. "I assure you, the young men in Poromont are even more afraid of me than the ones here." He reached for her hand again. To his relief, this time she uncrossed her arms and gave it to him. "I want you to get to go to dances and on picnics and all those things."

"And drink too much and kiss people?" She tilted her head to one side with an evil glint in her eyes.

"If you don't mind causing the violent death of some poor fellow so you can have a few kisses, go right ahead," Ari said, tension tightening his jaw.

"You're squeezing my hand too hard."

"Sorry," he muttered, easing his grip.

"You realize that's not fair."

Ari shrugged. He didn't care if it was fair or not. No one was allowed to kiss his fiancée but him. He noticed the satisfied gleam in her eyes, the slight quirk to her lips, and realized she'd been hoping for just that reaction. "Look, why don't we agree that neither of us will go around kissing anyone but each other?"

"I thought that was implicit in our engagement."

"It should have been. I'm sorry."

"I know." Ispiria sighed. She smiled at him, a real smile. "I can tell you're sorry, and I really do believe you that it won't happen again. After all, you're the noblest knight in the realm. You've proved as much."

Ari returned her smile, although he'd never really accepted that prowess in battle meant a person was in the right. Still, it was a longstanding tradition of the knighthood. Ispiria's smile grew a little wider. "What?" he asked.

"You really are a knight now."

"I am." He frowned. He had been since the spring tourney a year past. She should know. She was there.

"I haven't really gotten accustomed to the idea. You look more grown up, you know. You act more grown up, too. You even give orders to people."

"I guess so." Ari felt a little awkward about that. He'd been obliged to learn to. He'd just spent the past year in Wheylia in charge of Princess Siara's retinue, including a whole contingent of men.

"But not to me," she added.

"I wouldn't dare," he said, a little confused. "Are we done fighting now?"

"Not if you spoil it by asking."

Ari shut his eyes for a moment. Ispiria squeezed his hand. He looked down at their clasped fingers, hers so slender and white, while his were thicker, calloused and tan. "I'd hoped we could be married by now. I'm sorry I have to go away again."

"It's important to find out who murdered your parents." She shook her head. "Which is awful. I know you thought they must be gone, but murder . . ." She shuddered. "You're the greatest knight in the realm. You can't let someone get away with that. Although, you do realize the killer might already be dead or something. It was a long time ago."

"I suppose that's true." They were moving onto shaky ground, though she didn't know it. He knew Tal Mraken wasn't dead, but there was no way to explain that to Ispiria without breaking multiple vows. He searched for a change in topic that wouldn't make it obvious he was redirecting her. Now that they weren't fighting anymore, maybe he could get her to kiss him.

"Do you really think I should go to the capital?" she asked. She frowned slightly, two lines creasing the smooth skin between her brows. "I don't have anyone to chaperone me, now."

"I'll write to Siara. One of her ladies was killed in Wheylia, so she needs a new one." Ari winced. That hadn't been the right thing to say. "Don't worry. I, uh, saw to the people responsible."

"You mean you killed them?"

"Well, sort of. Queen Reudi had some of them beheaded, as well." He was never going to get her to kiss him this way.

"How many people did you kill last year?" She stared at him with wide green eyes. They looked over-large, the way she had her hair pulled up so tight.

"Not many," he assured her. "I don't suppose you would take your hair down? I really don't like it that way."

"You didn't like it the way they did it in the capital, either. If I'm one of the princess's ladies, they'll do my hair that way, and make me obey all sorts of ridiculous little rules and protocols and it shall be ghastly boring and stuffy." Her face thoughtful, she tugged her hand from his and started pulling out pins. Red curls sprang free, seeming happy to be unconfined. "I really would like to go there again. I never go anywhere. Maybe your mother's family could chaperone me."

"My . . . Who?" Ari stammered. "How can I ask them for that when I've never even met them? They're only now learning I exist."

Ispiria tossed a pile of pins onto the table. Standing, she pulled apart her braid and shook her head. Wild red curls tumbled around her shoulders and down her back. "Better?" she asked, smiling.

Ari nodded. He'd forgotten how very beautiful she was when she was happy. Yes, he'd imagined her smile often enough, but the reality of it was infinitely better. She walked around the table, stopping beside him. She held out both her hands and he pushed his chair back to stand, taking them. Up close, he could see that the silky black fabric of her mourning dress shimmered with a green iridescence.

"Ari, aside from the royal family and Sir Cadwel, you are the most famous person in the realm," Ispiria said, looking up at him. "I'm sure they'll be more than happy to take me in. Do you suppose you have any cousins around my age? I shouldn't want to be lonely. You will write them, won't you? I can't think of anyone else I've a connection to."

"I will." The more he thought about it, in so much as he was able to think with her standing so close, the better an idea it seemed. Much better than asking Siara to chaperone Ispiria. The princess might still have her ideas about separating them, and what if Siara mentioned that she'd kissed him? Ispiria would be livid.

He realized then that he didn't plan to tell her. Really, there was nothing to tell. It hadn't been a real kiss. It was part of his mission for the king. Besides, he couldn't stand the idea of another fight. They'd only just made up. His gaze drifted down to take in her full lips and he couldn't pull it back away.

Ispiria stomped her foot. "Lord Aridian."

"What?" He returned his focus to her green eyes.

"This is the part when you kiss me."

"It is?" He grinned.

She stomped her foot again, but before she could formulate another complaint, Ari complied.

***

It had been such a nice kiss, Ari reflected as he rode Stew up a steep mountain trail. Rather, kisses. An improper number of them. A smile flickered across his face. In truth, they'd been more improper than any unmarried couple had a right to be. He supposed it was a good thing they'd been in Sir Cadwel's study, where anyone could find them, or things might have gotten out of hand.

That evening, Ispiria had worn his favorite of her green dresses, looking altogether like her usual self. They'd danced for hours. During his year in Wheylia, as he'd been responsible for escorting Princess Siara to any number of events, Ari had become rather good at dancing. He hoped he'd made an impression on Ispiria. He didn't want to be far from her thoughts when she was in the capital, dancing with other men.

The cry of a hawk brought Ari back to the reality of the rocky trail. He, Cooro, and Lord Kenmar were nearly to the village of Hawkers, where they would meet Hawk Guardian Mirimel. Glancing up to the bright blue sky above, hemmed in by pine-shrouded peaks, Ari took in two Sorga Hawks making lazy circles. He dropped his eyes. Before him, the trail disappeared from view. On either side, he could see guards, marking where the roadway dipped into the valley that sheltered Hawkers.

Ari waved to the guards as he rode past, starting down the long incline into the valley. The wood and plaster buildings spread out below him and he was surprised by how many people moved about. It almost seemed as if the devastation of two years ago hadn't happened.

Only, he knew it had, he thought as his eyes picked out Mirimel waiting for them at the bottom of the hill, her orange hair making her easy to spot. Mirimel had lost her entire family, except Ispiria and their great-grandmother. Now the old woman was gone, too.

Mirimel held up her arm and a hawk dropped from the sky to land on the leather wrist guard she wore. Ari could see her lips moving. The hawk dipped once and she raised her arm, sending it soaring upward. Ari looked over his shoulder, following its path south. He had no doubt that, soon, those in the keep would know he and his companions had reached Hawkers.

"That enchanting creature is to be our travel companion?" Cooro asked, maneuvering his mare up alongside Ari and Stew.

"Enchanting?" Ari repeated.

He studied Mirimel's bright orange locks, taking in her forest garb of green breeches and tunic, tall brown boots and leather bracers. She had a quiver of arrows at her belt for the short bow on her back, and wore a broad bladed hunting knife. He'd seen her shoot the top off a daisy from a distance that almost rendered the flower invisible. Her face was pretty but, though less than two years his senior, Mirimel had a hardness to her and a lack of ease in her nature that didn't encourage notions of romance or love. "If by enchanting you mean dangerous, sure."

"Dangerous?" Cooro repeated, his tone scoffing. "She is a flower among women. I should have known, with the beauty your lady possesses, that her cousin would be equally lovely, but I confess, tales of her prowess in battle disinclined me to believe it."

"What?" Ari could never follow Cooro's thoughts when the swordmaster expounded on things romantic.

"Practicing flowery speech for the lady?" Kenmar asked, riding up on Ari's other side.

"Flowery speech Mirimel?" Ari shot Cooro a pitying look. "I really wouldn't, were I you, and I don't recommend calling her a lady, either. At least, not to her face."

Cooro didn't speak again as they closed the remaining distance to Mirimel, but he wore a speculative, longing look that Ari knew could only be trouble. The swordmaster, being handsome, accomplished and a favorite of the queen's, was accustomed to finding himself charming to women wherever he went. Ari was pretty sure he knew what Mirimel thought of charming.

Stew stopped before her and Ari slid down. He could see Cooro and Lord Kenmar dismounting as well. Mirimel glanced at them before turning back to him.

"Ari." Her tone warm, though she didn't smile. She held out her hand and they clasped wrists, as equals. Mirimel wasn't much for recalling his titles. "You made a quick journey of it."

"Mirimel," he greeted. "These are the companions I wrote to you about. This is Lord Kenmar."

"My lord." Mirimel made a perfunctory bow.

"Hawk Guardian," Kenmar said, returning the bow.

"And this is Swordmaster Cooro."

Mirimel looked him up and down and stuck out her hand. Instead of greeting her as he would have a brother in arms, Cooro took hold of her fingers and lifted them to his lips. Mirimel raised her eyebrows, drew back her free hand, and punched him in the gut.

Ari coughed, trying to contain a laugh as Cooro released her, doubling over.

"My lady," the swordmaster gasped.

"It's Hawk Guardian Mirimel," Mirimel said, her tone hard. "Come, I'll show you to your quarters. I already sent a bird advising Sorga that you've arrived." She spun on her heels and strode away.

Ari picked up Stew's reins, for show. He patted Cooro on the shoulder, taking in the Whey's red face and rasping breath. "You're lucky."

From his crumpled position, Cooro looked up. "Lucky?" he wheezed out.

"I thought for sure she'd break your nose. Come on," he added over his shoulder to Lord Kenmar, who had a look of mild amusement on his face.

Kenmar nodded, already holding the reins to his sorrel gelding.

Ari grinned as he led the way into Hawkers. He hoped Cooro was a fast learner.

Chapter 10

Ari felt a quickening in Stew's steps and wondered if they were near the end of the mountain range. They should be. At least, that's what Mirimel said. Her hawk had returned to them with long sheaves of last year's grass, intermingled with a few green shoots. For days, she'd been sending him over each peak they approached, and he'd come back with small pebbles and pinecones. The grass was something different.

Ari looked up at the white-capped pinnacles before them. He could see blue sky beyond, beckoning him forward. The sun was bright on the scraggly pines clinging to the mountains surrounding them, but the day was cool. He wasn't sure how warm it ever got this far north. Stew's race must be a hardy one indeed, to dwell on the plains.

The descending trail began to curve about the peak before them, and Ari leaned forward, as impatient as Stew to reach the grassland. As they came around a final outcropping of rock, Ari gazed, for the first time, on the land that men referred to as the endless northern plain. His eyes traced the trail they must take, meandering down the side of the mountain and into the few rolling foothills, until his gaze alighted on the vastness beyond.

West, to Ari's left, the sun filled the afternoon sky, almost low enough to begin streaking it with color. There was no other landmark. Everywhere he looked, save behind him to the south, was a sea of yellow stalks. Patches of green peeked through, but they only served to emphasize the vastness before him. There weren't even hills, beyond the few crowded against the mountains. The plain stretched away east, west and north until it met the sky, forming an indistinct horizon far in the distance.

Ari would have stopped, daunted by the endless expanse, but Stew was obviously eager to leave the mountains. He increased his pace again, trotting down the steep slope. Ari realized they were leaving the others behind, Lord Kenmar especially, as he wasn't an accomplished rider. He didn't think it was his place to stop Stew, though. Ari didn't even know how long it had been since Stew had seen his home.

Together, they rode out to the plain. As soon as they left the foothills behind, Stew stopped. He tossed his head. Ari could all but feel his desire to run.

"All right, I get the message." Ari dismounted.

Stew nipped at his sleeve, pawing the ground.

"I'm working on it," Ari said, amused. He pulled off saddlebags, saddle, blanket and bridle. He would have brushed Stew down, but as soon as he was unencumbered, Stew galloped out onto the plain. He stopped, bucking and jumping, looking for all the world like a fox toying with a mouse, and then sped off again.

Ari watched as Stew galloped in a wide circle, his tail and mane streaming. He'd never seen his horse so happy. A hard lump formed in Ari's throat as he realized this might be the last journey they took together. If Stew was so happy here, would he really want to leave?

He heard the others ride up and dismount. Nearly silent footsteps approached on Ari's left and he glanced over to see Mirimel stop beside him. Her orange locks and forest green tunic were splashes of color against the dry grass of the plains. Her traditional hawk guardian outfit served her well in the shadows of the pinewood, but seemed out of place in the grassland.

"Stew looks happy," she said.

"He does."

"Any idea where we go from here?"

He turned to face her. "You're the guide."

"This is as far as I've ever come. Actually, up the trail a ways. I've looked over these plains before, but never left the mountains to set foot on them. My people are superstitious about treading here." The blue eyes Mirimel cast toward Ari were almost the same color as the afternoon sky. "How about your cartographer? Does he know anything about where we are?"

"I don't think so." Ari shook his head, wondering if he should ask about the superstitions. Would it matter? Mirimel obviously didn't think so, or she would have brought it up before. "That's why he's here, to map it."

"Doesn't look like there's much to map." She gestured to the boundless flatlands stretching out before them, where Stew still frolicked. "I don't know why you brought him. I don't trust him," she added in a low voice. Not seeming to notice she did it, she reached up and toyed with the pendant she wore, a delicate likeness of a hawk carved from striated brown stone. The item was a gift from Larke and, like the one he'd made for

115

Ispiria, imbued with magic to offer Mirimel some protection from Empty Ones. She turned her eyes back to Ari. "Do you trust him?"

Ari shrugged. He'd be worried, but Mirimel didn't trust anyone. Lord Kenmar seemed harmless enough, with his piles of parchment and breakable jars of ink wrapped in wool, carefully arranged in his pack.

"Seriously, I--"

Ari cut her off with a quick shake of his head, turning to face Lord Kenmar as he walked toward them, leading his horse. The last thing he needed was for the cartographer to overhear her. If Mirimel hurt Kenmar's feelings, it would only lead to awkwardness among them.

"Aren't you afraid he'll not return?" Lord Kenmar asked, watching Stew gallop.

"He'll be fine," Ari said, hoping it was true. He glanced at the sky, realizing it was growing late. With the sun's rays so unobstructed, Ari suspected the days would seem overlong, but night would fall quickly.

Cooro came up to stand on Ari's right. He, too, held his horse's reins, as if worried the piebald mare might run off. Only Mirimel seemed unconcerned with her mount. Of course, the packhorse was tied to her saddle, and her hawk now perched on the saddle horn. He supposed she'd have enough warning if the encumbered beast tried to leave.

"Do we have a plan?" Cooro asked, sounding a bit pensive.

Ari realized the vastness of space about them, for all its openness, was having an oppressive effect. He felt it too. It made the task he'd set them suddenly seem daunting. He'd assumed finding a large herd of horses wouldn't be difficult.

Now, his eyes on the plains, it seemed much more monumental.

"We'll set up camp here tonight," he said. "Mirimel, will your hawk be able to seek the Questri? Do you have a way to make him understand what we want?"

"I can try." She shrugged, giving Ari a hard look.

He suppressed a sigh. Mirimel was probably right. Maybe he shouldn't have brought Lord Kenmar. He didn't know what he'd been thinking. Mirimel and Cooro were deep in Ari's confidence. If it were just the three of them, Mirimel might be willing to speak openly about her special link with the hawks. As it was, they had to make sure not to reveal to the graying lord anything that ought to be kept secret. He wondered what Kenmar would say if asked to return to Sorga.

"We're going to run out of firewood quickly out here," Mirimel said, looking around.

"I offer my services to keep you warm, Lady Mirimel," Cooro said, grinning.

Ari shook his head. He would intervene, but experience had already taught him that Mirimel took it as a personal offense if Ari stood up for her. Nor did he need to. She was fully capable of dealing with Cooro herself.

"I'd rather sleep with my horse, and I doubt cuddling up to you will cook our meals."

"We could try, my lady. I'm quite hot blooded."

"I'm not a lady," Mirimel snapped, for what Ari was sure was the five hundredth time since they'd met with her in the village of Hawkers.

"Beauty such as yours infers nobility. In fact, I can hardly rest my eyes upon you, so bright is the halo of loveliness enshrouding you."

"I'm standing between you and the sun, you idiot. Here, let me move. Maybe if you stare directly at it for long enough, you'll spare me the trouble of putting out your eyes."

"Cooro," Ari said. "Could you please clear a space for the fire? Try to get down to the dirt. This place looks like a giant tinderbox."

"I'll prepare dinner," Lord Kenmar said. As he moved to unpack their cooking utensils, he started whistling. He did it so poorly, Ari couldn't tell what the tune was.

They fell into a familiar rhythm, setting up camp for the night. Every other line out of Cooro's mouth was an innuendo directed at Mirimel, each meeting with a scathing response. At first, the bickering had bothered Ari, but he now realized Cooro didn't mean anything by it. It was also the most he'd ever heard Mirimel talk, and he'd caught her grinning at a few of the swordmaster's more outrageous compliments. It wasn't the same as traveling with Larke and Sir Cadwel, or Peine, but it wasn't bad.

"You call that down to dirt?" Mirimel said, inspecting Cooro's work. She held an armload of sticks from the packhorse.

"My lady, have I failed you yet again?" Cooro scuffed the area with his boot. "I shall lie upon the earth and beg you to set the fire on me, for I cannot live with the shame."

"Or you could move out of my way." She set the sticks down and began arranging them carefully.

"Do you know," said Kenmar, who was carefully peeling the wax coating off a block of cheese. "Across the ocean, in Jondor, they carry camel milk in camel bladders, and it turns to cheese, and they squeeze it out and eat it."

Ari looked over from where he was brushing down the horses, except Stew, who was still running in circles. "What's a camel?"

"It's what they ride," Cooro said. "They're reputed to be larger even than knight's horses."

"Yes." Lord Kenmar nodded. He pulled out a long knife. For all his seeming ineptness in many ways, he sliced their food with effortless precision. "And they have humps, you see, which are thought to be where they store their water for long desert journeys."

Mirimel looked up from where she knelt, trying to strike a fire. "Have you seen these camels with your own eyes?"

"I intend to someday." Kenmar looked wistful. "But no, I've only read of them and seen sketches."

"Well, I'll believe in your giant humped horses when I see one."

"Do you never believe in that of which you have no physical proof, my lady?" Cooro asked her, sitting down on the other side of the unlit fire.

"I prefer not to. There's enough I wish I hadn't seen, without adding all that imagination can conjure." She struck a spark into the tinder and bent down, blowing gently on it to bring a flame to life. Feeding it twigs, she sat back on her heels, her expression turning contemplative. "Not that I haven't come across a few things one must take on faith."

"You speak of love." Cooro leaned toward her. "Now we're getting to the heart of things."

Mirimel shook her head, returning her focus to the fire. "You're an idiot."

"They say that, in the far north, there are times in the summer when the sun never sets," Lord Kenmar said.

Ari glanced over to find Kenmar gazing west, where the sky was showing the beginnings of a dazzling display. He could see Stew trotting back toward them, a silhouette against the lowering sun. As Ari moved to brushing the packhorse, he decided it was good to have Kenmar with them. If not for the lord's seemingly endless string of facts, there'd be nothing but Cooro and Mirimel's bickering, or flirting, or whatever it was they were doing. He wondered, with a slight smile, what Larke would think of it. Even though the bard was beyond vague about his relationship with Mirimel, Ari suspected his friend wouldn't be pleased.

They passed a pleasant evening and turned in, with Mirimel drawing the first watch. Cooro drew the second, which was the worst, leaving Ari last. Lord Kenmar, they let sleep. Ari told him it was because he wasn't trained as a man at arms of any sort, but it was really for Mirimel's benefit. Ari knew the hawk guardian wouldn't sleep while Kenmar was responsible for their safety. In truth, he also doubted the graying lord really would stay awake for a whole shift.

Ari was pleased he drew final watch, for he preferred it. He was fond of the sunrise, though first he had to get through the tail of the night. After Cooro woke him, he stretched, then began to walk in a slow circle around their camp. He stayed just close enough to see the slumbering forms of his friends, but far enough out so his movements wouldn't wake them.

As he paced, his mind turned toward Ispiria. He'd been dreaming about her, as he often did. She would be in the capital by now, meeting his family. A family he'd never met. Ari felt a surge of jealousy. He wasn't sure who he envied more, his fiancée for getting to meet his family, or his family for getting to spend time with his fiancée.

What if he did have cousins about their age? What if one was a young man, like him? If they were cousins, he might look like Ari, and act like him. Ispiria might prefer a version of Ari who didn't run off to the ends of the earth hunting for a stone so he could kill an age-old enemy he'd only just realized he had.

Sometimes, he wondered what it was he was even doing, out there in the middle of nowhere. Maybe he should go back. He could ride to Poromont, find Ispiria . . .

He drew in a deep breath. No. This was for Ispiria. How could they marry and have children when he knew the very world they inhabited was woven with magic that would seek out his offspring? Yes, he could ask Larke or the Lady to make them amulets, but the Lady was right when she said that wouldn't really protect them. Ari couldn't hide his wife and children away as the Lady had done with his family for so long. His sons would be heirs to a dukedom. They couldn't disappear into the cloak of obscurity.

He wished it morning already. The sooner a new day came, the sooner he could find the herd. How he would communicate with them or get them to give him the stone, he didn't know, but he'd find a way. Hopefully, they would want to relinquish it. The Sorga Hawks had insisted Ari take the one they'd guarded. Of course, they were just as much citizens of his dukedom as the humans inhabiting it were, though very few of those humans knew it. In contrast, Ari had no idea how the Questri might feel about a human lord from Lggothland.

Ari glanced toward the stars to assess the time, and his breath stilled. He'd been so caught in his musings he hadn't noticed that the endless plains came with an endless sky. His head tilted back, he turning in a slow circle, but it was impossible to take it all in.

Their small cooking fire had long since gone out, leaving no light but that of the moon and stars. For its part, the moon was a thin sliver, hanging low on the horizon. Spread out above Ari, stars filled the night sky. Stretching from horizon to horizon, they formed a dome broken only by the mountains to the south.

The more he looked, the more he saw. Bright stars gave way to darker patches, spattered with streaks of color and light. He took in the familiar patterns, augmented by so many more glimmering specks than he'd before realized. His eyes sought his favorite constellation, Verillia. As far north as they were, it dipped low on the horizon, seeming to ride slowly across the perimeter of the plain like the glimmering sailing ship it represented. On the northwestern horizon, he saw unfamiliar clusters. He wondered if Lord Kenmar's maps included one of the night sky.

Ari stood the rest of his watch with the stars as his companions, though they eventually dimmed with the false dawn. It wasn't until that, too, had faded and true sunrise threatened, when Ari was about to wake his companions, that he felt the rumbling. Stew moved to stand beside him, facing east, and Ari turned his gaze toward the new day. As the ground began to tremble more violently beneath him, he felt the stirrings of alarm, but Stew seemed calm. Behind him, he could hear the others stirring.

"What is that?" Mirimel asked.

"I recommend you hold onto me for support, my lady," Cooro said.

"They suffer bouts of quaking earth in the Eal la Oraan Desert, on the great southern continent across the South Sea," Lord Kenmar said. "They say the grand city of K'Orge was once atop a tall peak, but was rattled loose and slid down to rest beside the sea."

Ari looked over his shoulder, wondering if the shakiness in Kenmar's words came from the trembling earth or fear. Their other horses, eyes wide, pawed the ground in agitation. Cooro moved toward where they were picketed, gathering up their reins.

"Yet we are a long way from the fabled Eal la Oraan Desert," Cooro said.

Ari squinted toward the rising sun, but he couldn't make it out. He glanced upward, judging that dawn had broken. He realized a cloud hung low along the plains, obscuring the horizon to the east. It took him a moment of wondering at the strange weather pattern before he grasped that it was a cloud, yes, but one made of dust.

Mirimel came up alongside him, her bow held loosely in one hand. She raised the other to shield her eyes, peering east. "Are those . . . horses?"

"I think they are," Ari said, squinting.

Beside him, Stew shook his mane.

Lord Kenmar moved to stand next to Mirimel. "That's a lot of horses."

"Well, at least we solved one problem," Ari said.

"Yes." Lord Kenmar's tone was slightly amused.

Ari glanced at him, surprised the scholar didn't sound afraid.

"You were going to say that we solved the problem of how to find the herd, weren't you?" Kenmar asked. "I didn't mean to preempt you."

"It's all right." Ari grinned. Having a herd of hundreds of horses charging toward him was infinitely better than the despair he'd felt looking across the plains yesterday. "It's just, you're supposed to wait for me to say it, and then you get to say something about how we have a new problem."

"I see. I'll try to keep that in mind for next time," Kenmar said.

For all his light tone, Ari could see Kenmar's fists were clenched. He glanced at Mirimel, finding her gazing intently eastward. She'd fitted an arrow to her bow, but still held it down at her side.

From where he was endeavoring to soothe their mounts, Cooro snorted. "Yes, next time we're standing around, waiting for hundreds of horses to trample us, do try to keep to the prescribed banter, my lord."

"Will you three grow up?" Mirimel snapped. "The Questri have arrived."

Chapter 11

To Ari's relief, the herd slowed before reaching them. More horses than he felt anyone could easily count filled the plains to the east, all facing their small camp. Their eyes weren't like those of normal horses. They were filled with intelligence, like Stew's, and having hundreds of them trained on him was very disconcerting.

There was a ripple of movement in the herd. To Ari's surprise, the horse that emerged bore a rider. Looking about as the dust settled, he realized he could see other humans astride some of the horses, spattered throughout the herd. The dark stallion bearing the first rider moved out at a walk, flanked on one side by a graying mare and the other by a vital looking roan.

As the three outriders drew near, Ari could see that the person astride the stallion was a slender girl, perhaps thirteen. She wore a loose undyed smock and had a blindfold over her eyes. Her pale blonde hair was pulled back and her feet bare. She rode without the aid of a saddle, bridle or any other tack.

"Thrice Born," the girl said when the three Questri stopped before them. Her voice was oddly devoid of inflection. "I am Clanmaster of the Faesten Clan. I have come to greet you at the behest of the blue lady, and to offer you the opportunity to earn a boon from the Questri."

"Don't look at her," Lord Kenmar whispered, at Ari's shoulder. "It's rude, you see. I've read an account of this. She is . . . his translator. It is the Clanmaster who speaks."

Ari nodded to show he'd heard the advice. He pulled his gaze from the blindfolded girl's face, meeting the intelligent eyes of the stallion. He wondered if the blue lady was, in fact, the Lady. "I greet you, Clanmaster." Ari bowed.

"It is as your companion advises," the girl said. "The child upon my back is the voice of Clan Faesten. She has no words of her own, nor does she bear a name. She is a servant of the clan."

"Thank you for explaining, Clanmaster," Ari said, feeling instant anger. What right did they have to subjugate this girl? He looked out over the sea of horses again, picking out dozens of other riders spread through the vast herd. Were they all similarly voiceless and nameless? Where did they come from?

"You shall journey with us to the heart of the plain," the girl's voice said. "There, when the day is longest, you will be offered a chance to earn your boon. Know that we do this not for you, but as a favor to the blue lady." The stallion shook his mane.

Ari nodded. So, the Lady had already been here, paving the way for him. He wondered if that had been before or after he'd agreed to seek the stone. He supposed it didn't really mater. She'd known he would have to do as she wished.

126

"I shall remain with you as your guide," the girl's voice continued. "The herd wishes to run. Soon, the day of the equinox shall dawn, and they are eager to commence the Spring Folly. As your unthinking cannot run with the herd, we shall travel behind."

"Unthinking?" Ari had no idea what the girl referred to, or if she meant that she would stay, or she and the stallion. He was having trouble keeping his eyes on the Questri when it was the blindfolded girl who spoke, and too many questions were building up in his mind. What was a Spring Folly? Did the longest day mean the summer solstice? That was months away. "That is, who are the unthinking, Clanmaster?"

Stew snorted, pawing at the earth.

The Clanmaster looked to Stew for a moment, then turned back to Ari. "Those on which your companions ride. The unthinking. They are but shadows of the Questri."

Though the girl's voice still lacked inflection, Ari got the distinct impression that the Clanmaster felt disdain. Behind him, he heard Cooro murmur to the horses soothingly. "Ah, right, the unthinking," Ari said.

He felt decidedly out of his element. He wished Larke could be there. He would know how to deal with the Questri. Ari had thought it would be easy, like being around Stew. He hadn't anticipated such formality, or coldness. Maybe it was just the girl's way of speaking.

"Will it trouble you if we saddle our horses and ride them?" Mirimel asked.

The Clanmaster's head swiveled toward her, then back to Ari. "You permit this female one to speak?" the blindfolded girl asked.

Ari could practically feel anger radiate off Mirimel at that question. "We are, all four of us, equal and may all speak." He hoped that was clear enough.

"The blue lady spoke only of the nobility of the Thrice Born." The stallion turned first to the mare on his right, then the roan, as if consulting them. "We will answer only the Thrice Born."

"Fine by me," Mirimel muttered, leaving his side to go stand with Cooro and the horses.

Stew pawed at the ground, snorting again. The Clanmaster turned to him. "Your opinion was not sought, young one," the girl said.

Stew dropped his head, taking a half-step back.

"Er, so, is it acceptable if we saddle the unthinking ones and ride them?" Ari asked, intervening. He'd always loved horses, but they were large, powerful beasts. He'd never realized just how menacing one could look, until now.

"Do as you like with them. The unthinking are less to us than the servant astride me. Know, though, that I do not believe your Questri companion will wish to come bridled before the herd."

Ari looked at Stew, who still stood with his head down. "Uh, may I ride without a saddle or bridle?" If not, he supposed there was always the packhorse, if they redistributed its load.

Stew stared at him and Ari wished, not for the first time, that he could communicate with the Questri. Larke managed it with ease, but Larke had the magic of the Aluiens at his disposal. Ari only had his and Stew's friendship, and it wasn't nuanced enough for him to know the Questri's thoughts without trying to ride. Ari didn't want to embarrass Stew.

"He will permit this," the blindfolded girl said. "There is no shame for him in bearing a rider. All shame belongs to you, for to ride is to serve."

Ari nodded. "Thank you," he said to Stew. Ari didn't care if he was diminished in the eyes of the herd, so long as Stew wasn't.

Stew tossed his mane, but Ari wasn't sure how to interpret the gesture. Agitation was evident in the tension rippling through Stew's flank, but was it tension over Ari's request or over the condescension of the Clanmaster?

"These others, then, shall accompany you?" the girl's voice asked.

"Yes, we're all going, Clanmaster."

The stallion swung his head in a slow arc, scrutinizing Ari's companions. "The human ones shall partake of the Blessing of the Mare. No human creature can dwell long on these plains without it. They will wither and die. As these humans belong to you, Thrice Born, we shall honor them with the blessing." The stallion looked to the young roan, who dipped his head once in a sort of bow before spinning and galloping toward the herd.

"Ah, thank you." Ari contained a wince. He was sure Cooro and Lord Kenmar would shrug it off, but Mirimel wouldn't take kindly to the stallion's phrasing.

Ari watched the roan as he reached the herd and disappeared into the mass of horses. The heat of the rising sun roused a soft breeze. It flittered across the plain, making the long yellow grass tremble. The stirring of last year's blades seemed unnaturally loud in the cold silence that stood between Ari and the stallion. Out on the plains, the herd moved restlessly.

Finally, the roan and another Questri emerged from the throng of horses. Ari could see a rider on the back of the

129

second Questri, a white-socked bay. Reaching them, the roan retook his place beside the Clanmaster, but the bay walked past Ari, to where Cooro and Mirimel stood with their horses. The woman astride her was gnarled and old, her long gray hair bound back, a blindfold over her eyes.

The old woman dismounted with astonishing agility, not even using her hands. She unslung a water skin from about her neck, producing a cup hardly larger than a thimble from her robes. Pulling the stopper from the skin with her teeth, she poured a whitish liquid into the cup and held it out to Cooro.

The swordmaster looked to Ari. "What is it?"

"It is the Blessing of the Mare," the old woman said, her voice a rusty creak. "You must partake of it or return to your mountain home."

"I've read of this, as well," Kenmar said, leaving Ari to join Cooro and Mirimel. "I didn't truly credit it, but the drink is supposed to be enchanted. It won't hurt you, by all accounts."

"Then you have the honors," Mirimel said. She'd put up her bow, but her arms were crossed over her chest, her features pinched together in suspicion.

Turning to the old woman, Kenmar took the cup from her hands. He peered in it for a moment, shrugged, and downed the contents. The grimace he gave showed what he thought of the taste, but, as he handed it back, he appeared otherwise unaffected.

"That good?" Cooro asked, reaching to take the cup as it was offered to him, refilled. "Here's to not withering and dying." He raised it in salute before drinking.

Cooro gagged a bit, handing the cup back and moving to collect his water skin. The old woman turned to Mirimel, offering the strange drink once more.

"How do you know where I am with that blindfold on?" she asked, not taking the cup. She peered at it. "Has that thing ever been washed?"

"The voiceless does not need to see." The old woman pressed the cup into Mirimel's hands as she spoke. "I am her eyes. I am within her, mind and limb. She is but a means."

Mirimel turned a hard stare on the bay. She sniffed the cup and frowned, looking over to Ari. He shrugged. Cooro and Kenmar seemed fine, after all, and the Clanmaster would probably be offended if they didn't all drink it.

"It won't harm you, my dear," Kenmar said.

Mirimel didn't acknowledge the cartographer's words. Glaring at Ari as if this was his fault, which he supposed it was, Mirimel drank. Her face remained expressionless as she did so, as if she wouldn't give the Questri the satisfaction of a grimace. She handed the cup back.

The old woman stoppered the skin, taking the cup and licking it out before returning it to her robes. Unaided by anything but a grip on the bay's mane, she swung back astride.

"What about me?" Ari asked, turning back to the Clanmaster. If the bit about the effect of being on the plain was true, Ari didn't want to wither and die any more than he wanted the others to.

"Only human ones need partake of the blessing," the girl atop the stallion said. "Though it does no harm to those no longer considered as such."

The stallion swung his head, eyeing Ari's companions. Ari kept his gaze forward, his neck heating. He could feel his friends' scrutinizing him.

"See to your unthinking," the girl said, the stallion returning his gaze to Ari. "The herd departs. The Questri wish to run."

131

At that, the old mare, bay and roan turned, powerful strides carrying them back toward the herd. In an undulating mass, the Questri began to move, the three outliers curving to merge with the oncoming wave of horses. The plains shook as the herd galloped past, leaving Ari, his friends, their mounts and the Clanmaster behind. Dust rose into the air, once again obscuring the still-low sun.

"I'll help Cooro saddle the horses," Mirimel said from behind Ari. "Permit the female to speak, indeed," she muttered.

When they were ready to depart, Ari and Stew rode alongside the Clanmaster and his passenger. They took the journey in slow stages, heading south and east. A large cloud of dust out on the plain marked where the bulk of the Questri frolicked. Behind him, Ari could hear Mirimel, Cooro and Kenmar talking, but the stallion next to him remained quiet. He wondered if the Questri didn't engage in casual conversation, or if he was supposed to be breaking the silence.

Finally, he decided he'd better speak. If he was supposed to, he was being very rude. If the stallion didn't wish to converse, Ari was sure it would soon become apparent. "What is the Spring Folly?"

"In the spring, the blood of the herd runs fast, especially in the young," the girl said in her inflectionless voice.

Ari glanced at her out of the corner of his eye. She sat straight, seeming almost statue like, except for the fluid movement of her form, which matched to perfection that of the Questri she rode.

"Between us and the Orate Tree are many obstacles upon which the herd may be tested and prowess proved."

"Will we be able to pass?" Ari added Orate Tree to his list of questions.

"We shall take the overlooking route, with the old and sick."

"I'm sorry we're keeping you from the, ah, Folly," Ari said, not sure how to put it.

"I do not partake of the Spring Folly. Those who bear the voiceless never partake. If I die, the voice of the clan dies, and a new voice has not yet come to us."

He wanted to ask how they got the people who rode them, but he was worried he didn't really want to know. He also wondered if something called a folly could really be so dangerous that Questri died doing it. Dangerous or not, Stew likely wanted to test himself, and Ari had no right to detain him. "Stew, do you wish me to ride the packhorse so you can join in this Folly thing?" He said it hoping the Clanmaster would answer.

"The young one does wish to do so, but worries you require him." The Clanmaster looked at Ari askance. "Such loyalty inspired by you, Thrice Born. Perhaps as I come to know you, I shall comprehend it."

"Thanks," Ari said. The stallion certainly hadn't become Clanmaster based on his charm. "Stew, I know you haven't been home in a great while. I think you should join in the Spring Folly." Stew shook his mane and Ari could feel the lightness in his step.

The next time they stopped, Ari redistributed the packhorses' load. Stew watched, standing a little apart but seeming reluctant to leave. Before Ari mounted, he crossed to his horse. The tall dead grass rippled around them. Ari was struck by a sense of mournful foreboding. "Good luck in the Folly. I guess I'll see you where it ends."

Stew dipped his head.

Ari wanted to pat Stew on the withers, but he didn't know if that would humiliate him. "Good luck," he said again instead, stepping back.

Stew shook his mane. He turned, his pace reluctant at first, but speeding up. Soon, he was galloping across the plain toward the roiling dust that marked the location of the herd. His dark brown tail and mane streamed behind him. Ari had never seen him look so free. He sighed, walking back to the others.

Chapter 12

They traveled with the Clanmaster for several days, and his disposition didn't improve much. His rider, the voiceless girl, dismounted each night and slept beside him. She would have looked peaceful, if she wasn't so motionless and wearing a blindfold. Sometimes, when the stallion left her standing alone for a moment, Mirimel would speak to her, but the girl resisted all attempts at communication, giving no evidence she could perceive anything outside the Clanmaster's hearing.

Mostly, it was easier to view her as an extension of the Questri, though Ari felt guilty each time he realized he was doing that. He could tell from the look on Mirimel's face when her eyes were upon the girl that the hawk guardian didn't see her as an appendage. Mirimel's tendency toward perpetual anger seemed to have found a new focal point in the Clanmaster.

Eventually, nearly imperceptibly, the ground around them began to rise, the shallow rivers striating the plain meandering through the low points. Lord Kenmar noticed the subtle change in elevation first. He brought out his instruments and took various arcane seeming measurements, squinting from horizon to sun and jotting the results down in his journal as he rode. Then the ground grew steeper yet, undulating in rolling hills, each coming down a gentler slope than it went up. To the east, where the herd ran, Ari could see the land drop away from them.

As they traveled farther east, they were joined by others. The bay bearing the old woman with the Blessing of the Mare rode nearby, as did a little over two dozen other stately looking Questri bearing riders. Ari supposed they were leaders of other clans, but no attempt was made at introductions.

They were also, as the Clanmaster of the Faesten Clan had suggested they would be, surrounded by the lame and old. Few of the Questri Ari saw fell into the former category, though. He wondered if this was due to an inherent heartiness, or if those who were injured didn't survive for long.

In time, they turned fully to the south. The days grew in length and the air warmed. Ari didn't have Lord Kenmar's exactness, but he felt they'd come far enough south that they would be in Sallsburry, were they still on the peninsula of Lggothland and Wheylia.

He could count with exactness, though, and knew they were nearing the spring equinox. He looked about for some indication as to where the Spring Folly, this set of obstacles on which a Questri could test himself, might be. Yes, the area they were in now was hillier, but it was still just an endless sea of grass and shallow waterways. It was getting greener.

He could have asked the Clanmaster where the Folly would take place, but he didn't really enjoy talking with the stallion. Ari rode oddly alone among the regal and old of the

Questri. He could hear his friends talking amongst themselves, their tones hushed as if human voices did not belong on the plain, but his place at the Clanmaster's side kept him from joining them, except when they stopped riding.

Finally, on the morning of the equinox, they swung sharply east, trudging up a steeper than average hill. As they reached the top, the plain dropped away before them into a wide, deep valley. Ari stifled a gasp as the stark landscape below came into view, a harsh scar gouged into the grassland.

Narrow at both ends, the fissure widened into nearly a circle at the center, like a snake that had eaten a very fat rat. All about the valley were strange pinnacles, as if, when the rest was carved away, flat-topped fingers of stone had been deliberately left. There were also cracks and cuts in the valley floor, ranging from a foot wide to what Ari would guess was nearly twenty feet, all too deep to see the bottom of. It was a strange, menacing landscape, and Ari felt unease stir within him as he looked out over it.

"The fastest way is down the neck, from pass to pass," the girl atop the Clanmaster said.

Ari flinched slightly, her voice taking him by surprise. Usually, the Clanmaster didn't speak unless Ari did first. He eyed that route. It was clear, even from their perch high above, that running through the center of the valley toward the pass at the far end would be terribly dangerous. He glanced at the northern end, seeing the herd moving restlessly at the opening to the valley.

"Each of us must decide our own route in the Folly, as in life," the Clanmaster continued. "The closer to the edges, the less risk, but there is little glory to be had in skirting the center."

"Where did you ride?"

137

"Near the center, but not down it. To take that route is to court death."

The Questri at the head of the valley pawed the earth, a restless mass.

"What are they waiting for?"

"For the sun to reach its peak."

Cooro, Mirimel and Kenmar rode up, positioning themselves along the valley rim to Ari's left.

"By all that's sacred," Cooro breathed.

Kenmar started muttering to himself, scribbling furiously in his journal. "Who knew? All this here. Who knew?"

"Is that Stew?" Mirimel asked, pointing.

Ari peered downward, but his far sight wasn't as keen as Mirimel's. He couldn't pick Stew's glossy brown hide out of the undulating mass of Questri. He shook his head.

"There," she said. "By that black mare."

"My offspring," the girl atop the Clanmaster said.

Before Ari could sort out where Mirimel was pointing, the herd gave a sudden lurch. Questri surged forward, spilling into the basin below. The rumble of thousands of hooves rose up toward them, shaking the valley walls, though the rocky ground below put up little dust.

Questri veered off, swarming through the basin at varying angles, most surging toward the far edges. A powerful mass kept closer to the center, though, and it soon became quite obvious where Stew was. He, alongside a stunning black mare, galloped forward alone, right up the center.

Ari's eyes sped out ahead of them, taking in the pinnacles and fissures in their path. He swallowed a cry of protest. Was Stew mad?

"Foolish mare," the girl atop the Clanmaster said. "She shall shame me with her death."

Ari swallowed again, hoping the Clanmaster wasn't right.

Below, Stew and the mare galloped headlong at the first spire of rock. Ari cringed, unable to see what course they would even take, for the finger of stone stuck up from a deep hole in the valley floor. There was no way to jump that gulf, or, as they drew close, to go around it. It seemed his horse would either run flat out into a wall of rock or plummet to his death.

It took all of Ari's will not to turn away. At the last moment, Stew and the mare both leapt. Ari realized they would not go around the spires, but intended to use the ascending pinnacles spanning the chasm as a sort of broken bridge. A gasp sounded in his ears, but he didn't know if it was his or came from one of his companions.

Stew and the black mare both landed atop the first rocky spire, their paces not slowing as they worked to steady their strides in time to leap to the next. Ari felt as if he couldn't breathe. Stew ran, jumped, skidded, and ran again. The mare beside him, Stew leapt the next gap, and the next. Soon, he had four flat-topped fingers of stone behind him, and four to go.

Each was separated by a wider gap than the last. With each jump, it seemed Stew had less time to recapture his stride before he needed to leap again. On the second to last pinnacle, he skidded so far, Ari was sure he didn't have good enough footing to make the final leap. His hooves seeming almost to push off the edge, Stew sailed through the air, suspended for a moment over a vast nothingness. He clattered down onto the final spire, nearly sliding off the other side before jumping the remainder of the vast gully.

"Bravo," Cooro cried, clapping.

Ari shot him an incredulous look, but the swordmaster was intent on the scene below. How could he possibly be enjoying watching Stew risk himself like that?

139

"Splendid performance," Lord Kenmar murmured.

Ari realized the lord had stopped making notation, his eyes riveted on the scene below. He turned his gaze back to the valley as well, skimming over Mirimel where she sat beside him. Her eyes were wide. She appeared to be holding her breath. In the sky far above, her hawk winged in a slow spiral over the deep gully.

All around the valley floor, most much closer to the edges, Questri galloped in a flowing river of bay, chestnut, gray, black, dun and every conceivable variation thereof. They leapt obstacles, surged up rocky outcroppings and galloped across open ground. Ari didn't know if it was a race or if the goal was simply survival, but Stew and the black mare were in the forefront.

The two charged across a section of even ground toward the far neck of the valley. All around Ari, their movement bringing them to his awareness, the various clanmasters of the Questri backed away from the edge. Along with the lame and old, they walked across the grassy hill, taking up formation on the southeastern side of the outcropping on which they stood.

Ari looked at his friends and shrugged, unsure where the Questri were headed. They started forward and he watched them for a moment before urging the packhorse to follow. He sometimes found the packhorse difficult to ride, for he'd forget he had to convey what he wished to do. Stew always knew what they were doing.

Urging his timid mount through the ranks of the Questri, Ari returned to the side of the Clanmaster of the Faesten Clan. Mirimel, Lord Kenmar and Cooro lined the rim of the valley to his left, for they'd left him a space next to the dark stallion and his voiceless rider. Looking down, Ari saw Stew and the black mare careening around a sharp turn.

Ari realized that what he'd taken for the end of the valley from their first vantage point was a turn. Spread out before him was a second bloated crater of land. Cut across the valley floor, widest below them, were more bottomless looking fissures. It was as if an unfathomably large creature had taken its two massive clawed paws and raked them down the valley floor.

Ari grimaced as Stew and the black mare angled for the edge where the fissures were widest. Just as with the pinnacles, each fissure must be jumped, and the thin slices of valley floor between them offered little room to recuperate and make the next mad leap. Ari would have called out beseeching Stew to stop, if he thought it would do any good.

In nearly perfect stride, Stew and the mare leapt the first gap, and the second, and third. Ari started to breathe again, for this didn't look as difficult as the flat-topped spires. It wasn't until they'd cleared all ten that he thought to look ahead.

Stew and the mare entered into a field of boulders, jumping some, dodging around others. They became separated, the mare slowing slightly as she circled too many of the giant stones, leaving her facing west. Her mad pace carried her toward the sheer clifftop from which Ari, his friends and those few Questri who weren't within the valley observed. She swung in a skidding turn, careening around a large boulder to head south once more.

Ari returned his attention to Stew, who was coming out the other side of the boulder field to an area crisscrossed by toppled pinnacles. Striations that were horizontal along the valley wall skewed at odd angles on the fallen stone, creating a dizzying effect that Ari hoped Stew was immune to. His pace not slowing, Stew leapt the foremost, landing with a clatter before speeding toward the next.

The mare reached the fallen spires, leaping the first one. Though they were high above, Ari could see her gait falter as she jumped, her hooves brushing the top of the rock. He realized she must have injured herself in her last sharp turn, among the boulders. He winced as she leapt over the next obstacle, her hooves once again grating across it.

She shook herself as she landed, charging forward with a bearing that could only be called resolute, though Ari wasn't sure he'd ever seen resolution in a horse's expression before. She cleared the rest of the jumps, but none cleanly, and was now far behind Stew.

The Clanmaster beside him backed away from the drop and crossed to the southernmost edge of the overlook. Ari followed, urging the packhorse into a quicker walk. Stew was taking the turn into what Ari hoped was the final valley. Many of the Questri onlookers didn't follow this time. Ari realized the rest of the herd was still navigating the central gorge.

As if to emphasize that point, a horrible squeal rose from the valley behind him. A tremble went through the Questri atop the hill. Mirimel appeared at Ari's side, her lips pressed together in a thin line.

"One of the horses just missed a jump. Only its front hooves made it to the other side." She shuddered slightly.

Ari took up his place beside the Clanmaster and his silent rider, finding he needn't have hurried. The valley before them contained only one thing, a giant fissure, a crack that rent the earth. In despair, Ari watched as Stew lined up in the center of the valley, where the fissure was widest. His eyes went to it, knowing it was an impossible distance. What was Stew trying to prove? Even a Questri couldn't have the power for that jump.

Stew didn't rush toward the obstacle, as he had with the others. He slowed to a stop, looking back. The mare trotted into the valley. Ari could see the awkwardness in her gait as she came up to Stew.

Stew ducked his head, pawing at the ground. The mare shook her mane. They stood in what Ari could only assume was silent communication. Finally, the mare shook her mane again, turning toward the fissure. Stew let out a distressed whinny.

Seeming to ignore whatever it was Stew was telling her, the mare fixed her gaze on the center of the fissure. Stew cast a look upward, his eyes meeting Ari's. Fear shot through Ari at the look. It was one of apology, maybe even a goodbye.

Turning to stand beside the black mare, Stew pawed the ground once. They both leapt forward, heading straight for the widest part of the cleft in the valley floor. Ari glanced at the Clanmaster, but the stallion remained expressionless.

Galloping faster than Ari had ever seen him, Stew seemed almost to fly toward the drop, the mare falling behind. At the last possible moment, Stew pushed off, hurtling himself into the air. He hung, suspended, his stride full open. After an endless, frozen moment of fear, Stew crashed down onto the far lip of the valley floor.

His back hooves skittered, seeking purchase. He pulled them in, finding his footing. Ari let out his breath, coughing at the raggedness in his throat, as Stew slowed his gait. He swung in a wide arc, circling back to face the fissure. Following his horse's gaze, Ari turned just as the black mare leapt.

With her injured gait, she hadn't managed to reach the tremendous speed Stew had. Even as she jumped, Ari could see she wouldn't make the far side. She sailed in a low arc, fear bright in her eyes.

Ari caught a movement to his left, a flickering glow. He swung his head, but found only his three companions. Mirimel, her expression horrified as she watched the mare's ill-fated leap. Lord Kenmar, his gaze intent. Beyond the cartographer was Cooro, looking stunned.

Mirimel gasped, her face breaking into a smile. Ari wrenched his head back around, seeing the black mare skidding to a halt on the far side of the fissure. He blinked in surprise, astonished. Cooro let out a loud cheer.

The Clanmaster swung his head toward them. "Intervention was not needed," the girl astride him said, not turning.

"Fortunately," Mirimel muttered.

Ari wondered what could even have been done. To the best of his knowledge, the Questri had no overt magic. One had died already today, after all.

"You should be congratulated on the performance of your offspring," Lord Kenmar said.

"I shall reprimand her as a foolish mare," the girl's voice said.

It still disconcerted Ari, how she would speak without facing them, while the Clanmaster did. He preferred to converse when they rode side by side, so he could ignore such things. "Congratulations, Clanmaster."

From the valley behind them, there was another squeal of death. Ari grimaced. The Spring Folly, it seemed, was more serious than the name implied. The mare looked up at them, then dropped her head and began to limp away. Stew matched his stride to hers. As more Questri surged into the view, Ari turned the packhorse away, not wanting to watch in case more fell.

To his surprise, the Clanmaster turned as well. "Come," the girl atop him said.

Though her tone was expressionless as always, Ari took mild exception to the commanding nature of the request. Shrugging off his annoyance, he looked back at his friends. Mirimel was already moving to follow, as was Kenmar. Cooro's gaze remained fixed on the display below. Another horrible cry rose from the valley. The swordmaster shuddered. He looked over his shoulder at Ari and shook his head, backing his piebald mare from the edge.

They met Stew and the black mare at the bottom of the hill, which rolled in a long, gentle slope to join the flat grassland south of the valley. The Clanmaster walked up to the mare, his eyes cold. She dipped her head, looking miserable.

Ari rode over to Stew and jumped down. At the last moment, he thought to restrain himself to patting Stew on the withers, rather than flinging his arms around his horse's neck. "That was amazing. You were incredible." He leaned toward Stew's ear, lowering his voice. "I'd appreciate it if you wouldn't do it again, though. I was about to keel over in fear."

Stew tossed his head, his eyes bright.

Mirimel rode up beside them. "I believe you are to be congratulated, Stew."

Over her shoulder, Ari could see Kenmar and Cooro nearing.

"With the end of the Spring Folly, the herd shall revel," the blindfolded girl said.

Ari turned to see the Clanmaster looking his way.

"It is not safe for you among the revelry, nor do we wish onlookers to our jubilations. You shall escort this mare to the village, where you may, on the longest of days, attempt to earn your boon. As punishment for the shame she brings on her clan, my offspring is forbidden our celebration."

"Ah, we'd be happy to escort her." Ari had no idea why the stallion was so displeased with his daughter, but he didn't mind going with her. He'd seen enough of the brutal ways of the Questri herd. He didn't know what their jubilations were, and he was pretty sure he didn't want to. Anything else aside, the Clanmaster was likely correct. Humans shouldn't be around hundreds of reveling horses.

Stew took a step forward, dipping his head toward the Clanmaster.

The Clanmaster pawed at the ground, snorting.

Stew shook his head.

Ari wished he knew what they were arguing about, for, by their demeanors, it did seem to be a disagreement.

Finally, the Clanmaster reared slightly. "Go with the disappointing mare, then," the blindfolded girl said as the dark stallion whirled away.

The Clanmaster of the Faesten Clan galloped back toward the end of the valley, where more Questri had spilled out. The girl on his back leaned forward over his neck, her blonde braid bouncing. Ari hoped she would be safe during the revelries.

He shook his head slightly, turning toward the black mare. "It's nice to meet, you." He said it even though he knew she couldn't answer. "I'm Ari."

The mare dipped her head in acknowledgment before turning away. Not looking back, she started to limp south. Ari sighed, hoping she wasn't as arrogant as her father, and urged the packhorse to follow.

Chapter 13

Ari was pleased Stew accompanied them as they headed farther south. He and the mare walked side by side, setting a slow pace. It seemed both to suit her injured leg and to accommodate their less tireless, normal mounts.

That evening, after they'd finished eating, they sat in a circle around the remains of their small fire. It was warm enough that they didn't need one for anything except cooking, which was fortunate as they'd long since run out of wood and been forced to learn how to gather up dead grass, twisting it into dense bundled for a sustained flame. The horses were picketed in a line, downwind, and Stew and the black mare stood across from them, as if not wishing to be any closer to the unthinking than required.

Cooro leaned on his elbows in the now green grass, his eyes flicking around to look at the rest of them, obviously formulating a plan for amusement. Lord Kenmar hunched over his parchments, scribbling away. Ari lay back and looked up at the sun-streaked sky. He hadn't realized how exhausting it had been to be in the constant company of the Clanmaster.

Mirimel stood and walked toward the black mare, Ari tuning his head to follow her. She held out a hand. The Questri shied away. Mirimel dropped her arm, looking to Stew.

"Stew, tell her I'm a friend. I want to look at her leg. I may be able to help."

In the sky above, Mirimel's hawk gave a lone cry, drawing Ari's gaze. The hawk folded his wings, diving. Mirimel held up her arm as the little brown raptor dropped down to alight on her leather-encased wrist. He looked at her, giving his odd little chirp, and then turned to administer a like sound to the mare. The mare swung her gaze between Mirimel and the hawk before turning to Stew.

Mirimel sighed, looking at her hawk. "I wish . . ." Her voice trailed off and she shrugged.

Ari knew what she was thinking. She wished she could do more than sense the hawk's emotions and try to convey hers. She wished she could truly speak to him and to the mare, inside their heads, the way Larkesong could. Ari felt the same, both for her and for himself and Stew. It was frustrating knowing they traveled with beings as intelligent as they, but with no means to communicate. Especially when he had so many questions.

"I wish I could at least know your name," Mirimel said to the mare.

The mare took a step toward Mirimel. Her hawk turned back to her as well, dipping in almost a bow, and launched himself into the air. Crossing the distance between them, Mirimel knelt down to examine the mare's leg.

"Such grace," Cooro murmured. "I've never seen her like."

Ari pretended he didn't hear, hoping, but doubting, that the swordmaster was referring to the Questri. He might have to take Cooro aside soon and explain to him . . . Ari frowned. What was there to explain, really? That he had a vague feeling that Larke, a magical being who was currently confined to the caves of the Aluiens for two more years, might, possibly, have some sort of affection for Mirimel?

The only sign Ari had that Mirimel was at all inclined to return Larke's feelings, which may or may not exist, was that she wore the necklace he'd given her. As the pendant was a beautifully carved rendering of a hawk and imbued with magic to help keep Mirimel safe, it wouldn't take love to get her to wear it. Did Ari really have anything to go on other than an inexplicable feeling that the bard and hawk guardian shared a connection?

Ari smiled, knowing what Sir Cadwel would say. The knight hated making any sort of decision based on vague feelings. Cooro probably wasn't even serious in his pursuit, anyhow. He had to pursue someone, after all, and Mirimel was the only woman they'd seen in ages who wasn't blindfolded and mentally subservient to a horse.

On top of that, Mirimel hated anyone intervening in her affairs. Ari relaxed. No, in this instance, he had no responsibility to do anything. It was a nice change.

"I have a salve that I think may help," Mirimel said to the mare. "I use it on similar injuries in hawks, and myself."

The mare regarded her with unreadable eyes.

Stew snorted.

Mirimel shrugged, rising effortlessly. "I'll get it and show it to you. Then I'll try to apply it. If you don't want me to, just move."

"You said you've read about this land, Kenmar?" Cooro asked, though his gaze followed Mirimel, watching her drop to one knee beside her saddlebags.

"I have, yes, long ago." The cartographer looked up, his pen poised over the page he was writing on.

"What can you tell us?" Ari had all but forgotten, in the long days since he'd felt like they could speak freely among themselves, that Kenmar had said that.

"It didn't have a mention of that amazing geographical formation through which the herd ran." Kenmar shook his head. "And there were those who said there was nothing of note on the plains. Little did they know."

"Truly," Cooro said. "But if I may ask, what did the account you read contain, other than an absence of information on the Folly pit?"

"Let me see." Kenmar tapped his pen against his lips, frowning thoughtfully. "It was a detailed account, but the author didn't observe the Spring Folly, you see, and, somewhat past where we are now, he left our world. He wouldn't drink the Blessing of the Mare. He did, indeed, wither and die, but, before now, I counted it a coincidence."

"How did you come to read it if the author died here on the plains?" Cooro asked.

"I thought you said you'd read it was safe to drink that stuff." Mirimel's tone was sharp. She closed her saddlebag and stood, a small jar in her hand.

"Yes, yes, it is. I said as much. You see, my dear suspicious hawk guardian, the man had his servant drink the brew. It said so in his journal. The servant showed no ill effects."

"Of course that's what he did." Mirimel shot Ari a withering look.

Ari grimaced. He would have drunk it, given the opportunity.

"So, the man died," Ari prompted, mostly for an excuse to look away from Mirimel's accusing stare. Once he turned his head, he could hear her walk back to Stew and the mare.

"Yes, you see, he grew very ill and turned back, but he didn't make it. His servant returned with his possessions, including the journal. The servant could neither read nor write, but he knew it was precious to his master and that the man wanted it shared."

"How faithful of him," Mirimel muttered where she tended the mare.

Ari decided to ignore her. "So, did it tell us anything else useful?"

"It did speak of a village," Kenmar said, after a moment of thought. "It could be the one we travel toward. I feel there can't be many, out here. His map making skills were atrocious, however, so I can't say with any certainty. You see, he didn't seem to realize that, when you travel great distances, different celestial bodies appear in the sky. He kept trying to apply his constellations to the stars over the plain. It's a common error in very old works, and can be corrected for to some extent, but his skills were such that . . ." Kenmar trailed off, looking between Ari and Cooro. "Yes, well, be that as it may, he did write some little concerning a village, and a tree atop a high pinnacle."

"A tree atop a high pinnacle?" Ari repeated.

"Indeed. It sounded fanciful to me, or like fevered ravings. A round, lush tree, with bright yellow flowers that bore no resemblance to any other flowers he'd seen. He described it as perched alone atop a high spire, with hardly enough width to hold it."

"That does sound a bit fanciful," Ari said.

"Yes, well, of course I'd discounted it, but in view of some of the things we've seen, it may be we shall find this tree erelong."

"Did he say anything about the village?" Ari asked.

"Is it a village of horses?" Cooro added.

"Of Questri? No, I think not. I believe of people, though that is where he saw, by his words, the most stunning steed ever to walk the lands, so maybe it is a village of both?" He set to tapping his pen once more. "I shall meditate on it, endeavoring to recall the details of what I read. I'm afraid it was some time ago. In view of the lack of geographical integrity in the report, I've long since set it aside."

"Thank you," Ari said. "Let us know if you remember anything. It might be nice to have some idea what it's like there."

"Of course. Honored to help."

"Do you wish to spar, my lord?" Cooro asked, turning to Ari.

Ari looked up at the sky, showing streaks of pink and orange. It was a bit late to start sparring. He glanced over at Cooro and grinned. "Sure."

***

Ari and his friends journeyed for what, to him, seemed an interminable time. They had to ration their last bits of dried fruit, eating mostly small game Mirimel and her hawk caught. Green grasslands rolled before them, and behind, and to the east and west. They went on forever, as far as Ari could tell. The days grew longer, and his eighteenth birthday came and went.

No one mentioned it. He suspected none of them knew when it was, though Mirimel must have some idea. Ari didn't mind, though it made him miss Ispiria all the more. He recalled her saying once that she would change the time of her yearly visit to Hawkers so she could always spend his birthday with him. So far, that hadn't worked out well for them. He wondered, if he managed to rid the world of Tal Mraken, if he and Ispiria could finally be wed and spend some time together.

Mirimel made progress in befriending the black mare, and healing her leg. Ari and Cooro sparred daily, an activity that seemed to entertain the others, including the two Questri. Cooro spent considerable time trying to teach Ari to flip in the air, but, strong and agile as he was, Ari didn't seem to have the knack for it. He supposed he was built with too much bulk. A form suited to wearing the full regalements of a knight didn't seem to lend itself to the almost magical feats of acrobatics Cooro could undertake.

After what seemed an endless journey over infinite plains, two things marked their approach to the village, which, so far, Ari had no name for. He wasn't sure there was one. There seemed to be only the one, so why would it be called anything other than The Village?

The first sign was the tree. An indistinct smudge on the horizon, it grew daily in both height and distinction. As they neared, it formed itself from a blur into what was recognizably a tree. A very round one, in fact, not tall and pointed like the pines they'd left. It also loomed farther and farther above the landscape, rising up on a singular pinnacle of rock.

Ari could understand why, reading the description of it, Lord Kenmar would have dismissed it. It was an impossible seeming placement for a tree, with so little soil or water and constantly barraged by sun and wind. It could only be the Orate Tree, sustained by magic. It seemed to be flecked with yellow, but Ari couldn't tell if the flecks were fruit, flowers, or unhealthy leaves.

What marked the greater immediacy of their destination, however, was when the grassland ended and tilled fields began. First, they were empty stretches of turned earth, but these soon gave way to areas that were planted. People toiled in them, alongside bright-eyed young Questri. They cultivated what Ari thought, from his vantage point on the wide, well-trodden roadway, was grain, perhaps oats and barley. People and Questri alike looked up as Ari and his friends rode past, but they never left their labors to speak with them.

The Questri were uniformly yearlings, barring a few who seemed to stand as overseers. Ari could only assume the foals of the previous year didn't run with the herd. Though he knew they were sentient, it was strange to see horses hard at work in fields, but without drivers. They toiled near the humans, who were clad in homespun, undyed fabric, but seemed to engage in entirely different tasks.

They traveled for so long through the fields that Ari started to despair they would ever reach a village. When it finally took shape on the horizon, he felt a surge of relief. The days were getting long and warm, the summer solstice nearing, and he was becoming a bit weary of the road and of riding the packhorse. It was a pleasant enough creature, but riding it didn't compare in any way to the sheer joy to be had riding Stew.

The low, sloping structures in the village seemed to be made mostly of straw, which Ari supposed made sense. There was little else to be had on the plains. Mud bricks were also in evidence, outlining small gardens and wells. Even from where they were, walking down the overly-wide roadway between the fields, Ari could see that the buildings were placed well apart, much more removed from each other than in a typical human town.

There was no wall around the village, nor a gate of any sort. Who would they defend themselves from, after all? The Questri ruled the plains and, if what the Clanmaster had said was true, humans couldn't live there long without the aid of the Questri.

Still, two striking, well-muscled stallions stood to either side of the road, at the point where ordered fields gave way to the packed earth and low grass of town. Stew and the black mare led the way, passing between them. The stallions watched with hard eyes, but didn't intervene.

Running through the center of the village was a wide swath of open space, almost too broad to be thought of as a road. It stretched out before them, and Ari could see it ended at the base of the tall spire on which the tree stood. The spire was centered in a vast open area, large enough, perhaps, for the whole herd to gather in. Ari craned his neck back, his gaze traveling up the spire. The Orate Tree, resolved now into a bright splash of green leaves and yellow flowers, loomed high above them.

Stew and the mare didn't slow their pace upon entering the village. Around them, humans and Questri paused in their tasks to stare at Ari and his friends, but none moved forward. Ari was sure he heard at least one child, in a scandalized voice, blurt out the term unthinking, only to be quickly hushed. He patted the packhorse on the neck, feeling the disdain of Questri and human eyes alike. It wasn't the docile gelding's fault he wasn't as intelligent as a Questri.

They marched down the over-wide avenue in awkward silence, the murmur of the townsfolk washing over them. Reaching the far side of the hut-lined boulevard, they entered the vast open space, passing between an honor guard of stallions who could only be described as menacing. Muscled flanks rippled, and lips were pulled back to reveal strong teeth, although each member of the guard kept his head forward. Still, their eyes followed Ari, and he could feel the weight of them.

The base of the pinnacle on which the tree stood was as impossible as the rest, for it was hollow. Four natural looking, yet symmetrical, arches were cut into it, each facing one compass point. They left the spire supported by thin corners of stone, the sight so unnatural, it made Ari uneasy to be near it, as if it could topple at any moment.

Within the domed chamber beneath the spire stood a shimmering gray stallion. His coat glowed with so much luster, he seemed wrought of fine silver, but he exuded too much vitality for the impression of a statue to take hold. Though he was sheltered from the noon sun by the tower of stone above, he reflected back light, making the chamber in which he stood seem almost to glow.

The silver stallion, alone of all the Questri Ari had yet seen, bore ornamentation. A single, nearly fist-sized, blue crystal glowed on his brow. The gleaming strands of his forelock partially obscured it, and Ari had no idea what held it in place.

Stew and the mare stopped before the silver stallion, who Ari could only assume was the king of the Questri. Both horses bowed. Ari hastily slid from his saddle and did likewise. Behind him, he could hear the others dismounting. He could only hope they would bow, too.

"The Thrice Born shall come forward," a child-like voice said. Even though the voice was young, there was a cadence to it, a regal tone, that couldn't be mistaken.

Following that voice, Ari was surprised to see a young boy, perhaps five, standing beside the stallion. With how still the

156

child had been, the Questri's magnificence had rendered him nearly impossible to see.

Stew looked back. He and the mare stepped aside. Ari belatedly realized he'd been given a command.

He strode between them, bowing again, hoping he didn't look too disreputable after so many days of travel. "It is an honor to come before you, Your Majesty," he said, unsure how to address the Questri.

The Questri king regarded him with amusement deep in his eyes. Ari was struck by the familiarity of the gaze. This magnificent creature, this silver-toned icon of equine perfection, bore a striking resemblance to Larke's horse.

"The correct form of address is Herdlord," the boy said. "We shall forgive you your ignorance."

"Thank you, Herdlord. You are generous." This once, it wasn't difficult to look to the Questri, not the speaker. For one, the small boy's features were completely obscured by his blindfold, rendering him faceless. For another, it was hard not to stare at the Herdlord.

"You have journeyed far, Thrice Born. Tell me what you seek."

Ari opened his mouth, but closed it again. The Clanmaster of the Faesten Clan had made it seem as if the Questri knew exactly why Ari was there. The Herdlord couldn't wish a reiteration of that. Something in his wording, and the intensity of his gaze, gave Ari the feeling this was a test.

What, then, did the king of the Questri wish to know? Would a wrong answer mean Ari couldn't get the stone? Was this the chance to earn a boon the Clanmaster had spoken of? It wasn't yet the solstice, and Ari had assumed he would have a warning when the time came to earn the stone. He'd been anticipating some sort of feat. Could it be this simple? Or rather, he thought, looking into the stallion's gleaming eyes and realizing he didn't know what to say, this difficult?

"Weigh your answer carefully, Thrice Born, for you may speak only the truth to me," the Herdlord said, as if knowing Ari's thoughts. "Speak falsely, know not your own heart, and these shall be the last words between us."

Ari nodded, swallowing, and tried to see what was in his heart.

Chapter 14

"I seek peace," Ari finally said.

"Yet you pursue a means of destruction."

"Because I must." Ari shook his head. "It's been made clear to me that if I don't hunt down my family's enemy and kill him, he will come for me, and my future children. I can't marry knowing that. I don't even know if it's fair to remain Duke of Sorga with such a threat looming before me. Part of being duke is to ensure the line carries on, to stave off war."

"And what of revenge?" The eyes of the silver stallion locked with his.

Ari suppressed a shiver at the intensity of the Herdlord's gaze. He took a steadying breath. "I love my parents, or the idea of them, for I never knew them. I love my fiancée and the children we might someday have, and Sorga and the people there." He shook his head again, trying to rattle his thoughts into a discernable order. "I know all that my enemy has done, and I know the things I've done, but I'm not Sir Cadwel. I'm not even Hawk Guardian Mirimel. If my enemy was here now, before me, asking for forgiveness, I don't know if I could kill him."

He heard his friends stir behind him and hoped his words didn't make them think he was weak. "I've never been the type of man Sir Cadwel is. I don't know if I have it in me to keep the peace as he has. Yes, I've killed, and I know I will again, but it's always been to protect those who need protecting, or to save those I care for. The Lady would have me hunt down this Empty One and slay him, and I will, to keep my world safe, but I didn't ride all this way for vengeance or hatred. I don't know if any good can come of those feelings, and I want to do good."

He choked a bit on those final words, realizing the truth of it. When he'd dreamed of being a knight, his dreams had been of valor and glory, his foes faceless. He'd never realized the king's champion might have to do something like plan to kill Larkesong if he tried to run away with the queen, as Sir Cadwel had done long ago. Nor had he thought good people did things like try to force two lovers apart, as the Lady had tried to do to his parents.

Ari understood sometimes hard decisions had to be made. Horrible things had to be done to ensure safety and peace. He didn't think he was strong enough, though. He hoped he'd never be tested.

"It is as the blue lady has said," the eerie high voice blindfolded child said.

Ari looked up, once again meeting the silver stallion's gaze.

"Your intentions are pure, Thrice Born. Only those who come before me in worthiness may be offered a chance to earn the boon."

"Thank you, Herdlord." Ari bowed. He suppressed a sigh, feeling worn thin by his admissions. He supposed it had been too much to hope that answering the stallion's question honestly was enough to win the stone. "May I ask, what form does this chance take? How may one earn the right to ask for a boon of the Questri?"

"You may ask, but I shall not answer." With that, he lifted his head, seeming to enter into a deep contemplation of the sky.

Stew turned to Ari, walking forward to usher him back. Ari bowed again, but the Herdlord gave no sign he saw. A blond young man, dressed in the same loose, undyed fabric as the other villagers they'd seen, appeared at Ari's side.

"The Questri master is trying to tell you your audience is at an end," the man said, nodding toward Stew.

Stew dipped his head, as if in agreement.

Ari turned to look between Cooro, Kenmar and Mirimel. She gave him one of her inscrutable, but disapproving, looks from where she stood holding the reins of the packhorse he'd been riding, along with those of her own mount. The young man, about Ari's age, held his arms wide, seeming to herd them back toward the village. Ari took the reins Mirimel handed him and they led their unthinking horses back between the rows of Questri. Stew and the black mare trailed behind.

"I'm Tewlar," the villager said, casting curious, slightly horrified looks at their mounts. "I've been summoned to be your guide."

"It's our honor to meet you, Tewlar. I'm Ari, and those are my friends, Cooro, Kenmar and Mirimel." He pointed to them in turn, deciding to leave out their titles. Hopefully his friends wouldn't complain. It was easier, and their Lggothian and

Wheylian stations didn't matter on the plains. "Did I do something wrong, just now?"

"The Herdlord does not answer questions," Tewlar said with a shake of his straw-blond head. "He poses them."

"I see." Ari suppressed a grimace. Hopefully the stallion would extend his forgiveness of Ari's ignorance to cover that mistake, too. "Am I allowed to ask you questions?"

Tewlar grinned, and Ari felt some of the tension leave him. "That's what I'm here for. Would you like to eat? It's a bit past lunch, but I know you've been traveling."

Ari nodded. "Thank you, but first we need to see to our mounts. Is there somewhere we can put them, out of the sun, where they can have food and water?"

Tewlar eyed the four unthinking horses, looking uncertain. "They must be tied?"

"Or closed in with a gate." From what he'd seen of the village so far, though, there were no gates.

"I think, maybe, there is a place." Tewlar changed direction slightly. "The harvest is not yet in, so there is space in the storage barns. Does each require a private space?"

"Not really. They'll be happier together. It depends on how much room they have, though."

Tewlar led them to a row of wider, taller structures, though still with the sloped roofs they employed in the village. Stew and the black mare didn't stop when their guide did. Stew had his head angled toward her, not even looking at Ari as they passed. Ari sighed, turning back to the other humans. Even though Stew had traveled with them, he'd felt oddly removed from his horse during the journey.

Tewlar stayed with them, however, helping them assemble feed and buckets of water. He watched, peppering them with questions, as Ari and his friends removed the horses' tack, brushed them down, and inspected their hooves. Before long, for they were well rehearsed at caring for their mounts, their horses were settled.

Ari turned to Tewlar. "Shall we go eat, then?" In truth, he was rather hungry. He also wished to get away from the horses and all of the queries they seemed to raise, for he wanted to be the one doing the asking. He had questions enough of his own.

"They aren't smart enough to eat and drink on their own?" Tewlar asked as he led the way from the barn.

"They'd wander around and eat and drink things they found. I can't guarantee they wouldn't take something they shouldn't, or wander away from the village."

"They aren't even smart enough to stay here?" Tewlar was clearly shocked.

"At home, they will usually return to their stable, but this is a new place."

Tewlar led them to one of the long sloped huts and Ari followed him inside. As soon as they stepped in, dim though it was, Ari realized he would only be able to stand in the center of the dwelling. Ducking, he made his way to the end of a table centered in the room. A second door was at the back, leading to some other part of the structure. A blonde rosy-cheeked young woman looked up at him from where she was setting out plates.

Tewlar made his way down the table, stopping to kiss the girl on the forehead. "My wife, Mia. Mia, this is Ari, and Cooro, Kenmar and Mirimel."

Mia nodded to each of them as Tewlar introduced them. Ari nodded back. When their guide reached Mirimel, Mia's eyes went wide.

"Is that a bird?" she blurted, the remaining plate she was holding clattering to the table. She pulled up the apron she wore, covering her face.

Ari looked over to see Mirimel's hawk perched on her shoulder. He was so accustomed to the creature, he hadn't given any thought to it coming inside with them. "He's a Sorga Hawk." He tried to sound soothing. "He won't hurt you."

Mia peeked over the top of her apron. "Is he fierce? Does he bite?"

"He does bite," Mirimel said.

Ari shot her a quelling look.

"He won't bite you, though," Mirimel said, her tone kinder. She walked halfway up the table. "Really, he's a very well-behaved hawk."

She held up her arm and the little hawk jumped to her wrist. Mia lowered her apron a bit more. The hawk tilted his head to the side, looking at her. She gave a tentative smile.

"He does seem well-behaved." She let go of her apron, smoothing it. "I'm sorry. We have only the great plains vultures, you know. We . . ." She glanced at the hawk. "We tell the children stories of how they swoop down and carry off babies or toddlers who are left unattended or run outside alone." She blushed.

"I don't think this one is large enough for such a feat," Cooro said. He bowed, somehow still fully elegant in the cramped space. "I, Cooro, have long traveled with this paragon of a hawk. I personally assure you, he will not abscond with any babies."

Mia turned her tentative smile on Cooro, then looked up at Tewlar, as if to assure herself all was well. He put an arm about her shoulder.

"Sit, friends. I shall dine with you, and answer questions."
Tewlar grinned. "Mia, I think, already ate."

"I did," she said quickly, though she'd put out enough
plates to include herself. She turned and lifted a squat
earthenware pot from the floor, setting it in the middle of the
table, which bore the plates, bread and nothing more. "I'll
return later."

Mia kissed her husband, gave them all another nod, and
hurried away. Ari noticed she circled around Tewlar, walking
down the side of the table away from Mirimel and the hawk.

"As if you'd want her babies," Mirimel murmured to the
hawk as she pulled out a chair with her free hand. She gave a
little toss of her wrist and he flapped his wings. Half flying, half
hopping, her hawk perched on the back of the chair beside
hers.

Cooro eyed the hawk, then took the seat opposite Mirimel,
Kenmar sitting down next to him. Ari sat at the foot of the
table, while Tewlar took his place at the head. The blond young
man pulled out his chair, but didn't sit, proceeding to ladle out
what looked like cooked oats onto their plates.

Ari stared down at the oats, which actually smelled good.
He could detect some spices, and some sort of dried berries.
Discreetly, he looked about for a spoon. He could see the
others doing likewise.

Just when he was about to give up and pick up his plate,
planning to try to pour the oats down his throat, Tewlar
reached out and ripped off a hunk of bread. Using it in place of
a spoon, he shoveled a scoop of the cooked grain into his
mouth.

"Please, eat," Tewlar said, pushing the loaf of bread down
the table.

Mirimel took it, breaking off a piece, and passed it to Cooro. By the time it got to Ari, only the end was left. Watching Tewlar's technique, Ari was fairly sure the end was the most useful part.

They ate for a moment in silence. Mirimel offered the hawk a bit of bread, which it didn't take. Ari found the fare a little bland, but it tasted well enough and it was filling. He wondered, thinking about the endless fields, if barley and oats were all the villagers ate. He'd seen no livestock yet.

"What do you call this place, this collection of homes?" Kenmar asked, breaking the silence.

Ari looked to the older lord. He seemed more worn than usual, and worried. Ari wondered if there was anything amiss, or if Kenmar was just tired after so long in the saddle. Hopefully, for a few days at least, they would be able to rest. By his count, they'd arrived just in time, for the solstice was in two days. After he did his best to secure the stone, they would return to Sorga. Ari wasn't overjoyed with the idea of the long ride back through the empty grasslands. He thought it would take less time, though, for they'd swung quite far east for the Folly.

"This place? This is the village," Tewlar said, confirming Ari's earlier suspicion that there would be only the one.

"I see. What, then, do you call these plains?" Kenmar asked.

"This land, you mean, on which this village stands?"

"All of the realm of the Questri, north, south, east and west of us."

"We call the plains Tybrunn. What do your people call them?" Tewlar's eyes were bright with curiosity.

166

Ari realized it must be an interesting thing, to meet people from outside the realm of the Questri. If it was true about the Blessing of the Mare, visitors must be very uncommon.

"We call them the great northern plains," Kenmar said. "But, you see, I've realized that name is inaccurate. Great they may be, but we are quite far south now. We've simply left our peninsula, or we would be near Poromont."

"Peninsula? Poromont?" Tewlar repeated, making the words a question. "What's it like there? Is the grass as high, the sky as blue?"

"There are forests," Mirimel said.

"And mountains," Cooro added.

Tewlar looked back and forth between them, his expression one of confusion. The conversation devolved into a discussion of geographic features, with Cooro waxing on at length on the magnificence of the Wheylian range. Tewlar was clearly entranced, though Ari wasn't sure how successful his friends were being at imparting an accurate description of things like mountains, lakes and seashores to someone who had never even heard of some of them.

Finally, Ari cleared his throat, interrupting Cooro, who was expounding on the beauty of snow encased peaks. "What is this chance to win a boon from the Questri? Is it a competition?"

Tewlar nodded. He leaned back in his chair, pushing away his empty plate. "It is, yes. Each year, all those who wish a worthy boon are permitted to compete. When the longest day is at hand, the competitors stand in a ring about the stone spire on which the Orate Tree stands. As the sun surmounts the rim of the plain, the flowers become fruit at the touch of its rays, and the men of the village climb. Whoever first brings the Herdlord a fruit from the tree is awarded the boon."

"I have to climb that spire?" An image of it, looming taller than anything he'd ever seen other than a mountain, filled Ari's mind. "Are there ropes?"

Tewlar shook his head, smiling.

"Do they need the fruit?" Kenmar asked. "Can more than one man return with it?"

Mirimel leaned forward, propping her elbows on the table. "And why is it called the Orate Tree?"

"The Orate Tree bears the Orate Fruit." Tewlar looked bemused. "The Questri masters told me you know nothing, but it is hard to understand such ignorance of important things. Only one fruit may be picked. The moment one is removed from the tree, all others wither. The Orate Fruit is given to the first born babes. In the few survivors, it opens the mind to the voice of the Questri. It is those chosen few who become the voiceless."

"Opens their minds to the voice of the Questri?" Mirimel repeated, her eyes narrowing.

Ari raised his eyebrows. He was much more concerned with the other things Tewlar had said. He didn't like the idea of having to climb up a sheer rock face to retrieve a strange fruit that would be fed to babies and make most of them not survive. How could he be a party to poisoning infants? No one would do such a thing. He must not have understood properly.

"Do you mean, it makes it so you can speak with the Questri?" Mirimel pressed.

"I don't know." Tewlar shrugged. "We don't speak with the voiceless. They have no voice."

"But they can hear the Questri, in their heads?"

"The Questri masters inhabit them."

Mirimel frowned.

"What do you mean, given to the first born babes?" Ari asked. A glance at Cooro and Kenmar showed worry on their faces as well.

"Each new family must present their first born child in the spring. They shall be fed the Orate Fruit, and some few will live on as voiceless to the clans."

"And those who do not become voiceless?"

"They depart this world."

"Every first born?" Cooro asked, his features showing he was horrified.

"Yes, but it is only the first child." Tewlar's tone was reassuring. "The Questri masters ask for no others."

"Why do it?" Ari asked. "Why not refuse?"

"It is our way." Tewlar shrugged. "The Questri masters are generous in return. For this one sacrifice, they give all future born the Blessing of the Mare during the solstice celebrations. Without the Blessing each solstice, all of us would die, not just the first borns. It is the duty of the eldest to make this sacrifice for the rest. Any sibling would do as much, I think."

Ari shook his head, appalled the Questri would ask this of people. To give up their children so the clans could have mouthpieces? It was nearly unfathomable.

He thought of all the people, over two dozen, he'd seen among the herd. How many children had died for the Questri to have that paltry number of voiceless, sightless slaves? He stared at Tewlar, stunned.

Turning to his friends, Ari saw they were similarly disturbed, except for Mirimel. The hawk guardian wore a contemplative look, a dangerous glint in her eyes. Ari scrubbed his hands over his face, his meal of cooked oats suddenly seeming a heavy weight in his gut.

The Lady must have known. She must be aware of what task would win Ari the boon. He wasn't sure if he could do such a thing, retrieve a fruit to poison babies. Not for a stone. How could she ask him to take part? Were there any lengths to which she wouldn't go, or force upon him, to see Tal Mraken dead?

Chapter 15

Ari stood from the table, everyone turning to look at him. "Can we go see the Orate Tree again? I'd like to look at this pinnacle of rock I'm supposed to climb." Maybe a walk would clear his mind. He didn't feel as if he could think straight. All of the revelations of the day rattled about in his head, each seeking attention.

"Yes, of course," Tewlar said, rising as well.

He picked up his plate, walking to the corner and ducking low to place it into a bucket of water. Turning back, he held out his hand expectantly. Ari passed his plate down, as did the others.

"What of this?" Mirimel asked, pointing to the nearly empty pot of oats.

Tewlar looked over from where he was depositing their plates. "Please put the lid on. Mia will be along to collect it."

Mirimel nodded, complying, and they made their way back outside. Ari stretched, squinting into the bright afternoon light.

He hadn't realized how dark it was inside the hut. Mirimel lengthened her stride to pass him, coming alongside Tewlar as he led the way back toward the Orate Tree.

"Is it permissible for my hawk to hunt in your fields, or shall I ask him to fly farther out?"

"He hunts?"

Ari could hear the underlying worry in that question. He shook his head. It seemed odd for anyone to be afraid of a Sorga Hawk. The small brown hawks were as intelligent as people, and had worked beside them for generations.

The hawk, perched on Mirimel's shoulder, issued one of his little chirps. Tewlar flinched. Mirimel reached up to stroke the hawk on the head, more to apologize to it, Ari guessed, than to reassure Tewlar.

"He hunts for small rodents, like mice or voles. I assure you, he really isn't interested in eating children."

Ari detected only a hint of sarcasm in her tone. He was proud of her.

"I worry, even small as he is, that if he dives down as raptors are known to do, it will strike fear into the workers," Tewlar said.

"What about the outermost fields?" Ari asked. "The ones that aren't planted yet."

Tewlar glanced back at him, frowning, until understanding erased the expression and he turned his gaze forward once more. "You mean the firebreak."

"Firebreak?" Mirimel asked.

Behind him, where Cooro and Kenmar walked, Ari heard the latter mutter, "I see."

"Many years, before the snow comes, the grasslands burn. That ring of land, past the fields, is what keeps our crops and village safe from the fires."

"It must be an amazing sight," Kenmar said.

Tewlar shrugged. "I think the hawk must go to those fields, or beyond, please."

"I'll let him know." Mirimel held up her arm and the hawk jumped onto her wrist, cocking its head as she spoke to it in soft tones. Ari knew none of the others would be able to hear her, but his Aluien-enhanced senses could pick out the words.

"Don't let these idiots upset you," Mirimel whispered. "Hopefully we won't be here long. Just try not to go near their children." She murmured something else, too low for even Ari to make out.

The hawk dipped his head and Mirimel tossed him into the air. He spiraled up. Ari could hear a few gasps from around the village, and the squeals of children. Quickly becoming nothing more than a speck in the clear blue sky, he winged his way south, toward the Orate Tree.

"Are these great plains vultures really so fierce?" Ari asked, moving up to walk on Tewlar's other side.

"You shall see." Tewlar was leading them in a wide arc, going around the honor guard of horses leading up to the Orate Tree and the Herdlord. "Behind the tower of rock on which the Orate Tree stands is a large slab of stone. On it, we set the first borns of the previous year. They are fed the fruit and left. It is then the vultures come."

"You leave your babies out for vultures?" Cooro asked, clearly appalled.

"In truth, the birds offer a mercy. They never take those whose minds are opened by the Orate Fruit. For the others, it is a painful death, for the fruit is poisonous. The great birds offer a quicker release. No one knows how they can tell which babes to cull and which shall survive the transformation, but the Questri masters assure us they know."

Ari stopped walking. He didn't want to hear any more. Cooro and Kenmar halted immediately, but it took Tewlar and Mirimel a moment to notice his defection. They turned to look at him. Mirimel's eyes were dark with anger. Tewlar wore a questioning look.

Ari turned to face the Orate Tree, on its high tower of rock. They were east of it now. Underneath, in his vaulted chamber, Ari could see the flank of the Questri king, his stunning silver hide rippling with muscle. South of the pinnacle sat a large slab of rock, streaked with dark stains.

Ari swallowed, his eyes skittering away from that rock. Seeking something else to fill his attention, he lifted his gaze up the spire of stone. It would be a difficult climb, even for him. He was strong and agile, yes, but he had no experience attempting such a feat. Maybe he wouldn't make it. Maybe he wouldn't be the one to return with the fruit.

Glancing at Tewlar, Ari wished the villager's face didn't show so much confusion over their obvious disquiet. "Have you ever made the climb?" Ari asked him, his voice rough. He cleared his throat.

"I tried, once, but few succeed." Tewlar turned, looking up at the tree. "Often, many years pass without someone claiming the fruit."

"If no one brings it down, the children must be spared." Kenmar's tone was hopeful.

"No." Tewlar shook his head. "All first borns go to the rock. If none can harvest a fruit, there isn't even the scant hope of them becoming voiceless to console us."

"And you just live like this?" Mirimel asked, harsh accusation in her voice.

Ari couldn't believe the Questri demanded such sacrifice. He looked back at the silver stallion, his eyes traveling up the

174

ranks of powerful Questri who formed the honor guard. Did human life mean so little to them?

"It's how we live, yes," Tewlar said. "It's how we've always lived. The Questri masters are good to us. The yearlings help in the fields, we're given the Blessing so we may survive. I gather our ways are not your ways, but they are the only way here, on the Tybrunn Plain."

"Why not just up and leave, man?" Cooro demanded. His head swiveled between the distant ranks of horses and Tewlar.

Tewlar shrugged again. "Some few do. Some ask, as their boon, for one of the Questri masters to bear them away, beyond the plains. Who knows what becomes of them, in your world, without a village or family?"

Ari had no idea. He'd never met anyone from the plains. What would happen to them? They would come to a town and live, he supposed. They wouldn't have any money. Would they have skills? How would they eat and where would they sleep?

He looked to the others, wondering if they'd met anyone from this village. Mirimel was eyeing Tewlar like he'd just crawled out from under a rock. Cooro's gaze was turned toward the spire on which the tree stood, his look contemplative. Lord Kenmar met Ari's eyes and shook his head slightly, as if he knew what question Ari would ask.

"What other boons do people ask for?" Ari finally said, to break the silence. He may as well know what hopes he would be dashing, if he took the fruit.

"Usually, anyone with a first born climbs, of course, to ask their child be spared."

Ari nodded. He'd expected that.

"Young men climb to impress young women."

"I thought the Herdlord said it had to be a noble cause, or something like that?" Mirimel said.

Tewlar cast her a wry smile. "To the Questri masters, seeking the best mate is a noble cause, and, I think, it entertains them to see us try. They call a man a yearling until he climbs." He cast Ari a companionable smile before returning his gaze to the tree. "No one with that as their goal climbs long. We start, hoping we won't be the first to give up and climb down, or fall. Once a few men give in, the rest come down. We don't want to get hurt, just to impress the womenfolk."

"So women can't climb, then?" Mirimel's tone was as sharp as Ari had ever heard it. "I suppose they're called yearlings until they meet some criterion as well?"

Beside her, Kenmar took out his notebook. He began turning in a slow circle, muttering to himself and jotting things down.

"Girls are fillies, until they have their first child." Tewlar's tone was amused. Apparently, he didn't notice the venom in the look Mirimel was leveling at him. "Occasionally, women do climb, but not often. Why would they? No woman could ever beat the men. She would risk herself for nothing. Less than nothing, for no man would want to marry the sort of woman who would climb, and any husband would be shamed before the whole village if his wife did."

"I see," Mirimel said, ice in her voice.

"Er, so, did you do well the year you climbed?" Ari broke in. The last thing he needed was for Mirimel to decide to beat the amusement out of Tewlar.

"I got Mia, didn't I?" Tewlar grinned.

"And a fine prize she is," Cooro said, slapping Tewlar on the back.

Mirimel shot the swordmaster a look that very well ought to have stopped his heart in his chest. To Ari's surprise, for he wouldn't be as brave, Cooro smirked at her. Ari shook his head.

"I'm going for a walk," Mirimel said, turning away from them.

"I say, it's awfully bright out here," Lord Kenmar said. "Good for transcribing. Do you have a table I could use?"

"Yes, of course." Tewlar looked between Kenmar and Ari, obviously waiting to see what Ari wanted him to do.

"I'm going to have a word with Hawk Guardian Mirimel," Ari said. "You three may as well head back." He gave Cooro an apologetic look, hoping the swordmaster didn't mind what was practically an order.

"Is it acceptable to ask the Herdlord for permission to climb?" Cooro asked.

Ari wasn't sure if the Whey was asking him or Tewlar.

"Of course," Tewlar said. "I shall find your friend a table and then we will seek an audience, but you must not ask. Rather, wait for him to question your reason for approaching."

"What reason will you give?" Ari asked Cooro, frowning.

"Why, that I want to impress a girl." Cooro's face splitting into a grin.

"Good luck with that." Ari doubted it would work. "I'm going to go try to placate her before she shoots someone."

Cooro nodded. He took Lord Kenmar by the arm, for the cartographer seemed too busy with his papers to notice Tewlar was trying to steer him to the requested table. Ari hurried after Mirimel.

It took him longer than he'd expected to catch up to her, for she was walking quite fast. As he drew near, he realized she was also muttering to herself. His boot sent a stone skittering away from him and she whirled, her hand going to the knife at her belt. If her face wasn't indication already, Ari knew her well

177

enough to realize that reaction meant she was in a terrible mood.

"Ari." She relaxed her grip on the hilt of her hunting knife. "Are you here to give me some sort of speech about accepting this culture?"

Ari raised his eyebrows. "No. I came to ask your advice."

"Oh." Her hand dropped to her side. "About?"

Ari looked around, but they were quite alone in the vast dirt field that surrounded the Orate Tree. His eyes skimmed over the slab of stone, north of them now, and he wrenched them back away. He shoved a hand through his hair, too long and tangled by the wind. "I don't know if I can climb up there and get that fruit."

"Of course you can. You're stronger and faster than any other man alive. If these village weasels can do it, so can you."

He shook his head. "Rather, I mean, morally. I can't get a poisoned fruit so they can feed it to babies. How can I do that?"

"They're going to kill those babies either way," she said, her tone harsh. She looked over his shoulder.

He knew her eyes were on the stone slab. "That doesn't mean I have to help them. And I'll be taking any chance anyone else has to gain the boon for their child."

Mirimel pursed her lips. Finally, her eyes moved back to him. "They climb to save their first borns. You climb to save your entire family. You climb for Ispiria and all of your future children."

"Theoretical children. These first borns are real."

"And they won't have even the hope of becoming voiceless slaves to these Questri if no one gets up there and brings down a fruit."

Ari sighed, turning back toward the tree. She was correct about that. Looking up the tall finger of stone, he was surprised anyone ever came down with a fruit. He wasn't even sure he could do it. He frowned, wondering if he was afraid. It really was a long way up. "Do you think we're allowed to practice?"

"I doubt it." She stepped up beside him. "Ari, I know this is all very awful, but it's been going on for years and will keep going after we leave. You'd best get the fruit, ask for your boon, and we'll go. I can see why Stew left."

Ari looked around, realizing he had no idea where Stew was. He missed his horse. Not that Stew was really his. A sentient creature couldn't be, could it? Just as Peine, or Mirimel or any of Ari's other friends, Stew traveled with Ari out of his own volition. Ari hoped he wouldn't decide to stop.

"Speaking of leaving, I think Larke's horse is related to the Herdlord," he said, his eyes moving to the gleam of silver beneath the spire.

"How is Larkesong?"

Ari glanced at her, but her face was expressionless. Still, he imagined he heard a slight wistfulness in her tone. "He was well enough, when I saw him this spring."

"Two more years. Three years seems quite a time to be confined, but I suppose it isn't so much when you're immortal."

"I think it seems a long while to him anyhow."

"That's because he's of a flighty, unpredictable, flittering nature. Like a butterfly."

Ari smiled. He didn't think Mirimel meant that as a compliment. Larke invited the comparison, though. Not just because of the way he acted, but his manner of dress as well. Ari knew it for the act it was, though. "Have you ever heard him sing that very sad song, the one about a long ago queen and her lover?"

Mirimel shook her head, turning to him with a question in her eyes. "I can't say I have. He always seems to be singing silly things, or songs of battle." Her eyes got a faraway look. "Do you mean the melody he played to the hawks, that time in the aerie? He didn't sing the words." She refocused on his face, looking suspicious. "Why?"

Ari shrugged. "You may want to ask him to sing it for you someday. Few have ever heard it."

"That's a fascinating suggestion, but I have no idea what you're going on about. What does that song have to do with Larke being flighty?"

"It will show you another side of him, is all. One I think, maybe, you should see."

"If you insist," she said, returning her gaze to the Orate Tree.

They stood in silence for a long while. Ari replayed their afternoon in his mind, but he couldn't settle any of his dilemmas. "I'm going to head back," he finally said.

"I think I'll continue my walk. I'm finding our guide and that Whey you've saddled us with rather intolerable right now."

"Cooro is from a world where women are in charge of pretty much everything. He doesn't believe women are prizes to be claimed. He only said what he did to torment you."

"I know."

"Why are you so angry, then?"

"Because it worked."

Ari stared at her for a moment, having no idea what that meant. Her orange curls, so like Ispiria's red ones, blew loosely about her face. Though they did share similar features, Mirimel was over a year older than Ari and Ispiria, and she'd seen much more evil in her life than his fiancée had. Mirimel's face was harder, with a more angular look to it. Her blue eyes were often reminiscent of ice, a very different tone from Ispiria's laughing green gaze. Mirimel, Ari thought, might be the better for a little bright, flittering butterfly-like spirit in her life.

"You'll be well out here?" He didn't know why, but the intent look on her face, as she gazed up at the tree, worried him.

"Yes. I hate this flatness, though. I'm going to keep walking. Eventually, I might find something to shoot at. You'd best warn that Whey I'm looking. He's not very tall, but he'd be more challenging to hit than a rock."

"Uh, all right. See you in a while, then."

"Ari," she called as he started to walk away. "I know you'll do what needs to be done, and what you do will be what is right."

He looked back, nodding. He wished he could be as sure.

Chapter 16

The herd arrived that afternoon, filling the small town with a rumbling that was met with cheering from the villagers. Ari felt it was another reason for the low, sloped shape of the buildings. He was sure the arrival of hundreds of horses would shake a post and lintel structure apart. He stepped out of the dwelling Tewlar had left them in, watching the revelry of Questri and humans alike. Their joy only made him feel more removed from the people and Questri surrounding him.

While the inhabitants of the Tybrunn Plain frolicked, Ari availed himself of a bucket and well to get truly clean for the first time in months. He then set to washing his spare set of clothes, which were now only slightly cleaner than the ones he wore. Halfway through that activity, Mia appeared. She looked on for a brief time, then shook her head ruefully and took the items from him. Later, when he returned to their hut, his clothes were waiting for him, clean, folded and smelling of the grasslands and sun.

He'd hoped to sleep well that night, bathed, warm and with a soft pallet beneath him, rather than a blanket on the ground. He hoped in vain, though, for his dreams were filled with images of the Orate Tree, its yellow flowers transformed into evil, glowing eyes. Finally, near dawn, he rose and went for a walk.

He was forced to walk north, up the roadway they'd first come down, for the village and the great open expanse around the tree were filled with sleeping Questri. They lay on thick straw mats. Ari supposed the villagers must weave them as part of their service to their Questri masters, as Tewlar put it. As Ari neared the last row of dwellings, he saw that two different guards stood at the northern edge of the village, their dark hides melding with the lack of pre-dawn light. He nodded to them, but they didn't act as if they saw.

He walked north, his eyes tracing the fading stars. He knew Sir Cadwel would climb the spire a morning hence. In truth, Sir Cadwel might ask Mirimel to shoot down anyone who was outpacing him, to ensure victory. To the knight, the outcome was of more value than the course taken to reach it.

Ari had learned a lot from his mentor, but that was a lesson he didn't seem able to absorb. It mattered to him, what he was forced to do to win. Sir Cadwel had grown up in a shattered and desolate kingdom, burdened by generations of war. The great knight would have done anything to end the suffering of the people of Lggothland.

That seemed worth it, to Ari. He would lay down his personal honor to save a kingdom of people. What was his ability to sleep at night compared to thousands of lives? This, though . . . this was different. He was being asked to go against what he felt was right so that he could seek out a faceless foe. Of course, Tal Mraken had ordered over a hundred people murdered, simply for being related to the Lady. He'd also sent the Caller to attack Hawkers and Sorga, killing hundreds more.

The trouble was, he didn't seem to be doing anything evil right now. Ari could rise to a challenge and defend those in peril, but could he help poison infants as part of a long-reaching plan like this? The children were the ones in immediate danger, and not from Tal Mraken. They hadn't even found the third stone. If the Lady and Larke couldn't locate it, gaining the second wouldn't matter.

Ari scrubbed his hands over his face. He turned around, toward the village, his mind no clearer than when he'd set out. Walking back, he watched the first rays of daylight hit the Orate Tree, wondering if the climb the following morning would start at that moment, or when the sunlight was full upon it. He supposed he would know soon enough.

He'd gone farther than he'd realized, almost out to the firebreak. Long before he made it back to the village, he saw Mirimel's hawk spiral upward. He waved when it passed, but the lazy arc it made through the sky over the village didn't alter, so Ari had no idea if it saw him.

A lone figure trudged up the broad roadway. It took Ari a surprised moment to realize it was Lord Kenmar. The graying lord waved, stopping and waiting for Ari to reach him. He'd bathed as well, and donned clean clothing, but he still had the disheveled look of someone who didn't pay much attention to his appearance, other than to ensure the necessary warmth and decency.

"I thought you should know, first thing this morning, Hawk Guardian Mirimel went to ask permission to attempt to gain the fruit tomorrow." Kenmar's worried tone and lack of a greeting were clear indication of his distress.

"What reason did she give?" Ari wasn't surprised. More than likely, she wanted to prove to the men of the village that a woman could beat them. It wasn't as if she could outpace Ari. She must know that.

"I don't know. I was still breaking my fast. I didn't realize that was her intention. As far as Tewlar can tell, no human was near enough to hear her conversation with the Herdlord. The village is buzzing over her inclusion, though."

Ari shook his head. "Cooro gained permission yesterday so he can impress Mirimel. Mirimel gained permission this morning, likely so she can show up Cooro and the rest of the men. Are you planning to climb as well?"

"Me?" Kenmar blinked at him. A slow smile replaced the confusion wreathing his features and he chuckled. "Not I, no."

Ari tried to match the cartographer's smile, but he knew his attempt fell flat.

"You still are, though, I assume?" Kenmar asked, his amusement fading.

"I think I must."

"Tell me this, what if leaving the fruit up there meant all of the children would be spared? Would you climb then, to bring the fruit down and claim your boon?"

"No, I wouldn't climb then. I couldn't."

"Of course, I suppose no one would," Kenmar said, almost to himself. "That the fruit offers at least some hope, and claiming it earns a redemption, is what perpetuates the event."

"I can't believe the Questri watch this climb, where people may die, as a matter of entertainment, and then take this poisonous fruit and murder infants with it. I wouldn't have thought it of Stew's people."

186

"Do not we race steeds, or joust with them, for a similar amount of amusement?" Lord Kenmar asked. "We also eat them, and wear their hides."

Ari stared at him. He hadn't thought of it that way. He looked down at his leather boots. No one in the village wore any leather. What must they think of him? "That's not the same," he said, a bit defensive. "We don't do it to Questri. Humans are sentient, as they are."

"Do you think most men would make the distinction?"

Ari grimaced. What was Kenmar doing? Ari had enough to trouble him without contemplating the philosophical treatment of man and beast.

"You raised the issue," Kenmar said, his tone apologetic.

Ari was once again struck by how well the other lord could follow his thoughts. They must have similar minds. He recalled Kenmar's advice about apologizing to Ispiria, which had been quite sound. "What would you do, if you were me?"

Kenmar looked away. "I am not so deep in your counsel, Lord Aridian. Not as Hawk Guardian Mirimel or Swordmaster Cooro are. I am likely not privy to all I would need to know to answer that question." He turned back, his eyes troubled again. "I know you seek a weapon, for the Herdlord said as much. Yet, I see no ready danger. I've gathered you wish to fell a villain you feel threatens your future, but I know not on whose word you pursue the man, or woman." Serious eyes locked with Ari's. "I do know, though, that every tale has more than one side. Likewise, I know the one thing as permanent as death is being the man who administered it."

Now it was Ari's turn to blink in surprise, for the intensity of Kenmar's gaze, coupled with the strange advice, confused him. "So, you don't think I should do it?"

"I think you are a good man. I don't know if you can remain that way all of your life."

Ari looked down, oddly embarrassed. "I'll climb to make sure the children get the chance to live, even if it is as voiceless, but I don't know what boon I'll ask. Maybe I could pick a babe to spare, but how would I choose?" And how could he go back to Sorga knowing he'd brought strife down on his people and his future offspring so that he could save a stranger's child?

"I don't envy you your decisions."

Ari nodded. Who would? "We should get back. Maybe Mirimel will tell me what her plan is."

"Yes, of course," Kenmar said, matching Ari's pace as he started south. "I should be working on my map, I suppose, though I don't know that I'll ever share it."

"No?" Ari asked more out of politeness than any real concern.

"It seems to me, in view of all we've learned, that a map of Tybrunn would only lure people onto the plain, where they will likely die."

"People will be lured onto the plain with your map or without." Ari shrugged. "There will always be someone who can't settle for not knowing. If they use your map, it doesn't mean you made the choices leading to their death."

"Just as, if you get the fruit, it doesn't mean you killed the babes?"

Ari grimaced. He didn't have an answer to that.

They continued toward the village in silence. Ari nodded to the hooved guards again, two different Questri than when he'd walked out before dawn. Though daylight made it obvious they could indeed see him, they seemed no more inclined to acknowledge his greeting than the previous two.

He and Kenmar were almost back to the dwelling they'd been provided when a small procession blocked their way. It was headed by a lean young man, not much taller than Cooro, with a noticeably arrogant countenance. As Ari watched, young women threw themselves at him. He kissed several, casting smug looks at a nearby group of other men, who glowered. He seemed to be making his way toward Ari.

"Padro," Tewlar's voice said. "He claimed the fruit last year, and the year before."

Ari looked to his left to see their blond guide beside him. "I take it he was climbing to impress girls?"

"No, to save his son, at least the first time." Tewlar pointed.

Ari took in a miserable looking young woman standing off to the side of Padro's crowd. She had a toddler by the hand and carried a baby in her arms. Ari raised his eyebrows. "And the women he's kissing?"

"Other people's wives. A woman will barter a lot to a man who can spare her child. He will compete this year, and save the child of his favorite."

"I see," Ari said. This boon of the Questri business grew less savory by the moment.

Padro brushed aside the women flocking around him, his eyes on Ari. He puffed out his chest as he walked over. Ari sighed, recognizing the look of dislike in the other man's eyes. He squared his shoulders, standing to his full height. Padro came up to his chin.

"A big man like you will never have the strength to reach the top," Padro said. "Your own muscles will weigh you down, outsider."

"Hello," Ari said. He extended his hand in greeting. "I don't believe we've met. I'm Ari."

189

Padro eyed his hand, making no move to take it. "I know well who you are, outsider. I know you've come not to spare a child, but to take that hope from my people."

There was a murmur of disquiet at this. Ari had to congratulate the tactic. "I suppose that will be decided tomorrow." Ari dropped his hand. "The Herdlord wouldn't have given me permission to climb if he didn't think my quest worthy."

"The Questri masters are wise," Tewlar said. "The Herdlord, the wisest."

This was met with another murmur, but of agreement. Ari shot Tewlar a grin.

Padro looked about, frowning. "The Herdlord knows I shall claim the fruit, as I do every year. This is why he allows outsiders to compete, because it matters not."

"Well, you have nothing to worry about, then." Ari gave Padro a friendly smile.

Padro mulled that over for a moment before nodding. Obviously unsure how to respond, he spun on his heels and walked away, his crowd of admirers following. Beside Ari, Tewlar chuckled.

"He wanted to incite the crowd against you, but you gave him no purchase," Tewlar said. "I can see why you are a great lord where you come from."

"Who said that?" Ari asked. He looked about, but Lord Kenmar had disappeared.

"Everyone speaks of it." Tewlar shrugged. "It isn't hard to tell. You walk like a lord, and ponder as one whose decisions carry weight. The women say you are handsome like a great prince, and all can see the nobility within you."

Somehow, Ari doubted that. His eyes narrowed. Was Tewlar trying to flatter him? "Do you and Mia have a child, Tewlar? A first born?"

Tewlar looked down, flushing. He nodded.

"Good luck tomorrow, then," Ari said, his decision made. He would get the fruit, and he wouldn't ask for the stone. He would ask to spare Tewlar's and Mia's child. He couldn't refrain from saving a child simply to gain possession of a magical stone he may never even be able to use, to fight a foe he hoped never to meet.

"Thank you. I have hope. I'm a strong climber."

"Good." Ari wouldn't want Tewlar to fall and get hurt. He spotted a flash of orange among the general mass of straw-colored heads. "I'm going to go speak to Mirimel."

Mirimel saw him long before he reached her, but made no move to cross the crowded central road. He supposed, with all the people and Questri milling about, there was no point in meeting in the middle. He finally pushed his way through to where she leaned against the wall beside the door of the dwelling they were staying in.

"I see you met the village idiot," she said, nodding in the direction of Padro and his mass of followers.

"I was glad to see Mia wasn't in that group of women chasing him around."

"She may be afraid of birds, but she isn't a total fool."

"I hear you went to see the Herdlord this morning." Ari strove for a casual tone.

"I did."

"Are you going to tell me why?"

"Nope."

"Mirimel--"

"It really isn't any of your concern, Ari." Her eyes still following Padro through the crowded street. She fingered the fletching on one of the arrows in the quiver at her waist.

"You listened to my conversation with the Herdlord," he said. Once the words were out of his mouth, he hoped they didn't sound as petulant to her as they did to him.

Mirimel cast him an amused glance. "I guess life isn't fair. When you're my age, you'll realize that."

"You're barely older than I am." He glowered at her for a moment, but she either didn't care or was good at pretending as much.

"They say there's a celebration tomorrow evening." Mirimel's gaze was back on Padro's crowd, far across the village now. Not too far for Mirimel to shoot him, though, if she wanted to.

"I suppose that makes sense," Ari said, though he didn't think the climb and the fruit worth celebrating.

"There will probably be drinking, and dancing."

Ari had been letting his glower slip, but he recommitted to it. What he'd thought was an attempt to change the topic was beginning to sound like the start of a lecture. In the months they'd been traveling together, Mirimel hadn't once brought up his trouble with Ispiria. He'd come to the hopeful conclusion she didn't know about what he'd done. "Oh?" he finally said, unable to formulate any other sort of reply.

"And temptation." She turned hard eyes on him. "Lots of pretty blonde-haired girls who, apparently, like to kiss the man who climbs down with the Orate Fruit."

"It wouldn't make sense for them to kiss me," Ari said, channeling his annoyance into baiting her. "I have a boon in mind and I won't be here next year to climb again. Although, they may not realize that. I should ask Tewlar not to tell them."

"Ari," Mirimel exclaimed, looking, for once, truly shocked.

Ari grinned at her. "You deserved that. How long have you been waiting to dress me down? I'd decided you didn't know about that kiss. You let me ride down the hill into Hawkers without shooting me full of arrows, after all."

"That was my first inclination, after reading Ispiria's letter."

"But?"

"I received one from Sir Cadwel, as well. He seems to think your behavior was exemplary." She wrinkled her nose, looking for a moment quite like Ispiria. "If you're exemplary, it makes me wonder how he behaved while he was married to my aunt."

Ari shrugged. It was impossible to say. He hadn't even been born then. Certainly, since the death of his wife, Sir Cadwel had made his love for her very clear.

"Why did you kiss that girl?"

"Not for any real reason." Ari shoved a hand through his hair. He really needed to get someone to trim it. "I drank too much and it just sort of happened."

"And you'll never do it again?"

"I don't plan on it."

"You realize that if you break my little cousin's heart, I really will shoot you full of arrows?"

Ari would have laughed, but he knew she was completely serious. "And I'll stand still and let you."

"A moving target is more fun."

"Siara kissed me, too." Ari glanced at her, gauging her reaction. "I didn't tell Ispiria that. I was going to, but she ran off. Later, well, we'd just stopped fighting . . ."

Mirimel shrugged, looking unconcerned. "Sir Cadwel said as much. Something about the princess kissing you to confuse a

193

serving girl. I wouldn't tell Ispiria, if I were you. There's no reason to upset her. Not over nothing."

"Why does everyone dismiss Siara kissing me so quickly?" Ari asked, a bit annoyed. No one seemed to realize how much it had affected him, though the feeling had dwindled down to a dull confusion, especially after seeing Ispiria.

"Shouldn't we?" Mirimel turned narrowed eyes on him. "Princess Siara is magically bound to love Prince Parrentine or die. Why wouldn't we dismiss her kissing you?"

"Ah, you would." He contained a grimace. Even to Mirimel, his closest friend now that Peine was gone, he couldn't reveal the feelings Siara's kiss had stirred in him. "I just find it odd that the one kiss is so upsetting to people and the other not," he added, to cover what he was truly thinking.

"Take your blessings where you find them." She gave him a half smile. "You should be glad your princess is bound to her husband. I wager it made your last year much easier. Imagine the chaos in the realm if she was able to fall in love with you, and did, and Lggothland's paramount knight ran off with the future queen."

Ari shuddered, sobered by the thought. "It doesn't bear thinking of."

Why, indeed, would he ever want anyone to take Siara kissing him seriously? He didn't want to contemplate the devastation any love between them would cause to the kingdom, or to Ispiria and Prince Parrentine. Not to mention that Sir Cadwel would likely break his vow to the Aluiens, come out of retirement, hunt Ari down, and kill him.

"Speaking of unbearable things, you'd best do something about that idiot of a swordmaster," Mirimel said. "Spar with him to keep him from trouble, or something. He's been gadding about the village, showing off his acrobatic skills and attempting to suborn women."

"Jealous?" Ari asked.

The look she gave him could have curdled milk. "Picture yourself riddled with arrows, Ari. Riddled." She turned and walked away.

Chapter 17

That night, his last thoughts on his resolution to spare Tewlar's baby, Ari slept deeply. He didn't wake until the door to the hut opened, the hour seeming very early. Steps came in and it closed again.

"Ari, Cooro, Mirimel," Tewlar's voice called. "You'll want to rise and make ready. We have to be there when the light touches the flowers."

There was some grumbling from Cooro, who'd still been out when Ari retired, but soon enough they were all ready. As they emerged into the dark street, Ari saw Mirimel had dressed in all her accoutrements. He wasn't even wearing his boots, having deemed bare feet would be better for climbing, let alone carrying his weapons. He fell in beside her as they joined the stream of young men walking toward the tree.

"Won't the bow and quiver slow you down?" he asked in a low voice. It seemed too early to talk very loud.

"You worry about your climbing, Ari, and I'll worry about mine."

He nodded as she quickened her pace, following Tewlar. He wondered if her sharp whispered tone was caused by the stress of today or if she was angry over the occurrences of the evening before. She'd still been up when he'd gone to sleep. He hadn't asked, but he'd sensed she was waiting for Cooro.

Lord Kenmar fell in beside him, yawning. "I say, this is early, isn't it?"

Ari nodded. "You don't have to be up, really."

"And miss the climb? I think not." Kenmar glanced at him. "If you don't mind me asking, have you decided on a boon?"

Ari nodded again. He shot the cartographer a smile. "Tewlar's and Mia's baby," he whispered.

Kenmar's face registered shock and he stumbled. Ari caught him by the elbow, letting go as the other man regained his stride.

"You're going to sacrifice your family for . . ." His quiet voice trailed off. He regarded Ari with wide eyes.

Ari shrugged, embarrassed by Kenmar's incredulousness. "It's the right thing to do." He turned away from the other man, heading for the rows of Questri who formed the honor guard for the Herdlord.

Cooro, Mirimel and Tewlar in front of him, Ari fell into the queue that formed, moving up the aisle created by the Herdlord's guards. All around, villagers and Questri moved, filling the vast cleared space surrounding the pinnacle on which the tree stood. They left an empty circle at the center. Each man in the line, and Mirimel, bowed to the Herdlord before taking a place around that circle. When it was Ari's turn to bow, the Herdlord held his eyes for a moment, his gaze that same mixture of amusement and condescension Ari recalled from their first meeting.

Those who climbed formed an incomplete circle, more in the nature of two half circles. No one stood directly before the silver stallion who ruled the herd, and none stood on the south side, either. Ari didn't know if it was some sort of sacrilege to cross the blood-stained stone to reach the rock spire, but it looked as if no one planned to. He certainly didn't want to set foot on it.

Men clustered at the ends of the half circles, jostling a bit for position, and Ari realized there would be a funnel effect. Everyone must start out at one of the corners, as the rest of each of the four sides forming the base of the spire were empty archways. He moved toward the northeast corner. Mirimel and Cooro, however, both stood due east. Cooro started working through a series of stretches, limbering up his muscles. Mirimel stood with her arms crossed. Above, in the darkness, Ari caught sight of something flying. He hoped it was her hawk. It looked too small to be the vultures Tewlar and Mia had described.

The sky lightened and a hush fell. Questri and humans stilled, falling silent. Somewhere back in the village, a child cried. Ari wished now he'd selected the southwest corner, for the sun was coming up behind him. He'd been on the plains long enough to know that dawn arrived quickly in this flat world. He didn't want to miss the mark.

The air was split by a horrific wave of sound as every Questri on the plains let out a piercing whinny, as one. The sound catapulted Ari forward. He could hear other men running too, behind him, but didn't look back. He didn't even look up to confirm that the sun had touched the tree. Across from him, he could see men running toward the spire.

He hit his corner as, on the southwest side, Padro reached another. Ari started up, digging his fingers and toes into rocky crevasses. He caught a glimpse of Cooro out of the corner of his eye. The Wheylian swordmaster made a running jump, vaulting over the tall arched opening and latching onto the side of the stone pinnacle, his grin giving Ari the fleeting impression of a deranged insect before he scurried upward.

Ari didn't try to watch Cooro, or Padro. He concentrated on climbing, falling into a steady rhythm of moving hands and feet, never in unison. The first mad dash, spurred by the ear-splitting cry of the herd, gave way to steady breathing. He knew this climb wasn't a sprint. Given the height of the spire, it was more about endurance than speed.

A cry sounded below him, followed by a bone-crunching crash and a gasp from the human onlookers. Ari winced, but didn't look down or slow. He could hear the men behind him growing farther away, but he could also hear Padro's somewhat ragged breathing coming from the other side of the spire. Out of the corner of his eye, Ari saw Cooro as he passed him by. The swordmaster's pace must have slowed for Ari to have overtaken him. Cooro's grin had been replaced by a look of determination. Of Mirimel, Ari saw nothing.

The world brightened around him. Glancing up, the spire Ari climbed filled his vision. It seemed almost to tilt toward him as he clung to the side. He was nearing a line of light, dropping down to meet him as the sun rose.

He realized the tree must be fully in the sunlight now, though he couldn't see anything above him, save a wall of rock. Fleetingly, he wished he'd witnessed what must be a miraculous transformation, the large petals of the yellow flowers contracting inward, or falling, or whatever they did when the sun hit them and they turned into fruit.

His fingers and toes ached and he fought the urge to rest. If he could hold one or two limbs away from the wall for a moment, his enhanced healing would have time to restore them, he was sure, but he could hear two competitors near him. Glancing down to his left and seeing a dark head, he knew one was Cooro, who could likely be counted on to ask for whatever Ari requested. The other, the one he couldn't see, Ari knew must be Padro.

Ari crossed the line of sunlight, the searing heat of sun-bathed stone slamming into him. Squinting, he angled his gaze upward again, seeing green. His breathing sped up as he realized he was almost there.

It seemed to Ari, as he pulled himself over the lip of the spire, that Padro's blond head appeared at exactly the same moment. They locked eyes and Ari exerted his strength, hoisting the rest of his body over the edge. Below, distance melding them into a wave of sound, voices cried out and cheered.

Ari knelt on smooth stone, trying to gather enough strength and steadiness to stand. His breath was harsh in his ears. His hands curled into pain-ridden, immovable claws of muscle and bone. Sweeping his gaze across the gnarled roots of the tree, which rose from the rock in an impossible seeming way, he watched Padro struggle to pull himself over the lip.

Ari was in the shade, he realized. The branches of the tree spread above him. Dangling a few feet away was a bright, shiny yellow fruit. Ari stumbled to his feet.

A thrumming sound swept by his head and an arrow buried itself in the fruit, knocking it from the tree, sending it sailing out into the air. All around Ari, there were thudding sounds. Rotten Orate Fruits rained down. Ari watched, his mouth gaping open, as Mirimel's hawk appeared in the sky. It

201

grabbed the fruit-bearing arrow before it could drop out of sight.

Behind him, Ari heard Cooro's awed curse. Padro let out an anguished cry, reaching out, though he had no hope of capturing hawk or fruit. His cry turned to one of fear and pain as he lost his grip.

Ari lunged across the open space below the tree, pulverizing rotten fruit as he slid toward the edge. His own body sliding halfway off the rock, he caught hold of Padro's forearm. Still skidding, Padro's weight adding to his momentum, Ari tried to dig in his toes.

"Ari," Cooro yelled, and Ari felt the Whey grab him by the feet.

They shuddered to a halt, Ari hanging half over the edge. Padro slammed into the side of the pinnacle, his grip on Ari's arm going slack. Ari didn't let go.

"Can you pull?" Ari called to Cooro. The smell of rotten fruit filled his nose.

"I can hardly hold on," the Whey yelled.

Ari could feel how tightly Cooro grasped his ankles, the swordmaster's grip shaking. Taking a deep breath, Ari mustered his Aluien-enhanced strength. He gritted his teeth, raising the front half of his body until it was parallel with the ground, suspended over nothing. Padro dangled from his right arm. He reached back with his left, grasping the lip of the drop off and pushing upward while folding his body. Retracting himself into a kneeling position, he dragged Padro along.

It was the hardest thing he'd done since moving the giant stone that had trapped Mirimel in an underground chamber. He winced as his movement dragged the semi-conscious Padro over the lip, the stone gouging lines in his chest. Releasing Ari's

202

ankles as he sat up, Cooro rushed forward to help pull the villager to safety.

He and Cooro laid Padro out. Ari fell back on his heels, trying to catch his breath. Cooro dabbed at Padro's torn flesh with what was left of the villager's shirt. None of the wounds seemed deep, but they were wide and full of dirt and dead fruit. Ari looked down at himself. He was similarly smeared, though he knew his abrasions would heal cleanly and disappear completely within a day.

"Damn her," Cooro said, looking up at Ari.

Ari could read neither his tone nor his expression. His exclamation wasn't vehement, though. "Why's that?" he finally asked, still a bit out of breath.

"She could have shot the thing down before we climbed all the way up here."

Ari glanced over the edge, seeing the ground a dizzying distance below. He nodded. "We'll have to speak to her about that."

Cooro left off tending Padro and peered over the edge. "I've never seen anyone make a shot like that. The angle doesn't even look possible, and the wind . . ." He trailed off, his gaze turned toward the bright orange of Mirimel's hair far below.

"I told you she's good."

The Whey nodded.

Ari didn't like the look forming on Cooro's face. It was awed, almost worshipful. "Cooro, I think she may be taken."

"She's taken when she tells me as much."

Ari shook his head, reminding himself he'd decided not to intervene.

"Wheylian women don't fall in love," Cooro said.

Ari glanced at him. A cooling wind buffeted Ari's face. He had his breath back now. Soon, he'd be ready to climb down. He really needed to change his blood and rotten fruit coated shirt. "Yes they do. They love one man for always. Everyone knows that." Though he hadn't. Not when he'd first met Princess Siara. He'd thought she could get over Prince Parrentine and learn to love someone else.

"That's why they don't fall in love. They're outrageous flirts, and no women are more entertaining companions, but they never let themselves fall in love. They resent the power it holds over them."

"How can someone keep themselves from falling in love?"

Cooro shrugged. "They're raised to it, from birth. It's just our way. They're quite good at it."

Ari wasn't sure he believed it was possible not to fall in love, though he knew Queen Reudi had somehow succeeded, for her husband was dead and she hadn't withered with his passing. "What does that have to do with Mirimel?"

"A woman like that, she would let her heart go. When some man wins it, it's going to be his, completely his, and she'll be proud to give it."

"That's the same as winning the heart of a Wheylian girl." Ari decided he definitely didn't like where Cooro's mind was. Nor was atop an impossible spire of rock on a windswept plain the time or the place to be having such a discussion.

"There's glory in winning something freely given, and in keeping something that can be lost."

"Ah, are you going to be ready to climb down soon?" Ari said, having no desire to continue the conversation. "What should we do with our rival here?"

Cooro didn't take his eyes from Mirimel. She was surrounded by a sea of Questri now. They appeared to be steering her toward the Herdlord. Ari wanted to get down there and hear what was happening. He had no idea what boon the hawk guardian would ask for, but he was nervous to find out. He wished he'd told her and Cooro, before going up, that he didn't plan to ask for the stone. He reached out and shook Padro by the shoulder.

The plainsman groaned, his eyes opening. He sat up, wincing, and turned suspicious eyes on Ari. "You saved me."

"It seemed like the better of the two choices."

"Thank you," Padro muttered. He moved his left arm and went pale.

"Are you going to be able to climb down?" Ari looked about. If they could tie Padro to his back, and the other agreed to stay still, he could probably carry him down.

"Of course, outsider." Padro reached out and picked up a fistful of rotten fruit, rubbing it on his shoulder.

"Did his head slam into the rocks when you caught him?" Cooro asked.

Ari glanced over to see the Whey watching Padro with the same confusion that must be on his own face.

"The dead fruits numb your pain." Padro's tone was disdainful. "You outsiders know nothing."

Ari looked down at his chest. He didn't feel any pain from the scrapes there. He'd attributed it to his quick healing, but maybe there was more to it than that. "So you think you can make it?"

"I'll be down before you, outsider." Padro stood and moved to the edge.

"So much for his gratitude," Cooro said.

Ari flexed his fingers, feeling good as new, though he was sure he didn't look it. "And you can make it down, you're certain?"

"Of course I can make it down." Cooro looked offended. "I'd boast I'll get down faster than you as well, but that seems like an inauspicious claim to make when standing atop something this high."

Ari chuckled. "It really does, doesn't it?"

"Ari," Cooro said, his eyes turning serious.

Ari suppressed a sigh. Cooro was never going to let him off this rock.

"Do you really think she loves someone else? Who is this man who has managed to capture her heart? I've noticed that pendant she wears, that she often caresses."

Ari stared at him, decidedly uncomfortable with Cooro using the word caress in a sentence applying to Mirimel. "I honestly don't know if she has any feelings for any man, let alone the one who gave her the pendant."

"So it was a gift, and you know who he is," Cooro said, triumphant.

Grimacing, Ari realized he'd been tricked. "Cooro, we have to get down there before she does whatever half-mad thing she's planning."

"Right." The swordmaster rose in a fluid motion and strolled to the edge. "We'll continue our conversation anon." With that, he dropped out of sight.

Ari stood more slowly. He turned in a circle. It was cold standing in the shade under the tree, the wind whipping past with much more force than it held on the plains below. He glanced up at the oddly shaped leaves, thick with veins. Now that he stood beside the Orate Tree, he could see the bark was smooth and a strange pale gray. He hadn't known what to expect, but the tree seemed hardly real, more crafted than grown.

Turning his back on it, he moved to the edge. He raised his gaze, taking in the plains spread out below him, going on forever. Out in the sky, below him rather than above, Mirimel's hawk circled. It hit Ari that this was a view few had ever seen, and one he would never witness again.

A glance downward showed him Cooro already a quarter of the way down, and Padro far below that. Taking a deep breath to steady himself, for it was a very, very long way down, Ari dropped onto his belly and eased himself over the edge.

Chapter 18

Ari slid the last ten feet or so of the climb, half on purpose for speed and half because his fingers and toes were going numb from the unaccustomed activity. He landed with a thud on the northeast corner of the spire, his bare feet sending up puffs of dust. A ring of Questri surrounded him, most with blindfolded voiceless on their backs, but he could see over them to the Herdlord.

Mirimel, Cooro and Padro all stood before the silver stallion, the two men flanking and slightly behind her. She held a bright yellow Orate Fruit out before her, the morning sun lighting up her orange curls. High above, her hawk issued a challenging cry, setting the villagers to murmuring.

"The successful have returned. She who has captured the Orate Fruit shall request her boon."

The clear voice of the boy who spoke for the Herdlord rang out in the morning air, startling Ari. He couldn't see the small figure standing on the other side of the Herdlord, but he could picture the blindfold-wrapped head.

Mirimel cast Ari a strange look over the backs of the horses and his stomach sank. What did she have planned? He should have worked harder to drag the information from her.

She turned her gaze back toward the Herdlord and bowed. "You know what boon I would ask, Herdlord."

"The dark boon," the high-pitched voice of the child called out.

At first, it was almost as if the words were echoing, but then Ari realized they were being repeated. An excited babble rose from the mass of villagers. The dark boon, the dark boon, they murmured, sounding almost like a flock of excited birds.

"Bring forth the Thrice Born," the boy called, the silver stallion swinging his head toward Ari.

The ring of Questri surrounding him parted. Ari looked out over the crowd, wishing Tewlar was at his side. He had a feeling he'd need to know what this dark boon was. The people sounded excited and pleased, but the name was nothing if not dire. He strolled forward, coming to stand beside Cooro. The Whey's face was pinched with worry.

"As this female is your creature, Thrice Born, her boon belongs to you," the child on the other side of the Herdlord said. "Will you permit her to decide it?"

Mirimel shot him a startled look, which rapidly turned into a glare.

"First, I would need to know what the dark boon is, Herdlord," Ari said, careful not to phrase it as a question.

"Bring forth the guide," the Herdlord commanded.

The crowd shifted. Tewlar pressed his way between the Questri near Ari. Ari was pleased to see the villager unharmed, for he knew at least one person had fallen from the spire. Tewlar hurried to his side.

"I'm sorry," he said in a quiet voice. "I couldn't get through."

Ari nodded. "What's the dark boon?"

"It's when someone asks that all of the children of the year be spared." Tewlar looked to Mirimel, hope in his eyes.

Ari stared at him, then at her. She frowned, obviously trying to convey that she would be very displeased with him if he didn't allow her to do this. Ari shrugged. It seemed like a wonderful idea to him.

"Hawk Guardian Mirimel is not my creature, but her own, Herdlord," Ari said, raising his voice. "If this is the boon she wishes, then she has every right to ask it. She, not I, retrieved the fruit."

The Herdlord regarded him for a long moment, that same look of smug amusement in his eyes. He turned back to Mirimel. "Let it be known, then, that the dark boon has been claimed and the female, the Mirimel, has agreed to pay the price of it."

"Wait," Ari cried. Everyone turned to look at him. "What price?"

The Herdlord's condescension grew. "You forget yourself, Thrice Born."

"I beseech your pardon, Herdlord." Ari bowed, for good measure. He turned to Tewlar. "What price?" he demanded in a low voice.

"The person who evokes the dark boon must consume the Orate Fruit. It may not be squandered."

"Mirimel has to eat the poisonous fruit?" Ari looked at her.

211

She raised her chin, her defiance clear. It was obvious she'd already known about the price she must pay. No wonder she wouldn't tell him her plans.

"I will not allow it," Cooro cried. He lunged for the fruit, reaching to grab it from Mirimel's hand.

A wall of air slammed into Cooro, knocking him backward. Ari was spun around, caught by the edge of it. He fell to one knee, dust coating him. He blinked, trying to clear his eyes.

Squinting through the grit, he could see Cooro sprawled on his back, yards away. The Whey tried to sit up, his expression dazed, but fell back to the ground. Menacing Questri stood over him, looking ready to tread on him the moment the command was given.

A hand appeared in Ari's vision, reaching down. Ari realized it was Tewlar, his face creased with concern. Ari took the offered hand, though he didn't need it. Tewlar pulled him to his feet. He turned back to the Herdlord. The crystal on the silver stallion's brow glowed brightly.

"The fruit shall not be defiled," the voiceless of the Herdlord said. "It is only because you, this day, are a champion of the spire that you remain alive, Whey." The Herdlord turned to look at a group of Questri. "Confine him."

Ari stifled a protest as the Questri stepped back and a group of men came forward, dragging a barely conscious Cooro away. The Herdlord had said to confine him, not kill him. Ari hoped the command meant what it seemed to.

"The female Mirimel shall relinquish the fruit," the Herdlord said. His voiceless child stepped forward. He walked up to Mirimel without hesitation, as if he didn't have a heavy cloth wrapped about his head. The little boy held out both hands and Mirimel placed the fruit in them. Ari resisted the urge to dive for it, as Cooro had.

The Herdlord's voiceless returned to him, the Orate Fruit disappearing into the long sleeves of his undyed smock. Ari wondered if, to the Questri, a voiceless was like a saddlebag, or a glorified pocket. Somewhere to store things. He grimaced at the thought.

"Please, Herdlord," Ari said, turning back to the silver stallion. "Allow me to eat the fruit. I rescind my permission for Hawk Guardian Mirimel to request the boon. I shall request it, and I shall pay the price."

The silver stallion regarded him for a long moment. Amusement had left his gaze, replaced by annoyance. "This permission, once granted, may not be rescinded."

Glancing at Mirimel, Ari could see she was pleased.

"At dawn, the female Mirimel will consume the fruit in the stead of the first borns. I decree this to be so," the Herdlord said.

Ari stared at the silver stallion, frustration filling him. He was sure the Herdlord had looked amused before. He'd found Ari's consent diverting. Mirimel eating the fruit would be a source of entertainment for the herd. Why had she sought such a thing? Did she really believe Ari wouldn't have eaten the fruit to save the children if she'd told him about this dark boon? Ari's fists balled at his side.

"Bow," Tewlar whispered.

Ari realized his gaze was locked with the silver stallion's.

"Ari, bow," Tewlar pressed. "Or you'll end up in the pit with your friend."

Ari bowed, though the movement was stiff. "Yes, Herdlord." He didn't know what the pit was, and he'd have to find out and ensure Cooro was well, but he did know he

213

couldn't take on the whole Questri herd. Diplomacy was the only way. "It is my wish we be allowed to tend Hawk Guardian Mirimel after she eats the fruit, to do what we may to aid her."

Ari hoped this, at least, the Herdlord would grant him. How could Mirimel plan to deliberately poison herself? What could he do? He wondered if Kenmar was versed in healing lore, and recalled his own oft made, but never pursued, vow to better educate himself in the field.

"The devouring of the Orate Fruit shall take place at dawn, atop the slab," the Herdlord said, looking out over the mass of people and Questri. "Once the fruit has been consumed, I order none hinder the Thrice Born's futile attempts."

"Thank you, Herdlord." Ari had to work to make his tone resemble graciousness. He bowed, gritting his teeth.

Plans swirled in Ari's mind. Perhaps he could break Cooro free from this pit they'd confined him in. Then, they could take Mirimel and run. Of course, their steeds would never be able to outrun the herd. Stew could, but Ari hadn't even seen Stew today. Looking out over the myriad of hides and blond heads, Ari realized he didn't know how to find Stew in the sea of Questri.

A new thought came to him, and he wondered if he'd be able to pick out one specific blond head, were it near. He'd never asked, but he couldn't help but think Larke would have marked Mirimel. If she was marked, Larkesong should appear near the time of her death. Maybe he could heal her. Ari didn't know if he would, as it would violate the rules of his people, but Larke could usually be counted on to do what was right, rules or no. Even if he didn't heal her, he would at least cause her to be reborn as an Aluien. Ari was sure of that.

Ari looked around, seeing the eyes of the Herdlord upon him, infinitely knowing, as if the stallion read his very thoughts.

The amusement had returned to the Herdlord's gaze, and Ari mistrusted it. He wondered why no one had moved yet. Was he supposed to ask permission to leave? He couldn't. That would be a question.

The Herdlord swung his head toward Padro, who Ari had all but forgotten about. "Human, you are a champion of the spire. As this is your third year of success, your name shall be added to the counting, to live forever in history. You are among the few humans to be immortalized in Questri lore. This is our reward to you."

Padro bowed. "Thank you, Herdlord. I live to serve my Questri masters," he said in a dull voice.

"He's forbidden to climb again, now that his name is added to the counting," Tewlar whispered to Ari, his tone a touch smug. "No more stealing favors for Padro."

Ari raised his eyebrows. The Herdlord was obviously amusing himself by making what was tantamount to a punishment sound like a reward.

"Thrice Born."

Ari contained a grimace at once again being the recipient of the silver stallion's consideration. No good seemed to come of it. He glanced at Mirimel, but she stood straight, like a soldier at attention, her eyes forward.

"You saved this villager's life," the voiceless boy continued, speaking for his master. "You allowed your creature to request the dark boon, then offered to take the price on yourself."

"And I willingly shall." Ari knew he was interrupting, but he couldn't help it. He had to try.

"You are also a champion of the spire," the voiceless went on, speaking over Ari's blurted words. The look the Herdlord gave him was flat with anger. "It is our assessment that the blue

215

lady was in the right. You are a noble being and a fitting recipient of the stone we have so long guarded. It is our way to give some reward to all who reach the top of the spire, and your request to aid a doomed companion is as nothing. Instead, revealing the stone shall be our gift to you."

"Please, Herdlord, allow my reward to be paying the price for Mirimel's boon." Ari had been ready to give up the stone for Tewlar's baby, and certainly would for Mirimel.

"I have decreed the female shall consume the fruit," the voiceless boy's voice rose in pitch. "Dare you gainsay me before my herd? Do you wish my gift to you to instead be the freedom one knows only in death?"

Ari looked at Mirimel. She cast him a hard glance, shaking her head. What could he really do? He felt a wave of futility course through him, scalding his guts with an almost physical pain. Why was she doing this? Swallowing down his emotions, Ari turned back to the Herdlord, dropping his gaze.

"I am sorry, Herdlord," he said, humbling his tone. "I beg your pardon for my words. I thought only of the pain of losing a friend, and not the nobleness and glory of you, master of all Questri. Please forgive me." Ari had to grit his teeth to get the words out. He kept his eyes downcast, for he knew he wasn't master of what emotions lay within them. He realized his fingers had gone numb again, his fists were clenched so tightly.

"You speak wisely, Thrice Born."

Ari risked a glance, finding the stallion's eyes shadowed with thought.

"You speak to your credit, as well, not only offering to take the price on yourself yet again, but showing your devotion to a companion. You risk my wrath, and obtaining that for which you have come. Know that the Questri hold much respect for the powers of the blue lady. I am pleased we need not destroy one of her creatures because it cannot see reason."

"Thank you, Herdlord."

Was the Herdlord saying he was partially sparing Ari out of fear of retribution from the Lady? What could the ancient, delicate Aluien do against a herd of Questri? If they were that afraid of the Lady, had they planned to give him the stone all along? Had this all been for their entertainment? Ari resented the bitterness that washed over him. He hated feeling like he was playing someone else's game, not knowing the rules, all of the players, or even the objective.

"Know you, Thrice Born, that you are not permitted to pay the price of the dark boon, no matter how desperately you plead. This is not only because I have decreed it so, though that is enough, but because you are one for whom there is no price. The fruit would open your mind to our voices without testing you, for the Thrice Born is inured against harm as no mortal man can be."

Ari's head whipped around, his gaze going to Mirimel. She kept her face forward. Now, he understood. She wanted to pay the price. Nearly certain death was worth it to her, for the scant chance the fruit might be able to open her mind. He was sure, though, that it wasn't the Questri she longed to communicate with. It was the Sorga Hawks.

He stared at her, shocked by the desperation of the plan. They didn't know what opening her mind to the Questri even meant. The voiceless no longer had thoughts and actions of their own. They were puppets.

He recalled the times Mirimel had pressed the voiceless of Clan Faesten, trying to get the blindfolded girl to speak. There had been that intent look in Mirimel's eyes, just as when she'd listened to Tewlar tell them about the fruit. Did she really think eating it might allow her to speak to her beloved hawks? Was such a scant hope worth pursuing?

He could tell by the set of her jaw she thought it was worth it. So much, he realized, for any thoughts of sneaking off in the night, even if they could come up with a way to outrun the Questri. He and Cooro would have to knock Mirimel on the head and carry her if they wanted to take that route.

Tewlar elbowed him in the side and Ari realized everyone was staring at him. Everyone except Mirimel, that was. Hundreds and hundreds of human and Questri eyes waited for his reply.

He bowed as low as he could. "Thank you, Herdlord. I am honored you have made things clear to me. I bow before the wisdom of the Herdlord and seek only to receive any small boon you wish to bestow upon me above permitting me to care for my friend tomorrow. Or no other at all, for I am hardly worthy of more."

Ari hoped his words made more sense to everyone else than they did to him. His mind was in no state for pretty speeches. It was only a year of practice in Wheylia that allowed words to leave his lips at all.

"I do not rescind that which I have offered," the Herdlord said. "We shall make ready for the summoning. The stone shall be brought forth. It is for you, Thrice Born, to retrieve it."

The silver stallion raised his head, a long high neigh leaving his mouth. It dug into Ari's ears, searing into his brain. He clenched his jaw, working hard not to bring his hands up to cover his ears. Beside him, Tewlar seemed to shake.

Then the sound ended, and the villagers and Questri began to move.

Chapter 19

Ari took a step closer to Mirimel as the ground about them began to shake, Tewlar at his side. Padro's eyes went wide. He bowed in the direction of the silver stallion before bolting. Ari cast a glance up, wondering if they were in danger from rocks falling off the pinnacle towering above them.

He caught Mirimel by the arm as the villagers and Questri withdrew from the vast open area before the Herdlord. "Why didn't you tell me what you were going to do?"

"Would you have tried to stop me?" She pulled her arm free.

"Of course I would have. You're mad. We don't know what that fruit really does, except kill almost anyone who eats it."

"We know it does something, and I'm stronger than a newborn, Ari." She glared at him.

He glared right back. He was livid with her. How could she make a decision like this without at least talking to him about it? Did she really think there was any way he was going to let her eat that fruit in the morning?

"You aren't going to stop me." She folded her arms over her chest in an obstinate manner. In the air above, her hawk gave a cry, hardly heard over the mass of hooves and feet.

"We should move," Tewlar yelled at them.

"What?" Mirimel asked, turning from Ari.

"Move," Tewlar yelled, backing away from them.

There was a surge of silver from Ari's left and he dove at Mirimel, tackling her to the ground as the Herdlord burst forth from his arched shelter, nearly trampling them. It went through Ari's mind to wonder what the Herdlord was thinking, for why bring forth the stone if he ran Ari down first, but the thought was scattered by the realization that he was lying on top of Mirimel, their faces inches apart.

"Get up you idiot," Mirimel said.

Ari scrambled up. He offered her a hand, which she ignored. She came to her feet and checked her bow, dusting herself off. She shot Ari another glare.

"We'll talk about me and the Orate Fruit later. Right now, I think you'd better pay attention to whatever that is." She nodded north, the direction the Herdlord went when he leapt at them.

Even though the sound of hooves was rising to a thunder behind him, Ari didn't turn immediately. Over Mirimel's shoulder, he could see the voiceless of the Herdlord standing in the center of the empty space carved from the base of the pinnacle. Without the Herdlord near, the blindfolded boy would be like a statue, as the voiceless of Clan Faesten had been when the Clanmaster she rode left her standing among them. He could walk up to the child and take the fruit. No one would ever know.

Something sharp dug into Ari's gut. He looked down to see Mirimel's hunting knife pressed against his middle. Raising his gaze to her face, he could see the hard lines there.

"Watch the horses, Ari," she said.

Shaking his head at her tenacity, Ari backed away from her knife and turned toward the thunder of hooves. It took him a moment to grasp the whirl of movement on the plain before him. In the vast open space where the Questri slept at night, and the Herdlord's honor guard stood in twin lines during the day, chaos seemed to reign.

Questri galloped before him, dust rising about them in waves. Their paths were not, as he at first thought, random. As his mind sorted out the swirl of manes and hooves, he realized that the leaders of the clans ran in a circle before him, riderless. Within that circle, traveling in the opposite direction of the clan leaders at an unfathomable speed, was a blur of silver. Far beyond, the rest of the Questri and the villagers had formed a wide ring. They swayed like stalks of grass in a rippling breeze. The villagers chanted, but Ari couldn't understand the words.

The Herdlord's pace grew faster and faster, until the inner circle was a streak of bright silver and glowing blue light. Within the ring of clanmasters, the swirling dust spiraled tighter, turning into a funnel of sand-filled air. It rose before them, a violent whirl of debris. It didn't tower as high as the Orate Tree, but it was as tall as one of the king's towers in Poromont.

Ari ducked as an ear-splitting crack rent the air, pulling Mirimel close to shield her. In the center of the circling horses, the earth burst open, the debris from the explosion joining the whirlwind. Elbowing him in the ribs, Mirimel pulled away. He could sense her scowl, though he didn't dare take his eyes from the display before them to confirm it.

Something bright rose from the fissure. Ari could hardly see it, small as it was, but he couldn't take his eyes from it. It glimmered with a white, glossy glow and he knew it was the second stone. Instead of getting caught in the swirl of dust and rock, it rose in the center of the whirlwind, glinting brightly.

The silver streak of the Herdlord shot over the backs of the galloping clanmasters in a startling, amazing leap. Ari stood, transfixed by his glory, as he ran straight at them once more. He truly was magnificent. His silver mane and tail streamed out behind him. His grace was peerless. The blue stone on his brow glowed bright, its light transfixing, reminiscent of Orlenia.

Ari stared at it, drawn to that alluring miasma of power. Beneath the stone, the eyes of the Herdlord were deep, ageless pools of knowledge. Then, as his hooves hit the ground, those eyes glinted with a savage glee and the stallion barreled down on them. Mirimel wrapped both hands around Ari's arm and yanked him out of the way. He realized she'd been yelling at him.

"What is wrong with you?" she snarled.

"Run, Thrice Born," the high pitched voice of the blindfolded boy yelled. "Run to the circle. Dive into the storm. See if you can claim your prize. Run."

That last, screeching command sent Ari surging forward. He pelted toward the ring of galloping horses, his eyes keeping pace. Ari knew he couldn't jump over them, as the Herdlord had, and wished he'd cooperated better when Cooro had tried to teach him such tricks.

For most, it would be impossible to dive between them. It would take perfect timing, and incredible speed. Ari adjusted his pace as he drew near, readying himself for the leap. Inside the circle, the maelstrom of dirt grew, reaching out until it brushed the hides of the running stallions. It swelled upward, twisting and bending as if trying to break free.

Ari moved his legs as fast as he could, bending his knees as he hit the final stride. He launched himself into the ring of horses, flying through the interval between the moments of their passing. He yanked his legs up toward his chest as his body made it through, but still felt the pain of hooves hitting his feet.

Then he was in the storm. He crashed to the ground, skidding sideways in the gale of wind. He reached out, sliding across the ground toward the ring of hooves, but there was nothing to grab onto. Just as he thought he'd be flung out to be trampled, the force of the wind took him careening in a different direction.

He felt himself being sucked upward, and knew the storm was trying to take him. Rolling, Ari wrenched himself from the outer storm and closer to the center. He pulled his shirt over his face, squinting eyes already filling with blood and sand. Above him, in the center of the storm, he could make out the glimmer of the stone.

Unable to breathe, even through the fabric of his rapidly shredding shirt, Ari crawled toward the second stone. He could feel his skin being abraded off of his exposed flesh, and knew his light breeches and shirt wouldn't protect the rest of him for long. He coughed, gasping, but there was no clean air for his lungs.

A shape moved on the other side of the fissure the stone had risen from. Ari blinked away blood, trying to screen his eyes with his hands. The shape seemed to be surrounded by a red glow, keeping the sand and stone from it. That, or the red glow was simply the haze of blood in his eyes.

The silhouette of a man angled into the middle of the storm, where the stone glinted. Ari crawled forward, sure the goal of the other was to take it. Before he could claw his way to the center, his opponent was there, reaching out. Ari's arm came up as he mimicked the movement from where he half sprawled on the ground.

As soon as the other man's hand closed around the stone, the world stopped. The hooves of the Questri stilled. The hole in the earth Ari was crawling toward snapped shut. Even as the man retreated, still surrounded by his red haze. Dirt and stones rained down around Ari as the towering maelstrom collapsed. Something hard thunked against the back of his head. A haze of darkness was added to the red.

Ari collapsed on his face. Sand and stones continued to pelt him from above. He knew he needed to raise his head, to escape the dirt clogging mouth and nose, but he couldn't move. Everything was dark. He didn't know if his eyes could no longer see or if he had them squeezed shut, or both.

He heard hooves running toward him, perhaps two sets. They slid to a halt beside him and he felt something touch the back of his head. He wasn't sure how long after, but soon footsteps ran up, first one set, then another.

"We have to dig him up. He can't breathe," Mirimel said somewhere above him, her voice hazy to his ears.

"He's covered in blood. Do you . . . do you think he's alive?"

Ari's mind struggled to place the less familiar baritone. Tewlar?

"Stew, get someone to help us," Mirimel said. "We have to carry him inside and get him cleaned up. Tewlar, do you have a healer?"

"Oh my. Oh dear." It was a new set of footfalls, and a new voice. Lord Kenmar's.

Ari felt hands on him and groaned at the agony. Every inch of him was pain. Someone took him by the shoulders and yanked his head up. He gasped in the fresh air, even as he resented the treatment. He couldn't see, but he was sure it was Mirimel. Anyone else would have been more careful.

"I have some small skills with healing," Lord Kenmar said.

"We have a woman who sets bones and keeps the herbs." Tewlar's voice was shaky. "This may be beyond her."

"He'll be fine," Mirimel said. "Ari, nod if you'll be fine."

He tried to nod. He hoped it worked. His head buzzed inside, like the sand had gotten in through his ears, nose and mouth and was continuing to swirl around in there.

"See?" Mirimel said. "Just get someone to help me carry him inside and we'll clean him up."

Ari was flipped over and he heard gasps. He couldn't imagine what his face looked like. Or rather, he could, as he could feel every inch of it on fire with pain. He ground his teeth together to keep from crying out. Someone took a few steps away and retched. Ari couldn't get his eyes to open to see who.

"He's useless," Mirimel muttered. "Where is that idiot of a Whey when I need him? Stew, can you please ask someone to help carry him? Lord Kenmar and I can't lift him alone."

Ari heard the hooves leaving. He wished he could speak, or see. Or move.

He knew he must have fallen from consciousness, because the next feeling was the pain of having his clothing peeled off. He had just enough sanity left, tucked away deep inside the pain, to hope the person doing it wasn't Mirimel. Probably not,

225

he thought, for though the pain was excruciating, the hands were gentle.

"I know it hurts," Lord Kenmar said.

Ari tried to open his eyes at the words, but to no avail. He was in too much agony to tell, even, if he had them open or not. Either way, he couldn't see and he didn't want to move his arms to reach up and feel for lids.

"I'm afraid this next part will hurt even more, my young friend," Kenmar said.

A wet cloth was laid over Ari's leg. The pain that shot through him was so intense, he didn't have to bear it for long. Seeking the refuge of oblivion, he passed out.

Ari awoke to darkness. For a panicked moment, he thought he still couldn't see, but then he realized he could feel his eyelids. All he needed to do was open them. As he did, outlines formed, and then shapes, and sight returned.

With sight came the knowledge he wasn't in pain. He sat up carefully, finding his body draped in clean, damp cloths. He held up his hands. There were still some deeper nicks, appearing half-healed, but his skin was mostly smooth.

How fast had he healed, he wondered. He knew he'd been in a sorry state, his skin scoured clear off, but none of the injuries had been deep. Pain still lingered at the back of his head and he reached up to find a half-healed lump. Flexing his limbs, he realized his foot was still hurt where it had been kicked when he'd jumped through the ring of galloping Questri. That had probably broken the bone. Hopefully it was mended enough to walk on.

A surge of panic filled him as his mind became reacquainted with memories of what had happened. Had it been more than one day? Had Mirimel already eaten the fruit? A glance around the room showed Lord Kenmar asleep in his cot, but Cooro was missing. Ari swung his feet to the floor, wrapping one of the towels about him as he stood, indecisive.

Should he go to Mirimel's room to check if she was there? His throat clenched at the idea of her having already eaten the fruit, and died, all while he was asleep. He fought down a surge of panic.

"Ari?" Lord Kenmar sat up. He squinted in the dark. "Are you well? Can you see? We were worried about your eyes. Not, of course, that anyone can see without light."

Ducking, as he didn't want to bash his head on the low ceiling, Ari walked to the other end of the room and lit a candle. He lifted it, turning back to the older lord, who now sat propped against the wall behind his cot.

Kenmar gaped at him.

"How long have I been asleep?" Ari asked, resisting the urge to charge off to Mirimel's room. If she was well, odds were she wouldn't appreciate that sort of behavior.

"You have eyelids."

Ari blinked. "I do. What day is it? Was I unconscious for long? Has Mirimel eaten the Orate Fruit yet?"

"It's the same day." Lord Kenmar was still staring at him. "Rather, the next, as it's past the mid of night, you see."

Ari nodded, letting out his breath. He set the candle on a table, sitting down beside it. "So she hasn't done it yet."

"Hawk Guardian Mirimel?" Kenmar shook his head. "She hasn't eaten the fruit. It's hours till dawn." He eyed Ari. "She told me you would heal quickly. I admit, though I know she isn't given to flights of fancy, I didn't credit her that it would be this fast."

"Ah, yeah." Ari glanced down at himself. Like his hands, most of his flesh was smooth, though scored by dozens of deeper gouges. They would likely fade by dawn, leaving just a

227

dull ache in his head and a bruise on his foot. "Cooro is still in that pit?"

"Swordmaster Cooro and I spoke. To call it a pit is an understatement. It is a deep fissure in the ground. They lowered him down. You must yell to him, so nothing you say is private. I told him what happened."

"He can't get out of there? Where is it?" Ari pushed a hand through his hair. Sand rained out. He'd have to dunk his head in a bucket. He wished he had Larke's magic whirlwind. Then again, after the day he had, he didn't really want even a small, cleaning whirlwind.

"He was of the opinion that he could climb out, just as he climbed the spire." Kenmar looked down, appearing abashed. "I told him to stay down there, you see."

"You did?" Ari was surprised. Usually, Kenmar didn't have much of an opinion.

"Well, they said they would release him just before dawn. He said, that will be too late. I said, where would you go if you got up here? There are Questri standing guard over the pit, and you can't outrun them on the plains. He said some unflattering things I shan't repeat, some of them being in the nature of curses, you see."

Ari smiled slightly. "Yes, I'm sure I do see."

"He said, I don't care if they kill me, I just want to save her." Kenmar shrugged. "It was at that point that I was forced to inform him Hawk Guardian Mirimel desires to eat the Orate Fruit. I said, you see, in view of her stubborn nature and Lord Aridian's indisposition, it would be quite difficult to stop her. He then informed me, at length, what he thinks of Hawk Guardian Mirimel's mental state."

"Thank you for speaking with him. I'm sorry you had to subject your sensibilities to it."

"It was my pleasure to be of some small help on this journey. It isn't as if he used any words I haven't heard before, although some of his hyperbole was quite inspired."

"He sometimes uses words I don't know," Ari said, though his mind was no longer on their conversation. What could he say to Mirimel to stop her, assuming what she'd put in motion could be stopped? Lord Kenmar's words echoed Ari's own thoughts of the day before. How could they run from the Questri, especially on the Tybrunn Plains?

"Yes, well, sheltered though my life may seem to you, I am a deal older than you, so it only makes sense I should have encountered a great deal more words, of every sort."

Something in Kenmar's tone caught Ari's attention. Some hidden amusement. It reminded him of the Herdlord. He locked gazes with the cartographer. "How much older?"

Lord Kenmar stared at him. "I . . . I don't know. Older?"

"More than twice my age?" Ari pressed.

"I should think so."

"Why don't you just tell me how old you are, and we'll know." Ari stretched out his legs, trying to seem casual, though he was anything but.

"I, that is, I lose track sometimes, you see."

"Lose track? Of your age?" Ari frowned. "Well, in what year were your born?"

"Yes, I lose track." Kenmar shook his head. "Since, you know, the blight I spoke of, that took my family and left my son forever unwell. I stopped counting then, you see."

Kenmar looked down, his gaze on his toes. His hands, fingers interlaced, shook where they rested on the blanket he had wrapped around him. He was the very picture of misery.

229

Ari sighed. Why couldn't anyone be what they seemed? Was Kenmar Larke's replacement, sent by the Aluiens to try to keep Ari out of trouble while Larke was confined?

"The pit, as they call it, is actually right in the center of the town, you know," Kenmar said. He looked up at Ari, his gaze pleading. "You asked where it is."

"I did," Ari agreed. Whoever the aging cartographer was, he didn't seem like a threat. Ari supposed he could keep his secrets, for a little longer. "I also said we need to find a way to stop Mirimel from eating the Orate Fruit."

Silence stretched out between them. Ari realized he was rather tired. He was grateful for all of the gifts he'd been granted by the Aluiens, however unwittingly they'd awarded them. He just wished those gifts had included a lack of need for sleep.

"Never have I found a way to temper the rashness of youth," Lord Kenmar said, his gaze clouded. "She is strong willed, and her will is set on this thing."

Ari nodded. He didn't like it, but he knew it was true. "Not to mention, as you said, we can't escape the Questri now. If we run, there will be blood on both sides." He pushed his hand through his hair again, letting lose another shower of dirt.

"One might argue, even, that Hawk Guardian Mirimel has the right to make this decision," Lord Kenmar said hesitantly.

Ari grimaced. Of course she did. Mirimel was perfectly capable of making her own choices, and had been for years. He didn't like her choice, though. Didn't that give him some right to stop her?

"It may also be argued that though we do not agree with her choices, we have no right to intervene," Kenmar added.

Ari sighed. "Did I hear you say you have some skill with healing?"

"Some, yes."

"Well, then, I'll concentrate on keeping Cooro from doing anything that will get him locked in that pit forever, and you can promise to do everything in your power to save Mirimel after she eats that poisoned fruit."

Lord Kenmar pressed his lips into a thin line, but he nodded. "I promise," he finally said.

Ari nodded. He stood, returning to his cot. He didn't know if it would work, but he knew he should try to get some rest. His mind was so filled with worry for Mirimel, it wasn't until he was drifting off to sleep that he remembered the stone, and the dark silhouette of the man who took it.

Chapter 20

The sound of someone calling his name penetrated Ari's awareness moments before a hand reached out and shook his shoulder. Ari opened his eyes, pleased to find his vision in good working order. Lord Kenmar was leaning over him, his face somber.

"It's time to wake," the so-called cartographer said. "It's nearly dawn. A group of women already came to take Mirimel away, to ready her."

"Ready her?" Ari sat up as Kenmar stepped back.

"I gather there is some form of ritual cleansing and there was some talk of what she must wear, for the babes are laid upon the rock naked."

A vision formed in Ari's mind and he quickly dispelled it, feeling his face heat. "Is Cooro back yet?"

"I think they will bring him directly to the . . . event."

Ari swung his feet to the floor. The older lord looked tired, and anxious. Ari was feeling well after his sleep, but he couldn't deny the anxiety coursing through him. He dressed, grateful Mia had cleaned all of his spare clothes after he'd changed into the first clean set. He was wondering how he could repay her, for the village didn't seem to use coin, when he realized that Mirimel was about to pay enough for all of them.

Belting on his sword, and still feeling a bit guilty for all of the leather he wore, Ari joined Lord Kenmar in the front room. He sat down at the table, but couldn't get himself to eat. It didn't seem as if Kenmar could either. The cartographer served himself from the pot of warm oats that someone, likely Mia, had left, but he pushed the food about on his plate.

A knock at the door caused Ari to start. He realized he'd been staring at Kenmar's plate and looked away. He felt singularly helpless. He couldn't stop Mirimel from doing something she wished to do, and his sword was no match for the poison that would take hold of her when she did it.

"Lord Kenmar," Tewlar called as he pushed the door open. "Are you ready? It's--"

Tewlar's eyes fell on Ari and he broke off, his jaw going slack. He blinked several times. Finally, he pulled his mouth closed, but his eyes were still wide, almost afraid.

"Good morning, Tewlar," Ari said, standing.

Tewlar took a step back. "It's true, then," he whispered.

"What's true?" How could rumor of his recovery traveled during the night, Ari wondered.

"You are not a mortal man." Tewlar backed up another step.

"Uh, I am. Of course I am." He realized he hadn't even thought of taking pains to hide his recovery, as he would have in Lggothland or Wheylia. Here, in this remote village, there seemed no point. No one came here and few left. Not to mention, the Questri had referred to him as the Thrice Born

234

repeatedly, and pointed out he wasn't normal enough times that he didn't even wince anymore when they said it.

"Your skin was flayed from you," Tewlar said. "Your eyelids gone, and the eyes beneath ruined. How are you healed?"

"I, ah, heal quickly, but I am a mortal man."

Tewlar shook his head, looking dubious. Then his face lit with hope. "Can this healing of yours save Mirimel? The village feels joy to have our children spared and the Blessing of the Mare given without cost, but we despair so noble a lady must die for us."

"I wish it could." Ari cleared his throat. "It doesn't work that way."

The hope slid from Tewlar's face and he looked down. "I'm sorry that your friend must die to spare my son. It isn't right."

"Mirimel made her choice," Ari said. "Once her mind is set on something, there's little anyone can do to change it." He decided not to tarnish the gift she was giving the villagers by admitting to Tewlar that Mirimel had her own reasons for eating the fruit.

"No, it cannot be changed," Tewlar said, fear in the eyes he lifted to meet Ari's. "The Herdlord said Mirimel shall eat the fruit and our babes will be spared."

Ari could hear the desperation in Tewlar's voice and realized the villager was afraid it could, indeed, be changed. Tewlar feared Mirimel would back down. There was raw agony on his face. Ari could only guess at the emotions pummeling Tewlar. The joy of someone offering salvation for his child. Guilt over it. Fear for them. Fear that salvation would be ripped away at the last moment, and guilt for hoping it was not.

Lord Kenmar looked between Ari and Tewlar, his face pinched.

"Mirimel will eat the fruit," Ari said.

He didn't like it, but he knew it was true. He also realized there had never been any chance of running away from this, even if they'd thought of a way. They couldn't snatch such hope from these people, forcing them to wake into a morning where their children would, indeed, die. The only course Ari could have taken was to sneak out at night and try to get the fruit, to destroy it or eat it himself, but it was too late for that. If only he hadn't been so incapacitated by his attempt to get that worthless stone the Lady wanted him to have, he might have--

"We should go." Lord Kenmar's quiet voice broke into Ari's self-recrimination.

Tewlar nodded, still looking miserable. "It is time."

They left the hut and made their way through the village. Though the sun was not yet up, it was already light enough to see fairly well. Everyone Ari passed stopped what they were doing to gawk at him. He tried to look straight ahead, keeping his face bland. He thought smiling and nodding might be better, but he couldn't muster a smile.

A crowd converged, following them. As they drew near the base of the Orate Tree's spire, Ari realized a crowd was already gathered there as well, on the south side of the stone. Outside the ring of people was an assemblage of Questri, forming a half circle that filled the plain south of them. The silver stallion was turned in that direction as well, facing the stone slab which normally lurked behind him.

Looking over everyone's heads, Ari could see Mirimel already stood on the slab. They'd clad her in a simple, homespun dress. Her hair was lose and hung down her back in long orange spirals. Ari was struck by how pretty she was. He realized this was the first time he'd ever seen her not dressed in her green and brown forest garb, bow, boots, quiver and knife. She looked younger, much more vulnerable, and not a whit less stubborn.

Ari searched the crowd, hoping for a blond head to stick up higher than the rest, for Larkesong was taller even than he. Or for a hat. A bright garish colored hat with clashing plumes. His ears were alert as well, seeking any hint of music. If Mirimel was about to die, surely Larke would be there.

The crowd behind Ari was still murmuring, spreading the news of his miraculous recovery. Their agitation seemed to communicate itself to the swarm of villagers surrounding the stone. Soon, they turned to look at him as well, and a path opened from him to Mirimel. All along it, heads turned toward him, eyes wide.

Now that the way was clear, Ari could see Cooro knelt between the silver stallion and the broad flat rock on which Mirimel waited. His hands and feet were tied round with rope, and another was about his neck. Ari clenched his teeth, outraged to see the swordmaster so bound. Cooro didn't turn toward him, his eyes on Mirimel.

She saw Ari, though, defiance flickering through her otherwise composed gaze. She tilted her chin up, her jaw set, as if to challenge for her right to do as she wished. Ari shook his head, wishing he had the power she seemed to think he did, the power to stop her.

"Look," Tewlar said, pointing upward.

Craning his neck to look up and over his shoulder, Ari could see shapes moving along the rim of the flat-topped pinnacle on which the tree stood. One spread its wings, a dark outline against the colors streaking the predawn sky. Ari was stunned by the size of it. The bird, which he could only assume was a great plains vulture, looked large enough to carry off a boy of twelve. He glanced back at Mirimel, wondering how much she weighed out of her accoutrements. It couldn't be much.

"They came yesterday afternoon," Tewlar said in a quiet voice. "After you . . . after you were taken away. They like to eat all of the rotten fruit from beneath the tree. They make a terrible noise up there. Sometimes they fight. It's said the blood of the vultures nourishes the tree."

Ari's eyes moved to the tree, pristine and picturesque. He shuddered. Who or what had created it, he wondered. How had all of this come into being?

"We should go to them," Kenmar said, glancing from Cooro and Mirimel to the lightening sky. "Dawn draws near."

All inflection was gone from the older lord's voice, leaving only resignation and a lurking sorrow. Ari nodded, starting down the aisle of villagers. They murmured as he passed, the words thrice born rustling through the predawn. Some reached out to touch him. Their fingers were like blades of grass brushing him as he walked by. He suppressed a shiver, unsettled by their behavior.

"I see the Thrice Born approaches," the Herdlord's voiceless said in his childlike, yet stern, tone. "You have come not too soon, nor too late, upon this morning. It further shows your courage, for there were those who whispered you would not be brave enough to watch this female die."

Ari bowed stiffly to the stallion, trying not to be struck by the Herdlord's stunning equine perfection. "You said I would be allowed to help her, once the fruit is consumed." He had to force the words out through clenched teeth.

"So you shall, futile though I know it to be. Once the act is done, I will release both the Whey and the female into your care, for you are a friend to the Questri. Tell the blue lady we did you this kindness, for we wish to make amends, though it is no fault of ours a creature of hers was unable to reach the stone."

Ari gazed on the Herdlord through narrowed eyes. Should he ask who took the stone? Of course, asking would get him nowhere. The silver stallion did not answer questions.

Ari wished he knew if the red glow he'd seen about the man who took the stone had been real or an effect of the destruction of his eyes. Empty Ones didn't glow red, though, and neither did Aluiens. Someone with power must have taken the stone, but who? More importantly, why? If it was to stop Ari from completing the set, the man had most likely been a minion of Tal Mraken.

"Thank you, Herdlord," Ari finally said. "I will tell the Lady of your generosity." He bowed again before turning his back on the stallion.

Ari moved to stand beside Cooro, helping him to his feet, though it was obviously difficult for him to stand with bound legs. The swordmaster shot him a frantic look, and Ari realized he was gagged. Ari followed the rope about Cooro's neck, finding a strong looking villager at the other end, on the edge of the crowd. Cooro made a pleading sound in his throat.

"She wants to do it," Ari whispered to him. "I cannot stop her. She thinks it will make it so she can speak with her hawks."

Cooro shook his head, training his gaze back on Mirimel.

Ari looked over his shoulder again, finding sunlight touching the top of the spire, inching its way down. He could see the vultures in perfect detail now. They were great, rangy beasts, looking more made of scaly hide than feathers. Their bright eyes were on Mirimel, their hooked beaks clicking. As he watched, they jostled for position, snapping at one another. He dropped his gaze slightly, to the long talons with which they gripped the rock edge, before lowering it farther, to track progress of the sun.

The line of light inched down as the sun rose. Ari was so tense, his lips felt numb. The crowd of villagers and Questri stilled and a breeze stirred, as it was wont to do at the break of day. Far out, past the open expanses and fields surrounding the village, likely beyond the hearing of any but Ari, the gentle rustling of the wind made the grassland sing.

The shriek of a Sorga Hawk split the air as the sun crested the horizon, falling full upon Mirimel. It lit her orange curls like a flame. Beside Ari, Cooro groaned. A glance showed tears sliding down his cheeks.

As the echoes of the hawk's cry faded, the eerie silence returned. His footfalls nearly soundless, the small boy who spoke for the Herdlord walked past Ari and Cooro, the bright yellow Orate Fruit held carefully in two hands. He stopped at the edge of the slab, which was waist high on him, and held it up.

Mirimel knelt with a fluid grace. Her skirts billowed around her, to splash down in a pale pool on the reddened stone. Reaching out, she accepted the fruit. She stood, her gaze sweeping those before her. She gave Cooro the slightest smile before turning her blue eyes to Ari. Looking at him, she shrugged, and bit into the fruit.

It wasn't large. It took her only five quick bites. Ari could see it had no pit, or stem. There was nothing to leave behind.

When Mirimel swallowed the last bite, the villagers cheered. The Questri raised their voices, letting lose boisterous whinnies. Movement erupted around them as celebration broke out. Ari was peripherally aware of Mia rushing from the crowd to embrace Tewlar. The man holding Cooro's rope turned to a woman beside him, dropping the offending restraint to the ground as he swung her into his arms.

"Keep an eye on Mirimel," Ari said to Kenmar. He didn't want to take his eyes from her, but he had to untie Cooro. Quick glances while he worked showed Mirimel still standing in the center of the stone slab, a perplexed look on her face. Ari stripped the ropes off Cooro, ripping them open more so than untying them.

Mirimel gasped. Cooro, his hands free now, tore off his gag. Ari turned toward the slab to see Kenmar hovering beside it. Mirimel, to his surprise, had brought both hands to her head. For some reason he'd thought the poison would begin its work on her heart, or gut. He rushed to the rock, Cooro at his side.

"What can we do?" Cooro asked, his tone frantic.

Ari shook his head, looking to Kenmar.

"I don't know. I don't know what's wrong yet. Mirimel, can you hear me?" Kenmar called.

Mirimel squeezed her eyes shut, her fingers digging into her skull. Beads of sweat started to form on her forehead and her breath became more ragged. She gritted her teeth, her face squeezing into lines of pain.

"We have to get her off that rock," Cooro said.

"Will it harm her to carry her?" Ari asked Kenmar.

"I don't know. I shouldn't think so. It seems to be working in her mind, not her body."

Mirimel let out an anguished cry, falling to her knees. Ari lifted a foot to the slab, ready to go get her, but stopped as a chill ran up his spine. Over his shoulder, he heard a riotous, hissing shriek. Cooro jumped onto the stone, coming to his knees at Mirimel's side. Shadows swirled over them. Ari looked up. The vultures dropped like stones, hurtling down from above.

Chapter 21

Ari launched himself onto the stone slab. He pulled free his sword, the blade whistling through the air. High above, he could hear Mirimel's hawk screaming. He hoped the little hawk wouldn't try to take on the horse-sized vultures. Like Mirimel, there was probably no way to stop him.

The vultures dove with the speed of raptors. Ari was once again struck by how they seemed more lizard than bird, though their lithe bodies were clad in coarse feathers. It was only their necks, heads and legs that were leathery.

Talons the size of kitchen knives outstretched before it, one plummeted toward Mirimel. Ari jumped in front of it, bellowing. He swung, using the flat of his blade, trying to knock it aside. Evil as the creatures looked, he wasn't sure he should kill them.

His blow hardly seemed to faze the brute before him. Its scaled neck snaked forward. Ari snapped his sword back around, catching the hooked beak before it could reach his face. Realizing it had been going for his eye, Ari decided he should try to kill them after all.

Cooro let out a yell and Ari whirled. Mirimel was curled into a ball, her arms wrapped about her head. Cooro, weaponless, punched at a vulture. It dodged the blows, hopping agilely from foot to foot where it loomed over Mirimel. As Ari watched, it landed a hit, taking a deep gouge out of her forearm. He could see Cooro was bleeding as well.

Pain stabbed the base of his skull and Ari whipped back around, his sword leading the way. He caught the vulture behind him with a glancing blow as it winged backward. His sword skittered off the scales on its neck, seeming to do no damage.

Seeing it lift itself beyond his reach, Ari turned back to Mirimel and Cooro. The vulture menacing them had landed another blow on Mirimel, this time to her side. Blood spread in a dark ring around the tear in her dress.

Another of the giant birds landed beside the first. Ari lunged for it before it could find its footing. This time, he aimed the point of his blade for the center of the creature's chest.

It winged backward, but he struck true. His sword sank into the feathered body, colliding with bone as hard as rock. The giant vulture cried out, writhing in pain as it launched itself. His sword tore a long hole down through it as it lifted.

That vulture retreating, Ari swung at the one still pecking at Cooro and Mirimel. He didn't chop for the neck this time. He'd already learned how impervious the scales were. Instead, he angled his blade to slice into the base of its neck, where leathery skin met feathers.

Though he swung with enough force to cleave a man in two, he only succeeded in a shallow gouge. He did gain its attention, though. It turned from the nearly defenseless Cooro and launched itself over Mirimel, at Ari.

Gripping his sword in two hands, Ari braced the pommel against his chest, diving forward to meet the vulture as it cleared Mirimel's crumpled form. The force of their collision dropped him to his knees, his blade buried in the monster.

The vulture thrashed, widening the hole he'd stabbed into it. It tried to wing backward, as the last one had, but the sword was lodged in the bones of its chest. Seeming to understand its predicament, its exertions grew more frantic, nearly wrenching Ari's blade from his grasp.

Exerting his strength, Ari surged to his feet, dragging his sword upward. Still stuck, it cut through the giant vulture at a cruel angle. Twisting his blade to break it free, Ari heaved the vulture onto its side, sliding the weapon out through its flank.

The thing let out a gurgling screech. Its body gave a tremendous shudder. Ari saw the light go out of its eyes. Air escaped it as it seemed to sink, flattening into the pool of blood beneath it.

"Ari, Cooro," Kenmar yelled behind him.

Ari whirled, sword ready, but Kenmar was pointing up.

Dozens of the giant vultures circled above them. As Ari watched, they started to dive. He realized there was no way he could fend them all off. Even if Cooro had his swords, this was a battle they would lose. His eyes dropped, finding the silver stallion in his arched shelter, watching.

Holding his sword out so he wouldn't hurt her, Ari dove for Mirimel. He swept her into his arms just as the rock slab shook with the impact of the first vulture hitting it. Cooro staggered to his feet from where he'd been kneeling beside her.

"Cooro, run," Ari yelled, springing from the rock.

245

He could hear Cooro's harsh breath and rapid footsteps following and he ran headlong out onto the plain. Questri and villagers stood in groups and Ari realized many had stayed to watch the scene unfold. Resentment flared in him for their lack of help, though he didn't suppose any of them were much of a match for the giant birds.

It took him several moments of running to realize what he didn't hear, or see. No shadows sped toward them, cast by vultures attacking from above. He couldn't hear their great sweeping wings. Ari slowed, turning back. Cooro skidded to a halt beside him, gasping for breath.

On the slab, the vultures fought, squabbling for purchase. Feathers and blood sailed through the morning air. Ari realized they were ripping apart the one he'd killed. Scaled necks shot skyward with each mouthful, as if to allow the torn off pieces to slide down their throats. They screamed and fought over the morsels, trampling the corpse into the slab as they ate, shredding it with their giant talons.

"We better get her inside before they finish it," Cooro said.

The Whey was streaked with blood. He'd been gouged several times on his arms, and a trio of long gashes raked his chest, mute testament that he'd taken a hit from the creature's talons as well. Ari nodded, not bothering to speak.

He handed Cooro his sword, for there was no way to sheath it without putting Mirimel down, and no way to carry her safely while he held it. He hoped his mad dash from the stone hadn't done her too much harm. Holding her in both arms, Ari used long steady strides to walk in a wide arc back toward the village.

Kenmar caught up with them as they passed the spire on which the Orate Tree stood. He was wringing his hands, shooting worried glances at Mirimel where she rested in Ari's arms. She still had her hands clenched around her head, her face contorted in pain. Ari wasn't sure if she was conscious or not. He was just glad she was still breathing.

"What can I get?" Tewlar asked, jogging up beside them.

"Water, clean, of course, and cloth for bandages," Kenmar said. "I'll need a fire and boiling water as well, and those bundles of herbs I asked the healing woman to prepare."

Ari clamped down his anger, knowing Tewlar couldn't really have helped fight off the vultures. He was surprised to learn Kenmar had been to see the healer. He seemed to recall, hazily, mention of a healer when they'd come to get him after the whirlwind.

"Will the herbs help?" he asked in a low voice.

"I don't know," Kenmar said. "I need to examine her. I don't know what the fruit did, you see."

Ari nodded. A shadow streaked over them, darting across the ground as they entered the village. He ducked, curling his shoulder inward to protect Mirimel. The anguished cry of a raptor split the sky above. Ari looked up, realizing it was Mirimel's hawk. The little brown creature winged downward, its flight wobbly.

"Hold up your arm, Cooro," Ari said, for he couldn't.

Cooro cast him a surprised look, then glanced up at the hawk. Switching Ari's sword to his other hand, he held out his arm. The Sorga Hawk alighted on Cooro's wrist, the Whey wincing as its small talons dug into his skin, for he didn't wear the protective garb Mirimel normally did. The hawk chirped at Cooro before turning serious eyes on her.

Once again, people watched them as they passed through the village. Though most of their faces showed worry and respect, Ari had to fight down the urge to curse at them. He was glad, he thought sarcastically, that he and his friends had arrived to bring such entertainment to this remote town.

That thought caused him to look about again. Where was Larke? The bard should be there. Mirimel needed him.

They reached their dwelling to find Stew and the black mare outside. Ari stopped, Kenmar and Cooro flanking him. Stew looked as worried as Ari had ever seen him, the mare similarly so.

Stew shook his mane.

Ari shrugged at him, unsure what the Questri wanted him to say.

"I'll fetch what you need, and send Mia to assist you," Tewlar said, jogging off.

"We have to take her inside," Ari said to Stew. He didn't, though. He stared at his horse, wishing he had something to say, or knew what Stew wanted. "We'll do all we can for her. I'll come out and let you know what's going on."

Stew glanced at Lord Kenmar, Ari following his gaze. The cartographer looked worried, a frantic glint lurking in his eyes. Odd as it was to Ari, Kenmar looked like nothing so much as a rabbit his older cousin Jare had brought in once, in a wooden cage. Ari had freed the poor creature once Jare had gone to sleep, having already been forced to stomach an afternoon of his cousin tormenting it through the bars. When Ari had opened the cage door, it had stared at him with that same cornered look for a moment, until it realized it was free.

The mare pawed the ground nervously.

Stew dipped his head.

Shaking his, Ari carried Mirimel inside, Cooro behind him.

Kenmar hurried ahead, returning to the main room with a pile of blankets before Ari could cross it at his careful pace.

248

The cartographer spread them on the table. "Lay her here, please."

Ari gently placed Mirimel on the table. Her hawk hopped from Cooro's arm, landing beside her head. He rubbed the side of his beak on the back of her hand, where it still clutched her brow. Ari wished he could tell if she was conscious. Her breathing was very shallow, her skin waxen.

Kenmar cut away the side of Mirimel's dress, tending to that wound first, before moving on to her arms. Fortunately, she didn't seem to be badly hurt. Not by the vultures, at least. Cooro handed back Ari's sword, pulling out one of the chairs and slumping into it.

Tewlar and Mia entered while the cartographer was working. Mia helped Cooro clean and bandage the gouges in his arm, blushing as he took off his shirt so she could work on his well-muscled chest. Tewlar ran about, fetching anything anyone asked for.

Ari sat to the side, feeling useless. As soon as the fighting was over, he became about as needed as rain during a spring flood. When Mia was done with Cooro and the swordmaster had gone to change into clean clothing, she crossed to Ari.

"Do you need my help?" she asked, her eyes downcast. "Your wound must be hard to reach."

"I was wounded?" he said, trying to remember.

"One of the birds landed a blow to the back of your head." She shuddered when she said the word birds.

Ari couldn't blame her. The great plains vultures were a great deal more formidable than he'd anticipated. He wasn't sure he would look on anything with feathers quite the same way again. The meaning of her words penetrated his musings. He reached up to touch the back of his head.

There was a sticky mess there, but he could tell the wound, though tender, had already closed. Now that she mentioned it, though, he was aware of a trail of dried blood down his back. He recalled Tewlar's words from earlier and wished he could, indeed, share his gift with Mirimel. Cooro too, for that matter, and the little hawk, he thought, glancing at it. One of its wings hung at an off angle, probably wrenched. Likely Mirimel was the only one of them who knew how to fix it, though Ari would ask Kenmar.

"I'm well enough," Ari said. "I just need a wash and clean clothing, although I seem to be ruining it at an alarming rate."

"I can clean the blood, though it will likely stain. I'll bring you a shirt to wear."

"Thank you."

She nodded and went to see if Kenmar needed her. Ari stood, feeling stiff. He supposed he ought to get cleaned up. He wasn't helping anyone by sitting around in his own blood and sweat. First, he ducked outside to see Stew, letting him and the black mare know that nothing had changed yet.

When Ari returned from his ablutions, wearing a borrowed homespun shirt and clean breeches, he found Cooro sitting beside Mirimel, holding her hand. Her eyes were still closed and she appeared hardly to breathe. Kenmar sat on her other side, looking worried. Her hawk perched on a chair, near her head. They all looked up at Ari when he entered.

Cooro's face was stricken, his eyes bloodshot. "She's dying, Ari."

Ari looked around the room, stunned by both the idea and that Larkesong wasn't there. "She can't be."

Cooro shook his head. He stroked the limp white hand he clasped. "Denial is no cure," he choked out.

Ari turned to Kenmar. "But she looks better, somewhat. She isn't holding onto her head anymore. Did she ever wake up?"

"I gave her something to numb the pain." Kenmar's voice was tired. "I think, examining her, that the trouble is inside her mind. It seems to me, you see, that the fruit opens all minds and that is what causes the pain."

"What of those who live? Do you mean they're strong enough to overcome it?" Ari demanded. "Mirimel is strong. She's strong enough, I'm sure of it." Desperation twisted in his gut. He ruthlessly tamped it down.

"I think, that is, I mean the opposite. A weak mind gives up and is extinguished, allowing the Questri entrance."

"The voiceless are those few whose minds are snuffed out," Cooro said in low tones. "Our Mirimel, her mind won't allow itself to die. It will fight, and in the fight, ruin itself beyond repair. That's why they say what the vultures do is a mercy, for the babies that fight do so in vain, only to die a slow, mad death."

Ari stared at them. He recalled similar words once, from the Aluiens. They'd said Clorra's mind was beyond repair. Prince Parrentine had been forced to kill her, to end her insane suffering.

His gaze returned to Mirimel's face. There was absolutely no way he would allow Mirimel to suffer a similar fate. It was unfathomable. He glanced at Kenmar, catching a flicker of guilt, quickly buried, in the older lord's eyes.

"How can you know these things are true?" Ari asked. "She hasn't woken up, has she. You're guessing. You can't know what's inside her mind. Cooro, may I speak to you outside?"

251

Cooro blinked at him. He nodded, gently placing Mirimel's hand on her chest, where the other rested. He slid back his chair and stood. Mirimel's hawk watched him go, but Lord Kenmar kept his eyes downcast.

Ari led the way outside, surprised at how early it was. It wasn't even midday yet. He felt as though it should be the middle of the night, so much had happened since dawn. He looked around, but Stew and the black mare were gone. "What can possibly entice you to believe this verdict?"

"Kenmar sounds so sure, and he's an educated man," Cooro said. "You know I am not one given to despair, Ari, but there is no hope."

Ari nodded, his mind whirling. Cooro truly wasn't given to despair. In fact, his words were so unlike him, they only served to fuel Ari's suspicions. He should have known better than to leave his friend, a mortal man, alone with someone he suspected was an Aluien. "I'll talk to him. You go inside and sit with Mirimel."

Cooro nodded, his shoulders slumped with despair. He turned and headed back into the hut.

"Kenmar," Ari called through the open door. "May I have a word?"

Lord Kenmar emerged with halting steps, that same trapped look lurking in his gaze. He glanced up at the sun, which seemed almost to shimmer in the sky. As it did most days, the morning breeze had stilled, leaving the air around them dry and hot.

"It's not kind to beguile your travel companions," Ari said in a quiet voice, closing the door between them and Cooro.

Kenmar winced. "Beguile? What an odd word."

252

"Not to you." Ari contemplated Kenmar's evasive answer, realizing the older lord went to lengths not to lie. "Though I do respect your effort not to deny what you've done."

Kenmar looked down at the ground, his lips pressed tightly together.

"Yet evasiveness and secrecy are, in their way, as false as any untruth," Ari said.

Kenmar raised his chin, his expression strained, but still didn't meet Ari's gaze. "Cooro was very distressed. I was merely trying to soothe him by resigning him to her fate, so he wouldn't become rash. What you heard is true. She is dying. The struggle not to allow her mind to be snuffed out, leaving her an empty vessel, will destroy it. She'll be left mad. The Orate Fruit leaves no survivors."

"Did you know that before she ate it?" Ari asked, trying to stop his hand from crawling toward the hilt of his sword.

Kenmar shot him a startled glance. "Of course not. I didn't know what it would do. I've never observed the effects before. There's no other tree like it."

Ari nodded, relieved. "None of this tells me why you're breaking your promise to me."

Kenmar pressed his lips into a thin line once more. He paced away, then back. "I've done all a healer can do," he blurted, still pacing.

"You've done all a mortal can do," Ari said, his voice low. "I believe you promised to do everything in your power to save Mirimel. Not most things. All of them."

Kenmar swung around to face him.

For a moment, Ari thought he might run. He tensed, unsure if he could catch a fleeing Aluien.

Instead, Kenmar strolled toward him. He stopped when they were nearly toe to toe, glaring at Ari even though he was half a head shorter. "Then you promise me something, young Aridian. An oath, on your word of honor, on everything you hold sacred."

Ari frowned. That was not the capitulation he'd expected. "What sort of oath?"

"You need only to swear that you'll protect me." Kenmar's eyes were intent as they burrowed into Ari's. "Swear you won't let any harm befall me if I can mend Mirimel."

"Can mend?" Ari asked, his heart sinking. "You aren't sure you can do it?"

"You yourself said I make an effort not to lie to you. Know this, I have never done so. When I said I haven't seen a poison like this before, I spoke the truth. It could be that all of my powers cannot save her." He looked down, his shoulders slumping. "It wouldn't be the first time I've failed."

Ari recalled Kenmar's story about his family, and how most of them had been struck down by a malady of some sort. He nodded. "You know I can't promise to protect you forever. I am the king's man."

"Is that who you owe your allegiance to?" Kenmar asked, his tone bitter. He shook his head. "Fine, then. Give me one turning of the moon. When next it waxes so near full as now, you may abandon me, but swear you will do everything in your power to keep me unharmed until then. If you make that vow, I will fulfill my promise to do everything I can to save her."

"An oath given under duress--" Ari began.

"Is much what you extracted from me, though I daresay you didn't fully know it. I shall count on your chivalry, and what I have come to know of your heart."

Ari nodded. It wasn't that much to ask, after all. He always protected his companions as best he could. All they would be doing when they left the village was traveling back to Sorga, hopefully with the surety of Kenmar's maps, for he doubted the clan would escort them all the way home. If Kenmar was afraid of defying the Aluien council and changing the course of a mortal life by helping Mirimel, Ari was happy to offer to protect him from them, though there might be little he could do in the face of a mass of angry Aluiens.

Ari squared his shoulders. "I swear, on my honor, if you do everything in your power to save Mirimel, I shall do everything in my power to protect you for one turning of the moon. So I swear, so it shall be, or my life be given pursuing it."

They locked eyes for a long moment. Kenmar searched Ari's gaze. Finally, he nodded, turning away. "Then let us proceed." Kenmar pushed up his sleeves as he marched back into the building.

Chapter 22

Ari followed Kenmar inside to find Cooro sitting beside Mirimel once again, tears sliding down his cheeks. Her little hawk was by her shoulder, hunched into a ball of feathers. His damaged wing stuck out at an odd angle, and Ari thought it looked worse. He supposed it was setting up in some way, and wondered how to treat it. If Mirimel woke to find they'd allowed her hawk to suffer too much damage to fly again, she'd fill them all full of arrows.

Kenmar moved to the head of the table, looking down at Mirimel's face. Her orange curls pooled about her head, emphasizing her pallor. She looked small out of her hark guardian gear, lying there in her borrowed dress and draped over with a sheet.

"Has she grown worse?" Ari asked, eyeing the hawk. It was shaking, though it was by no means cold inside the hut, and its eyes were dull and glossy.

Kenmar placed ink stained fingers on her temples, closing his eyes for a moment. "She slips ever further away, but we still have time."

"Would it take long to heal her hawk? I mean, is that a thing you can do? I know it wasn't part of our bargain."

Kenmar looked at the trembling little creature, his features softening with sympathy. He reached out, placing a gentle finger on its head, and it flinched. "All will be well, little one."

The hawk turned its head to look over its shoulder at him.

Kenmar closed his eyes, murmuring in a language Ari had never heard before. It had harder edges than Wheylian and was sharper than the bumbling tongue of Ari's people. It stirred something in him, though, for he'd heard words that seemed to fit with it. Ari swallowed, eyeing Kenmar with dawning horror.

The little hawk stopped trembling. Looking surprised, but showing no sign of pain, it turned its head to eye its wing. As Ari watched, the damaged appendage visibly righted itself, sliding back into place. With a shake, the hawk stood, extending its wings and angling them this way and that.

Ari's fear was replaced by awe. He'd never seen even Larke do anything like that. Larke had told him that he could speed healing, but not effect an instantaneous remedy. Ari glanced at Cooro, but the Whey was too immersed in his sorrow to have noticed the hawk's miraculous cure.

Kenmar dropped his hand, opening his eyes. The whites were black as night, sending a chill down Ari's spine. He gripped the tabletop where he stood by Mirimel's feet, to keep from reaching for his sword. Kenmar blinked and his eyes were normal once more.

"What does Tal mean?" Ari asked in a quiet voice.

"It's an ancient word for lord." Kenmar's tone was equally quiet. His frame was filled with tension, as if he might bolt at any moment. "From a time long before your people came to our land."

Ari stared at him. An Aluien would know that, he thought. Yet, Kenmar had drawn no runes, called no Orlenia to bear. Nor, Ari realized, relaxing slightly, had he made the obscure gestures used by the Empty Ones.

He looked down at Mirimel. Her skin had taken on a strange gray tinge. Her breathing was so shallow, Ari didn't think anyone but he, and possibly Lord Kenmar, would be able to hear it.

"Shall I proceed?" Kenmar asked.

The movement stilted, Ari nodded. "Do what you can to save her. I will keep my vow." Though he had no idea what it would cost him.

Ari looked down, pressing his eyes closed, his fingers biting into the wood of the table. He would not allow himself to believe the man before him was his greatest enemy. It didn't seem possible. How could it be? They'd traveled together for months.

"Ari."

Ari looked up, forcing himself to open his eyes. The same rumpled, graying cartographer he'd come to know stood before him.

"There are two sides to every story," Kenmar said.

Ari nodded.

Kenmar drew in a slow breathe. Closing his eyes, he placed thin fingers on Mirimel's temples. In a quiet, soothing voice, he began to murmur in that ancient tongue.

At first, nothing seemed to change. Ari locked his eyes on Mirimel's face, scouring it for any sign of improvement or, his fears whispered, suffering and pain. So infinitesimal that Ari was forced to blink, thinking something was wrong with is

259

vision, swirls of color began to radiate from Kenmar's fingertips.

Shimmering lines of blue, green, orange and red formed, fading almost as quickly as they appeared. The luminous pale blue Ari was familiar with. He was sure it was Orlenia. He could almost smell it, taste it on his tongue, and he had to tamp down the familiar desire to reach for it. He looked at Cooro, wondering if the Whey could see what he could, but Cooro's head was bowed in grief.

The red caught Ari's eye, and he recalled the outline of a man in the storm. It had shimmered red. Where was Kenmar then? If he was who Ari feared he was, of course he would have taken the stone. Ari tasted bitter bile, realizing that must have been Kenmar's goal all along. Get Ari to work for the stone, and then take it. What better way to prevent him from assembling the whole set?

He raised his gaze to scrutinize the rumpled lord. Kenmar still murmured. His eyes were squeezed shut and lines of sweat trickled down his face. Whoever or whatever Lord Kenmar was, he looked to be trying very hard. Ari just hoped he was actually working to save Mirimel. There wasn't really any way to know for sure, but Ari was certain she would die without some intervention.

"Ari?" Mirimel said, her voice questioning and small.

Ari dropped his eyes to her face, relief shooting through him strong enough to make his legs wobbly. Kenmar released her forehead, little sparks flying from his fingertips. He staggered backward, sinking into a chair. His eyes still closed, the so-called cartographer sucked in deep breaths.

"That was more difficult than I thought it would be," Kenmar muttered. "The tree is powerful."

Mirimel looked up at Ari, her blue eyes confused. She tried to raise her head and winced. Letting it fall back against the blankets on the table, she raised her arm instead, inspecting the bandage. She grimaced, probing her similarly wrapped side.

Ari stared at her, fighting back the desire to weep, irrational now that she was doing better. Her hawk hopped from foot to foot, twittering and flapping its wings excitedly. Mirimel turned her head toward Cooro, who still held her other hand and wept.

"What's wrong with you, Whey?" Her voice came out weak. She grimaced, clearing her throat. "Is there any water in this furnace?"

Ari realized it was very warm in the hut. It must be the middle of the day, or there about, and the door had been closed all morning. "I'll get you some," he said, but he felt too shaky to move.

"Don't flap your wing like that," Lord Kenmar said from his chair, frowning at the little hawk. "You must treat it like it's just come out of a cast. It's tender."

"Why?" Mirimel's voice was stronger already. "What happened to his wing?"

"He hurt it." Ari moved up the table, sitting opposite Cooro. "Probably fighting the vultures."

"Vultures?" Mirimel frowned. Her eyes went wide. She looked between Ari and Cooro. "I ate the Orate Fruit."

"Yes, you did, and you nearly died." Ari bit back the more angry words he wished to add.

"Oh, my poor sweet hawk guardian, a woman whose boundless grace shall know no equal," Cooro said. "I cannot stand that you should die. Why must it be so?"

"I'm not dying, you idiot." Mirimel pulled her hand from his grasp. Grimacing, she propped herself up on her elbows. "What is wrong with you?" she asked Cooro.

"This voice, this lovely siren's call, it sings to me from beyond the grave." Cooro's eyes were wide and staring.

"Kenmar." Ari gave the cartographer a pained look.

Lord Kenmar raised his chin, looking over from where he slumped in his chair. He gave a rueful shake of his head. "Sorry. I forgot." He snapped his fingers.

Cooro's eyes went blank for a moment. He started blinking.

"You're right, Lord Aridian. One should not beguile one's friends," Kenmar added.

"What's going on here?" Mirimel asked, her tone stern.

Beside her, her hawk set to chirping again, clearly excited.

"Mirimel." Cooro's cry broke into the little hawk's display. "You're alive. Praise be given to all the gods, high and low, large and small. You have returned to me." He glanced at Ari. "I don't understand. I was so sure, that is, I was certain . . ." His voice trailed off, confusion flittering across his face.

Mirimel sighed, laying her head back down on the table. She raised a hand to rub her temples. "Someone had best tell me what's going on," she said, though her voice lacked its usual asperity.

"What's going on is that you have returned to me." Cooro reached out to take her hand. "And now I shall never let you from my sight again. I have been a fool, playing my games, toying with the idea of winning your heart. No more. The great Cooro has made up his mind. I shall love you always, Lady Mirimel. I, Cooro, swordmaster of the queen, now belong to you." He dropped to one knee, still holding her hand.

Mirimel shot Ari a horrified look.

Ari stared at her, then Cooro, then her again. He realized his mouth was open and snapped it shut. "I can't take this," he said, standing. "I'll be outside."

"Ari," Mirimel called as he strode toward the door. "You can't leave me to deal with this."

Ari ignored her. He very well could leave her to deal with Cooro. It was none of his business. He did think, though, that Cooro could have employed better phrasing. Ari knew that, given any reflection, Mirimel would be angered by the Whey's declaration that he'd made up his mind they should be together.

Ari closed the door carefully behind him, squinting against the glare of the noon sun. He tried to get his mind to go over all he knew of Lord Kenmar, to ascertain if there was any way the bumbling, genial, rambling cartographer could possibly be the lord of Empty Ones, Tal Mraken. He couldn't, though. His thoughts were too jumbled, his emotions worn too thin.

He considered that his inability to concentrate could be the result of a spell, but he didn't really believe it. His mind and heart were simply exhausted. It had seemed such a simple task, to ride out and ask for the stone, but it hadn't turned out that way. Of course, nothing was truly simple when the Lady was involved.

Voices rose behind him and he moved farther away, so he wouldn't be able to make out Cooro's and Mirimel's words. A short while later, the door to the hut burst open. Ari turned, seeing Cooro charge out.

The Wheylian swordmaster looked about, his gaze quickly finding Ari. He marched over, fists clenched at his side, a scowl on his normally cheerful face. "I sat all night in a pit for her. I climbed a spire. I wept the heart's most bitter tears as she lay dying."

Ari nodded. "True enough."

"Do you know what she says to Cooro? Do you know?"

Ari shook his head, glad he hadn't listened. He didn't even want to hear what had transpired between Cooro and Mirimel once, let alone have to listen to it and then have it repeated.

"She says, I didn't ask you to do any of those things, and then she calls me an idiot. I once thought that her way of showing her affection for me, but now I pause to wonder."

"I'm pretty sure she never meant that lovingly. She just thinks you're an idiot."

"Well, Cooro is not an idiot. Not for any woman, no matter how glorious." His scowl deepened. "And how do you think she took my declaration of love? My heartfelt proclamation of my intentions for us?"

"Poorly."

"She said I do not get to decide to win her heart."

"I believe you told me part of her allure is her ability to give and take her heart as she chooses," Ari said, not sure why he was even trying to mitigate the situation,

Cooro glared at him. "True," he muttered. He drew in a breath, a slight smile turning up his lips. "Though I am not sure I realized, then, what it would be like to live with the fear of her reclaiming it."

"She can't reclaim it." Ari endeavored to make his tone kind. "She hasn't given it."

Cooro folded his arms over his chest, his gaze traveling around the village. People peeked at them, looking up from their tasks, obviously curious what the outsiders were doing now. Ari resisted the urge to scowl at them.

"I shall not give in so easily," Cooro said, his tone soft.

"I really wish you would." Ari knew it wasn't tactful, but he didn't need Mirimel and Cooro at odds. Not on top of all of his other worries.

"You don't think I can prevail?"

"I think we may be in more danger than we realize, and I need you and Mirimel ready. I think something that was just an amusement, to make the hours of travel speed by more quickly, has become something of an obsession for you. Not every woman must be taken in by your charms, must they?"

Cooro shrugged, though he looked a bit guilty. "Don't you think she wishes a grand love in her life? She is a young woman, no? Not more than a score of years have passed her."

"I think Mirimel has other things on her mind."

"Minds can be changed."

Ari sighed.

"We shall agree not to agree on this score, my young friend," Cooro said. "Not all of us have your great fortune, to find the woman who suits us to perfection, making us long for no others. The rest of us must seek and strive, hoping for a glimmer of the happiness you know."

Ari rolled his shoulders, trying to ease the tension those words created. He wasn't sure if Cooro meant them to torment. The Whey wasn't usually spiteful, and Ari did love Ispiria and knew she was the one woman for him. The door to the hut opened and closed, footsteps coming up behind them.

"Ari," Lord Kenmar said.

Ari turned, scrutinizing the older lord intently. He still looked kind. He still looked harmless. What was he, though?

"You said, you see, that it's in bad form to beguile ones travel companions," Kenmar said.

"And I stand by that." Suspicion surged in him.

"Beguile?" Cooro looked back and forth between them.

"It's Hawk Guardian Mirimel," Lord Kenmar said. "At her request, I explained to her what happened today. I told her there's no way to know if she'll be able to communicate with her hawks, not until the damage the fruit did to her mind is healed. I told her, the harm to her mind is like a newly dressed wound, and that striving to share thoughts with her hawk is like ripping the bandage off too soon." He cast an anxious look back over his shoulder, toward the hut.

"But she won't listen to you because she's stubborn, willful and infuriating?" Ari pushed a hand through his hair.

Kenmar nodded. "I know what you said about beguiling, and I know we both agreed she can make her own choices, but in this, I think her tenacity will not be an asset to her."

Ari nodded. "You have a suggestion, then?"

"I'd like, with your permission, to make her sleep for a while."

"Do what?" Cooro bristled. "What are you, Kenmar? More than a simple cartographer, it very much seems."

Ari held up a hand and Cooro fell silent. "How long do you think she needs to sleep before she's healed?"

"A day or two. Maybe three. She won't be restored fully, but the danger of sending herself back into the struggle I wrenched her from will hopefully be over. She'll be strong enough, by then, to do herself no lasting harm with her attempts, succeed or fail."

"Two days." Ari said, making up his mind. He didn't like the idea of deciding things for Mirimel. Kenmar was right about that. The cartographer was also right in saying Mirimel wouldn't listen to reason. If she would, she wouldn't have eaten the Orate Fruit in the first place.

"Ari, can we trust this one?" Cooro eyed Kenmar. "If he has such powers, think of how much he's already deceived us."

Kenmar looked down, guilt all but radiating from him. "Only through silence."

266

Ari turned to Cooro. "When someone takes a wound to their side as she has, the healer often gives them a draught to help them sleep while they heal. You know as well as I, for some wounds, those afflicted must be kept asleep for a time to increase the chances they'll survive."

Cooro looked back and forth between him and Kenmar. Finally, he nodded. "There is truth in what you say, and the girl is stubborn."

"Do what you have to, Kenmar," Ari said.

"But after that, you're going to offer us an explanation for these newly revealed skills of yours," Cooro added in an implacable tone.

Kenmar shot Ari a worried look before he turned and hurried back toward the hut.

Running footsteps rang out behind them, coming nearer. Ari closed his eyes briefly, wondering what could possibly be wrong now. Facing the sound, he was surprised to see Tewlar and Padro rushing toward them.

"Is Mirimel well?" Tewlar asked as he stopped in front of Ari and Cooro, a bit out of breath.

"She will be," Ari said.

"So the female will not die?" Padro's worried tone softened the words.

"Better yet, she will live," Cooro said.

"Then you should hurry, for the petitioning began at noon," Padro said.

Tewlar nodded. "I am sorry. I didn't think to tell you. To my discredit, I thought Mirimel would succumb, but Padro saw you here, not sorrowful, and came to get me."

"What petitioning?" Ari asked. "For what?"

Tewlar blinked, giving Ari that look that meant he was again surprised by how little the strange outsiders understood.

"The petitions of the Clanmasters. They vie each year, while they wait for the survivors to be made ready."

"What do they vie for?" Ari asked, mustering all the forbearance he could.

"For who shall have the survivors as their new voiceless," Padro said, his face filled with worry.

Chapter 23

All Ari could do was stare, working through the exchange in his head to make sure he understood it properly. Now the Questri wanted to take Mirimel and turn her into one of their blindfolded slaves? Were they mad?

"Impossible," Cooro roared.

Ari put a hand on the Whey's shoulder to still him. He looked back and forth between Tewlar and Padro. "You're telling me that the Clanmasters are, right now, deciding who will get to keep Mirimel?"

"No." Tewlar shook his head. "The Herdlord is deciding. The Clanmasters are presenting their cases."

"But Mirimel isn't a voiceless. Her mind wasn't wiped clean. She's still Mirimel."

"I'm not sure what that means," Tewlar said. He glanced at Padro, who shrugged. "All I can tell you is our ways, and it is our way that the Clanmasters vie for the survivors."

Ari wasn't sure he had enough forbearance to deal with that, no matter how hard he tried to muster it. "Let's go. I'll explain to the Herdlord that Mirimel is still in full possession of herself."

He turned south, setting out with long strides that made the other three have to jog to keep up. He knew it was inconsiderate of him, but he felt a deep anger broiling inside and he hoped the rapid pace would help dissipate it. There was no way, he reminded himself, he could take on the whole of the Questri herd, so reason would have to be his ally, and anger was no friend to reason.

"Who is likely to win?" Cooro asked as he trotted along beside Ari.

"It is never certain, of course," Tewlar said, his breath ragged. "I believe Clan Faesten will prevail."

Ari grimaced. He didn't have enough experience with any other clan to like or dislike it, but he already knew he wasn't very fond of the dark stallion who led Clan Faesten.

"The clanmaster we came south with?" Cooro asked. "Why him?"

Why indeed, Ari wondered, grinding his teeth. Likely just to entertain the Herdlord. After taking in the Herdlord's endless amusement with the struggles they'd undergone since arriving, Ari had a terrible suspicion the silver stallion had told Mirimel of the existence of the dark boon. He was sure the Herdlord would have dangled the idea of being able to speak with her hawks and save children, alongside heartfelt-sounding warnings about the dangers. He was equally sure the silver stallion wouldn't have mentioned this part. Mirimel wouldn't have agreed to something that would make her into a slave.

"Clan Faesten now has the fewest voiceless," Padro said, answering for an obviously more out of breath Tewlar.

270

"They're due, and they gallop the border with your land. That region, far in the north, is the territory of Clan Faesten. Their Clanmaster will argue they have the greatest drought coupled with the greatest need."

"Wonderful." Ari muttered, but he didn't think they heard.

When they reached the twin lines of the honor guard, there was a queue of Questri waiting to speak with the Herdlord. Most had voiceless upon their backs. Others, many of whom Ari recognized as clanmasters, stood to the side in small groups. They looked like courtiers in any king's hall, petitioning and politicking, thinking only of their own gain.

The Clanmaster of the Faesten clan stood to one side of the Herdlord, a younger dark stallion, who could only be his son, beside him. Ari would have said they listened to the other petitioners, except he still had no idea how Questri communicated among themselves. If it was as silent as it looked, no conversation would ever be overheard.

Finally, Ari and his companions reached the front of the line. Cooro moved to stand beside him, but Tewlar hung back. Glancing over his shoulder, Ari realized Padro had disappeared. Apparently, saving a man's life was worth a little pertinent information, but not the loyalty of sticking by while Ari went up against the Herdlord.

Ari bowed to the silver stallion as he approached, Cooro doing likewise.

"Thrice Born," the voiceless of the Herdlord said. "Have you come with news on the state of the female?"

"Yes, Herdlord. I have come to tell you Hawk Guardian Mirimel is recovering well and her mind is still as strong as ever it was, her self entirely intact. I know this news will be joyous to you."

271

"You are in error, Thrice Born, for this presence of mind shall make the transition to voiceless go hard on her indeed. Struggling against her new master will only cause her to suffer."

Ari took a deep breath, trying to ensure, in the face of the Herdlord's continued amusement, that his tone would be even. "It was my thought, Herdlord, that perhaps Hawk Guardian Mirimel should not become a voiceless. She is a woman grown, not a babe, and was not rendered an empty vessel by the Orate Fruit."

"This may well have been your thought, Thrice Born, but you think in error," the piping voice of the Herdlord's voiceless said.

On the plain around them, Questri shifted, some making small sounds. Ari wished he knew what they were saying. Unable to tell if he had any support, he was forced to conduct himself as if the Herdlord had the full weight of the Questri behind him. In all likelihood, he did.

"You will not release my friend to me?" Ari asked in a low voice. He realized his hand was on the hilt of his sword and forced himself to drop it to his side. Two men with swords, even be they him and Cooro, were no match for hundreds upon hundreds of horses.

"I will not violate our ways for you, Thrice Born. We have been more than generous with you."

Ari wasn't so sure about that. He'd provided them with entertainment, he knew, and what had he gotten in return? His friends had received the Blessing of the Mare, keeping them alive. He'd been given a chance to claim the stone, but failed. What did he really have to show for these many months of questing?

In framing his answer, he called on nearly a year spent in Wheylia, learning to be diplomatic. "Attempting to retain Hawk

272

Guardian Mirimel may be construed as making us less than friends." Ari was sure Sir Cadwel would have offered to run the Herdlord through.

"Do you threaten me, Thrice Born?"

Ari could hear the rustle of agitation that went through the twin lines of stallions behind him. "I am not in a position to do that, Herdlord. I simply wish you to have knowledge of the various elements at play."

The Herdlord looked to his right, where the Clanmaster of Clan Faesten stood with his son.

"Cease your insults before we must trample you, Thrice Born," the blindfolded girl atop the dark stallion said. "The Mirimel female shall go to my son. His mind will break hers, emptying it of thought. She is our creature now."

At Ari's side, Cooro let out a low growl. Ari held out his arm, across the Whey's chest, in case Cooro decided to lunge for the dark stallion. Beside his father, the younger stallion threw his head back, neighing. His look was every bit as arrogant as his sire's.

Ari stared at them, his mind searching for any threat he could make or bribe he could offer to save the situation. He cast a look at Cooro. He could tell by the Whey's face that, if the Questri tried to take Mirimel, Cooro would fight. There was no help for it, Ari realized, his hand returning to the hilt of his sword.

There was an eruption of sound behind them. Questri snorted, pawing the ground and whickering. Hooves trotted across the hard packed earth. Ari risked a glance toward the sound.

From a cluster of mostly unmarked bay Questri, Stew emerged, shouldering his way out. He wore a determined look, walking forward until he was at Ari's side. He dipped his head

273

toward the Herdlord before turning to regard the Clanmaster of the Faesten Clan.

"It's good to see you," Ari said, but he didn't know if Stew was listening.

Glancing in the direction Stew had come from, Ari realized he bore a strong resemblance to that group of Questri. It suddenly struck Ari where Stew had been spending his time, with his family. It was much like how, when they reached Sorga, Ari would go inside to Cadwel and Ispiria, leaving Stew mostly to himself. Of course Stew was busy. He hadn't been home in years.

Ari resolved, if they ever got out of the mess they were in, he would be more aware of Stew's feelings in the future. It was wrong to leave him in the stable for endless hours, with no one to talk to save Goldwin and surrounded by a bunch of unthinking, regular horses. If Goldwin was anywhere near as grouchy as he seemed, their time together couldn't be all that interesting.

"Enough," the girl atop the Clanmaster of the Faesten Clan said. The dark stallion shook his mane. "You may issue as many challenges as you like, young one, but they shall go unanswered. The Herdlord has given the female to my clan, so to Clan Faesten she must go. There can be no challenge from you."

Stew let out a high-pitched neigh, rearing. Ari put a hand on his shoulder. There was no point in Stew being caught up in this. Ari was just glad he'd tried.

"The female will go to the mightiest in our clan," the girl atop the dark stallion said. "I decree this to be my son, with a surety that none shall gainsay me."

There was another disturbance among Stew's clan. Ari cast his gaze toward them, wondering what else they could mean to try. Perhaps Stew's father was still alive and would come to their aid. The stallion's whereabouts was something Ari should have thought to question sooner, for he'd helped Ari's mother and father, long ago.

It was not, however, a bay stallion who trotted free of Stew's clan. It was the black mare. Stew whickered at her and she shook her mane, moving to stand before her father.

"You would challenge your brother for the right to our clan's new voiceless, disappointing mare?" the girl atop the dark stallion said. "Know this first, least of my offspring, should you do this, succeed or fail, I shall denounce you. You will be cast from Clan Faesten, never to return."

The mare arched her neck. She was regal, yet more slender than Stew or her brother. What they had in bulk, she met with lithe grace. Ari looked between her and Stew, seeing the worry in Stew's brown eyes. He wondered what form this challenge would take, and if the mare could hope to succeed against her more massive sibling.

"Let it be so, then," the voiceless of the dark stallion said. "When this trial ends, you shall no longer be of Clan Faesten. You are no more to me than a carcass moldering on the plains."

The mare's arrogant stance didn't falter.

"Know as well, disappointing mare, that you would be wise not to cheat this time, for all eyes will be upon you. If your new friends seek to aid you in any way, as they did during the Folly, there will be a higher price than disqualification. In the presence of the Herdlord, I ask that price be death."

She tossed her mane, seeming unconcerned. Ari looked between the black mare and her father, confused. His mind called up an image, a flicker of blue catching his eye just before the mare reached the far side of a canyon she had no business trying to jump. Kenmar, he realized. Lord Kenmar had saved the black mare.

Ari felt his heart lighten. That wasn't the act of an Empty One. It certainly couldn't be the act of Tal Mraken. There must be some other explanation, another reason, for Kenmar's secrecy and strange magic. The Aluiens were endlessly guarded, after all.

All about them, Questri began to move, though the black mare and her brother stayed still, their eyes locked. Stew nuzzled her on the shoulder once, before backing away.

Tewlar pulled on Ari's arm. "We have to get out of the way." His tone was urgent. "They're setting up the challenge ring. Come on." Letting go of Ari's sleeve, Tewlar jogged toward the village.

"Challenge ring, ah?" Cooro said, glancing at Ari.

"We'd better go with him."

Cooro nodded, looking serious and drawn, and started after Tewlar.

Once they reached the village, Ari turned back, looking around. He could see people coming out of their homes, and the Herdlord's honor guards forming a wide ring of Questri. Unlike the one they'd formed to raise the stone, where they'd lined up head to rump so they could run, they all faced inward. Inside the ring stood the black mare and her brother. A glance at the silver stallion showed a keen brightness to his eyes.

"It doesn't look like enough space for racing," Ari said to Tewlar. "What form does this challenge take?"

Tewlar shook his head. "There will be a race, but first the bout. There are three challenges to be met."

"A bout? Is it dangerous?"

"Few are badly wounded in the bout. It is fought for the tally."

Ari nodded. It would be like when he jousted, then. The black mare and her brother would duel for points.

"It isn't until the final contest, the chasm, that those who face the challenge die," Tewlar added.

"What?" Ari sputtered.

He shot a look at Stew, who had returned to stand with his clan. Stew had been willing to risk death for Mirimel, and now the black mare would? Ari was so overwhelmed by gratitude and guilt, he didn't know which prevailed. He did know that Mirimel would want to fight her own challenge. Looking at the Herdlord's eager expression, he realized it was too late for that, even if there was a way and the Questri would allow it.

Ari closed his eyes, feeling the stiffness in his face, a combination of tension and a sheen of perspiration and dirt. He wished they could be off the Tybrunn Plain. Ever since they'd set foot on the grasslands, it seemed like things had spiraled out of control. Each decision he made was under duress, and always without a full understanding of the repercussions. He was reaching the far end of his patience for time spent among a race where he had no knowledge of custom and little ability to communicate.

A booming sound, accompanied by the earth shaking, caused Ari to open his eyes. The ring of honor guards was stomping their front hooves, the force of it enough to move the very earth beneath them. The rhythm increased. The stallion in the ring pawed at the ground. The mare stood unmoving, her head high and her neck arched. The Herdlord raised his muzzle skyward, the air about them ringing with his high pitched, piercing neigh. The black mare and the stallion leapt forward. The challenge had begun.

Chapter 24

Mare and stallion met in the center of the ring of Questri, coming together in a flurry of kicking hooves and gnashing teeth. They lunged and dodged, careening about the ring. Their attacks were so vicious, Ari could hardly keep track of what transpired.

Nor did he have any idea what constituted a point, or the number needed to end the mad fray before him. Several gashes were opened on both hides, blood streaming down their flanks. Questri and human watched intently, but Ari couldn't read much in their reactions. He could tell, though, that the two were well matched.

He could also tell when the bulkier stallion began to tire. He lunged at the black mare and she dodged away, whirling back to face him. He didn't pursue, his sides heaving. She was breathing harshly as well, her eyes bright as she circled him. Blood flecked foam dripped from the stallion's mouth.

"She only requires one more point to take the match," Tewlar whispered.

Ari nodded to show he'd heard, not taking his eyes off the combatants.

The mare lunged, causing the stallion to dodge. She didn't commit to her attack, though, shifting midstride to collide with him. Her teeth lashed out, tearing a deep gouge in the sleek hide of his shoulder. She jumped away as he swung his head around to retaliate.

"Match," Tewlar cried.

Around them, some of the villagers cheered, Cooro joining in. Questri shifted, but Ari was unsure if they were excited or uneasy. One whose emotions were not hard to read, though, was the Clanmaster of the Faesten Clan. The dark stallion snorted, his nostrils flaring.

At a signal Ari couldn't hear or see, the ring of Questri formed by the honor guard started to move back into two rows, as it usually was. They stepped in rhythm, creating a booming cadence that rang across the open expanse on which they stood. Ari guessed it was part of the spectacle. Still breathing hard, the black mare and her brother both trotted to the north end of the twin lines of horses, turning to face the Herdlord.

"Now they will race," Tewlar said.

The Herdlord let out one of his keening neighs, setting Ari's teeth on edge, and the mare and stallion leapt forward. They ran straight up the aisle created by the honor guards, neck in neck. Ari was thinking it would be a short and rather inconclusive race when they curved away from each other in opposite directions and went around the silver stallion under his spire. He turned his head to watch as they galloped south.

"How far will they race?" Ari turned back to Tewlar. "How will we know who wins?"

"I wouldn't put it past that stallion to cheat," Cooro muttered, his expression dark as he looked after the two trails of dust.

"No one may cheat. The Herdlord would know." Tewlar nodded toward the silver stallion.

A glance showed Ari the Herdlord was now surrounded by a nebulous blue glow. Still, he wondered how true it was, that the Herdlord was somehow watching the race. The glow could be for appearance, to strike enough fear to force honesty. Ari agreed with Cooro. The stallion didn't look trustworthy.

"Where are they going?" Cooro asked, pointing to a group of young men running toward the village.

"The race will take them around the village," Tewlar said. "They will return from the north and run the central lane, coming back to where they began. The yearlings go to ensure the street is clear of people and things, especially children."

Cooro grimaced, shooting Ari a disgusted look.

Ari had to agree. The Questri didn't treat their humans very well. He couldn't imagine two knights jousting wouldn't turn aside if a child ran between them.

"It is merely a precaution," Tewlar said, taking in their expressions. "Most Questri masters would jump over a playing child. Still, that might make them lose the race."

"Undoubtedly, a clearing of the streets is best for our cause," Cooro said. "For I say the mare would dodge or jump a child, but I feel an inclination to claim the stallion would not."

Tewlar shot the swordmaster a tight grin, the expression seeming one of agreement.

"How long do we have to wait?" Ari realized he was tapping his fingers on the hilt of his sword and forced himself to stop. He didn't like others to fight his battles for him. Not that he could race the stallion.

"We will hear them before we see them," Tewlar said. "Though, they may raise enough dust to alert us that they draw near. It's a dry summer."

Ari blinked. He hadn't taken the time to worry about the weather in quite a while. He wondered if it was similarly dry in Lggothland. In the village where he grew up, the farmers would come into the taproom on summer nights, complaining if it was too dry. Of course, if they had a rainy year, the farmers would come into taproom as well, complaining it was too wet. A smile flittered across Ari's face and he rolled his shoulders, easing some of the tension there.

Ari knew he heard the galloping hooves long before the other men did, for no one turned their heads save him. The Questri, though, swung long faces north, which the villagers soon noticed. As the sound grew in volume, Tewlar's predicted dust cloud rose. A hush fell.

It was clear from the moment they burst into view that mare wouldn't win. Ari clenched his fists, urging her to find some last reserve of strength. She was nearly a horse length behind her brother. They both ran flat out, and she couldn't seem to gain. Ari could see the mare straining as they crossed the finish line, her every muscle working to its fullest, but to no avail.

The two thundered by. The stallion was the clear winner by a half-length. They both slowed, trotting in circles to cool down. Dust caked the blood and sweat streaking their hides. The mare cast a look at Stew. Ari could read the apology in her eyes. Stew tossed his head.

Mare and stallion continued to circle in the open area before the Herdlord, their sides heaving. Resuming their rhythmic stomping, the honor guards adopted a stately pace as they swung outward, moving to form two new lines, flanking the Herdlord east and west. The other Questri and the villagers started walking as well, seeming to divide themselves into two groups, a northern one near the village and a southern one near the Herdlord and his guards.

"Come," Tewlar said. "We can't stay here."

Ari followed him north, to stand across the open square from the Herdlord. He wondered if the side they chose made any difference, but trusted Tewlar was steering them the right way. If there were sides, Ari was pretty sure he wanted to be on the one opposite the Herdlord and the Clanmaster of Clan Faesten, anyhow. "What happens now?"

"Watch," Tewlar said. "The Herdlord shall summon the chasm."

Ari turned his eyes back toward the silver stallion. A hush settled over the assemblage again, leaving only the rhythmic stomping of the honor guard. Then, the Herdlord stepped from his arched chamber and all went still.

The blue glow around the Herdlord intensified. The stone on his forehead became a pinpoint of light so intense, it hurt Ari's eyes to look at it. The silver stallion reared up, achingly beautiful in spite of Ari's growing dislike. His front hooves pawing the air, the Herdlord let out a shrieking whinny.

The earth shook, causing Ari to stumble. Beside him, Cooro held out his arms for balance. The Questri stood firm, and villagers grabbed onto one another for support, but no one seemed panicked. Ari turned his gaze back to the Herdlord as his front hooves descended, returning to the hard ground.

They touched the earth with a clear, almost bell-like sound. There was a loud crack, as if someone struck a whip inside Ari's ear. The earth before him split open in a long gash. Looking east and west, the fissure seemed to go on forever. Ari understood now why everyone had moved.

The black mare and the stallion stood to the south, on the side of the fissure with their father and the Herdlord. They both appeared recovered from their run, though Ari suspected the trials of the day had taken a toll on what strength and stamina remained to them. Turning from the Herdlord, they stood side by side, though not very near, and faced Ari across the fissure.

The honor guard stomped once, and both challengers surged forward. From where Ari stood, the crack in the earth looked deep, but not wide. He wasn't sure how any Questri could fail to span it, or how it would decide the winner. Ari was sure he could jump it without a running start.

The black mare and the stallion both sailed over with ease. They circled back to face the Herdlord across the fissure. He reared again, slamming his hooves down. The bell-like note rang out and the crack in the earth widened.

It still wasn't a long jump, but Ari had the idea now. He looked to Stew, whose eyes were locked on the black mare. It was clear why Tewlar said the final challenge could end in death. Ari didn't think there would be a draw. The two would keep jumping the widening gap until one of them fell.

Ari shivered, thinking of a Questri tumbling into that endless pit, clattering against the sides. He supposed the pit would be the loser's grave, for the Herdlord must plan to close it. How many brave Questri already resided somewhere deep below? Ari wondered if the Herdlord ever thought of them as he gazed, day after day, over the expanse of empty plain he'd cracked open.

Five more jumps were completed with relative ease, neither contestant showing strain. The seventh, a leap toward where Ari stood, his back to the village, seemed more of a challenge to both Questri. As they made ready to jump back, the chasm widening once more, the onlookers were forced to move aside to accommodate a longer run.

The black mare and the stallion reached the lip at the same time, hurtling themselves into the air. She cleared the gap cleanly, but he had to wrench in his hind legs awkwardly as his front hooves hit the other side, to ensure his back ones met with firm ground rather than open air. The villagers among the crowd gasped. Questri shifted uneasily.

They trotted toward the Herdlord. Ari realized they wouldn't be able to get as much of a running start as they'd used to cross the last time. Whereas the villagers and watching Questri would move aside to allow the two more room to run, the Herdlord and his honor guards seemed disinclined to.

The black mare and her brother lined up, their backs to the Herdlord. She looked at him, shaking her mane. He pawed at the ground, ignoring her. An angry nicker cut through the agitated rustling of the crowd. Ari looked to see the Clanmaster of the Faesten Clan glaring at them.

"She offered to allow him to concede," Tewlar said, his voice low.

"You can understand them?" Ari was a bit stunned, for he'd thought the only way the Questri could communicate with the villagers was through the voiceless.

Tewlar shook his head. "No, but it is the thing to do. When you see your opponent falter, as he did on the last jump, it is only kind to make the offer."

"I see." Ari realized it's what he would do. "I suppose the Faesten Clanmaster told his son not to give up?"

"I cannot say for sure, but it seems like what he would do."

Cooro snorted. "He'd rather see his son dead than beaten."

"He has several sons, but only one honor."

Honor or pride, Ari wondered as the signal was given and the two surged forward again.

The stallion must have gotten new vigor from his father's derision, for they both cleared the jump well. Ari wanted to believe angering his son had been a ploy on the dark stallion's part, but he wasn't sure. The Clanmaster of the Faesten Clan seemed to have little love for his children.

Making the crowd back up again, for eager villagers and Questri had moved closer once more, they both made the jump back. The mare stumbled slightly on the landing. Ari wasn't the only one to gasp. She trotted toward the Herdlord, shaking out the leg she'd injured in the Spring Folly.

They lined up again. This time the stallion turned to her. Ari wasn't sure if he could really read a horse's tone, but it seemed to him the stallion's questioning whicker was touched with derision. The mare stood stiffly, not looking at him.

The Herdlord reared up behind them, smacking his hooves into the earth once more, widening the fissure. Ari felt his eyes go wide as well, for the deep gouge in the earth seemed to widen three times as far as it had following other strikes. He shot a startled glance at Tewlar.

"The Herdlord grows weary of this." Tewlar's whispered tone was a study in neutrality.

The stallion pawed at the earth, fear in his eyes. He glanced at his father, who gave a harsh snort. The mare seemed oblivious to them. Her gaze was on the deep gouge in the plain before her. She shook her leg.

It was as wide as the one Stew had jumped in the Folly, Ari realized. The mare hadn't been able to make that jump after her injury. It was months healed now, but it was obvious she'd aggravated it. How bad it was, Ari had no idea.

Anxiously, he craned his head about, seeking Lord Kenmar. He'd helped the mare before. He could do it again. Ari knew they wouldn't win if they used magic to aid her, but they wouldn't win if she crashed into the other side of the giant crack in the earth and fell to her death, either. Of course, if Kenmar aided her, her father would demand her death.

The hooves of the honor guard crashed to the ground. Ari whipped his head back around to see the mare and the stallion charging toward the fissure. They reached the edge and the black mare leapt, sailing into the air in a graceful arc.

Ari was aware peripherally that her brother swung away at the last moment, skidding sideways to avoid falling into the pit before trotting back toward the Herdlord. He didn't take his eyes from the mare, though. She was stunningly beautiful, her well-muscled form stretched to its full length.

Her front legs extended, reaching out before her to meet the dusty earth. She pulled her back legs in, her hooves touching down a bare inch past the lip. They pushed off the moment they met dirt, launching her forward to gracefully prevent her from folding into a bone breaking roll.

Cheers erupted around Ari. It took him a moment to realize his were among them. Cooro pounded him on the back. Tewlar was clapping. Breaking free of the crowd, Stew went running toward her.

Across the chasm, the Herdlord was once again within his chamber, though Ari hadn't seen him move. The glow about him faded, the earth shaking as the chasm drew closed. His honor guard paced back into formation, leaving only the crowd's jubilation to mark that anything had happened.

Ari looked over to see Stew nuzzling the black mare, his eyes shining. Ari ran a shaky hand through his hair, wondering what choice his horse would make when the time came for them to leave. A time Ari hoped was soon.

The mare turned from Stew. The crowd quieted as she walked up the length of guards. Her father and brother waited, standing near the Herdlord. Ari touched Cooro on the arm, nodding that they should follow. Tewlar came with them and, somewhat to Ari's surprise, Stew fell into step beside him. It was comforting to have him there.

The mare reached the front and extended one leg, bowing to the Herdlord. With a gesture to the others to stay where they were, Ari stepped up to her side, offering his own abasement. Now was definitely the time to show respect, for Ari was sure the Herdlord wouldn't balk at breaking his own rules, should it suit him.

"Your champion has prevailed, Thrice Born," the voiceless of the Herdlord said.

"Yes, Herdlord." Ari glanced at the dark stallion out of the corner of his eyes. If ever a horse could look livid, the Clanmaster of the Faesten Clan did.

"This is a sad day for Clan Faesten, it seems," the Herdlord said. "They were awarded a voiceless, but have asked me to banish the clan member on which that gift shall be bestowed."

Ari shot the Faesten Clanmaster another look. He hadn't realized the dark stallion meant to have his daughter removed completely from the Questri. He'd thought it was simply a clan matter, meaning she would be outcast from her family, but not her home. As sad as Ari knew that must be for the mare, he felt a spark of hope.

He realized the Herdlord was waiting, but he didn't know for what. He had questions, like if the mare truly was banished, but he knew he couldn't ask them. He pulled his thoughts into order, remembering his training. "It would be my honor, and the honor of those who travel with me, if this mare, our champion, would become our companion until such time as she regains your favor and may be allowed to return, Herdlord."

"Then, knowing it is the wish of her Clanmaster and knowing, as well, that she shall be under the protection of the Thrice Born, I exile this most promising mare. She shall take her prize, the voiceless one once known as Mirimel, and leave this place at dawn. Only the gods know if she shall ever return to us."

The mare dropped her head, heaving in a deep breath of air before letting it out in a sigh. She bowed to the Herdlord and backed away. Ari could hear Stew turn to follow her.

"Thank you, Herdlord, for your wisdom and magnanimity."

"You, too, shall depart with the dawn, Thrice Born. I grow weary of the disruption you bring. I cannot speak to your reception, should you ever return."

"I shall bear that in mind, Herdlord. It has been to your credit to tolerate my companions and myself for so long. We will endeavor to quickly depart your domain."

"See that you do, Thrice Born."

Ari bowed, hearing the swish of air as Cooro and Tewlar did likewise. Turning his back on the magnificence of the silver stallion, Ari strolled toward the village. He felt at peace for the first time in days.

He hadn't gotten the stone and had no plan for how to find it now, but he was sure the Lady would know what to do

289

about that. He was still worried one of his travel companions might somehow be his mortal enemy, whom he'd sworn to protect for nearly twenty-eight more days. There must be a solution for that as well, though. The only real issues he needed to think on at the moment were saying goodbye to Tewlar and Mia, packing enough food, and how Mirimel could be awake enough to ride but not allowed to destroy her own brain.

Chapter 25

Tewlar and Mia brought them enough barley and oats, mixed with herbs and dried berried as the villagers ate it, to last twice the length of their trip back. Mia also brought Ari a new shirt to replace the ones he'd ruined. She and Padro's wife had embroidered the back of it with a stylized replica of the Orate Tree. Ari thought the gesture very kind, and thanked Mia warmly, though he didn't really wish a constant reminder of the tree and its purpose.

All through the afternoon and early evening, as they made ready to leave, villagers came to speak to them. Ari hadn't spent much time with anyone but Tewlar, but Cooro seemed to have made many friends. The Whey, released from Kenmar's compulsion and possessed of the knowledge Mirimel was recovering, had returned to his normal cheerful self.

"I'm sorry the Herdlord has said you must leave here," Tewlar said as he stood in the doorway to the room Ari, Kenmar and Cooro shared. Ari was carefully folding the shirt

Mia had given him. Cooro was outside talking, and Kenmar was checking on Mirimel to make sure her mind was recovering well. "You are the only outsiders to come here in my lifetime, or my father's, or his father's, and so on back. Some among us weren't even sure other peoples existed."

"Maybe, someday, you can convince one of the Questri to carry you to my home for a visit," Ari said, though he knew it was unlikely. As much as he longed to be off the endless grassland, it was sad to know he would never see these people again.

"Maybe."

Ari could tell by the mixture of amusement and sorrow in his eyes that Tewlar also doubted such a thing would come to pass. He came around the bed his possessions were strewn on and held out his hand. "It's been an honor to meet you, Tewlar. Thank you for the hospitality you and Mia have shown us. If you ever come to Lggothland, my home is called Sorga, in the north. You'll always be welcome there."

"Thank you, Ari." Tewlar clasped his hand. "Stories of your time here shall be told on the Tybrunn Plain for many generations to come." He grinned. "I believe you have immortalized me, for I was your guide."

Ari answered with a smile of his own. "I suppose it's the least I could do," he said, returning to his packing.

"I will go see how Mia comes along with packing for Mirimel." Tewlar left the room.

Ari didn't sleep well that night. Though he and Kenmar had agreed that Mirimel should be woken in the morning, a moment Ari assumed would be marked by her anger, and the other lord seemed as friendly and bumbling as ever, Ari was uneasy. It was obvious Kenmar was hiding something. If Ari had learned anything over the years, it was that people didn't hide good things for so long.

Ari rose early, giving up on sleep more than an hour before dawn. He dressed in silence, not wanting to disturb Cooro and Kenmar, and went to ready the horses. He wasn't sure how strictly the Herdlord meant his command that they should depart with the dawn, but he didn't want to test the silver stallion's patience.

The horses looked better for their several days of rest. He led the packhorse and Mirimel's mount out first, tucking their reins loosely into the sloped straw roof of their dwelling, for lack of a better option. Inside, Ari could hear movement and Mirimel's sharp tone, and smiled slightly. Hopefully, readying their horses for them was enough of an apology for leaving the other two to deal with her. He went back to get Cooro's piebald mare and Kenmar's docile gelding, who obviously found it too early to be awake and saddled. It wasn't until he'd secured them as well that he saw the lone figure hurrying toward him.

It wasn't dawn yet, but Ari could see better than most. Even could he not, he would recognize the tall, reed-thin man who approached in most any light. Though his clothing was creased and coated in dust, something Ari had never seen before, Larkesong's even features and elegant bearing were unmistakable.

Long strides carried Larke toward Ari. As he drew nearer, Ari could see deep lines etched into the dirt on his face. Larke wasn't wearing a hat, and didn't even appear to have his lute or the thin, decorative blade he normally wore. His hair stuck up at odd angles, dust dulling the blond. Ari had never seen Larke so distraught, nor so disheveled.

"Ari," Larke said as he halted. "I'm so sorry."

293

Larke's voice cracked. Ari was struck by the ragged edge to it. "Larke, what's going on? What are you doing here?" Ari despaired of learning what terrible thing had befallen the world now.

"What am I doing here?" Larke's voice was low and weary. "I don't really know, I suppose. I guess I want to see where she is buried, and to hear what laid her low."

"Mirimel?" Ari asked, realizing Larke must think she was dead. So she had been fated to die, and Larke hadn't come in time. How could that be?

Ari knew he should tell Larke that Mirimel was alive and well, but anger flashed through him. Larke was the one person Ari fully and completely trusted. How could he not have come to turn Mirimel into an Aluien? If she'd died, they would have lost her forever. "Why weren't you here? Didn't you mark her? Aren't you supposed to know when someone you marked is about to die, and come turn them into an Aluien?"

"Yes, we are. Of course we are." Larke's shoulders slumped. "When one travels with the Thrice Born, the turnings of their fate are not so simple."

Ari would have accepted that explanation. He would have taken it as truth, and told Larke all was well. That is, if the bard hadn't flushed when he said those hurried words, his eyes darting away to look at the ground. Larke wrung his hands.

"You've never lied to my face before," Ari said in a hard tone he barely recognized as his.

Larke looked up. "It isn't a lie."

Ari stared at him. "It also isn't the truth."

"It's a true statement." Larke sighed, seeming, if possible, even more miserable. "Ari, what happened to her?" he asked in a chocked voice.

"You and the Lady came when Sir Cadwel was about to die, the night I slew Lord Ferringul," Ari said, ignoring the question. "You were able to be there then, even though he was with me and my apparently ever twisting fate."

Larke swallowed, looking down at his dirt-encrusted boots.

"How do Aluiens reach those they've marked?" Ari pressed. There was obviously something Larke didn't want to tell him. Ari wanted to know why his friend hadn't been there to save Mirimel. There should have been no force in the world that could have stopped him.

"We know in time to set out." Larke's voice was flat. "That is hard, though, when a human travels with you, as I said."

"You must have another way." Days of travel didn't fit with all he knew of what Larke and the Lady had done.

Larke looked up, his eyes glowing brightly, yet dark with an anger Ari had never seen in them before. "Of course we have a way to reach our marks. There is a spell, one that will bring you to a person you have marked in mere moments of time."

"Why didn't you cast it?" Ari asked, dismayed that his voice faltered slightly. Larke was so angry, he actually looked . . . scary.

"The Lady prevented me," Larke whispered. Pain and confusion mitigating some of the rage marking his features. "I was nearly here when I felt my link to Mirimel falter. As I began the spell that would bring me at once to her side, the Lady appeared. She cast magic of her own. It was like a net of gleaming colors." He drew in a shuddering breath, the glow in his eyes fading. "It wasn't Aluien magic. I've never seen the like. I had no way to counter it. It stole over me and extinguished my power. I lingered in its clutches, unable to move or speak, for nearly the whole night, until finally it faded away."

"The Lady?" Ari stared at him. Surely there was some explanation. There must be a reason why, or a trick, or confusion. Why would the Lady stop Larke from coming to save Mirimel? "Why?"

"It's something to do with you, of course." Larke cast Ari a bitter look. "Sometimes, I wonder if any should be allowed near you and your unfathomable, warped fate."

"Me?" Ari felt a bit lightheaded. "The Lady wouldn't let you save Mirimel because of me?"

Larke shook his head, his already narrow features pinched with resentment. He closed his eyes, drawing in a deep breath. "I know it isn't your fault, Ari," he said in a calmer tone. "I know you didn't ask for any of this. The Lady did what she did, and you can't be blamed. It's only . . . Ari, I think I loved her." Larke's eyes grew abstract, his gaze turned somewhere over Ari's shoulder. "Maybe it is I who have a fickle fate, at least in love."

"Did she say why?" Ari asked, still unable to comprehend Larke's words. "You said it had to do with me. Why would the Lady prevent you from saving Mirimel?"

Larke sighed. "She said something about how you must be shown the true nature of your new friend. She said that you should know the man you travel with will never sacrifice his own ends, nor exert his will, to save. He is a villain who will let those you love die, if not hasten it along, and something along the lines of, the Thrice Born will know the error of his choices before the sun sets."

Ari gaped at him.

"I don't recall her exact words, Ari." Larke's shoulders slumped. "I was, well, very upset. I believe I was screaming. I begged her to let me go, of that I'm certain. I'm sure, had you been there, you would have found my behavior unworthy, but I tell you, I didn't care. I wanted only to reach Mirimel." Larke's voice cracked and he looked away, clearing his throat.

Ari could see Larke was struggling to hold back tears. Even through the jumble of pain, anger and confusion Larke's story stirred in him, he realized he'd let the bard suffer long enough. Whatever had happened, it didn't seem as if it was Larke's fault he hadn't appeared to save Mirimel.

"Who is this person you travel with, Ari? Why did the Lady do this thing?"

Ari realized, in that moment, how doubly stricken the bard was. Not only did he think he'd lost Mirimel, he'd been betrayed. Horribly betrayed, and by his mentor. By the Aluien who had saved his life, trained him, cared for him. Worse, the reason she'd given, if Ari could even bring himself to believe it, was that Mirimel's life was expendable if her death taught Ari to distrust Lord Kenmar.

There was no denying it any longer. Lord Kenmar must be Tal Mraken. Ari also couldn't deny, though, that Kenmar had saved Mirimel's life. Tal Mraken had saved her, while the Lady would have let her die, and Ari was sworn to protect him from harm.

"Larkesong," Mirimel's voice rang out.

Ari turned to see her and Cooro standing in the doorway to the hut, her hair glinting in the first blush of light touching the eastern sky. She stepped out, Cooro beside her. Her hawk launched itself from her shoulder, letting out a jubilant cry. Larke cast Ari a startled look, compounding his guilt, before rushing toward her. The tall bard swept Mirimel into his arms, pulling her into a tight embrace. Beyond them, Ari saw Cooro's expression go slack with surprise.

Larke let go, holding Mirimel out at arm's length to look into her face. "You're alive."

"No thanks to you," Mirimel said, but her tone wasn't as tart as usual. A smile turned up the corners of her mouth.

Larke pulled her close again, tears leaking from eyes he squeezed shut. He rested his cheek on her orange curls.

Ari cleared his throat, embarrassed.

"What happened?" Larke asked, holding her away once more. He reached up, resting long fingers on her temple. "Something is different with you."

Ari realized here, at least, was a worry solved. Larke would keep Mirimel from harming her mind, even if he had to beguile her to do it.

Mirimel held out her hand to Larke. "Walk with me and I'll tell you."

Larke looked at her hand, as if startled by it. He glanced around at the others, then back at her. She raised her eyebrows. Reaching out tentatively, Larke took her hand.

"Ari, we'll meet you up the road a bit," Mirimel said. "Please bring my horse."

Ari nodded. Before turning away with her, Larke shot him an angry glance over Mirimel's head. Ari grimaced. Larke probably wouldn't, and likely shouldn't, forgive him easily for allowing him to think Mirimel was dead while he probed for information.

"You look awful," Ari heard Mirimel say as the two walked away.

Ari couldn't hear Larke's reply, nor did he wish to. He generally tried not to eavesdrop, though his more acute hearing sometimes made it difficult. Turning from their retreating backs, he realized Cooro stood across from him, alone, his frame and features slumped in defeat.

"That was him, I assume." The Whey shook his head. "Cooro cannot compete with that."

"With Larke?" Ari glanced north, but they were out of sight already, obscured by the buildings of the village. As much as he agreed with the statement, he didn't understand why the weapons master was daunted by what he'd seen. Larke was too thin, thoroughly unkempt, and hadn't shown any of his usual eloquence or charm. Most men wouldn't be intimidated.

"With the look on her face when she saw him." Cooro's own face and tone were morose.

Ari tried to think of something to say, but all his mind seemed able to do was go over Larke's words. The Lady had prevented Larke from saving Mirimel. The Lady. She'd been willing to sacrifice one of Ari's dearest friends, a good person with every right to be alive, to prove a point. To make Ari hate Tal Mraken properly. To undo whatever rapport was developing between him and the man who had murdered his parents.

Ari felt dizzy. He'd somehow managed to forget that. He'd kept it out of his head. He raised his hands, squeezing them against his forehead to block out the pain and confusion threatening to overwhelm him.

"Ari?" Cooro asked, looking concerned.

Inside the dwelling, Ari could hear Kenmar's voice.

Cooro looked over his shoulder, through the open door. "I'll tell him," he called. "Kenmar wished a word with you before we go." He took a step toward Ari. "Are you well?"

Ari drew in a deep breath, dropping his hands. He nodded, though his whole body was trembling. He didn't even know why. He couldn't tell if he felt sick or angry. He managed to nod at Cooro. "I'll be well enough. Let me see what Kenmar wants."

Cooro eyed him, clearly concerned. "Do you wish me to accompany you?"

"No." Ari didn't know what to expect from Kenmar, but the swordmaster wouldn't be able to fight him, if it came down to it. Ari doubted even he could.

Trying to quell his trembling, he glanced at the sky to the west and the fading, but comfortably familiar, constellations there. It was almost dawn. The sky was already light. The sun would make its appearance in a few short moments. Around them, the village stirred. Soon, everyone would come out to watch them depart, he was sure. He had to finish this now, then. Taking another deep breath, he walked past Cooro and into the dark dwelling, where his family's mortal enemy waited.

Chapter 26

Even before his eyes adjusted to the dark interior, Ari could see Kenmar pacing beside the table. Though not as tall as Ari, he had to duck slightly to do it. As Ari closed the door, Kenmar whirled to face him.

"Ari?" he said, making the name a question.

Ari had to work not to put his hand on his sword hilt. "Tal Mraken."

Kenmar winced. "I've come to prefer Kenmar, you see."

"You know I can't possibly see," Ari said, his tone soft. He moved to the end of the table and sat down. He didn't know if it was a wise thing to do, but he'd already sworn not to allow anyone to harm this man, if he could be called a man. The gesture might be taken as peaceable, which was how Ari meant it.

Kenmar sat down opposite him. "Are you going to keep your vow?"

"I'm going to try."

Kenmar nodded. "We must leave here. The Herdlord is not known for kindness toward those who disobey his decrees."

Ari nodded. He pressed his palms to the smooth wood of the tabletop, spreading his fingers. He willed himself to stop shaking. "You wish to travel with us, then?"

"I would like the chance to tell you my side of this story."

Ari studied his hands, the fingers thick and bulky, made for holding a sword. Could he do this? Could he listen to this man?

"Every story has two sides," Kenmar reiterated, his voice quiet.

"How many different ways can you tell me that you murdered my parents?" Ari asked harshly. He looked up to see Kenmar wince.

"I ask only for my twenty-seven more days. Hear me out, Aridian." He cleared his throat. "You told the Herdlord what you really want is peace."

Ari blinked. He had said that. When he said it, he'd meant it. Now, sitting across from the man who had murdered his family, he wasn't sure what he wanted.

Kenmar didn't look any different. He was still rumpled. Ink stained his fingers. His hair was peppered with gray and somewhat disarrayed. His expression, as he looked at Ari, was sad, but touched with a desperate sort of hope.

"Twenty-seven days." Ari stood. "And I'll do my best to keep Larkesong from trying to kill you."

"Thank you."

Ari shrugged. "I'm doing it for him, not you. I know who would win that fight." He crossed to open the door. "Cooro, can you help me distribute everything between the horses?" he called.

"I'll get my things," Kenmar said, rising to hurry from the room.

Cooro stepped inside. "I'll take care of the saddlebags and whatnot."

Ari didn't know if he was pleased or dismayed to see the Whey was standing with his shoulders back, and glint of determination in his eyes. It was better than sorrow, but not by much. Couldn't Cooro let go of this idea of claiming Mirimel's love? There were too many other things for Ari to worry about. "I can get my bags, at the least."

Cooro shook his head. "Someone has come to speak with you. I was moments from entering to interrupt your conversation."

Ari turned toward the door, wondering who could be important enough Cooro would play the role of servant to give Ari time to converse with them. He went out, hoping it wasn't an unpleasant surprise. He was struck by how light the sky was, meaning it was time to depart, and by the number of villagers and Questri assembled. Stew stood waiting for him beside a large, bulky bay with a blindfolded voiceless on his back.

"Greetings, Thrice Born," the blindfolded young man atop the muscular bay said.

Ari bowed, for any Questri with a voiceless must have standing in the herd, but also because the bay bore a resemblance to Stew. "Greetings."

"I have come to meet the offspring of my onetime human companions," the bay's voiceless said. "Once, I rode with your father and his bride, at the behest of the one named Larkesong."

"It is an honor to meet you." Ari wished he knew if Stew's father was a Clanmaster or not. If so, it was rude not to address him as such. "Larkesong told me of how you helped my

303

parents, taking them to a place where they could live in peace."
He recalled, as well, his uncle telling him that his father had
traded Stew's father for a farm and livestock. He hoped the bay
stallion wasn't resentful.

"I only wish I could have been with them on that night,"
the voiceless man said. "Perhaps, with my fleetness, I could
have saved them."

"That is kind of you," Ari said, unsure how to respond,
but sure he didn't want to think about that night. Not with
Lord Kenmar walking around behind him, helping Cooro load
up the horses.

Stew looked at his father and the older Questri nodded.
"My son says I would have fought, not run, for speed is not my
strength. His, he gets from his mother." He looked toward
Stew again. "He also says your mother wouldn't have been able
to ride."

Ari nodded, supposing it was true enough. A woman likely
shouldn't get on the back of a horse mere hours after giving
birth.

"But sorrows of the past are not what brings me here," the
voiceless continued.

Ari glanced up at the blindfolded young man. He sat
straight, his face turned toward nothing. He brought his eyes
back to the stallion. "Regardless of your reason, I am glad you
have come. It is my honor to meet any of Stew's family." It
struck Ari that this might be his one chance to get the answer
to a question that had been plaguing him for years. "May I ask,
what is Stew's real name? Is it Stew?"

The bay stallion shook his mane, looking at Stew, who
nickered. "It is a part of his name. He has given me leave to
impart the whole of it to you, as you are his friend. Here,
among us, my son is called Gaustewlian."

"Gaustewlian?" Ari repeated, trying the name out, unsure how he felt about it. It was a bit cumbersome. He smiled at Stew. "I'm honored again this morning, to know your name, my friend."

Stew dipped his head.

"My son wishes me to tell you he shall walk by your side as you leave our village," the voiceless atop Stew's father said. "He asks this because he does not want you to bear the insult of being seen as his voiceless. Once removed from here, however, he wishes your relationship to return to what it once was, for he values your partnership greatly."

"So you're coming back with me?" Ari said to Stew. He smiled his first real smile in what seemed like forever.

Stew gave him a startled look.

"My son says he has always planned to return to your lands with you. He says you need him."

"I do," Ari said immediately. "Not only that, he's my friend."

The bay stallion nodded. "I am glad to have met you, Thrice Born. Trust in my son, as he does in you, and you shall both prosper. It may be that someday, in the grand turning of time, we shall meet again." He glanced over his shoulder, where the sun touched the horizon. "Now, I think, you must depart."

"Thank you for translating for us," Ari said. "I hope we shall meet again. I wish you and your clan prosperity."

He bowed, and the stallion lowered his head before backing away. Stew turned to his father, and Ari knew they were saying their farewells. Of the Questri arrayed to watch them depart, many were the bays of Stew's clan. Of the black mare, Ari saw nothing.

"Ari," Tewlar said, coming forward. "It is time."

Ari nodded. He looked around at the people and Questri watching him, glancing back to see Cooro and Kenmar mounted, each holding the reins of one of the other two horses.

Tewlar held out his hand. "We shall never forget you, Thrice Born."

Ari clasped it. "And I shall never forget you, Tewlar." He looked over the crowd again, raising his voice. "You shall be remembered in the halls of Sorga, where I am from. May your lives, Questri and human alike, be joyous."

Ari turned, Stew stepping up beside him, and started from the village. Cooro and Kenmar fell in behind. People called and waved, and Ari smiled and waved back. It reminded him a little of the parades in Poromont, but this was sadder, for here, he would likely never return.

The crowds dwindled as they left the village behind and entered the fields. No one worked yet, for the sun was only half above the horizon. Ari thought about how odd it was the villagers would all stay where they were and return to a life exactly like the one they had before he came. He was leaving changed, and maybe he'd changed some of them in some small way, but not their world. It would fall back into place and carry on.

Once the buildings had dwindled away and they were beyond the flat-eyed stares of the two Questri guards at the north end of the village, Stew halted. Cooro and Kenmar stopped as well, as they were following.

Ari turned to face them. "I'm going to rearrange the packs so I can saddle Stew and ride him."

"As you see fit, oh mighty Thrice Born," Cooro replied, but he wasn't even looking at Ari. His eyes were scanning the grassland before them.

Ari had been too, for he needed to speak with Cooro before they found Mirimel and Larkesong. "Kenmar, this is all going to be in the open erelong, so forgive me for speaking frankly to Cooro."

"Do as you think best, Ari." Lord Kenmar's voice was subdued.

Ari walked past Cooro to the packhorse and began rearranging their possessions.

"What is this?" Cooro asked, looking back at Ari. "What shall come into the open?"

Ari glanced at him, trying to decide how best to phrase the information. He shrugged. There really was no good way. "It turns out Lord Kenmar is secretly my mortal enemy, but he's come here to make peace. Larkesong will likely react poorly to seeing him."

Cooro stared at him. He blinked once, then shook his head. "I don't understand. Is this an amusement? Am I to laugh? Or am I to pretend to believe you, so that you may laugh at Cooro?"

"I'd rather if you just believe me." Ari carried Stew's tack to him. He realized Stew was staring at him as well. "Both of you."

Cooro swiveled to look at Kenmar, who fidgeted with his horse's reins, twisting them about in his hands. "Surely, this can't be true."

"I'm afraid it is," Lord Kenmar said in a quiet voice. "I am a most vile creature and I have done terrible things."

Stew turned toward at him, making Ari have to dance back. Stew pawed at the ground, snorting.

"Stew," Ari said. "I promised to hear him out, and not to let any harm befall him for twenty-seven more days."

Stew looked at Ari like he'd come unhinged.

Ari wasn't sure his Questri friend was too far off the mark. He shrugged.

"But, you healed Mirimel, and her hawk," Cooro said, his eyes still on Kenmar.

"And he saved the black mare," Ari said, readjusting the packhorse's load. "During the Folly."

"Why?" Cooro asked.

"It is my desire to begin making amends." Kenmar eyed Ari. "I offer no excuses for the evil I have done, but I would have you understand, at least, though you shall not condone nor, likely, forgive."

Ari looked back toward the village, then up the broad roadway. Squinting, he could see two mounted figures, one atop a black horse and one a silver-gray. "And I shall hear your tale soon, I hope, but first we must reconcile this with Larke."

"Why should this swain of Mirimel's care so much?" Cooro asked, his eyes narrowing. "Who is he?" He looked from Ari to Kenmar. "How did he even get here without the Blessing of the Mare? I saw no Questri bring him."

"It's all a long story, Cooro, having to do with men like the red knight and his master, and those who fight against them," Ari said. "I'm afraid the telling of it will break many of my vows, but it's time for you and Mirimel to know the whole truth. Your queen sent you here. Though I know not why, cannot even trust if it was for my good, you obeyed her and now you are a part of this."

"I thought we were on a mission to avenge your parents," Cooro said.

Behind him, Ari saw Kenmar wince. "It is all one and the same," Ari said. "This afternoon, once we are away from here, I shall tell you the whole of my story. All I ask, for now, is that no one do anything rash before we all have a chance to hear

Lord Kenmar out." He looked at Stew. "I ask this of you, as well."

Stew nodded.

Ari looked back at Cooro.

The weapons master shrugged. "My rashness is reserved for matters of the heart, not of the blade."

"The bard approaches," Kenmar said.

Ari looked back up the road to see Larke and Mirimel drawing near. Larke rode his gray, and Ari wondered why the Questri hadn't entered the village with him. Mirimel bestrode the black mare, bareback. Ari turned to Stew, nodding to him before swinging himself into the saddle.

"He is a bard, this man?" Cooro said, despair touching his tone.

Ari glanced at him. "What difference does his profession make?"

"Women love a bard." Cooro sounded glum.

"They love a swordmaster as well."

"We shall see, but I feel the disadvantages piling before me."

Mirimel's hawk cried out.

Ari looked up to see it spiraling above them, making their spot. "Let's go." He urged Stew forward.

Behind him, he could hear that neither Cooro nor Kenmar moved. Ari looked back. Cooro was adjusting the packhorse's reins. Kenmar sat looking worried, Mirimel's horse standing placidly behind his gelding. Stew kept going and Ari turned back around, hoping they would follow.

Mirimel and Larke continued to ride toward them. Larke had restored himself to his typical immaculate state, revealing his clothing to be as brightly colored as usual. He was still missing his hat, though, and his sword. His lute, however, hung from his saddle. Seeing Larke's gray, Ari was struck once again by his resemblance to the Herdlord.

"Here is the person who ordered me rendered unconscious for the past day," Mirimel said to Larke, her tone tart.

Ari stopped, as they did, facing them across a small stretch of road. He could hear four sets of hooves approaching behind him. He drew in a steadying breath.

"A wise man," Larke said, provoking a scowl from her, which he ignored. "Where, though, is this benefactor, this healer of the finest kind, who I must thank for finding you sound and still in possession of your lively wit?"

"That, I've been told, was all Lord Kenmar's doing." Mirimel pointed over Ari's right shoulder. "I suppose I shouldn't be surprised, as he's become a favorite of my cousins, or so her letters have said."

Larke looked past Ari. The smile fell from his face. His eyes went wide, a blue glow springing up around him, almost blindingly bright. "Ari, get away from him," he cried. He raised his hands, jumbled words spilling from his mouth as lightning flickered across his fingers.

So much for no one doing anything rash, Ari thought. Urging Stew to turn sideways, he firmly planted them between Kenmar and Larke.

Chapter 27

By the time Ari got everyone calmed down enough to see reason, they'd lost most of the morning. Though Larke was the most distraught, Cooro wasn't far behind. Having been confronted by the full reality of Larkesong as a powerful magical being, the Whey seemed to feel he no longer had any chance of winning Mirimel. While Ari privately agreed, he didn't like to see Cooro so unhappy.

Mirimel was angry with him, of course. She was upset he hadn't told her about Kenmar, ignoring the fact he hadn't had the opportunity. She was also, he knew, angry with herself for putting him in the position of having to strike a bargain with his family's enemy. Mirimel angry with herself was worse than her angry with anyone else, for it made her short with everyone, not just the focus of her annoyance.

Only Kenmar wasn't glaring at Ari with some level of aggravation. The graying lord looked contrite, and seemed to be making himself appear as harmless as possible. He kept casting

Ari guilty grimaces each time one of the other three, or Stew, berated him, though Stew did it silently.

"We shall discuss all of this when we stop to camp for the night," Ari finally said, raising his voice to be heard over the others. "I have told you of my vow. If any of you wish to challenge me, you may do so. If you dispose of me, by all means, attack Lord Kenmar." He glared around at them, meeting gazes ranging from angry to, in Cooro's case, sullen.

"We need to ride northwest, in a civil fashion, and we're going to start now. I'm doubtful the Herdlord considers the firebreak to be beyond the village." Ari gestured at the cleared grassland on either side of the broad roadway. "I would like to remind you all how important it is we travel well each day. It took us more than a season to get here, though we went out of our way to reach the Folly. If you'll recall, the Blessing of the Mare lasts only six months. I suppose Kenmar, Larke and I will be fine, but I'd rather not watch Cooro and Mirimel wither and die, if it can be helped." He eyed them again. Larke opened his mouth to speak. "We will talk about all of this later today, once we've put some distance between us and the village."

Larke's gray tossed his head, turning away without any urging. Ari had the distinct impression the Questri was on his side. He wondered again why the stallion didn't seem to want to be near his people. Maybe, Ari thought, he really was the Herdlord's son, and the Herdlord didn't make the best father. Ari found that idea quite plausible.

They rode for most of the day, walking frequently to rest the four unthinking horses. By late afternoon, when Ari called a halt, no one had said more than five words to each other. They all dismounted, stretching their legs, and set about caring for the horses in silence. Finally, when that was done and camp set up, Larke and Kenmar sharing a tense moment as both moved to do the cooking, Ari decided it was well past time for him to speak.

"I know some of you know some of this, maybe even all of it, but I think I'm going to start from the beginning." Ari glanced up at the sun. "It may take more than one night to tell it. When I'm done, we shall hear Lord Kenmar's side of the tale. I ask you all to withhold judgment in so much as you can, until then."

Over the next several days, after they ate each evening, they settled around their small cooking fire and Ari told what he knew of his story. He didn't tell it as well as it should be told, he was sure, but he did his best. He tried to state only things he thought were true. He started with his life, glossing over an uneventful childhood to his near death in the forest just before his fifteenth birthday, and his subsequent transformation at the hands of the Aluien.

He told of the Aluiens' rules and their deceptions, including the role Larke had been forced to play in keeping the truth from him. He detailed what had been done to Princess Clorra, and their failure to save her. He spoke of the Caller and his wolves, earning a stoic Kenmar many hostile looks, and briefly outlined his time in Wheylia.

Working to maintain his own composure, he repeated the Lady's tale to him and told them what had been done to his parents. He then summed up their current journey. Lastly, ignoring Larke's pained looks, he informed the others of what the bard had revealed to him, that the Lady had been willing to let Mirimel die rather than have Ari listen to Kenmar.

As it had with him, Ari could see this information swayed the others. Kenmar, hearing it, shook his head, a look of sorrow on his face. Finally, after days of speaking, Ari fell silent, with no small amount of relief.

"I am sorry I brought this on you," Kenmar said, breaking the stillness that reigned after Ari stopped speaking. "I did not mean for my presence here to endanger you, Hawk Guardian Mirimel. It is my hope that you know this."

"No one should be blamed for the evil of another," Mirimel said, not looking at him.

Ari was surprised she answered. Ever since he'd spoken of the burning of Hawkers and how the Caller was Lord Kenmar's creature, she hadn't once acknowledged Kenmar, accept to glare at his back, fingering the hilt of her knife.

"Especially when they have crimes enough of their own to answer for," Mirimel added, turning a bitter gaze on the so-called cartographer.

"I did not send the Caller to burn your village." Kenmar's voice was very soft.

"You can't expect me to believe that," Mirimel said.

Ari couldn't help but agree with her. Having finished his tale of all the evils that had come into his life in recent years, he was starting to doubt he could keep his mind open enough to listen to Kenmar's story. What could his family's oldest enemy possibly say to sway him? How could they know peace when it was obvious Kenmar must die, or kill Ari to stop him from accomplishing as much?

"I see not how you can trust either of these entities of which you speak," Cooro said, looking across their small fire at Ari. "Not your Lady, not Lord Kenmar. To my ear, both sound powerful and both sound evil. It is often the case that power does this, corrupting those who wield it until they can no longer see right from wrong. We Wheys know this well."

Ari knew Cooro referred to the despotism of the Witches of Whey of old. Their terrible reign had led to war, and the creation of the Curse of Whey, the binding magic that made it so Wheylian women could love only one man. It was the price they paid to keep their power. It was what held them in check, so they couldn't rise up and enslave the menfolk again.

Ari stared at the fire, contemplating Cooro's words. He'd been looking at this as a choice between Kenmar's side and the Lady's, but Cooro was right. Kenmar had said there was likely no way Ari could forgive him. Ari agreed. The real question was, did he have to? Could they come to terms, and could he trust Kenmar to honor them? Was securing peace moving forward enough of a boon to merit giving up the quest for vengeance?

He glanced at Mirimel. It wasn't really his quest, though, was it? Not his alone, at least. Even if he could live with not administering punishment for the death of his parents, there were still the people of Hawkers. There were those in Sorga who had died in the Caller's attack, and countless other deaths to be repaid, going back through the ages.

"Larke?" Ari looked at the bard, seeking his thought.

He trusted Larke, even if the bard hadn't been able to reach Mirimel in time. Larke had always tried to do what was right, no matter the cost to him. Even more so than Sir Cadwel, who would bend the rules of honor to accomplish what he deemed best for Lggothland and the king, Larke was decent and principled.

Yet, in this, the bard could hardly be considered without bias. The Lady, after all, had saved his life, taught him, molded him, and given him new purpose. He owed her everything, and had been her closest accomplice for over twenty years.

"You'll recall I told you I have not always been in complete agreement with everything the Lady has done." Larke's voice was low and musical, despite the strain in it.

"After what she did . . ." He trailed off, swallowing. He looked at Ari with troubled eyes.

Mirimel cast him an inscrutable look.

Larke cleared his throat. "After her recent actions, tracking me down and preventing me from going to Mirimel's side, I find my mind questioning what I have never questioned. There are things, commands and actions, that have shifting shades of meaning." Larke shook his head. "I have never felt myself so lost in all my years as an Aluien. Indeed, not since the night . . ." He glanced at Mirimel. "The night I joined their ranks."

"You're saying I should listen to Kenmar?" Ari asked, surprised.

Larke nodded. "You may as well, for your own oath prevents you from trying to kill him, as he likely deserves. For now, at least. I can see no harm in hearing him out. His lies shall be no worse than hers." Larke's voice was bitter. "I find myself leaning toward agreement with our Wheylian friend. Maybe the time has come to sever ties with both."

"I never thought the day could come, that you would cut ties with the Lady," Ari said.

"I never thought I would see the day she would sacrifice any innocent life, let alone one I hold so dear, to prove a point. Mirimel is not a chess piece in her endless game with Tal Mraken. Nor do I intend to be. Not any longer. The question is, do you?"

"Will you be able to return to the Aluiens if you no longer serve her?" Ari asked, worried for the bard. He'd all but forgotten Larke wasn't supposed to be there. Larke was still being punished for past violations of the laws of his people and was supposed to be confined to the Aluien caves. Ari was sure the council would have excused Larke to see to the gathering of one he'd marked, but this trip went well beyond that.

The last time Larke so egregiously violated their laws, it was only the protection of the Lady that kept the leader of the Aluiens from stripping Larke of magic and casting him out. Bereft of his magic and his home, Ari was dreadfully worried the bard would die. If he forsook the Lady, who would save him from the wrath of the council?

"I don't know," Larke said, his voice quiet. "I'm not sure, when I return, what will become of me." He looked off into the distance, at the glimmering constellations. "I have defied them again and again, to do what I consider right. You would think, if they are as noble as they wish themselves to be seen, what is right would more often align with their laws."

"So don't go back," Mirimel said, shrugging.

Larke shook his head, his gaze on the stars.

Ari thought about the bard's room. His instruments, his work, his collections of scrolls, books and oddities. All of the things he'd filled his days with since giving up a woman he'd loved beyond life itself and joining the ranks of the Aluiens. "If you don't return to face their judgment, will they hunt you down?"

"I am not sure if the council would. At rare times in the past, others have left. Some, even, have returned. Of those, one was allowed to remain among us, that I know of." He looked at Ari, his eyes dark with worry. "The Lady, though, she may not be willing to let some things pass. Especially not this." He gestured to Kenmar. "Me, sitting here, ready to listen to him. You know her. She will never forgive, and she will never forget."

"This could all be solved if Ari would take a long walk," Mirimel said. She leveled a glare at Kenmar, a hand on her knife. "While he's gone, Kenmar here could have an accident."

317

Ari shook his head, glancing at Kenmar out of the corner of his eyes. The rumpled lord still appeared as harmless as ever, but Ari recalled the evil they'd faced in his keep, high in the mountains of Sorga. Ari had been powerless before him, forced to run away, and Larke had fared little better. Cooro and Mirimel would be nearly useless against the magic of the oldest of Empty Ones. No matter how benign Kenmar was making himself appear, he was the nearly certain winner if it came to a fight.

"Please, try not to harden your hearts and minds against me completely," Kenmar said. "I ask only that you listen to my tale. I want only to be heard."

Mirimel shot him a glare. Larke's face was a mask of despondency. Only Cooro looked willing to listen. Ari dropped his head into his hands, scrubbing them over his face. When he lifted it again, he looked to Stew, who stood between Larke's gray and the black mare. His horse dipped his head in a nod.

"Ari." Kenmar's tone was pleading. "You said you would listen. In the name of peace, it is all I ask."

"Yes, I said I would listen, and so I shall, but not tonight. The hour is late. We are, I hazard to guess, all quite tired. You may begin your tale tomorrow."

"Thank you," Lord Kenmar murmured.

"I'm going to sleep," Ari stood, nodded to each of them, and retreated to his bedroll. Behind him, he could hear them moving, but no one spoke. Ari rolled himself in his worn blanket, the thick grass of the plains a soft cushion beneath him, and willed himself to sleep.

Chapter 28

They stopped early the next day, the afternoon hazy and hot about them. They'd been traveling for over a week now, keeping a trying pace, and Ari thought the old packhorse, especially, was thankful for the short day. The grassland provided soft terrain, but the tall shafts were sometimes almost as hard to push a trail through as snow. They tangled about the horses' hooves, making each step more work than expected.

They readied their camp in silence, Larke cooking. Without seeming to discuss it, he and Lord Kenmar had split the duty. When all were served an assemblage of warm oats and dried fruit, including the horses, they sat in a circle about the small fire, their eyes on Kenmar. He glanced around, then set his food aside untouched. Ari supposed eating was mostly for show on his part, anyhow.

"I think I must start at the beginning as well," the graying lord said. "In a time quite long ago, before even the tale Suyla imparted to you, Ari."

"Suyla?" Did Kenmar mean that was the Lady's name? Her actual, true name?

"Aye, for so she was called, a very long time ago."

Ari shot a look at Larke.

The bard shrugged. "She's never told me her name, and I've certainly never presumed to ask."

It seemed somehow almost wrong that the Lady should have a name. She was an entity, not a person. Ari turned back to Kenmar, nodding that he should continue.

"Long before your people came to the lands now known as Lggothland, my people dwelled there." Kenmar's gesture took in Ari, Mirimel and Larke, but not Cooro. "We did not have a country of our own, for we were but a collection of fiefdoms. We dwelled in moderate harmony, each lord looking to his own. My family's holdings were especially small, as the tradition of the time dictated that a man was foolish to oversee any lands and peoples he couldn't reach in a day's travel, and my home was in the mountains. May I?" Kenmar looked toward Larke, making a vague gesture.

Larke's eyes narrowed, suspicion clear in them, but he nodded.

"Thank you." Kenmar's fingers danced through the air, words leaving his lips in that strange tongue Ari didn't know. Above the small flicker of flames they sat around, the image of a castle formed.

Ari watched it coalesce in minute detail, awed. He recognized the place, he realized, though it was much changed. It was Lord Mrakenson's keep, where Larke had almost died. When last Ari saw it, the keep crouched atop a blunted pinnacle, dark and foreboding. In the image before him, it perched elegantly in place, its towers and sweeping walls a graceful complement to the beauty of the mountains around it.

Atop the turrets, which had stood bare when Ari visited, white flags with stylized brown mountains fluttered in an unfelt breeze.

"We knew of our Wheylian neighbors to the west, of course," Kenmar continued. A flick of his fingers sent the view of the castle sliding away, until a detailed map of the entire peninsula hung in the air before them. "We knew, as well, that unrest stirred among them, for the women of Wheylia were powerful sorceresses, and they'd all but enslaved the men." Kenmar sighed.

"Perhaps the troubles of our neighbors wouldn't have spilled into our lands, but we had magic of our own, for magic was plentiful in those times. One could reach it with the ease of scooping water from a well. In our land, any who studied hard could learn the arts. We used them for small things, like bringing rain to a garden, or healing a broken limb. As conditions in Wheylia worsened, men began to trickle across the mountain range that separated our two lands, seeking training. Had we been smart, we would have cast them back to the mercy of their womenfolk."

Ari didn't know if being smart had much to do with it. He'd heard some of the tales of the evils perpetuated in Wheylia in those long ago times. Would he have turned men like Cooro away?

"As was bound to happen, war came. I always believed its purpose twofold. Not only did the women of Wheylia wish to eradicate us and our magic from the peninsula, they also wished to fabricate an evil to unite their people against. Regretfully, that evil was us."

Ari shot a glance at Cooro, who listened with a rapt expression.

321

"The war went on for some time." Kenmar's map crawled with little masses of people. "I was already too old to go, but my sons went. Every morning, my wife and daughter would make offerings to the mountain gods around our home, asking for their safe return."

A round, kind-looking middle aged woman appeared before them, beside a girl with curly red hair and bright eyes. Ari swallowed, struck by her similarity to Ispiria. They knelt in a glade, placing crowns of ribbon woven with flowers onto a patch of thick moss beneath an ancient looking tree. Their clothing was simple, the colors muted.

"I do not know if it was the doing of the mountain gods, for I am not sure I can believe in any god anymore, but both of my sons returned home unharmed." The image shifted to two young men, one red headed and the other with wavy brown hair, like Kenmar.

"You see, the general of the Wheylian army had been struck down in battle, sending their forces into disarray and leading to a rout which pushed them back over the border. Her name was General Suyla." A mirthless smile flickered over Kenmar's face. "No, my sons had no hand in her death," he said, even as Ari began to formulate the notion. "They were not even a part of that battle."

"On our side of the mountains, we once again knew peace. With my sons returned, I devoted much of my time to studying the magic of our land, while they managed our holdings and provided for our people." The image of the two laughing young men disappeared, replaced by a startlingly realistic rendition of the glittering central cave of the Aluiens.

Ari cast a surprised look at Larke, seeing the bard equally startled. No one could conjure so accurate an image from the description given by another. Kenmar must have, at some point, seen the cavern for himself. Ari wondered if that was before or after the lord became an Empty One.

"What we did not know, couldn't know, really, was the world was changing," Kenmar said, his voice sad. "Magic was stretched too thin. It dwindled. I couldn't sense this, for there was still much untapped power in the mountains, but the women of Wheylia did. That, I later realized, was what drew them to such depths of evil as they would plummet to."

He shook his head and the image of the cave faltered. "But that is only somewhat a part of this story. What is important now, is the Aluiens. Once the most mighty race, they were fading. Humans were rising up to replace them, taking a greater share of the wellspring that fed their power. A choice had come before them. They could give up their magic and live out the twilight of their race, or they could keep their magic but would no longer be able to bear children."

Ari looked at Larke, trying to judge the truth of what Kenmar said.

Seeming reluctant, the bard nodded.

"I know not how long they argued, or any details of the exchange," Kenmar said, glancing at Larke as well. "I do know that those few Aluiens who wouldn't accept the price of magic and life eternal were sent away, south, over the sea. Those who remained were forever changed, and must, from that moment on, perpetuate their race by selecting those humans they wished to bring into the fold. The first such, for her grandeur in life and her prowess in magic, was Suyla."

Ari nodded, having expected that. The Khan Dar had said the Lady was the first of his children, and the Lady's words confirmed it. Ari found it interesting, with all the images Kenmar conjured for them, he didn't conjure one of the Lady.

"Of this, though, we knew nothing, and so we continued to live our happy lives, content in our ignorance. My children married, and grandchildren graced our halls. Those we watched over prospered, from human to sheep, glen to knoll. As my dedication to the arts increased my power, I saw to every difficulty my sons brought before me. Be it a sick ewe or a garden where nothing would spout, I aided our people."

While he spoke, scenes of mountain dwellings and steep, stone-lined fields flittered before them, along with running and laughing children, many with red hair. Kenmar's wife appeared again, older than before, smiling as she held a toddler, their daughter beside her. Happy as the images were, Ari felt sorrow rising in him. Ari knew that nothing of the village and people he was seeing remained in the mountains now.

"Then, one night, I was out in the pinewood seeking a restorative blossom that only opens in moonlight, and, to my great surprise, I was struck down." Kenmar's voice still sounded slightly surprised, as if, even now, he couldn't credit it. "My sons had reported some trouble with marauders, Wheylian men who'd run from their homeland and hidden in the mountains, but I hadn't paid much heed."

He conjured up a dark clearing, himself lying on the forest floor, a pool of blood about him. A glowing being appeared, coming to kneel at his side.

"He was so young looking, the Aluien who came to me. I think, in all likelihood, I was the first human he'd marked. I recall, even though my every sense flared with pain, thinking that I needed to form words. I needed to reassure this youthful, glowing apparition that he wasn't at fault for my death." Kenmar smiled slightly, his eyes abstract as they gazed on the past.

"Of course, I couldn't speak, but he could. He began working a spell, the intricacies of it fascinating me. It gave me something to focus on, to cling to, beyond the pain and the devastation of knowing I would never see my family again."

Ari could hear the pain in Kenmar's voice. Sweeping his eyes about the fire, he could see that everyone, from Stew to Mirimel, was caught up in the tale now. Ari suppressed a sigh, wishing he didn't have to wonder how much of the story was true.

Kenmar's eyes refocused, the forest image fading as he locked gazes with Ari. "Of course, you know what happened next," he said. "The marauder who struck me down wasn't the last of them. Another appeared, and I had not the breath left in my body to warn the glowing one. He, too, was struck down."

Kenmar dropped his eyes. "I thought, as darkness overtook me, that I was dead. It was not to be, for I later awoke to find my body whole. Whole, yet empty. So desperately, despairingly empty." His tone turned ragged. Pain crossed his features.

"I am ashamed to say the feeling drove me to madness. Days turned to weeks, and those to seasons. I roamed the forest as a mad, mindless thing, devouring any animal I could lay hand to. Yet, it never filled the void within me." He drew in a deep, shuddering breath.

"In time, I found myself in a particular glade. I know not how I came to be there, instinct or chance, but my wife knelt beneath the giant, ancient oak, a wreath of flowers in her hands, and wept. I knew she was asking the gods for my return." Kenmar cleared his throat, seeming to work to find his voice.

"She was older by then, of course. Not so much so in the time I was mad in the woods, but since our youths. Her face

325

bore many lines, each one so familiar to me. Each one as precious as a sweet memory." He looked up at Ari again. "When I saw her, I cried out, and her face lifted, her eyes meeting mine. Then I realized what I was, the monster I'd become. Before she could scorn me, I ran."

He closed his eyes, rubbing ink stained fingers across his forehead. "She came back every day, as did I. Slowly, through her love and my diligence, my sanity returned. I was restored to my family, surrounded by happiness once more, and all was right in the world."

This last he said with bitterness in his tone. Ari flinched, wondering what would go wrong. Would the madness of the Empty One return? Ari was almost afraid to listen.

"In time, it became obvious that, while I once again seemed myself, I was changed," Kenmar continued, his tone even now. "I felt the extent of my power when I practiced the magical arts. I didn't dare test the limits of it, for the allure of that struck fear in me, you see. Worse, it soon became obvious I no longer aged, while my wife and children still did."

A look of obstinacy flashed across Kenmar's face. "I suppose what I chose to do next can be considered wrong, but I ask you, what would you do if you were being forced to watch the one person you loved above all else wither and die?" His expression defiant, Kenmar looked at them each in turn. "I began working to replicate what the glowing being had done to me. First, I used small animals. Once I thought I had the process correct, I went down into our cellars and attempted it on a man we kept there. He'd been locked away for years, for he was too much a danger to himself and others to be allowed free. My spells worked on him as well."

Kenmar shot a guilty look toward Mirimel and Ari's eyes narrowed. Could the mad man the so-called cartographer had just admitted to changing into an Empty One have been the Caller? Kenmar looked at him and nodded. Ari was struck again by how the other lord seemed so able to read his thoughts. He put a hand to his amulet, but it was the same temperature as his skin, giving him no indication Kenmar was using magic on his mind.

"All went mad, though, after the changing," Kenmar said, sighing. "With the animals, it was not so bad. They regained normalcy quickly. The man . . . he did not, but he'd been mad to begin with." He shrugged. "In the end, my wife willed me to try. I think, really, she wished me to be able to gift our children with the powers and long life I seemed to have. She saw herself as the final test. A mother will always sacrifice herself for her children."

Ari wouldn't know, he thought, having grown up without one.

"It worked. She suffered the initial madness, but with me to guide her from it, it didn't last long. In time, as we knew not how begetting children would be effected, my sons and then my daughter, and their spouses, also underwent the change. We dwelled in infinite happiness, watching the young grow, anticipating that we should create an eternal family together.

"I knew, for rumor spread, that the Wheys were on the verge of civil war once again, but I didn't think the women would be able to work the same plan twice, uniting their people against mine to stave off internal war." He cleared his throat. "I also had no idea of what Suyla would do next. How could I fathom it?"

The image of Kenmar's keep reappeared, this time at night. Smoke rose in thin wisps from its chimneys, and from the homes dotting the mountain surrounding it. Sheep slept in fluffy clusters in their fields, and the moon shone down from where it seemed almost to perch on the top of a nearby peak.

Streaks of blue shot into the image. Screams arose from where they hit, from mountain homes and keep alike. Orange flames erupted, and lightning blasted away stone. Ari watched, horrified, as scores of glowing Aluiens marauded through Kenmar's lands, razing fields, burning homes, and killing human and animal alike.

Wrenching his eyes from the destruction before him, Ari took in Kenmar's tear-streaked face. The other lord closed his eyes, obviously unable to watch his own conjuring. As Kenmar sucked in a deep breath, the vision of the mountain village, with nothing left standing but the flame-wreathed keep, flickered and disappeared.

Kenmar's ragged breathing was the only sound as they all stared at him. Ari felt nauseated. He raised his gaze to the stars, realizing night had fallen while Kenmar spoke. The older lord pulled out a square of cloth, wiping his face. He cleared his throat several times.

"I was rendered unconscious by the strength of the magic I attempted to unleash and missed much of the battle, if it could be called such. Though I didn't realize it then, Suyla took my wife and children. She and her Aluiens slew my daughter's husband and my sons' wives, my grandchildren, and every other living creature on my land. All that was left was one old steward, who hid himself down a well, and the mad being we kept locked below the root cellars.

"I admit, I don't know much about what happened in the days that followed. The steward found me, and tended me. He didn't realize I can't die from lack of food or drink. Not even from the pain of a shattered heart, though I did my best to."

Silence fell as Kenmar worked to gather himself. Ari looked to Larke, finding a stunned, sick look on the bard's face. Tears streaked Cooro's cheeks, the swordmaster shaking his head. Even Stew, Larke's gray, and the black mare looked sad. Mirimel, alone, showed no sorrow, and Ari was reminded that what had happened to her home of Hawkers, at the Caller's hands, was every bit as bad as what had been done to Kenmar and his people.

"When my daughter returned . . . I cannot describe my emotions," Kenmar said. "I'd thought them all dead. I ran to her, my arms wide, almost impaling myself on the knife in her hand."

He stopped again and Ari considered calling a halt to the tale for the night. It was obviously even harder to tell than to listen to. Kenmar shook his head, drawing a deep breath.

"You see, as far as I was able to piece together from her raving, Suyla had tortured them, working various magic on them, turning them to Aluiens and then back to men and women of a more mortal ilk." He glanced at Ari. "I know not if she was experimenting for the sake of knowledge, or to hurt me, but she killed my wife and older son with her tampering." He pressed his lips into a thin line, and Ari saw his hands were shaking.

"She must have discovered I was alive, for instead of killing my daughter and younger son, she wrapped them in magic and returned them, one at a time, infused beyond my repair with a desire to kill me. My daughter was able to convey this all, even as she begged me to put an end to her life, for she dwelled in eternal torment of the hatred and love she bore me in near equal amounts."

"My daughter, I could not save." Kenmar's voice was barely a whisper. "But by the time Suyla sent my son, I had the keep ready, wreathed in spells. Never have I been able to cure him, but he cannot leave there."

"Lord Mrakenson," Ari whispered, glancing at Larke. "It wasn't you we met in your keep. It was your son."

"Aye," Kenmar said. "I don't often go there, you see. It's . . . I can't abide it. I return only when I think I may have found something, some new cure to try."

"I suppose you're going to tell us now it was your son who ordered the burning of my village, the murder of everyone in it?" Mirimel asked, her voice harsh.

"It was." Kenmar met her eyes. "And I am sorry for it, for I created the Caller, and I left my son there with only the steward to oversee him. I swear to you, Hawk Guardian Mirimel, if I had known what my son intended, I would have killed the Caller myself to prevent it. Yet, even as that is some small excuse in my favor, I cannot so easily plead away my other crimes." He looked at Ari.

"Suyla told you I created an army of Empty Ones and murdered her family." Kenmar clenched his jaw. "That is true. After she sent my poor, tortured children back, their minds abused to the point where they longed only for my death, I did exactly as she said. Know, though, that unlike Suyla's treatment of my children, we slew her people cleanly."

Ari wasn't sure how much difference that made. He tried to wrap his mind around what Kenmar had done. Was it much different, in its way, than Sir Cadwel killing the Lord of the Northlands and all of his men, after they sacked Sorga? That was the way of war. Each atrocity was met with another. Could it ever stop before all of them were dead?

"To my shame, though I shall likely never know the truth of it, I think I may well have played into Suyla's hands. This terrible thing I did, it reignited the war between my people and the Wheys. This time, they were merciless. Using their greater skills with magic, the Wheys scoured my people from the land, leaving it virtually empty."

Kenmar's shoulders slumped. "You know much of the rest. It can be nuanced, but the truth is that Suyla and I hunted each other, striving to harm those we each love, for hundreds of years." Kenmar's worried eyes found Ari's. "That is, until the night I sent the Caller to kill your parents."

Chapter 29

Ari sucked in a breath. All of the atrocities of which they spoke, barring the sacking of Hawkers, had been abstract. Though he felt it shouldn't be, for all life had value, it was different to hear Kenmar speak of the murder of his parents.

"Why did you do it?" Ari knew why, but he wanted to hear it from Kenmar's own lips, to look him in the eye when he said it.

"From the day I trapped my younger son inside our keep, I dwelled in a quagmire of evil. Gone was the eternity with my wife and family I'd envisioned. Gone were our people, whose lives we'd watched over for generations. All that was left for me was the desire to visit the same devastation on Suyla's family. The moment your father removed his amulet, I sensed him. I was far away, but the Caller was near, roaming the forests, collecting his wolves."

Ari realized he was breathing hard, his hands clenched at his sides. "She went there, you know. She went there not to save them, but to fight you."

Kenmar's lips twisted into a bitter rendition of a smile. "That is her way, I'm afraid. To her, humans are to be used."

Ari shook his head, still loath to believe it. After all, though she'd failed to save his parents, she hadn't abandoned him. She'd let the Caller go so she could take Ari to safety. He wondered, though, if she would have bothered with him if she'd found Tal Mraken himself there.

"I have no excuses, Ari," Kenmar said. "I had your parents killed. I didn't even see them as people, just as Suyla didn't. They were a part of our war, nothing else. It wasn't until the days after their deaths that I realized the depth of my mistake."

"In killing them?" Ari choked out. Killing his parents was more than a mistake.

"In all of it. In letting Suyla use me to restart a war between our peoples. In spending nearly two thousand years pursuing anger and death. Once your parents were gone and I thought it was finally over, I was left with nothing but the emptiness of my entire existence. For what had I brought to this world? What had I created?"

Ari stared at him. He couldn't even understand the questions. "You still don't see them as people. You still don't understand."

Mirimel nodded, her arms folded over her chest, her expression seething.

Beside her, Larke looked at Ari with sorrow in his eyes.

"But I do, now," Kenmar said, beseeching. "For sixteen years, I dwelled alone with my emptiness, and I came to realize the full folly of revenge. When the steward reported to me that my son had met one like himself, one brought beyond death and back, and that he was going to destroy him, I realized I had to stop it."

He looked about at them, his face desperate. "I went to my son, only to learn of his pursuit of the stones, and what he'd done to Hawkers." He turned to look at Mirimel. "I know it is my absence and neglect that allowed him to do this. Please, you must believe that I would have prevented it, if I could."

Mirimel glared at him, not responding.

"Please," he said again, looking about at them. "I don't ask that you forgive me, for I know I am beyond redemption, but I ask that you help me craft peace." He turned back to Ari, his expression one of desperation. "I know Suyla created you to destroy me. You are everything she could not make my son become. This can end, though, if you'll help me end it."

"I suppose next you'll tell him to give up seeking the stones he needs to destroy you, and we can all go home in peace," Mirimel said. She stood up, glaring down at Kenmar. "Well, I can't go home, not ever. My whole family is dead. The new village leader and his wife and children live in our house. His son sleeps in my old room, and his daughters practice in the back yard, where my father taught me to shoot."

Whirling, Mirimel stormed off into the night. Larke and Cooro both jumped to their feet. Larke cast the swordmaster a startled look before turning and hurrying after her. Cooro watched them disappear into the darkness. He sat down again, grimacing.

Ari turned back to Lord Kenmar. "Where is the second stone?" he asked, relatively sure he knew.

Kenmar grimaced. Reaching into his doublet, he pulled out a small, gleaming white stone. It shimmered like the inside of a seashell as Kenmar held it out. Ari put out his hand, and the man who was supposed to be his most unyielding foe dropped the second stone into it.

"An offering of trust," Kenmar said.

"Don't you need all three for them to make any difference in a fight?" Cooro asked. "It's not much of an offer."

Kenmar shot the Whey a look of annoyance. "Symbolically it is."

Cooro shrugged, his gaze wandering off into the night again, toward where Larke and Mirimel had gone.

Ari closed his hand over the small stone, which was much heavier than it looked. "You could kill me right now," he said, his voice quiet. "You could end this, as you say. I am the last of her line. I don't have the third stone yet. You know Cooro is right. I need all three to stand against you."

Kenmar's face was pinched with weariness.

Ari tried not to feel sympathy for how hard it must have been for the graying lord to relive his tale in order to impart it to them.

"Ari, I don't want to kill you." Kenmar looked off into the night. "I know we can't be friends. You may well think I need to die for all that I have done, but I must impress upon you that Suyla has done wrong as well."

"If we can't be friends and you don't want to kill me, why are you here?" Ari could see Cooro nod, agreeing with the question. "Why not just, well, avoid me? Even if I get all of the stones, I would have to find you to fight you."

"There are two reasons," Kenmar said, looking a bit guilty.

Ari shook his head. Of course there were reasons. Kenmar wanted something. "What are they?"

"One has come to me only recently, in my time spent in Sorga. You see, I could not help but become fond of Ispiria. She is so like my daughter was."

"So, you want me to live because Ispiria loves me?"

"It isn't quite that simple." Kenmar smiled slightly. "I knew Suyla would tell you of our rivalry. It has been my thought, since discovering you exist, that she shapes you into a weapon for the purpose of destroying me, so she would want you to know, to stir your hate."

Ari shrugged. He still wasn't sure he could believe the Lady had spent the past eighteen years plotting to make him into a weapon. Kenmar was right about her telling Ari of his evil deeds, though.

"Spending time in Sorga, and especially with Ispiria and Sir Cadwel, I learned through them what sort of man you must be." He eyed Ari. "I have to say, their opinions of you seem not to be exaggerated, though I hadn't fully credited them until you decided to give up asking for the stone to save Tewlar's child."

"You did?" Cooro asked, looking surprised.

Ari nodded, feeling a bit embarrassed.

"It became obvious to me, Ari, your honor would require you to give up Ispiria and Sorga, should you think the threat of your death and the deaths of those you love and protect, not to mention your unborn children, hung over your head. I can't let you do that. Ispiria loves you, and Lggothland needs you. I have watched your people struggle with the art of peace. I don't think they have mastered it quite well enough to do without a valiant king's champion."

Ari coughed, even more embarrassed. "Well, that's one reason for declaring peace. A good one. You must have had a reason before reaching Sorga, though. Before you came to know Ispiria and all that, you could still have gone the route of simply evading me."

"Yes, I had a reason of my own for coming to you. I don't wish just to make peace with you. I also wish a boon."

Ari eyed him, very leery of what the older lord might say next. Why was Kenmar working so hard to bring Ari to his way of thinking? He clenched his jaw, almost certain Kenmar was about to offer to help him get the stones, and suggest they then kill the Lady.

"I wish to help you get the stones," Kenmar said.

Ari's ears started to ring with the pressure building inside him. His hand crept toward the hilt of his sword where it lay on the ground at his side, sheathed. He looked about, wondering how far away Larke and Mirimel were.

"And then I want you to kill my son."

Ari's hand stilled. "Kill your son?"

"I told you once that he suffers a dire affliction," Kenmar said in quiet tones. "He is mad, and beyond mad. I have woven so much magic into that keep, to hold him there and protect him, that I cannot kill him alone. In my fear Suyla would come and take the last remnant of my family from me, I have outsmarted myself."

"Kill your son?" Ari repeated.

"He ordered the burning of Hawkers. He unleashed the Caller and restarted a war I'd thought done, and was happy to finally have over. He grows in power every year, and in madness. He captures unsuspecting travelers and turns them into his minions, sending them back out into the world to sow strife. I . . . I cannot permit it to go on. I have traveled the world over seeking a way to aid him. I have exhausted all avenues of repairing his mind. It is time to end his suffering and to free the world from the shadow of his evil."

"At least we can all agree on that," Mirimel said, striding back into the firelight, Larke trailing behind her. "Once he's dead, we can decide what to do with you."

Kenmar looked from her to Ari. "Does this mean, then, we shall have a truce?"

Ari shook his head. It was too much to think on. "I don't know. How many more days of my protection do you have?"

"I believe eighteen," Kenmar said, looking nervous.

"Well, then, we'll all agree to carry on in a civil manner, and I'll give you my answer in eighteen days."

Mirimel glared at Kenmar. "I say we take his help tracking down the stones and killing his son, and you make no promises to him."

Lord Kenmar looked down.

Ari wondered if there was a subtle way to explain to Mirimel that the unassuming older lord across the fire from her could likely kill them all while hardly exerting himself. Ari lifted the hand that didn't hold the stone, pressing his fingers into his temple. He didn't know when his head had ever been so full. It hurt. "Stone," he said, belatedly correcting her.

Mirimel turned to him with narrowed eyes. "I thought you failed to claim the second stone."

"Kenmar just gave it to me." Ari held it up between thumb and forefinger. "Actually, Larke, do you think you could help me add it to the hilt? I don't want to lose it." His borrowed shirt didn't have the special pockets he'd used to store the first stone.

Larke shot Kenmar an inscrutable look before nodding and moving to Ari's side. "Place the stone in one of the settings."

Ari picked up his sword. He held the hilt out toward Larke, carefully placing the stone into the empty middle socket.

He suppressed a sudden vision of accidentally dropping it into the tall grass, where it might never be seen again.

"Mirimel, may I borrow your knife?" Larke asked.

"Why?" She crossed her arms over her chest.

"So I can cut my finger." Larke's tone was patient, but the look he shot Ari begged for sympathy.

"I suppose that's a good cause." She walked over and handed it to him, hilt first.

Grasping it firmly in one hand, Larke slashed at a finger on the other, grimacing. Glowing blue Orlenia welled up like blood. Larke handed Mirimel's blade back to her.

"You could at least clean it off," she said, wiping the blade on the grass, though Ari could see nothing on it.

He watched in fascination, restraining himself from reaching out to catch the precious drops of pure magic as Larke squeezed his cut finger. Orlenia dripped onto the stone, seeping around it. At a gesture from Larke, the glow of both increased, then dimmed again. When the blue-white luminescence faded, the stone was adhered to the hilt.

"Just because he gave you that stone doesn't mean you can trust him," Mirimel said, sheathing her dagger.

"I know," Ari said, but he cast Kenmar an apologetic glance. It seemed wrong to talk about him as if he wasn't there. "I have eighteen days to think on this, and I shall. For now, though, I ask that we all try to continue to get along peaceably."

For the next several days, they did just that. Ari thought, and they traveled. If they were subdued, at least they weren't fighting. After turning everything he knew and all he'd been told over in his mind more times than he could count, Ari began seeking out his friends' opinions.

"I've had enough of my own thoughts," he said, riding up beside Mirimel one afternoon. "What is your advice?"

She glanced at him, her face set, before turning her eyes forward once more. "You know my advice. Use him to help find the final stone and kill his son, and then kill him. It's what must be done, Ari. He's done too much evil to be allowed to live."

Ari nodded. He wasn't surprised by her answer. What he was surprised by, though, was the lack of complete certainty in her voice.

The black mare on which Mirimel rode snorted, tossing her head.

From his perch on Mirimel's shoulder, her hawk chirped.

"Hush, both of you," Mirimel said.

Ari wondered if she'd been working on communicating with them, if the Orate Fruit had made it possible. He realized he'd been so caught up in his inner struggle, he hadn't even thought to ask. "Can you, that is, did the fruit alter your mind? Do you hear them?"

Mirimel shook her head. "Larke is working with me on it, slowly. He says Kenmar was right." She grimaced, obviously loath to say the words. "If I'm not careful, I shall unleash the full power of the toxin back into my mind. It's still there, apparently, but Kenmar helped my mind to lock it away. I need to let it alter my mind if I'm to learn to speak with them, but I must let it out slowly and learn to control it." She scowled. "It all sounds like lunacy to me, but Larke is sure I'm making progress."

Her hawk chirped, and her face softened.

"I hope it works," Ari said, meaning it. He knew it was important to Mirimel to gain the ability to speak to her hawks. Besides, he'd been put to an awful lot of trouble by her attempts. He'd prefer not to have to go through anything like that again in the future.

The following day, he approached Cooro for his thoughts, much less sure how the Whey would answer. He urged Stew to drop back and walk beside Cooro's piebald mare, something Stew preferred much less than keeping pace with the Questri Mirimel rode.

Cooro shot him an amused look as he drew abreast. "You have come to ask Cooro your question."

"If you'll answer it. I would like to hear your thoughts."

Cooro glanced at Lord Kenmar, who rode a bit away from the rest of them, reading a book. "These thoughts are too deep and ponderous for a man such as I. You are a lord and made for weighty decisions, my friend. I do not know what it is you should do."

"Then tell me what you would do," Ari suggested. He wasn't going to let Cooro off that easily. He wanted to make sure he'd considered all angles of the problem before him.

"I? I would challenge him."

Ari raised his eyebrows. That thought hadn't occurred to him at all. "Before or after I get the third stone?"

Cooro grinned. "Asking him now would test his honor, but I would say after. Otherwise, it isn't a challenge at all."

"So, you would let combat decide who is right?" Ari was intrigued, despite how implausible he knew the idea to be.

"Are you not a knight? Is not victory tantamount to righteousness?"

"I've always had my doubts as to the validity of that," Ari admitted. "So, your thought is, if Kenmar and I dueled in some way and he won, I would give in to his wish we kill his son and then leave each other in peace?"

"Precisely. It is the simple way to decide this."

"What would I get if I won?"

"What do you want?"

Ari frowned up at the bright blue sky. Want wasn't the correct word for what he felt must be done, and that was to slay Lord Kenmar's son. Assuming there was truth behind Kenmar's words, Mrakenson was the one who'd ordered the burning of Hawkers and the attack on Sorga, and who was unleashing Empty Ones on the world. For those things alone, his life was forfeit.

After that, Ari wasn't sure. He couldn't see himself turning to Lord Kenmar and declaring it was time for them to fight to the death. Yet could he, in rightness, not challenge this man? His mind returned to his endless question, were the evils Lord Kenmar had done any greater than those done by the Lady, or even Sir Cadwel? "Thank you, Cooro."

The following day, when he rode over to Larke's side, Ari could sense the bard's lack of surprise. "Larke."

"Ari." Larke nodded in greeting. "You have come for my thoughts."

"I have. Will you share them?"

"I think they are likely more jumbled even than yours, for right now, it is hard for me to put aside my anger with the Lady enough to think clearly." His eyes moved to Mirimel, where she rode point. Her hawk streaked though the sky above them.

"I don't know that I've actually gotten myself to believe the Lady would have let Mirimel die."

"Let?" Larke gave a bitter laugh. "She hoped for it, to turn you firmly against Kenmar. My greatest fear is the time we now spend, riding across this plain. Who knows what her next move will be, to get what she wants."

Ari's eyes went wide with shock. He hadn't even considered that. He had Kenmar here, where he could watch him, but there was no way to know what the Lady might be doing. "Why doesn't she just come fight him? She must know where he is."

"She's not sure she can win, or if any of us will intervene, is my guess. Lad, I don't know that you could kill our studious companion, even with the stones. I doubt the Lady knows, either. What is sure, though, is you would wound him enough to make her victory certain."

Ari swallowed bile. Would she really use him thus? Throw away his life, which she'd saved, to weaken her foe? "Larke, what should I do?" Ari was aware his tone gave away his desperation.

"I don't know, Ari, but I can tell you, I think, what your father would wish you to do, for I knew him well."

Ari turned to look at him, surprised by the idea. "Please do," he said, realizing Larke was right. It would be a comfort to know what his father would want him to do, for avenging his parents was one of the heaviest weights on his mind.

"He would side with peace." Larke's tone was certain. "Your father was a forgiving man. He was a painter, and his heart was one of the kindest I've ever known." Larke choked on the last few words, his eyes going to Kenmar.

Ari could read the same dilemma in Larke's face as was in his own heart. Knowing his father was a man who would forgive Kenmar only made his death that much more of a crime. Ari sighed and returned to his pondering.

He knew the moment the hour marking the end of his bargain to protect Kenmar struck. They were, by Ari's guess, about halfway back to Sorga. Kenmar rode his gelding out in front of Stew and turned him around to face Ari. Stew stopped. Ari could see Kenmar twisting the gelding's reins about in his hands, clearly nervous.

344

The others stopped as well, angling their mounts until they could look back and forth between Ari and Kenmar. Ari looked at each of them in turn, taking in the tension on their faces. Larke, closest to Kenmar, eyed him with apprehension. Cooro maintained a relaxed pose, but Ari knew it for the facade it was. Mirimel unslung her bow, laying it before her on the black mare's back. Ari cleared his throat, knowing the time had come.

Chapter 30

"We will not be seeking the final stone."

Surprise showed on every face.

"Lord Kenmar, I agree that your son must be stopped," Ari continued. "He can't be allowed to keep creating Empty Ones and unleashing them on the world."

"But, without the stone--"

Ari held up a hand and Kenmar broke off. "I think, if all here and Sir Cadwel are willing to help, we will be able to devise a plan to render your son impotent."

"Wouldn't the stones make that easier?" Mirimel asked, eyeing Kenmar.

"Without the third stone, I am only what you see before you," Ari said. "I admit, I don't truly understand the power the complete set would bring, but others do. I will not allow myself to be turned into more of a weapon than I already am. I think, perhaps, it creates too great a temptation."

Larke nodded.

Understanding showed on Kenmar's face. "You're worried for what others will force you to do."

"But no one can make you do anything you don't wish to," Mirimel protested. "With the stones, especially, you shall control the outcomes of any such confrontation."

Ari shook his head. "Until I can convince the Lady to let this war die, I fear there is little she wouldn't balk at, few she wouldn't endanger, to force my hand. Without the stone, though, I am worth little to her."

"But without the stone, there's no way to stand up to him." Mirimel cast a glare at Lord Kenmar.

"I don't think I need to. I don't think Lord Kenmar will continue this fight."

Kenmar was watching him closely, hope lurking in his eyes.

"You've always been too soft, Ari," Mirimel snapped. The black mare turned north. Mirimel glared at Kenmar as she rode by.

"If this is your wish in the matter, I stand by it," Cooro said into the silence that fell with Mirimel's departure. "I know not why my queen sent me with you, though, for I have yet to find anyone to fight." He nudged his mare, angling her toward Kenmar. "Welcome back into the folds of companionship, my lord." After an elegant half bow, Cooro rode after Mirimel.

Ari turned to Larke.

"I don't know, lad. I hope you're right. I hope this works."

"She'll have to meet with me now, to try to persuade me. Instead, I shall endeavor to sway her. This war cannot go on forever. We must all swallow our anger and pride."

Larke didn't look convinced. "You know I'll always stand beside you. I always do. Besides, I dare not return to the fold now, with all the trouble I'm surely in for gallivanting about after being ordered to stay put. Where better to while away my days than in torment of Sir Cadwel?"

Ari smiled slightly, appreciating Larke's attempt at levity. There had been very little laughter in his life of late.

Larke turned to Kenmar, squaring his shoulders and setting his jaw, as if faced with a difficult task. "My lord, I shall do my best to be civil to you for so long as you're among us, though I must admit, I hope it won't be long."

"That is understandable, Larkesong," Kenmar said. "Thank you for your civility."

Larke nodded. He looked at Ari, shrugged, and headed after the others. Ari let out his breath. His decision had been better received than he'd hoped. Now he just had to explain everything to Sir Cadwel, make sure he didn't try to kill Kenmar, and then take on the task of convincing the Lady. He couldn't imagine she would be immovable in this. After so many years, what did she or Kenmar have to gain by the other dying?

"I think they are not in total accord with your decision." Lord Kenmar's voice broke into Ari's thoughts.

"No. I didn't think they would be."

"Are you?"

Ari met his eyes. "I don't know, but I swear to abide by it."

"I could leave now. You are not going to seek the stone. You no longer threaten me. I am sure, if you convince Suyla to aid you, that she, you, Cadwel and Larkesong will be able to work out a way to destroy my son."

"Where would you go?"

Kenmar shrugged. "There is nowhere I can go where she will not, someday, find me."

"You don't think she'll agree to peace?"

Kenmar looked down. Ari could see the weariness on his face. "Maybe you can convince her, Thrice Born. You, after all, are the changer of fate."

Ari hesitated. "Are you leaving, then, or coming with us?"

"I think I must stay, if you will have me. Like your friend Larkesong, I do not trust what Suyla will do when she learns you refuse to carry out her bidding. I cannot leave you to face her wrath alone."

"What can she do? She can't force me to try to kill you without the third stone. It would be pointless. Beyond vague speculations about it being across the ocean somewhere, no one even knows where it is, so she can hardly force me to seek it."

"If we are fortunate, these are questions which shall go unanswered. Thank you, Ari, for this redemption. I shall not prove your trust misplaced."

Ari nodded, hoping that was true.

Kenmar turned his gelding, heading north with the others.

"Do you think I'm doing the right things, Stew?" Ari asked.

Stew shook his mane, setting off north as well. Mirimel was already a blur against the heat of the afternoon. Ari wasn't sure if Stew meant yes or no. Maybe, though, Stew was thinking the same think Ari was, right or wrong, the decision he'd made was the only one he could have.

The second half of their journey seemed less dire than the first. The air grew slightly cooler as they journeyed north, which appeared to improve everyone's mood somewhat. Though they saw the occasional cloud created by a herd of Questri, none came close. Eventually, a tentative comradery began to form amongst them, and they all treated it delicately.

It was with vast relief that Ari urged Stew off the Tybrunn Plains and into the mountains forming the northern border of Sorga. He knew they were still nearly a week out, but setting foot in the mountains already felt like returning home. He could see it on Mirimel's face as well, and feel it in Stew's gait. Only the black mare seemed reluctant, her steps slowing until, finally, she turned round to look back.

Stew, taking Ari with him, went back to stand beside her. She looked at Stew, and Ari could tell they were communicating in the way of the Questri. Stew shook his mane.

"All will be well," Mirimel said. "You'll like my home, and we can come down to the plain sometimes, if you wish. I can't imagine I'd wither and die that quickly."

The black mare huffed, turning away, and they headed up the trail toward the others.

It wasn't until they were near the cross-trail to Hawkers, with Sorga only a half day's ride away, that the hawks sighted them. At first, Ari thought they were just excited Mirimel was home, but a glance at her told him something was wrong. Nearly a dozen of them spiraled downward, converging from all directions. They swooped about, agitated. Mirimel's leapt from her shoulder, joining them.

"Something is wrong in Sorga," Mirimel said, holding up her arm.

Ari could see all of the hawks, save Mirimel's, had notes tied to them. Apprehension shot through him.

"They've all been sent, moments ago, to find us," Larke said, lines forming on his face as he frowned. "Calm down and tell us what's wrong. You're acting like a bunch of chickens."

Mirimel's hawk squawked, dropping down to land on her arm. He looked at Larke in an outraged fashion. Of course, he was the only one without a note, Ari thought, clenching his teeth.

"They don't know what's wrong," Kenmar said, looking from hawk to hawk. "No one told them. All they know is a bird came from the king and Sir Cadwel became very agitated. He sent all the hawks he had looking for Ari."

"One of you come here this instant," Ari roared, too worried to be civil. He may not be able to communicate with the hawks as Mirimel, Kenmar and Larke all seemed able to, but he assumed that would be clear enough.

Apparently, it was, for several hawks dove toward him, vying to be the one to land on his arm. "Thank you," Ari said to the one who won the position. He tugged the note free. "I need my hand now, please."

The hawk dipped in a sort of bow before launching itself skyward.

"You didn't need to yell at them," Mirimel said, stroking her hawk, which was back on her shoulder, peering out at Ari from under her hair.

"It seemed like I did." Ari unrolled the note. "All it says is, Ari, I don't give five hells what you're doing, get back here now, Cadwel."

"Eloquently put, but not very informative," Larke said.

"Mirimel." Ari turned to her. "I'm sure you can reach your village alone. I'm sorry for the abrupt goodbye but, as you heard, I must hasten to Sorga. I dare not even escort you the remainder of the way." He nudged Stew, assuming the rest of them would follow.

Mirimel and her black mare were beside him in moments. "If you think I'm going to return to Hawkers and sit around waiting to find out what's happening, you're sorely mistaken. Furthermore, I know these trails are narrow, but you act as if you've never met a Questri. Sir Cadwel said now. From the number of hawks he sent, I'd say he meant it."

With no signal Ari could see, the black mare leapt forward, breaking into a near run. Ari looked back at the others. He untied the packhorse's reins from Stew's saddle, letting them fall to the trail. Mirimel was right, and it was time Ari showed a little trust in Lord Kenmar, if he was ever going to.

"Cooro, Kenmar, I hate to do this to you, but could you bring Mirimel's horse and the packhorse to Sorga, please? She's right. Larke and I had best go as quickly as we can. I'm afraid your mounts aren't up to the task."

He looked each man in the eye, trying to impart his trust in them, and his apology. Kenmar nodded, seeming to acknowledge Ari's actions were a test. Not, he supposed, that Kenmar had sworn to stay with them, only said he planned to. His departure at this time would surely be taken amiss, though.

"If we're going . . ." Larke said.

Ari nodded. "We're going." He lifted his hand in a wave. Stew dove forward, Larke's gray a horse length behind him.

The harrowing ride put Ari in mind of the time he and Larke had charged down this same trail, trying to catch the Empty One who had stolen Ispiria. It wasn't a good memory, and Ari tried to dispel it, but he was overcome with foreboding. That day, they hadn't found Ispiria. Had, in fact, found only the dead. Those memories filling him with a growing sense of dread, Ari found himself urging Stew into greater and more precarious feats of speed on the narrow mountain trail.

When they finally sprang free of the mountains, Mirimel and the black mare already raced across the rolling hills before them. Chasing her, Ari could see the outer gates of Sorga were closed, never a good sign. They must have been recognized, though, for the metal-bound wooden structures began to swing ponderously open.

Mirimel and the mare disappeared inside, Ari and Stew close behind them. Stew, Ari had come to realize, knew no match among even the Questri when it came to speed. Unless, of course, it was in Larke's gray, for the bard was mere hands behind them.

The inner gates were almost open as they galloped across the smooth earth of the killing zone. All three Questri burst into the inner courtyard nearly side by side, Ari dismounting before Stew completely stopped. He ran headlong up the steps and into the keep, careening into Sir Cadwel.

"Ari." Sir Cadwel caught him half in an embrace of welcome, half to keep him upright. "I only just sent the hawks."

"They met us at Hawkers," Ari gasped, realizing he was nearly out of breath. Mirimel and Larke burst into the foyer.

Sir Cadwel glanced at the sky, obviously calculating the speed of their ride. "Come into my study. I see that bard's turned up again. What did you do with Kenmar and that swordmaster?"

"They don't ride Questri," Ari said, knowing that was explanation enough.

Sir Cadwel cast Mirimel a look over his shoulder, raising his shaggy gray eyebrows. "I see."

They filed into the study which looked, if possible, even more full of books. Ari glanced around, seeing Raven and Canid lounging in scruffy heaps by the fireplace, but Ispiria wasn't there. He wondered if she'd returned from the capital yet. He knew she was due back before snow clogged the roads. While it was only now nearing fall, he'd held onto hope she would be there, if for no other reason than to salve his worry.

"Sit," Cadwel ordered. "Natan left to fetch drinks when they spotted you from the wall."

Ari looked from Larke to Mirimel, and back to Sir Cadwel. "You made it sound urgent."

"It is." Cadwel crossed to his armchair by the fire.

"What did you do to your hounds, Cadwel?" Larke asked sharply, his eyes narrowing. He folded his long form onto one of the couches.

Mirimel settled on the other end of it. Ari moved to the one across from them, but didn't sit. He could feel the tension radiating off Sir Cadwel, despite the knight's apparent calm.

"Do?" Sir Cadwel's face was blankly innocent as he looked at Larke.

"You've infused your dogs with Orlenia. Do you think I can't tell?"

Mirimel shot Sir Cadwel an incredulous look, then turned to scrutinize the hounds.

"Do you have any idea how many rules you've broken?" the bard demanded.

"Coming from you, I'll take that as a compliment."

The door to the study opened. Ari jumped, his hand going to his sword. He turned to see Natan entering.

The chief steward had forgone a tray, holding a decanter of suspiciously clear liquid and a stack of small glasses. Natan's face was oddly pale, the muscles around his mouth clenched tight enough to tinge the skin gray. He stopped just inside the door, eyeing Ari. "It's nice to see you as well, my lord."

Ari dropped his hand from his sword hilt. "I'm sorry." He turned back to Sir Cadwel. "I don't mean to be jumpy, but it's clear to me something is very wrong, and one of you is going to tell me what it is before I--" He broke off, realizing he'd been about to threaten to bash Natan's and Sir Cadwel's heads together.

"I thought I told you to sit and wait for Natan and a drink," Sir Cadwel said, his tone an obvious command.

Ari sat.

Natan came around the couch and handed him one of the small glasses, filling it to the top with clear liquid. "I recommend not tasting it," he said, his face full of compassion.

Ari eyed the glass, trying not to let the liquid spill onto his fingers. It smelled vile. "Please tell me what's wrong." He felt himself moving from anger to panic.

"We've had a bird from the king," Sir Cadwel said, accepting a glass from Natan.

Ari was aware of Larke and Mirimel doing likewise and of Natan settling onto the other end of the couch on which he sat, but he kept his eyes on Cadwel. "And?"

"I can think of no easy way to say this, lad. Princess Siara has been kidnapped and taken away by boat, across the ocean."

"What?" Ari stared at him, aghast. A stray thought flittered through his mind. Across the ocean was where the Lady wished him to search for the third stone. What had he said to Kenmar, that there was nothing she could do to make him seek it?

Sir Cadwel cleared his throat. He knocked back his drink before meeting Ari's eyes once more. "They took Ispiria with her."

The End

ABOUT THE AUTHOR

Summer Hanford grew up on a dairy farm in Upstate New York. She earned her bachelor's degree in experimental psychology and went on to do graduate and doctoral work in behavioral neurology.

Turning away from long hours spent in research, Summer returned to her childhood dream of writing fantasy novels, although she enjoys turning her pen to science fiction, Regency and adventure as well. She is now a faculty member of the AllWriters' Workplace and Workshop and has launched her first fantasy series, Thrice Born, with Martin Sisters Publishing Company. To learn more about Summer visit www.summerhanford.com.